RUNE OF STRENGTH

RUNE-CHILD SAGA

BOOK 1

MICHAEL VERLAN

Book Cover Illustration: Reza Afshar, @rezaafshar.art

Developmental Edit: Erin Bledsoe

First Edition: January 2024

10 9 8 7 6 5 4 3 2 1

For my sister Lilya,

My first and best fan.

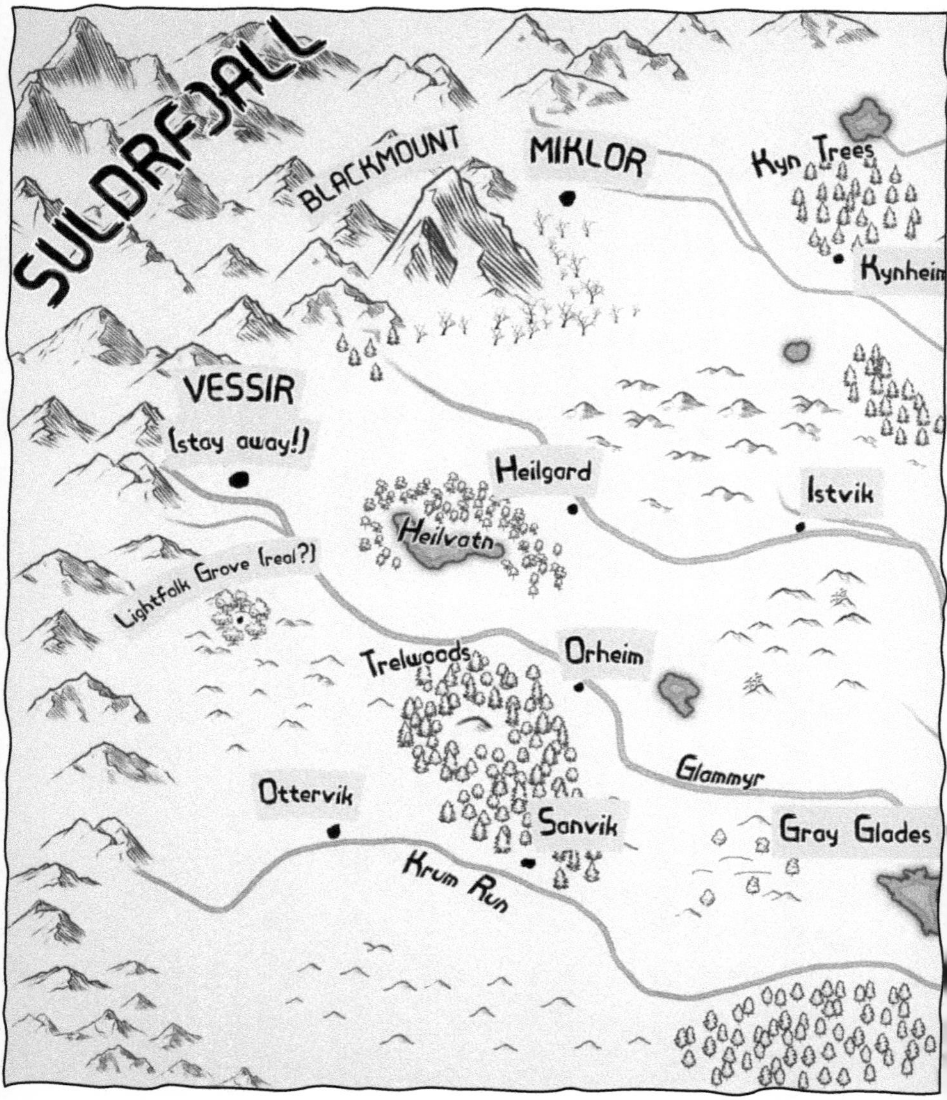

SULDRFJALL
BLACKMOUNT
MIKLOR
Kyn Trees
Kynheim
VESSIR
(stay away!)
Heilgard
Istvik
Heilvatn
Lightfolk Grove (real?)
Trelwoods
Orheim
Glammyr
Ottervik
Sanvik
Gray Glades
Krum Run

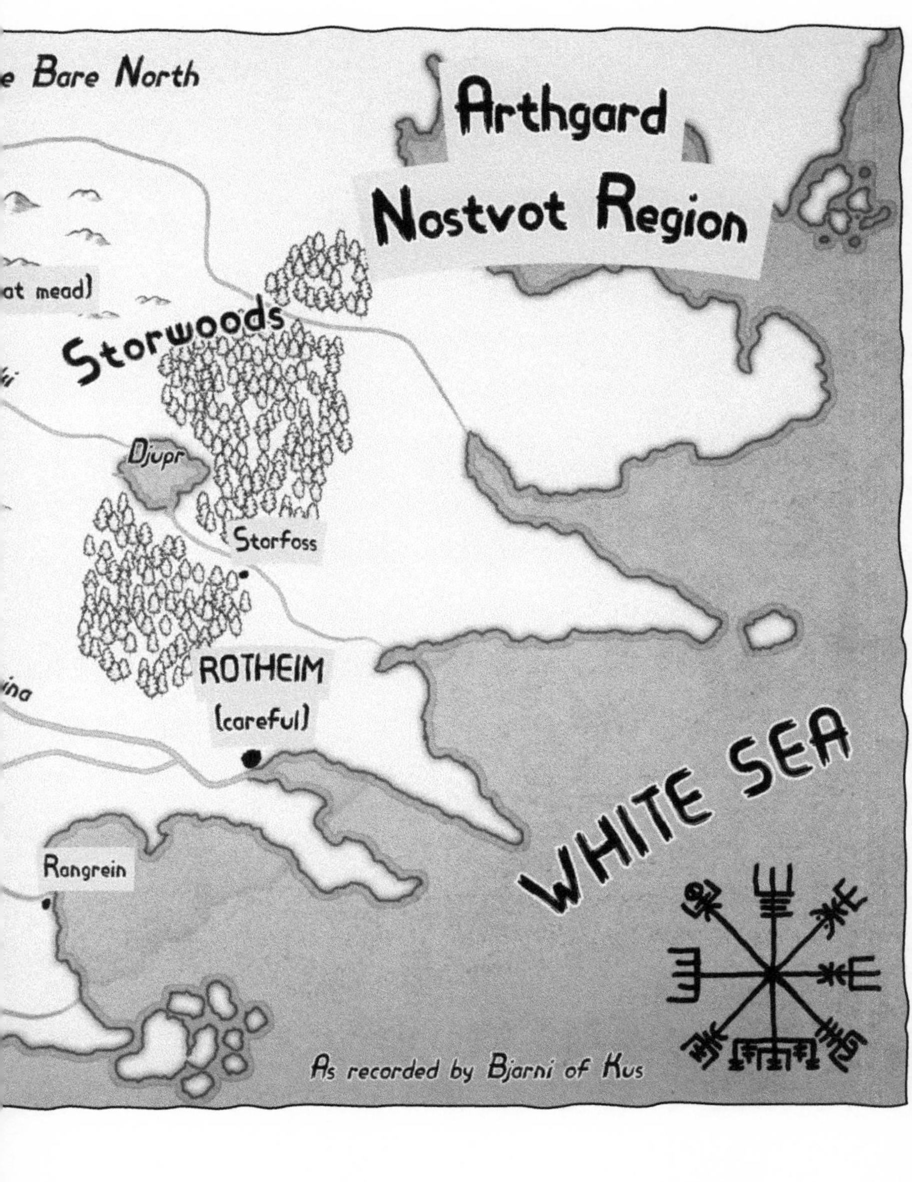
e Bare North
Arthgard
Nostvot Region
at mead)
Storwoods
Djupr
Storfoss
ROTHEIM
(careful)
Rangrein
WHITE SEA
As recorded by Bjarni of Kus

Prologue

The Madman

A gust of icy wind throws open the door like an uninvited relative, and the Visitor steps in. He has traveled far for his mission and has become increasingly careful as he nears his goal. Now he stands still in the crumbling hut, taking care to examine all before making his next move.

Snowflakes dust the floorboards as the door creaks closed behind him. Except for the flutter of rags covering the barricaded windows and the flicker of a candle in the corner, the room remains firmly undisturbed. Not even the hut's single tenant—who has weathered much more than a cold shiver—deigns to acknowledge the newcomer, or the uneasy winter outside.

Indeed, most are uneasy in these times. The trees are tense from the weight of the snow as well as a dark premonition. The frozen creek cracks reluctantly, as if afraid of shattering the precious calm. A single rat, an opportunist, skitters around the hut toward its lair, unmolested by the predators that would have escaped to safety months ago. And yet, inside the hut, all are still, save for the candle, next to which sits the Madman.

Why do they call him Madman? Because he thinks his leaning

hut is a fortress? Because sometimes he sits motionless for hours on a chair held together by a rusted nail and hope? Because all those who left the village called him a Madman, with his wild mutterings in the dark, his seclusion, his unnatural gaze?

"No," he utters, in a voice more gravel than man, "it wasn't no mutterin's." His lids peel open as yellowed eyes dart around the room in alarm.

"It wasn't no mutterings," he says louder. His eyes settle on the Visitor, speckled in snow and mud, except for the rune-marked axe hanging at the side. The Madman cannot see a face under the hood, though he would hardly care to, anyway.

"It was the stories," he continues, shifting slightly, "the stories makes them leave. The stories makes the winter harsh, see? The stories makes it all come crashing down. And not silly children's stories either—", the Madman prefers those best, "—or the garbage those upstart skalds serve nowadays. It was the real stories—ones to put fire in yer heart. Ones to drive ye mad, even. But I says... I says the madman is not one who tells the story like that, oh no. I says the madman is someones who...someones who would..."

The Madman trails off as he peers deeper into the cowl. He leans forward, and the old chair protests loudly. His eyes finally rest on two glimmers in the shadow, the Visitor's eyes weighing and judging. The Madman thinks the Visitor is not real, because no one would dare venture to Blackmount in the dead of winter. No one would brave the storms to visit him, and no one would be mad enough to—

"...listen to the story."

The Madman leaps up. He dons a maniacal grin as he marches to the other end of the hut, the floorboards whining under the weight. The Visitor's hand inches toward the axe, but the Madman pays no heed. He quickly reaches his prize: a half-empty bottle awaits in the junk on the decrepit shelf, wrapped in coarse wool. He snatches it, as if expecting someone to steal it before his eyes, knocking over other rubbish. An old axe handle with shallowly inscribed runes, and a cracked horn topple at the Madman's feet, who is already helping himself to a healthy dose of the brew. Finally, as he pulls the bottle from his mouth and smacks his cracked lips, he looks down at the half-instruments on the floor. His grin melts.

"The stories have consequences, is what they don't tell ye." He lumbers back to his chair, all of that impossible life drained once again. He eyes the Visitor and the axe, neither of which has moved. "But I suppose you want me to tell you anyway."

An odd silence fills the space around him, time itself stopping in anticipation.

"Fine!" He explodes, "By the nine gods, I will tell you everything. If it be the death of you, I'll tell you. I'll tell you of the reason for the fox's fear, the crow's silence, and the deathly snows. Oh, yes, especially the deathly snows. I will tell you of Yut the Strong, son of Eira, the blessed rune-child, the hero of Arthgard."

At the last title, the Madman's wild expression becomes more sinister. Shaped by the shadows of the candle's flame, the grin makes a grand return. "I will tell you the reason for our scourge, and a sorrow that would unseat the gods and break a heart. Listen close now, because there will be no repeats, no going back, and, most importantly, no spoilings."

The Madman settles back in the chair, the bottle of brew caressed by his arthritic fingers, as he begins to recount a lifetime in a new voice, a strong voice, a Speaker's voice.

"As with most great stories, this one begins in a far-away village, on a night of a great struggle..."

Chapter One

Strong Indeed

On the most important night of his life, Yut lost everything.

First, he lost his appetite. Half a breakfast sloshed around in his stomach, and was now aggressively exploring various escape paths. Then, when he stepped into the long house of his village, surrounded by everyone he ever knew, he lost his nerve. Weeks of building resolve to attain his manhood evaporated as soon as he saw the fighting pit. Finally, the first punch was thrown, and Yut lost his memory.

Thankfully, not all of his memories, just the ones he desperately needed now. Fighting stances, wrestling holds, and intimidation tactics he learned in the preceding weeks were mere glimpses lost in the noise and lights and pain. He risked closing his eyes for a moment, and his father's voice drifted in from the darkness. "*Remember, Yut, the bigger they are, the farther you should stay. But if you can't, then go for the legs.*"

Yut opened his eyes and dove for the attacker's legs. Unfortunately, his opponent has been wrestling smaller people his entire life, as is the natural case for all men his size. This is why he instinctively brought up his knee just as Yut met it with his face, showering Yut's vision with a thousand stars. As he lay on the sandy proving-pit ground, blinking away the lights and blowing the amassing blood out of his nose, he began to fly.

Ascending into the air, the world slowly spinning around him, Yut felt a deep sense of calm. An even deeper sense of dread immediately followed this, as other senses woke up and told Yut he was not flying, but, in fact, being lifted into the air by Keld like a trophy.

Faces leered at Yut, some angry, some disappointed, and others—most of them—wholeheartedly enjoying the show.

"Break his spine, Keld!" Someone yelled.

"Break his legs!" Came from the other end.

"Take his eyes!"

The people of Sanvik could be savage when beholding a scuffle, but the last one gave Yut pause as Keld held the youth above his head. *Dark below—Take my eyes? That sounds more tedious than...* The delirious thought cut off as Keld roared and *threw* Yut into the throng of people. Some toppled, others continued their jeering. Yet most did not recognize the mercy that Keld, Yut's alleged best friend, had just given him. Though the people weren't particularly nice, they were still softer than wet sand. This was not saying much, however, as a stray elbow caught him in the kidney. *Great, now I'll be humiliated* and *have to buy the oaf a horn,* thought Yut, gritting his teeth in pain.

Pulled to his feet and shoved back into the fighting ring, the bleary-eyed Yut took in his surroundings once again. The village long house was filled with patrons for the Proving Moon, the last full moon of summer. It was the night young men like Yut chose to prove themselves to the people of Sanvik. Some left the village to hunt a wild beast in the woods, swearing to bring back a trophy. Others, like Yut, decided to demonstrate their maturity through the People's Brawl. Though in this case, it was closer to the People's Beat-down. Broken or not, if the crowd approved of his showmanship and strength tonight, he would be allowed to taste strong mead, grow a beard, and be wed.

At this point, Yut's remaining hope was riding on showmanship.

Keld had already passed the Proving Moon winters ago, so Yut expected his friend to show at least a shred of sympathy on this important night. After all, Keld fought one of the strongest lumberjacks in Sanvik at the time. Yut was not tall enough to witness it fully, as the entire village gathered to see that fight, but they said he knocked his opponent out into the next morning.

"How did you do it?" Yut remembered asking weeks ago, at one of their games of tafl by the river. Anxiety about the Proving Moon had already begun to gnaw at him, so he gnawed his nails and watched the crystalline mountain waters rush past. As usual, Keld frowned at the playing board in complete concentration, as if he was angry at it. To be fair, Yut would be angry, too, if he lost nearly every game he played. But despite his friend's size or demeanor, Keld was one of the gentlest souls in the village, hardly ever raising his voice or fist against anyone. How could he ever pass the Proving Moon outright?

Eyes still affixed to the board, Keld nodded and decisively slid a piece forward. "I punched him."

Back in the proving pit, the big man closed in, wearing the same frown, though this was far from their peaceful tafl game. Keld came close enough to whisper, which is exactly what Yut thought he wanted to do. An apology for the obscene throw, or an idea for Yut to score some punches. But Keld seemed to transform into a different person when he stepped into the pit, so when his fist connected with Yut's stomach, it knocked all the wind Yut had left out of him.

As he sank to the sand again, he heard Keld holler, "Is he strong enough?!" It was the traditional phrase spoken during a People's Brawl. In a perfect world, the crowd would holler back "Strong indeed!" And the Brawl would end. In a perfect world, they would—

"Rip out his heart, Keld!"

Dark take it, cursed Yut, *should have hunted a deer*. He pulled himself up, wincing at the bruises already forming on his body. If he passed out now, then the people would never approve of the Brawl. Or worse, they would do so out of pity, which would follow him around like a foul odor. *Just a bit longer.*

Spitting onto the sand wet with ale, sweat, and blood from previous Brawls, he assumed the fighting form his father had shown him. His father did not fight often—he was a logmar, the judge and leader of Sanvik. Likewise, Yut expected to sit in his seat one day, solving conflicts with words rather than strength. Although his father did not have the time to teach him much, his mother proudly reminded him of his destiny at every opportunity. "*A leader needs to be strong, Yut, and true strength comes from the heart*," she would say.

And yet physical strength was what he needed now. He locked eyes with Keld, forcing the thoughts across the pit, straight into his friend's thick skull. *Dark take you, we practiced this. We practiced this!*

With a howl, Yut threw himself at his friend, throwing fists and knees wherever he could connect them. He hoped Keld would see his friend's desperate attempt at a final stand and go on the defense. Thankfully, Keld shared the thought with Yut for once, and brought up his hulking arms. He made a show of it too, flinching when a fist connected, giving ground as he lost momentum, growling in rage at the apparent burst of power. Yut almost began enjoying himself before he lost his feet and toppled, his scream inflecting at the end, as if his own spirit of rage was confused.

For the tenth time that night, Yut began picking himself off the floor, when Keld, flinging aside the quick bit of showmanship, threw himself onto his friend, pinning him in the Bear's Hold. Yut knew this hold, as he wrestled several other youths in his day, sometimes out of boredom, and sometimes for honor. He knew, everyone knew, that Bear's Hold, if done properly, was almost impossible to break out of. It involved grabbing the opponent from behind, restraining their legs with yours, and squeezing the neck until the desired result was achieved. Within seconds, Yut would lose consciousness. That is why he allowed himself a groan of relief, realizing the show would soon be over.

His vicious spectators knew what was about to happen: He would be called a boy, while those younger than him would be called men. He would lose his reputation, the reputation of his family, and his future as a respected logmar. In a word, he would lose his entire life. However, as Keld pinned Yut's arms together and immobilized his legs, Yut miraculously freed an arm and began pushing at Keld's elbow, which was lodged tightly against his neck. It seemed futile, but he kept pushing. Even if Yut the Young would never unfasten Keld's arm, and never pass his Proving Moon, he kept pushing. He gave a final howl, his face a mask of blood and bruises, as he *heaved* with all the strength he had left. The crowd, who had begun to lose interest, were caught in the spectacle of a heart-wrenching struggle, the force of will that only showed itself when one had everything on the line. No one would expect the young man to win, yet now everyone *wanted* him to win. Without realizing it, the crowd lost the noise of spectators, and gained the silence of witnesses.

Just as the young man's strength began to fade, Keld's arm began to lift. Still howling, Yut pushed the giant's elbow away from his neck and slipped his head out underneath it. Then, twisting his aching torso, he lifted his own elbow above Keld's sternum. He held it there for a moment, fully aware the crowd followed the movement like a starved man followed a chicken, before slamming it down with the force of thunder. Keld acted like it was the hardest hit he had ever taken, and let go of Yut.

The crowd roared.

Yut quickly rolled away, breathing in elated disbelief. *How in the dark did that work?* The exhilaration gave him enough energy to stand, though this time it proved more complicated, as the sand became water, his limbs joined in open rebellion, and the wild noise of the crowd became a muffled hum. Across the ring, Keld was already standing with his arms raised in a fighting stance. As their eyes met, Yut risked a quick nod of thanks. If the crowd saw collusion, then it would mean another long, embarrassing year of boyhood. Yet even though the two friends spoke about this night—and had a few practice rounds—Yut had not realized how passionate he would be about this. The pain and struggle were real, so the test, thought Yut, was real as well, even if some moves were rehearsed.

Dark take them, but the pain was real.

Splotches of darkness blinked into Yut's vision when Keld lowered his arms. Everything happened in blurred images: his friend was smiling and nodding at him, and then he was being attacked by the jeering crowd. They must have noticed the nod; they saw through the charade. Oh gods, they are coming for his eyes...

No, the crowd was cheering, hollering, and slapping his back. He was so focused on the next few seconds of his life that he almost missed the people yelling, "...Indeed! Strong indeed!"

As the realization dawned on Yut, he broke into a swollen half-grin.

By the nine living gods, it was over. He was a man now. The villagers crowded around him, offering half-heard congratulations and slaps of approval that were a little too hard. There were already three People's Brawls this night, but something told him this one was special.

Yut allowed himself to take it in. While he did not feel joyful or proud, an immense pressure was lifted off his chest as relief poured into him, nearly making him collapse. There was nothing left to prove, and no fights left to win. He was sure this was the hardest thing he would need to do in his life, and he did it well—no one could tell him that he didn't. After all, he withstood the trial, he has proven to be strong, and he was even about to say something to the crowd, before he puked the remains of his breakfast on the horrified villagers.

* * *

Sometime later, the new man sat at a table with a cup of strong mead in his hand, observing the rest of the Proving Moon. With the adrenaline gone, he rested in a sweet state of emptiness, even though the long house still brimmed with people and excitement. There were shouts and laughter from the sand pit as youths fought, punctuated by the occasional groan. The rest of the villagers were conversing and laughing in the slurred stupor of a people in dire need of a break. Some were even attempting to dance. Not everyone was drunk, but the smell of roasted meats seemed more intoxicating than the mead, making family of all.

Yut did not notice the harpa until it stopped playing, the skald of the night taking much-needed rest as he gulped down a full horn of ale. Yut turned back to Keld, and realized he was saying something. "What?"

"King Helgi's grunts," repeated Keld. "They've been coming around these parts. Big ones, too. Lookin' for fresh meat, is what people are saying. Lookin' to finish the war."

Yut shook his head, forcing his brain to start thinking again as he massaged his ribs. "King Helgi's... Didn't you see me out there?"

"Where?"

"In the Brawl, where else? I'm a man now, Keld. I mean, officially." Yut took on what he hoped was a more mature tone of voice. "Well done out there."

"Ah! Right, you were out for a while. It sure was somethin'," Keld said, casually taking a sip from his horn.

"A show it was, my friend. And when I brought down the elbow? I think Rothr and all of his hellish host were watching." Yut settled back into his seat, recalling the Brawl as if it was a fond memory from years ago. And, in a way, he thought that it was.

"Don't know about the god of battle," said Keld, taking another swig of mead, "But Ulric was watching."

Yut blinked. "Ulric? Ulric the Tall was in here? Ulric the Heisir?" Ulric the Tall was a leader of warriors from King Helgi, down in Rotheim. Though in these parts, he might as well have been king himself. Not only was Ulric the Tall born in Sanvik, he was said to have singlehandedly defeated a wulver using his sword, Staugr, and nothing else.

Keld kept his eyes on his horn of mead. "Yep. And then he said somethin' about you too, I think. You're a courageous spirit, he said."

At this, Yut nearly choked on his own drink. Ulric watching *him*? Perhaps even impressed by him? This could mean he had a chance to speak with him. Even though Yut had no large interest in soldiering, this was an opportunity of a lifetime. To be friends with Ulric would mean a life of adventure, becoming a band of something strong, something larger than Sanvik. Suddenly, Yut was a child in his parent's garden, a hefty stick in his hand, fighting beasts and searching for ancient treasure under the flowerbed. Like many children, he believed his life would be written in the sagas, and he would be loved by all. His heart tripled its pace as the forgotten fantasy emerged again, though he tried not to show it to his friend. "Gods below, Keld, you should have wakened me."

Keld chuckled. "Me? I thought you were dead, brother. Your face all messed up, starin' at everyone like they was a draugr. I just about carried you to the table."

"Damn, I don't remember a darkened thing. Did...did he say anything else?"

"Sure, plenty of things," said Keld, taking another sip, as if this wasn't news that Yut, or any man within a hundred miles, would have given a year's wages for. In fact, Keld was strangely docile. "Somethin' about looking for courageous spirits in the... what was it... the war against the Dark."

Yut set down his cup. This was unravelling too quickly. His entire life could be transformed by the next dawn. He often told himself that logmar was a worthy calling, but the gods put mankind on Arthgard for one reason: to drive back the great Dark before it consumed the world. Ulric was out there, on the edges of civilization, rooting out Seither-witches, wulvers, and other agents of the cursed Dark that infested their world. When the gods bestow blessings upon their children, they will bestow them on people like Ulric. But would they curse the people that abandon their fate as logmar? And what would his parents think of him? But what if he became a Heisir himself? Did Keld not realize what he was telling his friend? He had to find Ulric, or his parents, or—

"...the Jarl was saying something about marriage," Keld continued.

"Wait, the Jarl of Miklor was here too?!"

Keld buried his face deeper into the horn, which should have been empty by now. "Aye. The Jarl's daughter can't just marry some fool, he was looking for a real *man*."

Gods above. Yut had to act fast. Even if Sanvik was not the largest village, a logmar's son was still a logmar's son. Normally, if he did not find a good, wise girl shortly after passing the Proving Moon, then his mother would find one for him. And he doubted she would be placing good looks as a priority for his potential wife. "*Looks fade,*" she would say. But perhaps the Jarl knew Yut's father, and that is why he caught his eye. Perhaps... perhaps...

"Wait. I thought Jarl Floki doesn't have any daughters," Yut pointed out.

Keld made eye contact with his friend, and truly did his very best to swallow the mead in time. Alas, he did not.

He burst into uproarious laughter, spraying Yut with mead as he banged his arm on the table. *You have got to be kidding*, thought Yut. Unfortunately, Keld was. "The Jarl's... all his daughters!" Keld hollered between breaths as he wiped tears from his face. He eventually tapered down into soft wheezing as Yut watched him with death in his eyes.

"Ulric wasn't here," Yut said seriously.

Keld grabbed his nose as he snorted again, beginning another bout of blind laughter. "No, Ulric wasn't here," he conceded.

Yut was deadpan. The momentary excitement was swallowed by anger, shame, and returned awareness of physical pain. Mostly the pain. "That wasn't funny."

"What, that Ulric would want you in his command? That's not

funny, it's downright hilarious. Look, there is Bjorn the Mountain, who towers over all! *And behold*, there goes Ysolda the Bright, her braid sparkling with lightning. And, oh gods above, who is that by Ulric's side? Could it be...Yut the logmar's son!?"

"Never mind," said Yut. His friend was not being hurtful, he was just being right. A legend like Ulric would not take a dark-haired, skinny youth who had to cheat his Proving Moon to pass it. But that didn't make it easier to bear. He made sure to stomp out the fantasy of heroism properly this time, before burying it again. Every youth in Arthgard wanted to be in the legendary sagas. Probably most adults, too. So why should Yut be the chosen one? His only real skill was at tafl, though that was not saying much when you mostly played against Keld. No, he had his destiny, and he was content with it. Yut wiped his face from Keld's saliva as he picked up his cup again.

Keld stopped laughing when he noticed his friend's expression. "Aw, come on now, I was just having a laugh, brother. Ulric wouldn't take anyone from here, not even a hulking legend like me. Besides, the village needs you. More cool heads, more folks that can think. These young ones want nothing more'n to kill and get rich." He directed the last sentence at a few youths headed toward the warriors sitting in the corner. They tipped their horns to Keld, too drunk to sense the iron in his voice. He watched them pass, finishing the rest of his mead. "Darkened idiots. They'll come back without a limb if they're lucky."

"Gods above, Keld," slurred Yut, blinking the fatigue out of his vision. "You're almost too cheery. Aren't we supposed to be celebrating? The boys will be fine. They're strong boys."

"Strong enough for the Dark? The elders say it's closing in on us. They say it's all cause of the war. And there are monsters about now, too, beasts and worse. Can barely take a walk in the woods without riskin' your life. No mistake, this was the coldest summer we've had, and I reckon we'll see colder."

"Really, Keld, I think you're being just a little..." Yut paused as he regarded his friend, his famous frown on full display, "...paranoid. Sometimes summers are cold, and sometimes they're not. Sure, this year was tough, but we've survived tougher. And the Dark is out there, far past the mountains and the seas and far away from Sanvik. Besides, don't you think someone would have said something if they saw a wave of shadow, filled with monsters, swallowing up the earth?"

Keld's brows furrowed in thought. "Old Sten swears he's seen trelkin footprints in his chicken coop, and that's why his chickens been going missing."

"Yeah, but Old Sten is an idiot."

"Aye."

They sat quietly for a moment. There was cheering from the proving pit—another man had been born. On the other side, the youths were offering their horns to the Heisirs, who took it after openly inspecting the potential recruits. Keld was right; Yut had noticed them stopping by the village more often, speaking to Yut's father, their discussions growing longer and louder. Yut was proud of his father—the man was not big or particularly well-spoken, but he faced down fully armored Heisirs to protect the town. If it wasn't for him, Sanvik would be gutted of half its youths, enlisted to fight for the twin Jarls of Vessir or the Jarl of Rotheim. The other half would be drafted to battle the monsters of the Dark, wherever they were. Of course, his father did not repel them only out of the goodness of his heart. Sanvik was a lumber town, but it was nothing without its lumberjacks. Unfortunately, all Heisirs knew that if you could swing an axe at a tree, you could swing an axe at the enemy, be they man or beast.

Yut left his thoughts when someone placed a lamb's leg in front of them, still sizzling. The smell of spices and herbs on the dripping meat nearly made Yut cry. Keld left his world of monsters as well, and the two friends exchanged a conspiratorial look.

"Say, but that elbow was somethin'," said Keld, lamb spilling out of his maw.

Yut attempted to keep the food inside his mouth. "Ish wash good, wannit?"

"Oh, yeah. The crowd looked ready to jump when you brought it down. Dark above."

Yut thought back to the elbow as he thoughtfully gnawed on the bone. They hadn't practiced it before, but it felt right in the moment. "You didn't do too bad yourself, folding up like that."

"Genius, is what it was," said Keld, standing. "Another round? Look, some of my snot got in your cup."

"What? Where?"

"Kidding! Brother, you *gotta* to be less gullible."

Yut glanced around the long house again, recognizing familiar faces from neighboring villages, skalds from the cities of Miklor and Rotheim, and, of course, the Heisirs, watchful of potential killers emerging from the proving pit. They stood out like nails in porridge—all stone-faced, chainmail and axes glistening in the firelight, their gaze sharp. None were from Vessir, of course, not since the war began in earnest. And, unfortunately, none of the Heisirs were Ulric, and Yut swallowed that disappointment with the last of his mead.

He felt numb, his lip was swelling up, and the wooziness began to kick in, yet he tried to commit all the faces to memory. Most of the youths dreamed of fighting or sailing, and some snickered at Yut's "boring" destiny. Like his father, Yut was not a born fighter, but it didn't bother him too much, as being a logmar entailed a different type of battle. "*To die on a battlefield is a brave thing,*" his mother would tell him, "*but to lead a people in peace is the destiny of true heroes.*" They were not here, of course. Thanks to some tradition or another, parents of the Proving Moon candidates were not allowed to witness their children's fight. This was just fine by Yut, as he did not need his mother shouting fighting suggestions while he was in the pit. But they would be waiting for him the next morning, and his father would ask him who was at the long house, what they spoke of, and who they sat with. And, thanks to his performance, there should also be a feast. Yut allowed himself a smile. Yes, a feast and a celebration with his family and friends. Indeed, things were good now.

A rough slap on his pained back brought Yut out of his thoughts. "Atta boy, Eriksson, always knew you had it in ya," said the unmistakable scraggly voice of Tove, the village wisewoman. For such a small creature, she held surprising strength. Or maybe Yut's ribs were broken.

Yut struggled to enunciate through a swollen lip. "Thank you, withewoman."

She plopped down across from him, beads, bones, and jewels crackling in the movement. She wore her ceremonial garments, mainly a slightly cleaner assortment of her regular ornaments. Yut noted the people around them subconsciously take a step back, forming a circle around Tove. He could not tell if it was out of respect, or the cold summer.

She grinned mischievously while sliding a mug of hot something to him. "Nice fight. Interesting one, no doubt. Very interesting. And that elbow, my goodness. Must have practiced for weeks, eh?"

"Thank y—" The sluggish mind kicked into a sprint as her words reached Yut. Did she know? She couldn't, surely. He was hurt, he took a real beating. How could she know?

She smiled wider and winked. Dark take it all, she knew. He put his head in his hands. "Dark below..." he muttered.

"Mind the words in your curses, young man. Invoke the Dark and you only hurry its approach." And then she leaned in and whispered. "Relax, Yut, I'm a wisewoman, not the village herald. For what it's worth, I thought it was a fun fight. And I think you deserve the win."

Yut looked down at the mug in front of him, not sure of what to feel. All those weeks of planning, of practice. Did he deserve to be called a man at all?

"Eriksson, I said you deserve it, ya dolt. Now drink." She shoved the strange mug nearly into his lap. The fumes hit him then, and his eyes began to water.

"Dar—Gods, smells like cat piss. What is this?"

"Cat piss," said Tove. "It has healing properties, you know."

"Funny."

"Just drink it, and stop being such a baby. Tomorrow is a new moon and a new sun, and life will go on. For better or worse. Have my herbs ever steered you wrong?"

Yut brought the drink to his lips, hesitating. It was usually a bad idea to drink Tove's brews, but it was an even worse idea to refuse a wisewoman's offering. Yut heard of a lumberjack who had his leg broken by a falling log, and he swore Tove's herbs made him see the gods for nearly a week. But at least he did not feel the pain when they set the bone back in place. Closing his eyes, Yut forced the hot, salty liquid down his throat. Gods below, was it actually cat piss...?

"Be strong, boy," cackled Tove, "You'll need to endure harder things in this life."

"I..." Yut's head spun, and dark spots began appearing before him. What did the witch give him? The movement around him became images, the last sounds he heard were repeating in a loop. Then, lights began melding with each other, forming a brilliant display of orange and red. Everyone disappeared in the light, except for Tove, who was now somehow taller. She towered over him, the light not reflecting from her, instead forming an ominous silhouette.

"*Be strong, Yut.*" Her voice boomed and reverberated through the entire world, and they pushed Yut deep into the sea of red.

Yut did not know how long he sat there, but in time, the colors took on shapes again, and the sounds returned to their proper places. The skald was just beginning another saga, and like all sagas, this one began with the creation of Arthgard and the sagas of the gods that formed it.

Tove was gone, and Keld was talking to a few farmers' daughters by the mead barrels. As Yut moved to stand, he realized it no longer hurt to breathe. He gently felt his face—it was smooth, all the swelling was gone. What's more, there was a new energy in his limbs.

Cat piss indeed, thought Yut, spirits making a grand return. The night was young, and Keld looked like he needed help at the mead barrels. He stood and felt an indomitable confidence accompany his every step. Friends and strangers noticed him, nodding their heads and raising their horn. Even the Heisirs in the corner looked at him. He nodded at them, but not in an overtly friendly manner—his father did not trust them, and neither would he. Yes, he would be a firm logmar, but one with a heart of gold, like his mother taught him.

When the last fighter passed his Brawl, the night became everything. Yut was drinking mead with Keld, and then he was roaring the classic saga songs along with the skald and the rest of the long house. Then he was dancing, his mind melting in the lights, ale, and music. Someone punched him, but did not pursue the altercation after seeing Keld approach. Then someone kissed him on the cheek, but Yut was too drunk to see who it was or where they left to. The skald spilled drink all over himself and Yut laughed until he cried. He was given another horn, so he climbed one of the tables to give a speech, and they were chanting his name, and he did not know what he said, but they cheered him on anyway. And then Yut was watching them dance, caught in a blissful space where nothing and everything mattered all at once. These were the people for whom he would give anything. Yes, Yut will show them strong; he will show them hero. He just hoped Sanvik—no, the whole of Arthgard, was ready for him.

Interlude

The Madman

Far away from Sanvik, and many years after the Proving Moon, the Madman's hut shivers in the shadow of an ominous mountain. The Madman suddenly pauses his saga and eyes the waning day through a crack in the wall boards. "You might now know this," he tells the Visitor eventually, "but the Allwinter was much like this one."

The Visitor is leaning against the back wall, silently watching the old man while keeping an eye on the door and the windows. He does not show irritation at the sudden detour from the saga. After all, what else can you expect from a Madman?

"Yut's old man was born at the end of the Allwinter," continues the Madman, "but he knew how it was back then. Hunting for scraps, eating whatever root or bone you found, trusting none but the ones in your hovel, and n*ever* staying outside past dark. For three years, we waded in our torment, for three years, we lost our loved ones. First to the hunger, then the fever, then the wars. But when the gods finally brought spring, it was like being born anew. We didn't want to raise arms, we only sought peace, and life. That's right... we only sought life."

Tears crest the red eyes, but are blinked away instantly, and smothered with another swig of his foul brew. “The underfolk left at that point, and the lightfolk were nowhere to be seen, though it was said the Allwinter did not reach them. No, we had one another, and that was just enough. Now everyone is leaving again, for who knows how long the winter will last? And who will save us?” He looks at the Visitor again, grief mixed with hope. Then a husk of laughter escapes his throat, and madness takes his eyes again.

“I will, of course. Power in the stories, see? They’ll see. You’ll see. But first, see how Yut became what he became. Only then can you despise him.”

Chapter Two

Golden Eyes

Yut first felt the cold. Not the cold of a brisk walk through a winter's night, or even that of a morning wash in the river. This cold seeped into his very soul, paralyzing his body with a thousand pinpricks of pain. His lungs were aching, his fingers and toes were already numb, his hair was frosted solid. To move would be torture, though he tried anyway. He could not remember if he was shivering before he awoke, but his teeth were chattering now to the point that he had to clamp his jaw shut to avoid shattering them. Mornings in autumn could get viciously cold, especially after a cold summer.

Yut then felt the pressure. He was lying on a cold floor, and something—or someone—was lying on top of him. The pressure was not enough to cause severe pain, but it was enough to cover his torso as well as his face, allowing only the outskirts of his vision to see a faint light around him. It must have been morning. Through the mask of numbness, he could feel coarse hair on his forehead. So it *was* someone on top of him. But who? And why outside? And why were they not moving?

Flashes of memory began assaulting Yut's mind before he

realized he could not breathe. Whoever was sleeping on top of him was heavy and large, and while Yut may have been able to survive with what little breath he had while unconscious, the growing panic—and his increasingly frantic heartbeat—demanded more air from his lungs. He desperately tried to breathe, but the weight would not let him.

Yut fought with the weight, his lethargic limbs pushing and scratching at it. He heard a cloth rip, and the stranger's heavy arms provided firm but useless handholds. Yut felt like he was trying to lift a mountain, and as the slow realization that he might suffocate to death settled on him, he pushed even harder. He tried to yell and twist his body, but the weight was final, blinding Yut to anything around him. He scrambled, the panic becoming hysteria. He was going to die here. He was going to suffocate to death underneath another person, who might have been dead themselves.

What little strength he had begun to fade. Yut's heart beat even faster, but his chance of survival was flickering. There would be no morning feast, no logmar, no Keld, no family, no home. His new life would end as quickly as it began, and everyone would forget him.

His parents' faces, filled with mourning, passed before him.

Death was coming.

Sudden, savage strength ignited his frozen limbs, and he heaved again, knowing this would be his final chance. He pushed with his entire being, he *willed* the weight on top of him to rise. He could not die here. He would not die here.

As his shaking arms strained against the weight, Yut felt something shift. Things fell around him, the ground trembled, and the body on top of him inched to the side. Hope blossomed as more things began toppling on the floor.

Finally, he simultaneously pushed and twisted his body,

slipping halfway from underneath the massive weight.

He sucked in sweet, frigid air. It filled his lungs with fire, and he began coughing and heaving in uncontrolled bursts. The pain in his arms, legs, and lungs multiplied with each breath, but it did not matter, because he was still *alive.* His relieved laughter was broken up by the dry cough.

It took a few moments for Yut's eyes to adjust to the morning light. With a start, he realized he was still in the long house.

It had been burned to the ground.

A charred forest of planks leaned on each other, the roof had collapsed on one end and disappeared on the other. Ash and frost mixed on the burned floorboards and the destroyed tables. Yut's breath began to tremble as he stared at them, dumbfounded. He felt like he was in a vivid dream, though there was a horror building in his chest. Then he noticed a few black lumps strewn about, and his stomach twisted. Bodies. He looked away, forcing himself to focus on his breathing and think logically. Fires were not unheard of in Sanvik, but everyone should have been able to escape. Perhaps that explained the small number of corpses. Yes, that was it: a few unfortunate deaths in an accidental fire.

Bursts of memory flashed before Yut. It was a late night. There was action and excitement—the People's Brawl! He was a man now. Keld was getting a drink. But then...

Golden eyes.

Yut doubled over in another fit of coughing. He needed to get out of here and find his parents, they would be broken if they thought he had been burned alive.

As his cough subsided, he pulled his legs out from his death-prison, which seemed like the focal point of the collapsed ceiling, a mountain of planks and logs, and a body underneath it. No wonder it was so impossibly heavy. In fact, Yut was surprised—but no less relieved—that he escaped at all. He saw where some of the planks moved and broke as a result of his struggle. The body on top of him, however—

Golden eyes. They were slit like a cat's eyes. They looked beyond him, beyond his understanding, from the night sky. They stared *into* him, stripping him before an all-knowing mind far too intricate to be understood. They were filled with evil. And between them, a red sigil—a foreign rune—burning fiercely.

Last night, he stared into those eyes like everyone else in the long house, paralyzed as if the gods had torn open the roof. The roof... Yut looked again at the ceiling that was supposed to be there. It disappeared on the other side of the tavern. Yes, it was ripped, peeled away with the quickness of a retreating wave. Beyond the torn opening were the golden eyes, two golden moons encompassed in shadow. The light from the red rune revealed a glint of black scale.

Yut remembered teeth as long as his arm appearing below those eyes, and a deep rumbling sound in his chest. It felt like the beginning of an earthquake.

He remembered Keld running at him through the crowd of stilled people. The mouth of the being opened, and a glow emanated from its throat, a light at the end of the tunnel. A wave of warm air embraced Yut.

It was a fire drake, but that was impossible. Those things were half-legend and had no business invading small lumbering towns. Monsters like that were somewhere out in the Dark, in the depths of the mountains, and not in Sanvik. No, he must have drank too much, or it was the work of Tove's brew. Maybe it was still affecting him, and he was still unconscious, and this was the end of a horrible dream. That's right, and he would wake up any moment now. Any moment...

And then he remembered the blinding light. Keld ran into him from the front as the building collapsed. He heard a crash, then everyone screaming all at once, then nothing at all.

A slow, sickening realization crept up on Yut as he turned around and looked at the mound of planks. The body that trapped him, the body that nearly suffocated him... *No...*

He drew closer, his heart and teeth chattering. The body was burned on the back and impaled by several collapsed planks.

Please no...

He was big. Biggest in the village. And just big enough to shield Yut from the fire and the collapsing long house. Yut stopped breathing.

Keld lay underneath the wreckage. Yut's best friend died protecting him until the very end.

* * *

Yut stared at his friend. *This is not possible,* he thought. It simply could not have happened. His hands were shaking. What exactly did this? Why Sanvik? Why Keld?

He continued staring until he saw nothing else. Even though Keld was face down, Yut knew him too well—the bulk of his body, the rune marks on his forearms, the stark black hair. His back had been savagely burned, exposing frosted ribs and spine. Yut found himself hoping that the impaling planks gave him a quick death.

Yut's breath caught. *He is dead. He is truly dead.* The tears would not come, however. His hands continued shaking, but he felt still. Far away. He felt he should remove the debris. He should weep—collapse and curse the gods. But he continued kneeling there, quiet and unmoving, save for the trembling hands.

They will build a boat for him and send him along the Krum

Run to enter Rothr's realm for the honorable death he claimed. Everyone in the village loved Keld, so no expense would be spared. They would send him with the good furs, any pieces of gold they could find, and his lumber axes. Why would the gods take Keld instead of Yut? It should be him under those planks, not Sanvik's best lumberjack. Now, the others will look at Yut like a bad bargain, that his life was traded for Keld's. And Yut would have no choice but to agree.

He forced himself to stop thinking about that. Shamefully, he trudged to Keld's body, put his hand on his friend's shoulder, and whispered the rites of passage into the afterlife. Only those still living could send the dead to Rothr, as that was the way of things. "May the gods accept you in the golden fields, brother," whispered Yut, "and may we meet again."

After a few moments of numb silence, Yut's shivering had gotten so bad that he needed to find furs before helping Keld. Weren't people supposed to be here already? It must have been the second hour of the morning, at least.

He stumbled out of the burnt long house, and stopped, realizing what he had secretly been dreading. Ingvar's smithy, the hall of the elders, homes, stables... all were blackened, empty husks. More half-burned lumps of villagers were strewn along the main road as well. Some part of him was aware this was a horrible thing to behold, and that part wanted to break down and wither along with the husks. But Yut could not do that. He had to move. His parents would be worried about him. Gods above, his parents...

He sprinted with his head down through a village consumed by ash and silence, whispering prayers to all the gods he could think of. Empty houses passed before him like inquisitive skulls of some strange creatures. He decided not to look at the corpses after discovering some of them had not been fully burned. Several times

Yut tripped and fell into the ash, and getting up was growing more difficult. So much death, and yet he was still alive. Someone else had to be alive. They had to.

As he neared his home, he heard voices. Hope sparked somewhere, and he willed his numb legs to move faster. It was amazing how quickly the spirit could be lifted at the sound of a human's voice. In the deathly silence of the village, Yut almost gave up on hearing voices ever again.

Rounding a hill, Yut approached his house, where the voices came from. It was destroyed like the rest of the buildings, with the entire outer wall and most of the roof gone. That didn't matter for now, because some people were still obviously alive. In fact, as Yut saw several shapes moving in the collapsed house, his knees buckled in relief. They were moving the wreckage! They were rebuilding!

They were... not his parents, nor anyone he knew in the village.

Yut tripped again, falling behind an overturned cart. He shook his head as he tried to regain his breath. There were only a few of them, so who were they? Could this mean that the rest of the village had abandoned him in the wreckage of the tavern? Or was this truly all that was left?

It couldn't be.

Trying to keep his shivering contained, he peeked around the cart. The people were still there, speaking. One was a large, balding man wearing loud chain mail and a shield strapped on his back. Next to him stood a much smaller woman—barely reaching his chest—wearing dirty white robes and a peculiar band around her brown-red curls. She was waving her arms and insisting something to the man, who just grunted and pushed at a fallen timber pillar. Yut almost missed the second woman sitting on the ruined fence, to the side of the house. She wore hunting leathers, an assortment of daggers sheathed throughout, and the tightest white-blonde ponytail Yut had ever seen.

Something about her reminded him of a lightfolk. Or, at least, the way his mother described them. Young, fair skinned, light eyes, ethereal in nature, and untouched by the darkness of this world. The warriors of the gods. Yut noted those daggers looked like they've seen use. She was not lightfolk—those have not been seen for a hundred years. She was someone else.

And she was looking directly at him.

Yut shrunk back behind the cart. The strangers could be bandits, or maybe just pillagers. He could try to run—the lightfolk woman would need to get closer to launch a dagger at him. Come to think of it, she could be doing that now, or worse, she could be silently warning her fellows. The panic was returning. He escaped certain suffocation under a building to be killed by bandits. And yet, they could know where everyone went. After all, why would they hurt Yut? He had nothing, and he could not hurt them.

After a few more moments of panic-induced theorizing, Yut dared to peek out again. The young woman was still staring at him, though she hardly moved at all. After staring back at her for a moment, Yut realized she was looking in his direction, but not at *him,* as if there was something deeply interesting just behind.

Yut stole a glance behind him just in case. There was nothing.

He tried to gauge the other two. The big man relented his pushing and was now uncorking a flask as he walked to where the short woman was pointing. They were standing where his parents would sleep now, cots and furs ruined. Thankfully, the house was empty. The man took a swig as she kneeled and put her ear against the charred floorboards. Yut did not think she was young, though it was hard to place her age. She nodded, satisfied, and said something to the man, who took out a hatchet from a nearby knapsack. These were not bandits or pillagers—they were scavengers, hoping to find some funeral gold in the largest house of the village. It was not so large anymore, but they would not find anything. Yut knew his mother kept their silver in the forest.

Yet as the big man began hacking into the wood with a hatchet, it felt decidedly wrong to Yut. It was one thing to have your house burned down by something from the Dark itself, but another to watch someone rob your home.

With a couple more icy breaths, Yut gathered the courage to walk up to the house. He did not know what he would say, but he hoped he could improvise something persuasive—and quickly. After all, they would need to organize a funeral later that day. Many, many funerals.

Lightfolk's gaze followed him as he neared her companions, but she gave no shout or warning. *Excellent*, thought Yut, *all according to plan. Probably.*

He walked to within a few strides of the hacking man and cleared his throat. The woman in the white robes jumped and turned sideways to Yut. To his shock, he realized her band was not covering her forehead, but her eyes. *A blind scavenger?*

Yut sighed a breath of relief. These were not murderers, as murderers do not come in blind variety. At least, Yut did not think they did. They were usually big, and mean, and, well, men. That is how some poor travelers who stopped at their village described them, anyhow.

The big man, who did look like a bandit, continued hacking, oblivious.

"Olaf," said the blind woman quietly. Then she called to him again, louder. He finally stopped hacking, turned around, and jumped even higher than her.

"Eira! It's a draugr!" Yelped Olaf, his voice, though high in this instance, resonating with deep trepidation. He brought up his hatchet in a defensive stance. Yut couldn't blame him, he must have looked like death itself, covered in ash, dirt, and frost.

"P-p-please..." He tried enunciating the words, but speaking was difficult when you couldn't feel your face. The man grabbed his hatchet tighter, his eyes halfway out of his skull.

"N-not a d-d..."

"This is no ghost, Olaf," said the woman called Eira. Her words were tinged with a northern accent. The northerners made their hard sounds harder, so that it could penetrate through all the ice in their ears. At least, that's how Yut's father reasoned it.

"Even worse," breathed Olaf, "A restless spirit, come to haunt us from beyond a grave!"

"That... is what a draugr is, Olaf."

Olaf turned from Yut to Eira, and slowly back to Yut. He hefted his hatchet. "I knew it."

The blind woman whispered a curse under her breath as Yut backed away with his arms raised.

"No, child, he will not hurt you," she called. "Was this village your home? Whom do you seek?"

Olaf did not lower the hatchet, but something about the woman's voice made him believe her. How would a short blind woman harm him?

"Have you seen any of the others?" asked Yut, his neck spasming from the shivers. "T-they couldn't have gone far."

There was silence. What in the dark was wrong with them?

Olaf put down his hatchet, taking out the small bottle again. Eira continued looking down, though Yut wasn't sure if that was the right way of putting it. Was she listening more intently if she was looking down? Did it matter?

"Please, I need to find my par—"

"They're not here," said a voice behind Yut. Now it was Yut's turn to jump. The lightfolk woman stood not a stride from him, but she must have flown there. She spoke quickly and quietly, as if unwilling to spend unneeded breath. "You should move on."

"Please, the village was... I'm very cold," stammered Yut, tears blurring his vision, "You don't understand..."

"No, child, Sigrid is right," said Eira. "It is you who do not understand, and may never fully understand." She raised her arm, and Sigrid rushed to her, pushing Yut aside. Together, they approached him, and Eira put a hand on his shoulder.

She seemed ready to say something, but her mouth kept closing, and her eyebrows continued furrowing. It seemed her face could not decide which emotion to show, so it showed them all at once. But then she spoke a quick prayer, using words he understood and words he did not. She finished by loudly saying, "We are leaving, Olaf."

Suddenly, they began walking away from Yut along the road that led outside of Sanvik.

The big man looked as if he was about to protest, but glancing at Yut, he wordlessly picked up his pack of assorted weapons and joined his companions, shoulders slumped.

This was too surreal to Yut. He felt there was something he did not understand. No, he felt completely blind. Truly, these were the strangest scavengers he had ever met. He looked at the house, wondering if any furs were underneath the wreckage. He took a step forward...

And there they were, alive, beckoning him home, his mother fretting over the cold air invading the house, his father's usual face of concern split into a proud smile. The fire pit was smoldering, casting their home in a beautiful golden light, and Yut was sure he had never been more glad to be home. Keld was snoring in the corner, too, an empty bowl resting on his stomach. Yut's father arose from the table, upon which the steaming stew, fresh bread, morning pork and afternoon fish were all ready for him. His mother closed the door, and Yut could see tears in her eyes. "My strong man," she whispered, and gently embraced him. He heard his father laugh as he hugged him from behind. "You showed them, didn't you, son? You went for the legs?"

Yut could only nod as warm tears streamed down his cheeks. *You should've seen it, dad. You should've seen it.*

He stood there, suspended between shock and relief, barely breathing, until his eyes were drawn upward, where the ceiling should have been. Instead, he saw a wyrm's golden eyes in a black sky. They called to him, whispered to him, as the world began melting around him. He tried to hold on to his parents, but they faded as well, leaving him embracing air. He heard Eira's voice again—she was praying, but not in any known tongue. Still, he could almost understand it. Her whispering prayer engulfed him, and one word stood out clearly.

"*See.*"

And Yut opened his eyes, and he saw his village, his destroyed home, and the pair of burned corpses lying inside, and reality drowned him.

* * *

The sun was throwing its last reds across the blackened village. A soft breeze rustled through the nearby trees. Silent, empty homes leaned—some shedding a log or stone, while others quietly watched the lone youth at the edge of town.

Yut shivered under the scorched blanket. His fingers were crusted with blood, and he had lost feeling in his feet, but his attention remained fixed on a mound of bloodied stones in front of him. He remembered flashes of consciousness, though they were far away, as if the life in his memories was not his. He spent most of the day gathering stones for the mound. The process was painful, leaving his hands in tatters and his back numb with pain.

He couldn't dislodge Keld. It would have taken a score of men to uncover the collapsed roof, so he merely carved a rune of peace next to his body, making sure not to look at it.

Yut worked the entire day in silence. No one else was in the village, not a single living soul. He remembered bursts of weeping, utter hopelessness, and panic. He remembered retching as he touched his mother's hand.

Pain. He hoped they did not feel the pain. He hoped they were at peace when it happened. Gods, why did it happen? Why was he still alive?

He knew he was not fooling anyone. The entire village was burned alive. He may have escaped the fire, but he was no less dead. Yut the man indeed. Drinking strong mead and lumber quotas were infinitely inconsequential, forgotten, dead. No, that man—that boy—was dead. There was nothing left for him or of him.

Echoes of thoughts ventured to warn Ottervik in case the wyrm attacked again. Thoughts of starting a fire outside of town before he lost his feet, of scavenging useful items for the journey ahead.

Useless. There was no journey. Only the mound of stones—as large as he could make it, to give rest to the dead in case they were rejected from the golden fields of the gods. He imagined his parents clawing their way out, bent on avenging themselves, and instantly regretted it.

He stood up as the sun hid behind the trees, and started walking to the river to get away from the nightmares in the village.

He did not stop walking.

Chapter Three

Sigrid

Sigrid watched the landvaettir stride gracefully through the air. This one took the shape of a great stag, with glistening blue runes running down the length of its antlers, neck, and legs. From what she could tell, most vaettir took the shape of the local wildlife it protects, though they never seemed to match their appearance perfectly. In Sig's mind, this proved that even incorporeal spirits can be lazy. If you could change your appearance at will, why settle for looking *almost* like someone else? If she was an incorporeal spirit, she would just be a giant bear. And she would not allow anyone in her forest, no matter their reasons.

The vaettir stopped and grazed at a nearby patch of grass. It stood slightly above the ground, as if the laws of this world were a mere suggestion. The grass was undisturbed, of course, but the spirit must have had its fill anyway. It eventually drifted through the trees and into its own world. According to Eira, landvaettir did not actually touch the world of humans, rather they were observers. This did not stop Sigrid from picking at the handle of her best dagger. If the spirits lived in their world, then she figured they were ready to protect it as well.

When she was alone again, Sig kneeled, sliding her hands under the fallen leaves, into the cold soil, feeling the wet pebbles and moss slide against her palms. She breathed deep, focusing on the smells and sounds of this forest. Eira told her that this would help her focus, still her heart, and maybe even bring her peace. But peace was in short supply between scavenging for food and supplies, avoiding roving warbands, and not being eaten alive by wild beasts. Of course, there was a time when she was being hunted, and there was no peace at all. In those days, the landvaettir were a good sign, since it meant there were no people around. She never wondered why the spirits did not flee from her like they did from others. She was usually too busy looking for the next scrap of food, or running from the hunters' dogs.

Eira told her to take strength from her nature, to own and use it against her enemies. Sig did the best she could, but to be known for her past, and to look like a lightfolk, presented many dangers, not the least of which was the constant threat of capture. Sometimes they sought her for coin—apparently, she would fetch a good price on the witch market. Others had more respectable and honest reasons, such as simply drinking her blood for the promise of good health. The hunters usually made sure to announce their reason for chasing her, as if that would make her reconsider running. Thankfully, when others have been trying to trap you for most of your life, you figured out a thing or two about their methods.

She scanned the patch of trees in front of her. It seemed like the perfect place for a camp: Sheltered from the wind by the large tree trunks, dug in, well hidden from the outside. But the rustled leaves and marks in the dirt around the area would only fool children. This was a crude trap, where a canopy of leaves covered a hole in which, more likely than not, a few well-placed spikes awaited the victims.

The trappers themselves—drendir cannibals, probably—were not here. Times were rough, with the war and all. A scavenger had to spread their options. The drendir no doubt had several other traps like these in the area.

Sigrid noted the location of the trap but did not move to uncover it. She thought scavengers, whatever the sort, should maintain some sort of courtesy for each other. Otherwise, they would be no better than the jarls who drove them to scavenging.

After taking a moment to listen for dangers, Sigrid sat to await her companions. They agreed that she had the sharpest eyes of the three. This was not saying much, however, as one of them was blind, and the other a step above a conscious boulder. Still, her eyes have served her well in the past, and would fetch a handsome amount of coin to the right buyer. Or so she was told.

It was these eyes that caught the glimpse of a shadow behind a tree. A breeze brushed against the branches and fallen leaves, camouflaging his next move.

Sig held her breath as she gripped the dagger at her hip. One more movement was all she needed. One more glimpse, just to be sure of the target. *Breathe in...*

He peeked, and the dagger thudded into the tree, an inch away from Olaf's face. The big man recoiled, his sizeable pack pulling him off balance and sending him stumbling into the fresh leaves. "Dark!"

Sig breathed out, willing her hands to stop trembling. *That was close... or not close enough.* Of all the men Sigrid had seen in her life, none were as unremarkable as the warrior, with his balding head, unkempt beard, and rampant paranoia. He had been traveling with them for a fortnight, and Sigrid guessed he had some nightmares in his past—else he wouldn't be with her and Eira—but she did not prod him. He was an ox of a man, and might have looked fearsome when he was angry, but she could see the fear that drove him, as it drove most. As it drove her.

The second dagger impaled the ground between his legs. For the hundredth time that week, she thought about how much better things had been before he joined them. "You ought to drop a few dozen stones before trying that, idiot."

That got him to scramble up, a stupid grin on his face. "Not bad. You been working on that one all night?" She had, and a few more, but she'd save those for later.

"And I don't need to drop nothin', elf. I may be big as a bear, but I sure as dark run like one too."

"Sure smell like one. And I told you I'm not a lightfolk. If you call me that again I'll skewer you." She tapped the dagger resting at the small of her back, visualizing the trajectory, calculating the speed. Right below the chin, dead within seconds.

Be civil, Eira had told her. She relaxed.

It wasn't until he turned away, muttering something about just having fun, that she realized he was alone. "Where is Eira?"

Olaf looked around them, as if just noticing they were alone. "Right, I left her at the creek."

"What do you mean? By *herself*?"

"Obviously by herself, unless you people are into talking with trees."

She was already striding past him. "You left a blind woman alone in a forest."

"Hey, she *said* she'll be fine," Olaf called out, "She can summon spirits, or something. Hey! She said she needed to think!"

Sig smothered the rage building inside her. Eira said she cannot be controlled by rage, that is the way for the other side to win. *Her* other side. She needed to be like the landvaettir; watching and listening, but uninvolved. She also needed to be focused. If Eira walked anywhere by herself, she had to track her. It was easy to get lost in the forest if you could see, and much more so if you were blind.

Unfortunately, Olaf caught up to her soon enough, his armor, supplies, and weapons clanging as he jogged behind her. "Seriously," he wheezed, "She can hear very good. She can always tell which side the dice land on. She gets it right every time."

"And if a wulver catches her scent? Will he join her for a friendly game before tearing her apart?"

Olaf missed a breath. "There are wulvers here?"

She did not answer as they hurried back to the creek. Blessedly, Eira was still there, sitting on a rock, her fist under her chin, the image of contemplation. It was hard to tell how old she was—Sig never asked—with the wisewoman's dark hair merely touched by gray, and her hands mostly smooth. However, in the light of the overcast sky, she looked old and tired. She also seemed perturbed, as if trying to understand some complicated insult.

Sig realized she had that same look when she first saw Eira, years ago. She did not remember much from those days, but even then, she knew she would remember seeing the blind seeress wading through a forgotten swamp by herself. Somehow, she walked within an arm's reach of young Sig's hiding spot, and if she had come any nearer, Sig might have pounced just for the chance of finding food. But the seeress passed by unharmed, until she was at a safe distance. Then she turned around, and said, "*I'm glad you're still with us, child. Though, that will not last with that wound of yours—I can smell it even through the stench of the swamp. Heisir Sune coats her dogs' teeth with venom before going hunting. The dogs don't live long, but neither does their quarry. Come, let me see what I can do.*" And although all of Sig's frayed instincts screamed at her to run away from the strange woman, something in Eira's voice pushed her to simply... give up. Eira was the first person in a long time to make her feel like a petulant, awkward teenager, instead of a monster. At the time, that was all it took.

Before Olaf and Sig had time to catch their breath, Eira sprang up from her contemplation and stepped back into the creek, clutching her staff for support. Sig approached her carefully, the icy water gripping her feet once again. "You alright, wisewoman?"

Eira continued walking. "Do not be angry with Olaf, child. I needed to think. Something... something is happening. Or, already happened."

Nodding, Sig took Eira's elbow. The creek was fairly shallow in autumn, but the rocks underneath were no less slippery. Falling in would mean half of your body drenched with deathly cold, and night was coming. She did not worry for Olaf, who splashed loudly as he walked behind them, grumbling as usual. The man was so heavy that if he fell in, she would be more worried for the creek.

"What changed?" asked Sig.

Eira considered for a while longer. "The young man in the town. What did you think of him?"

Sig tried to remember the burned village. The sight wasn't unusual in their line of work. Plenty of villages nowadays were sacked, with dozens of Heisir groups bent on inflicting as much cruelty as possible in their jarl's name. Plenty of orphans and widows, too, desperately holding on to scraps of their lives. The scavengers had to collect what they could and be on their way, not committing the images to memory. Of course, few of these towns were razed by a living fire wyrm.

"The kid was no threat. I saw him walking from across town, but he didn't hold any weapons. He only noticed us—"

"No, what did you think of *him?*" repeated Eira more strongly.

Sig hesitated. The boy was detached—lost. An image of a little girl holding on to a stranger's hand flashed before Sig's eyes. The girl was crying, covered in fresh blood. "He was... I don't know."

"Then what does the Saga say?"

"...Right now?"

"Yes," said Eira, gripping Sig's hand firmer.

Taking a deep breath, Sig fell into that familiar space and focused on sound. The Saga was all around them, sharing its stories without end or beginning, through trees, rocks, birds, and creeks. So Sig listened, just as Eira had taught her. She could not listen to the bird songs or the skittering of squirrels, as those were too far, but the trees... The trees *spoke*.

Through silent sagas, they spoke of pain, tragedy, death, and strength. They drew her in, the stories of what they had heard and seen—closer to the source, to their burned brethren at that same village. Something important was in its center. She drew even closer, opening her mind and closing her eyes...

Which is when Olaf decided to release a belch so loud that Sig tripped on a root and nearly sprawled to the ground. "Poor kid," he continued, not missing a step. "I would give him three days. Then the wolves get him. I'd put coin on that."

Sig clenched her teeth. It was not often she could follow the Saga so clearly, but once her focus had been broken it was some time before she could get it back. She turned to Olaf. "You stupid, darkened—"

"The wolves won't come near a drake attack," interjected Eira, helping Sig with her balance, "not for weeks. But I believe the boy will leave the village."

"Huh? So even the wolves have enough sense to stay away from..." Olaf paused, and then chuckled. "This is what you do? Follow drakes around, pickin' up what's left?"

"Drakes," answered Eira. "Wulvers, trelkin, Seither-witches. Even soldiers. Anywhere the others won't venture."

"Smart," nodded Olaf, but, as far as Sig could tell, it usually took a minute for his thoughts to catch up with what he's heard. This time he slowed, furrowing his brow. "If the others don't come... it's because the wulver might still be there."

"They are usually not there," Eira said quickly, the corner of her lip curling slightly.

"Usually? How do you know?" asked Olaf, but Eira just walked on in silence. Sigrid's anger morphed into nasty amusement. She could almost see his imagination spring into existence and leap into the farthest pits of the Dark.

"Don't tell me... You think you'll hear them?!"

"And see them." Eira patted Sigrid's arm. "I have my eyes right here."

"But this is... what if they're sneaking around? What if they're flying? Or invisible? Gods below, I get wantin' good loot, but you're crazy, both of you. You're out here dancing with evils no one ought to dance with, bringing down the Dark on all of us poor—"

"The drake is long gone, Olaf son of Thoran," said Eira, her voice suddenly firm, "This I promise you. And no wulver or witch can sneak up on me. If you doubt my word, then I invite you to break yours and leave."

He did not leave, sadly. Sig was still unclear as to why Olaf was with them. When she first saw him, they were in an unremarkable town with an unremarkable name. Eira sent Sig to purchase provisions, and before she was done, Eira found her, Olaf in tow, and suggested that they leave at that very moment, and very quickly. Whatever his motivations were, Eira had complete confidence in his word, and that was that.

They walked on in silence, save for an occasional grumbling

from Olaf. *Good*, thought Sig, she preferred the silence. And she definitely did not want to break it by asking why Eira brought up the kid. And why they were going back to the village.

Chapter Four

Run

Yut walked along Krum Run, the river that ran by Sanvik on the Eastern side. Though the riverbank was one of the busiest spots in Sanvik, with villagers fishing and cleaning in its clear waters, he only saw one figure at the bank. He froze when he saw her face. She was slender, nearly as tall as him, with a dark red braid that matched the color of his own hair. His mother beckoned to him, and he appeared before her. She was in the middle of gutting fish, with her hands and apron covered in fish guts, when she motioned to a nearby bucket with her knife. "Are you going to gawk, or are you going to help?"

He was sitting, knife in one hand, fish in the other, when she looked at him again. Something was off, but he could not place it... He was forgetting something important, he had somewhere to be. He was running, yes, and something bad happened. His mother continued watching him, as the midday overcast darkened her face in shadow. "It's your fault," she said, her voice growing deeper. "My son, why did you kill us?"

Yut jolted awake. Emotions swirled within him as the world spun. His first instinct was to jump, roll away, scream, and he almost did, before remembering he had spent the night on a high pine branch. His entire body gripped the branch as it shook with his jolt. Yut waited in the silence of the dark morning as his dizziness settled. Then he heard another growl, and realized it was coming from his stomach.

Cursing himself, he began the slow descent from the tree. Memories crawled back. He was morose, dead, cursing the gods in the forest by himself. His village was destroyed. Dark above, his parents...

Before he collapsed in panic again, Yut forced the memories down. He was in a tree, he was running... he saw shadows. Shadows of drakes, wolves, the Dark itself enveloping him, and though his mind was suspended in darkness, he still had his legs. Yut did not give another glance at the village as he ran. He remembered then, through the fear and darkness, a deep need to survive. So, he ran, and continued running, until his legs and lungs were aflame. And when his body was about to give up, he sprang for the sturdiest pine he could find, clamped onto the branch, and tried to keep silent. Thankfully he still had his blanket, otherwise his chattering teeth would have given him away in the night.

He considered leaping down from the tree, but decided not to risk a broken ankle, so he slid and skidded to the ground. He was already out of breath. Gods, he needed food. He also needed water—when was the last time he drank anything? Couldn't have been since the Proving Moon...

Again he prodded at the open wound in his mind, but this time he recoiled faster. *No,* he thought, clenching his fists, *survive.* Somehow, he was still alive, so he had to... get through it.

He thought of Ottervik. He visited with his father before, the people there remembered him. They would take care of him—if they were still alive. His other option would be the family's farmstead, but that was a journey that took days longer.

Tightening the blanket around him, he ventured West—or where he thought was West, it was hard to tell through the overcast skies and the strange woods. He would make to Ottervik, hopefully passing a stream along the way, and berries. Perhaps even another farm. He only had his knife, with which he would be lucky to catch a squirrel.

Not that he saw any squirrels, and the berries he found were shriveled and sour. As he walked and chewed, a deep sense of dread began to take hold of his mind again. Yut stopped. Here he was, alone, with nothing but a blanket and a knife to claim for his own, in a forgotten patch of wood, lost amid a settling autumn. What now?

The berries fell to the ground, and he found himself running again. The still pines seemed to usher the running youth through their paths, offering no obstacle—only silent mourning—in exchange for a trail of tears left in his wake.

Chapter Five

Peace

The three scavengers stood on a hill overlooking the village, a dark scar upon the land. The charred wood and ash were stark against the pines surrounding it, the contrast given a sharper edge with the knowledge of what had happened here. Sigrid knew she understood this the first time they were here, but now, in part due to Eira's tone, she grasped the image fully. Several hundred lives burned away in one white-hot flash, seemingly without reason. Sig had seen plenty of violence, but knowing that a power like this existed, without anything to stand against it, made her shudder.

"Why in the dark are we back here?" grumbled Olaf. Sig noticed that his cursing increased the more afraid he was. "Dark take it, this place is death itself."

"Dark *has* taken it," replied Eira solemnly, "But there is something it has yet to take. Olaf, be a strong lad and help an old woman down."

Olaf started, looked at Sig, and reluctantly helped Eira descend the hill to the village entrance. Sigrid, understanding Eira's mercy, followed at a distance behind them. Something about this place instilled an eerie discomfort in her. There were no bird calls, no wind, and even the river felt too quiet against the sound of their footsteps and her breathing. She knew the animals would have escaped from the fire drake, but it was more than that. The Saga itself was twisted here, a hundred stories of people, animals, and trees overshadowed and cut off by something far more powerful. Sig stepped carefully.

Olaf shivered, weapons jangling against the chain mail. "I don't know about this, Eira. There might be restless dead here. Angry restless dead. Thirsty, angry... There's no point in waking them, right?" He continued peering in all directions as he guided the wisewoman to a mound of stones at the edge of the village. A wall collapsed nearby, and Olaf looked ready to launch an axe at it.

"Peace," replied Eira, "nothing will hurt us here, son of Thoran. No need to fear."

"I ain't afraid," he said, though his eyes continued darting, searching for moving shadows. For once, Sig could empathize with the big man, as her fingers brushed against the worn dagger hilt. Surely Eira felt it too? Who could feel at ease in a silence such as this?

An unannounced wind suddenly swept through the village, chasing away the silence as ash followed it through the air. Storm clouds gathered above the mountain tops in the West, and Sig figured it was quickly moving toward them. The sound of the wind brought the village back into reality, as if some dark spell was broken by the very forces of nature. Sig breathed a sigh of relief. She looked back to her party and noticed Olaf scowling at a mound of stones. "This wasn't here before," he barked. "Someone was here."

Eira let go of Olaf. "Report what you see."

Her quick tone seemed to awaken something ancient in the depths of the warrior's senses. Even at a distance, Sig could tell his eyes had become sharp as he leaned to inspect the stones and the drag marks around them. He looked like a hound that had caught the scent of its quarry, unrecognizable from the anxious man a second ago. "A mound of stones, enough for one, maybe two. No runes." He scanned the surrounding area. "The two bodies are gone."

"Then the young man buried them," said Eira quietly. "Though he could only give them the small rites."

She reached into her satchel and took out a small metal box. Opening it carefully, she dipped two fingers into the thick red mixture inside and touched her lips. Then she motioned with her index and middle fingers in the air, drawing the rune of peace, and whispered a prayer. Finally, she touched the mound, adding two droplets to the red-stained rocks.

Sigrid continued scanning their surroundings, as she had seen Eira give the rites of the dead many times during their travels. Death was common in their line of work, and proper burials were few. Olaf was paying rapt attention; however, once the ritual was over, his scowl at Eira was so defined that it could almost be heard. Eira scowled back at him. "What do you people want? You do not want magic when it raises the dead, and you do not want it when it gives them peace."

"It's because of the darkened magic that we even have to fight the Dark," he huffed back.

"Bah! Then keep living in fear, old man. Besides, that was a prayer to the gods. You pray, do you not?"

Olaf remained silent.

"Fine, then. Sigrid?"

"All clear."

"Good. Would you please find us some tracks to follow? Be quick about it—a storm approaches."

As if in response to her, thunder rolled behind the mountains and the first droplets touched the ash-ridden ground.

Sig searched the earth quietly, eager to get away from this place. Olaf spoke as she searched, uncorking his flask, "What's this kid to you, anyway? Plenty of orphans in other places, and we do *not* have food for them."

"Your logic is like a knife. Though perhaps we can save one orphan..." Eira said absently. Sig did not disagree with Olaf. After all, they were not in the business of saving people, and if they were, they could not save all of them.

She found traces of footsteps in the ground, taking a slow, uneven pace at first, but picking up speed as they descended to the river. "He went North," she said. The wisewoman seemed to be in her own thoughts, as if still pondering Olaf's question. When Sig took her by the arm, she thought she heard her mumble, "...and perhaps it will be enough."

Chapter Six

The Rune

Black spots of fatigue danced in Yut's vision as his legs turned to stone. He had run until the lashings from the stray branches began to bleed, until the dried lungs scarcely breathed amid the coughing. Even though his mind felt clearer, as if he had outrun some of the nightmares, he did not know how much more of this he could endure.

He wasn't sure why he ran, but he held a premonition that had he not, he would be overtaken by certain death. Had he stopped, his body would have been petrified, and all hope would have been lost.

His gasps steamed as he pushed himself from tree to tree. He was ready to collapse anywhere, but a small voice of reason penetrated through the darkness, saying he should at least find a spot out of sight of any wandering bandit or beast. Shouldn't be a problem—Yut loved to go adventuring in the forests around Sanvik, so he did not feel too lost in woods such as these. It was where he broke his first bone, falling from a tree. In the ensuing shock, he only found the way home thanks to the village kids that were with him.

No village kids to save you now, though, he thought.

Through blind luck, Yut found the perfect spot. He stumbled over to a small hollow surrounded by thick pines, covered with leaves, out of sight. It was not too large, but provided good cover. He made a plan to go for firewood later, and he half-remembered his mother teaching him how to start a fire a dozen years ago. They were home, his father was off meeting with the elders, and dinner had to be prepared. She put flint and steel into his little hands and helped him create a spark, which soon became a fire. In her usual way, she made that lesson about more than simply starting a fire, but he was too enamored with his newfound power to listen. Later that night, he took the flint and steel while his parents were asleep, and nearly burned down their house. He was not allowed to start many fires since then, but there was not much to it. All you needed was tinder, a spark, a little bit of—

His perfect spot collapsed under him. There was darkness, an impact, and a crack.

Yut couldn't breathe. He couldn't move. Gods, he was back in the burned long house. There was cold earth underneath him, and he closed his eyes against the swelling tears. *No no no no...*

He made a hollow gasp, forcing life into his limbs. Several hammering heartbeats later, he drew in a sip of air, and could feel his limbs again. *Just the wind knocked out, is all.* Warm tears still streamed down his dirty face as the tiny gasps resolved into regular breaths.

He rolled over with a groan, examining his ruined camping spot. Four wooden spikes pointed towards the afternoon light, and underneath him, he found another one, snapped in half. He looked at the drop, about double his height, and looked down at the spikes around him. He managed to land his limbs just around those, and to somehow snap the one that should have gone through his heart.

As he surveyed the trap, a soft golden glow drew his eye, one that came directly from his forearm. He swiped at it, backing to the pit wall, but it only brightened. Stupefied, he watched it slowly coalesce into a symbol that floated just above his skin. As he sat in the dark pit, transfixed by the light, Yut saw a rune he did not recognize on his forearm. It eventually dimmed to a steady glimmer, like a hovering, luminous rune mark.

He leaned against the dirt wall and looked up to the sky. Swirls of silver illuminated him in bleak light from above, mingling with the golden light on his arm. He was probably going delusional from the berries. No, he was going delusional from everything that had happened to him. No mortal was meant to survive that fire, which meant the gods were simply punishing him. But why? His family made their sacrifices of crops and livestock as much as anyone else in the village. They honored the gods during the sacred days and the seasons, and Tove never said anything about displeasing them.

And then he remembered what Keld said about the Dark. Perhaps it did arrive, and it began its destruction of the world with Sanvik. Perhaps everyone would be dead soon, unless the gods took pity on them. Perhaps it was already over.

And yet he was alive. He remembered the way his father led Sanvik. Those memories felt like cherished treasures now, so he made sure to hold them close. His father was pragmatic in everything. If livestock was missing, then it was most likely a thief or a wolf, not a trelkin. If the summer was short, then everyone would need to prepare for a long winter, not make more sacrifices to the gods. And if a wyrm attacked Yut's village, then...then...

Then he was completely useless. An accident, the wyrm's job unfinished. All he could do was try to survive, and find a town, and tell them what happened, and try to live with the nightmares of that night forever. Except he knew he couldn't. *No,* his father's logical voice drifted in. *Focus on the task at hand. Everything else will follow.* That's right, he had to get out of here, before the owners of this trap had their celebration turn into deadly disappointment of finding their quarry alive. And destitute. And exhausted. And, dark above, *thirsty.*

It did not take him long to escape the trap; the sharp spikes provided excellent handholds after he drove them into the walls. Soon he was trudging across the dense woods again, the glimmer of satisfaction at surviving the pit reflecting the strange rune on his arm.

The satisfaction faded, however, when he heard the thunder. He started running again.

Chapter Seven

Shadows

Before the day ended, and before they could find the kid, Sigrid was lucky enough to find a camping spot in the middle of a few underfolk tunnel entrances. Their ancient stone doorways jutted out of the earth like a giant's claw, protecting them from wind and onlookers. The crumbling tunnels sloped deep into the earth, until they reached the dwarves' trap-filled halls. Of course, most tunnels have collapsed now, and hiding in one of these entrances was a tempting but fatal mistake. You could run inward for a mile, but eventually you had to face the dead end.

Sig watched the rat sizzle. Plentiful eating in the forest, but a fire wyrm would send all living beings into a mad escape. Luckily for the group, the rats were not unlike them—scavengers, willing to go where no sane person, or animal, would want to be. All for a sliver of grub. Still, meat was meat, and even rats could be edible with a bit of spice and imagination. And though they had no spice, she had plenty of imagination. She watched Olaf tear into his rat, the fat running down his beard, and saw the wyrm tearing into the poor wretches in that village. The gods were truly savage beings, to allow such wanton slaughter. Except...

"The wyrm didn't eat anyone," Sig absentmindedly told the fire. Olaf glanced at her, then back to the rat skeleton in his hands, and put it down, frowning.

"You have to bring that up?"

"I don't expect you to have noticed that most bodies were reduced to pure ash. No chunks, no bones, no bits—"

"No, I didn't notice!" barked Olaf, "Because *normal* folk don't notice that. *Normal* folk don't go into dead villages lookin'... lookin' for some kid." He stared at Sig, then at Eira, who quietly worked on her own rat.

"'Normal' folk would... run away? Like cowards?" Prompted Sigrid, pointedly looking at him. It was a testing shot. She wasn't sure what weapons she had against this barbarian, but she had her suspicions. It seemed to pay off, as he adopted a quiet, threatening expression, made more menacing by the night shadows.

"Back off," he said.

She did. It was no use getting him angry now, but it was good to know. They stared at one another until Eira finally spoke.

"The wyrm did not come to the village to feast. In fact, fire wyrms rarely come to towns like this. They are usually content sleeping, or hunting bigger prey."

Neither the scout nor the warrior questioned Eira, as she wore the slightly-soiled white silks of a seeress, whose business it was to know things of such nature. The more Sig traveled with Eira, the more she realized how much respect seeresses commanded throughout all of Arthgard. And, for some reason, a blind seeress was even more esteemed, as if losing one's sight made one wiser. Commoners and jarls would offer their homes to her for the night, and when she spoke in her mystical way, even crying babies stopped to listen. Even so, Eira chose the vagabond life, to listen to the Saga in forgotten forests and ruins rather than the halls of jarls. She claimed there was less noise there, but Sig suspected Eira avoided cities after saving her, for which she was always grateful.

"Then why did it come down this time?" asked Sig.

Eira was silent for a tense minute, as was expected of a wisewoman about to reveal the ultimate truth of some ancient mystery. She took a breath as Olaf and Sig instinctively leaned in.

"I have no idea," she said, and, giving her rat remains to Olaf, promptly turned her back to them and curled into sleep.

Sig watched the fire a while longer, trying to drown out the sounds of Olaf's feeding. It was all strange: a fire drake descends on a village in the middle of the woods, takes nothing, incinerates everyone, and leaves. If it simply went mad, then they would have heard about its exploits elsewhere—there should have been smoke columns stretching through the entire countryside. Strange, all of it.

A movement caught Sigrid's eye. It stayed in the shadows, just behind Olaf, who was busy digging into seconds. She gripped her knife, but the silhouette did not move. It was, however, watching her. There were no footsteps, no eyes glinting in the firelight, but Sig knew all too well the eyes that did not need to see.

"*You know why it came,*" whispered a cold, familiar voice. "*You know the truth you are too blind to see. Too afraid to see.*" The shadow flickered and came back into sharper focus. Except now there were two of them, standing side by side.

Sig shut her eyes, her knife trembling. This usually happened when Eira went to sleep. Her *other* side came, twisting her mind like a wet rag. These were the only companions she had before Eira, and where the landvaettir signaled safety, the shadows nearly always brought about danger. She would be nauseous the next day, and jumpy. Depending on how bad this went, her vision could be blurred to near-blindness for days.

You have no power here, Sig wanted to shout aloud, but Olaf couldn't know. He couldn't see them, and so he wouldn't believe in them. So she tried to scream in her head. *You are lies!*

But the shadows did not respond. They simply jeered, and taunted, prodding her mind with cryptic whispers. There were dozens of them now, surrounding the fire. She could see their shapes—some were taller than others, while others looked like children. They were completely shrouded in shadow, save for the occasional reflection of firelight, which revealed gray skin and faces of swirling chaos.

"Too afraid to see... Wake up, Siggy. Wake up!"

"Eight gods of old, their saga is told," whispered Sig, forcing herself to focus on each word. "Rothr, and Orm, Hela, and Vae."

Through the shrieking laughter, she kept repeating the mantra Eira had taught her. It did not make sense, as there were nine gods, and the mantra only mentioned four. But it did not need to make sense. When she lay under dark skies, clutching Eira and the remains of her sanity, she repeated these words, until...

She was in the village—*her* village, somewhere in the East. There were not many people, but they all held torches, and their faces were swirling chaos. Then, she was covered in blood.

"Eight gods of old, their saga is told. Rothr and Orm... Rothr..."

The fire was fading, and a sharp cold gripped her. The shadows neared. "Eight gods of old. *Dark take it, eight darkened gods of old!*"

She was repeating nothing but jumbled syllables by the time the voices melted on the fire in her head. When she opened her eyes, the fire was dying, and Olaf was still speaking.

"...really prefer a fat rabbit, but nothin' beats a good—Oy." He looked at her like he just saw her swallow a rat whole. A rat he wanted to eat. "You alright?"

There were tears on her face, and she was holding the knife out, as if to protect herself. The episodes always felt longer than they really were. She wiped the tears away and sheathed the knife. The shadows were gone—they came and went, and now it was over. Yes, definitely.

But the human remained. Olaf's concerned eyes looked unnatural on his face. *Dark.* There goes any leverage she had before. Sig realized it was not concern in his eyes, but pity, like he was looking at a crippled dog.

"Fine," was all she could muster, before turning away, and curling up for another restless night.

Chapter Eight

Power

"What in all of the gods' names are you eating?"

Yut shot up and turned to the stranger, instinctively hiding the mushrooms behind him. His accuser was a short, ancient woman carrying a large bundle of firewood on her back. White wisps of hair stuck out from her knit cap, and she was bundled in at least three layers of coats and leathers. A thousand wrinkles formed in shock and indignation at Yut, and when she put her arms on her hips, he began to feel a deep, inexplicable embarrassment that only an elder can summon. Yut was made a toddler again, so he guiltily brought his hands forward, filled with delicious-looking gray and brown mushrooms.

She marched up and slapped them from his hands. Yut was dumbfounded—partially because the stranger just discarded his first real food in days, and partially because she was the first person he had seen since those scavengers in the village. To think that there were other people going about their regular lives after all that had happened to him seemed inconceivable. It was also strangely relieving.

"My mushrooms," stammered Yut.

"Never mind those, lad," she said, dropping a heavy waterskin into his hands, "Unless you don't want to sleep for the next week. Now, you tell me where you are from and where you're headed. I will not tolerate drifters in my backyard."

Yut looked at the waterskin in his hands and could not find the answer. He was in the same woods, running in circles, lacking energy or coherent thought. He recoiled when he saw shadows of crows pass above him, and triple-checked every spot that looked safe enough to sleep in. Though sleep did not last long, as paranoia and hunger kept him awake most of the time. He survived for two nights—he doubted he could survive much longer.

"I'm... I'm lost," he admitted. In response, the old woman folded her arms and studied him intently. She seemed to stand there for hours, weighing whatever was left of him, and Yut could not meet her gaze for even a second. He must have been quite a sight.

Finally, she gave a deep sigh, and turned to leave. "War will do that to you. Drink up. You will stay with me until we find a use for you."

Yut could not think of how to respond. He wanted to tell her about the wyrm attack, but he realized he must have looked like a crazed maniac, and he would rather not sound like one too. Perhaps later, when he had gotten some rest. He mumbled a thanks, and followed her through the forest, his sips from the waterskin soon becoming gulps. Gods, how he missed fresh water. He didn't actually know it was fresh, but after two days of licking rainwater from the ground, even bath water would taste like mead. Rivers and creeks should have been abundant in the Trelwoods, but his luck must have run out after the spike trap. At least, until now.

An hour later, his stomach continued grumbling, and though his cuts from the day before had stopped bleeding, they still hurt. His ankle made a clicking noise, followed by a sharp pain if he stepped on it wrong, forcing him to limp. Tough business, limping, especially on the uneven forest floor. At some point, he realized the strange rune on his arm was glowing again. He tried to keep his eyes on the path before him, but the rune, now sizzling with gold-white light, kept stealing his attention. He felt it should at least tingle. But the old woman did not remark on it, and so neither did he. He was hoping it would just go away, but during the course of the hellish march, it only seemed to glow brighter.

He painfully jogged to catch up to his savior. She was spry for her age, moving like someone who had walked the same forest path for decades. He could not quite focus on her face—when he tried, his gaze simply slipped off. At first, he thought it might have been the effect of her elder-stare and his great manners, but he expected that to lessen when he agreed to carry her firewood. Instead, he had to pin his eyes to the hem of her robe to not lose his way.

Eventually, Yut cleared his throat as gently as he could. "Excuse me, not that I am impatient—yes, thank you for the water, very kind—but do you think we will be finding your home soon now?"

She did not acknowledge the question. Instead, she murmured, "Dangerous out here, for you." At least, that's what it sounded like. Sound and light felt interchangeable, so her voice reached him a few seconds after she had already trudged on.

Embarrassingly, Yut was about to say that he finished the waterskin, but found the sack still holding a few horns in it. Didn't he finish it just moments ago? Gods, he was thirsty. And dizzy. The last thing he needed now was the old woman dragging him through the forest as he fell into delirium.

"Used to be better times, safer times," her voice echoed around him.

"I'm sorry?"

"Don't be sorry, lad, not your fault. You mark my words, the gods stopped speaking to us long ago, and now they have stopped listening. These woods are dangerous. They stopped listening too, see? The animals, the trees... we're not their masters anymore." As the words drifted past him, he glanced at his arm again. The rune sat just above his skin, as if painted on invisible armor. He was beginning to think it was real, though he was reluctant to tell her about it. Perhaps he would ask someone in Ottervik after getting some rest. He settled on nodding and saying "Aye" to her comments, few of which made sense to him.

They arrived at a hut after another excruciating half-hour. It sat at the bottom of a steep hill just outside the deep woods, at the edge of a ravine, beyond which stretched the tree-less hills. A trick of the light, or his weakening vision, made the hut seem out of focus, not unlike the hermit woman's face. It was like something out of a dream. A fever dream.

"Is that—?"

"Come now," she hushed.

Yut blinked and was at the front door, the woman gently pushing him inside. Darkness was closing at the edges of his vision, and the rune on his arm burned fiercely now. He imagined it had to be burning him, but he did not care anymore. He saw a bed, a fire, and was that the smell of fresh bread? Gods below, he had forgotten bread existed. The rune could wait a day or twenty.

Weak. So weak. He stepped up to the doorway and stopped. Inside the hut was a single bed, draped in furs, and a kettle boiling by the fire.

"You left the kettle on while you were picking firewood?" asked Yut.

The woman's eyebrows lifted in surprise. "I did not mean to take so much time. Now, in you go."

She pushed him gently again, and Yut wanted to go in, but

something was unsettling here. Did he even ask her for her name? Would he take her bed? He shouldn't take strangers' beds, that much his mother taught him. He could almost see her standing there, arms folded, shaking her head. "You're a logmar's son, Yut. There are plenty of animals out there, we don't need one inside, too. Be *polite.*"

He began to back away, but the woman's tiny hands proved to be too firm. "Young man... really an insult... soft bed..."

The words swarmed him, making little sense but overpowering his last reservations. He swallowed and stepped inside, as something warm and wet sprinkled the back of his neck.

He turned to find her head split by an axe.

She continued staring at him, her face twitching. Yut blinked and looked behind her. One of the scavengers from the town stood on top of the hill, about a hundred feet away—the scary one, Olaf, his arm outstretched in the follow up of the axe throw.

At that point, Yut's legs decided enough was enough, and ceased functioning. But his rear did not find the wood floor of the hut; instead, he landed on cold stone. As he looked around him the entire structure began to dissolve like a dry leaf on fire. The hut, or its illusion, seemed to have been suspended in midair, and Yut found himself inches away from a drop into a deep, rocky ravine.

He looked back again, his heart tripling in beat, and saw the hermit woman still standing there. Except her skin had gone a sickly green color, and she was growing taller. The axe in her head did not seem to hinder her as she turned to face her attacker. Yut blinked furiously to try and dispel these strange hallucinations, but without much luck.

He was still paralyzed when a low cackle began emanating from the... thing. As time slowed around him, he realized with building horror that he was nearly captured by a Seither witch. The sagas described them simply as old, ugly women that enjoyed boiling little children in a cauldron. Those who have seen their true nature must not have lived to tell the tale. Seither or not, she was now covered in various leathers, and her face became obscured by light cloth and hanging bones. Her attire almost reminded him of Tove's, except the monster's talismans were not shiny bits, but stained bones and dried animal parts. Yut gagged as the odor of rotting meat reached him, and he did not dare guess the reason for her smell. He had the feeling the new form was not created—rather it was being revealed, and his gaze did not slip off her anymore, unfortunately. The leathers made a long dress that covered her feet, while her limbs extended, jerking with wet snapping noises. Yut did not think he was ever more terrified of anything in his life. If his mouth was any dryer it would turn into dust.

But then she began to speak.

It was a tongue that Yut did not recognize, making Olaf cover his ears and topple back. Her chant seemed to take on a physical form as it drifted through the air, slithering toward Olaf while encircling Yut. He did not understand the words, but he knew they were magical. And powerful. It sounded as if she was speaking backward, harsh and guttural. As she continued intoning in the strange tongue, Yut regained blessed feeling in his legs, and realized this may be his one chance to escape.

Taking deep breaths, he bolted along the edge of the ravine, scrambling on all fours like a terrified dog, his body electrified. He thought he had gotten far, but as he looked back, he was still only a few feet away from his captor. Disbelief mixed with fear as he tried to stand and run and again found himself pushed down by an unseen force.

It was her. The Seither kept her arm stretched toward Yut as she chanted at Olaf. Gods, this was *real magic*. Gods below, he was dying. Again. His strength and consciousness began to fade, and that same desperate panic froze him.

And then another voice joined the chanting. This one was clear, strong. Yut saw the blind woman, Eira, appear over the hill beside Olaf, her white robes fluttering in the wind. She spoke her own strange words, and they collided with the foul chant like water on stone, light in darkness. Yut nervously surveyed the skies. If this was truly magic, the gods could come down any moment to strike them all down.

The wind became sudden and violent. The trees began to bend, as if the sky itself was pushing them down. The earth, too, became distorted as fissures formed and spread between the two women. The entire world seemed to be groaning under some unseen weight. Then Yut felt that weight on his own body, and it reminded him of Keld's weight on him, the crushing darkness, the lack of air...

There, in the midst of terror, he saw the soft glow of the golden rune. It was a mystery, an invitation, a promise. It lived somewhere beyond the forests, mountains, and clouds, but now it was here, and in that moment it felt like a warm fire for the drenched and cold. In the darkness, it waited for him. It spoke his name from the shadows, and Yut knew it would be his and his alone. It was power, yes, but also justice. Justice for him, and for all those around him, and in the darkness, it waited for him. All he had to do was reach for it, and grasp it, and hold it, just a bit farther, just a bit—

Fierce, savage strength flooded through Yut's body. The weight was gone, and he took a deep gulp of air. He sprang up, and his mind was suddenly clear. No fever, no dizziness, just... color. The vibrant hues of the dark brown trees, the soft tan of the witch's leather skins. Yut saw then that it was human skin, but the thought did not sicken him. He also realized it was not water that he drank, but that did not matter either. Nothing evil mattered now.

Suddenly, he was *alive.*

The rune on his forearm burned as he took in the bright world around him. Now he was focused. Now he was strong. The Saga of the entire world opened before him like a tapestry, and now he understood.

The two women were still locked in the battle of chants, but now the words they said made sense. He couldn't quite understand them, though he felt that he knew their meaning deep in his heart—these words came from the same place as his rune. They were hatred and love, corruption and life; words of creation itself, but each woman was trying to undo the other. It seemed ridiculous to Yut, and while he was filled with the strange strength, he strode up to the witch.

Her black, beady eyes took a second to register him through the veil on her face. Yut smiled as those eyes went wide with terror. She must have felt his strength, felt that something had awakened, and she was the only one to blame. Yut assumed the fighting stance his father showed him, planting his legs, winding back his fist, and putting the weight of his entire body into the punch. There was no point in trying to run. The Seither's eyes closed.

The impact and the shockwave ripped through the ravine. It was a deep, satisfying blow to the diaphragm, though he misjudged his strength. Instead of toppling into the ravine, the witch was launched across, her breath, scream, and lungs pulverized instantly. She impacted the opposite wall of the ravine, sending out an explosion of dust and rubble. In the settling silence, her limp body peeled away and tumbled into the swarming thorns below.

Yut breathed out as the color around him began to drain once more. He knew it was coming, it had to. The strength, the confidence, and the understanding were already fading as he turned and looked up at the scavengers. Olaf was awake and staring at Yut in shock. Eira pursed her lips, though he thought he caught the hint of a smile. The silent dagger woman, Sigrid, was also there, her stony expression giving way to honest surprise.

Yut was considering saying something heroic, but his attention was drawn to the cracks continuing to form in the ground. Cracks that extended to the place he was standing on, where the Seither stood moments ago, at the very edge of the ravine.

"You—" He managed, before the ground underneath him collapsed, sending him head-first into the thorn-filled ravine.

Chapter Nine

The Vision

Faces churned before Yut's eyes as his stomach twisted. Gods below, he was not ready for this. Watching the villagers, his friends, Keld, together, laughing, was like ripping open a festering wound and rubbing salt in it. He shut his eyes, and tried to will himself away from this place, as his family's shrieking filled his ears. Their smiles were too wide to be real, and their voices were not quite right. They crowded around him, their skin turning black as it burned, cracked, and peeled away, revealing bloodshot eyeballs and glimmering teeth. Yut screamed.

The laughter ended, and Yut found himself in an unfamiliar forest. Somehow, he did not feel lost or afraid, as the stars and the moon shone brightly, and it was not particularly cold. After walking for a few minutes along a well-worn path, Yut noticed the soft light of a campfire in the distance.

As he quietly approached, he saw several figures sitting around it, men and women, all intently listening to a hooded figure at the head. He could not see the figure's eyes, but heard his rich voice, brimming with joy, as he recited the saga of creation. The voice seemed familiar.

Yut was now sitting by the fire, warm, a cup of mead in his hand. It was just him and the storyteller, and even though the hood covered most of his face, Yut knew the man was watching him. He was wearing a deep, content smile, making Yut uneasy.

"Who are you?" asked Yut, and in response, the moon began to dim. He felt the awful shivering and nausea of fever pushing him back to consciousness. Somewhere, he was lying in a sea of thorns alongside a Seither's corpse, his body probably broken. *No*. This was more than a mere dream, Yut was sure of it, and he would not go back to reality until he found out why.

Forcing himself back into the vision, Yut set the cup aside and stood. "Tell me." There was silence. The fire and the forest sounds around them faded, as if anticipating the stranger's next words.

"*You have lost much, Yut, son of weakness and strength.*"

The voice was not deep, it was... vast. It resonated through the ground, the fire, through Yut. The storyteller continued in a measured, exquisite tone. "*You have suffered the grief of injustice, and now you walk the edge of the Dark itself. Many have walked it before, and many have fallen. Will you share their fate?*"

He knew he was speaking to a god, which made his emotions swirl even fiercer. He ought to demand justice for himself, for his family. He ought to be enraged. But through the clenched jaw, Yut could only whisper a cold, "Why?"

Orm stood, and the entire forest shrank away from him. His height had doubled, and each footstep toward Yut seemed to herald an inevitable doom. Yut forced himself to remain where he was and prepare for whatever punishment he deserved.

But no punishment came. Instead, the leader of the gods took a knee and put a giant hand on Yut's shoulder.

"*Be strong, Yut.*"

Darkness swallowed the world. And then the pain began.

Chapter Ten

Wisdom of a Seeress

Sig watched the kid writhe in Eira's cloak, his sweat reflecting the large fire they set for him. Dark below, they could have started the fire just from the thorns they pulled out of him. Sig could not decide whether his fever was from some sort of infection or whatever brew the Seither gave him, but she wouldn't give him many chances. If she was Olaf, she would put coin against his surviving the night. She was not annoyed that they had thrown away two days tracking the kid down, or even that they risked their lives against the Seither. She was annoyed that Eira still had not revealed the reason for all this.

It was her turn to watch him, as Eira slumbered a few feet away and Olaf was scouting for dinner. She watched his pitiful face, some fuzz sprouting under the nose and the jawline, the dark red hair cut short, the tanned skin, now yellow with fever. He looked like a dying rodent. Had he not been rune-marked, Sig might have suggested that they leave him here and let the gods decide his fate.

Except that he *was* a true, gods-sworn rune-marked, prancing around and punching Seithers. Sig had never seen a rune-child, but from the way Eira spoke about them, they were something to behold. Mortals blessed with a rune of the Saga, to shape the world according to its nature, whether it be through thunder, fire, or any other ability the gods decided to give them. Sig should have been grateful to see one, it's just that she expected someone older, and less wimpy-looking. No mistake, this is why Eira wanted to go back for him, but what were they supposed to do with him now? What was her plan?

The boy started coughing harshly, mucus seeping out of him as he shivered. Gods, he was the picture of pity. Perhaps the most merciful thing they could do for him now was to let him go peacefully, the rune be damned. A quick slice through the jugular, and it would be over before it started.

Eira suddenly jerked awake, felt her way to where Sig was sitting, and then felt the boy's head. "Dark above, Sigrid, he is freezing my hand off. Why is the fire so small?"

"It was hot—the kid was sweating waterfalls."

"He is supposed to sweat, you fool. Now find us more logs, quickly, and fetch me a waterskin."

Sig sighed as she began her search. Eira has been doting over him the whole night—no wonder why Olaf so graciously volunteered to go hunting through the night. He was probably gorging himself on mushrooms now. Or worse, he was sleeping.

"You didn't tell me anything about sweating," grumbled Sig.

"Didn't tell you to be an idiot either." Eira cast their last log into the fire and covered him with her own cloak. As the flame climbed, she took out her poultice of garlic and honey and stooped over the little bowl like some trelkin. She mixed it quickly and with well-practiced motions, occasionally adding herbs from hidden pockets in her vest. Then she felt for Yut, and began applying the poultice at the places where the thorns drove in the deepest, whispering continuous prayers.

Sig couldn't help but remember Eira healing a young girl in much the same way. Unfortunately, Sig was not unconscious when the seeress applied the poultice to the hounds' bites, and the pain released rivers of suppressed tears. They sat in the foul swamp while Sig tried to force the tears to stop. "*You're a strong one,*" Eira smiled, handing her a waterskin. Now Sig set the waterskin next to the boy, and was about to set off for firewood, but Eira grabbed a hold of her wrist. "Sig, I—"

"It would just be nice to know what we are doing here... with him. You decided something for all of us, but haven't told us what, or why. And now we are tip-toeing around some kid who won't even make it through the night—for what?"

As she said this, Eira gently dripped the cool water onto his lips. "Yut's wounds are not mortal, and his fever is not from any physical wound. He is fighting something. There is grief, sorrow, hope, and a rune of power all contending for his heart, and this battle is causing a physical illness. It may kill him, or it will shape him."

"Great," said Sig, folding her arms, "That sounds very noble and epic. I should have realized we had a thrice-blessed hero of the sagas leaking fluids on your cloak. And how do you know his name?"

"He is... like me, Sigrid. Like you," replied Eira. "He is a Speaker, and he is also rune-marked, as you have seen. Even more, he has been given the rune of strength. His life is already written in the Saga of our world."

"And what does that mean for us?"

Eira paused, taking a swig from the water flask herself. "What does it mean for you, you mean?"

"For *us*. It is hard enough scavenging with that walking armory—we were fine without him either, by the way—and now you want to drag the kid with us? We can work without them, Eira, like before."

"That's enough," said Eira, her voice hard. "If you do not wish to save his life today, then I can stay with him. I would not ask you to take his fate upon you, but before you stride into the woods, know this: Yut saved your life today. Yours and mine and Olaf's. And he will doubtless do so again. So, if you have no respect or honor for the gods or fate, then at least have some gratitude."

"Honor is a luxury," replied Sigrid. "No good for survival. *You* taught me that."

There was no response from the seeress, so Sigrid sighed as she began her hunt for firewood under the light of the moon, leaving Eira to whisper Yut to a fragile sleep.

Chapter Eleven

Wisdom of Olaf

Olaf awoke when the stars were at their brightest. Taking a second to remember where he was, he brushed the fallen leaves off himself, corked his flask, set aside the sack of mushrooms he hadn't finished yet, stood, and stretched. Hopefully everyone at the camp would be asleep at this point. Or better yet, hopefully the seeress abandoned him. Gods, there was a cheery thought.

He checked his weapons before he set off. The two axes on his belt, one on his back, protected by the shield strapped to the same clever loop he snagged a week ago. The sword was bound in the sheepskin sheath, the three knives sat firm on his belt. He felt for the fourth one in his boot, found it, and began walking.

Then he came back to grab the sack of mushrooms.

He set a slow pace for two reasons: First, he was groggy. There is no need to hurry a man in the morning. Or night. Whatever the hour was. The stars were bright, which meant there were at least a few hours before dawn. Plenty of time to get to the camp.

The second reason consisted of the growing need for Olaf to think. Most of his life was based on instinct—simple two-worded decisions: hide here, run there, eat this, and so on. But the situation had gotten out of hand. First, there was the problem with the girl. Olaf was half-sure she wasn't entirely human. Perhaps some demon bound to human form. Gods below, she was sharp, but not in a playful way, like the noble girls Olaf met in his youth. She was sharp like a... thorn. Yes, a thorn on a nasty, ugly vine that you hadn't noticed until you sat on it. And, apparently, she had something out for him. Better to keep the axes handy at all times.

Speaking of thorns, there was the situation with the boy. He wasn't going to survive the night; Olaf would put good coin on that. He was more bramble than flesh by the time they pulled him out of the ravine, with Olaf scoring more than a few cuts for the trouble. But the bigger trouble was that he could do magic, or speaking, or whatever Eira called it. And he was strong, like the heroes from the stories, even though he was skinny as a twig. Maybe he could replace Olaf. Who needs a mercenary when you have a guy who can punch witches across ravines?

Lastly, and most dangerously, the seeress could do magic. For all Olaf knew, Sigrid could too. They said nothing of it before. Honoring his word was good and all, but if the gods came punishing the whole group for the use of their magic, then Olaf intended to stay as far away as possible. And, according to all the sagas, it was only a matter of time before the gods *did* come down.

If they continued chasing down magicians, elf-girls, and seeresses, they would be bound to run up against something big—something even a hardened veteran like him couldn't handle. Though that witch must have been surprised with an axe to her head. One of his finer throws, thought Olaf. He didn't remember much of what happened after, but he was sure he weakened her for the kid. Maybe they would need him for a few more weeks after all.

Olaf popped another mushroom in his mouth and picked up his pace. Breakfast awaited.

Chapter Twelve

Beginning of the End

Yut awoke to a heavenly smell of watered-down stew. His nose seemed to lift him up from the nightmares, memories, and gods to something real, and delicious. He pried his crusted eyes open as he sat up, and found a large, blurry figure stirring a steaming pot over a fire. The same man from the village, and the hill. Names, places... Everything was foggy, and while Yut was trying to remember his name, the man finally noticed him.

"So, you're alive," he remarked, watching Yut expectantly.

"Uh."

"Olaf is my name. The snoring one by the tree is Sigrid, we call her Sig, or Siggy—she loves that one, and the snoring one behind you is Eira. You almost died."

Olaf paused again, watching Yut's reaction. There wasn't much to react to, but Yut somehow felt Olaf would not let him touch the stew if he didn't say something.

"Uh," he managed.

"You must be dim," said Olaf, returning his inspecting eye to the stew. "We pulled you out right quick, but the fever does that to the mind. You were shakin' like a leaf all night. Thought you wouldn't make it, if I'm bein' honest. Either way, you're safe now. Kind of. Had the shakes for a bit. Though if you're actually dead then let me finish my stew before tearing my throat out."

Olaf chuckled. Yut blinked.

Olaf grimaced. "It's a joke. Relax." He handed Yut a small, grimy bowl, and Yut took it with both shaking hands. Gods, he was pale and felt he hadn't eaten in years. He also took notice of a dozen cuts in his arms, covered in dried ointment of some kind. He thought it smelled of garlic.

"We've got no spoons, so you're gonna have to—" but Yut was already gulping down the steaming stew, wincing against the burning pain, but not slowing. Soon he was asking for a second, and Olaf hesitated when Yut asked for a third. He glanced at Eira, stirring awake, thought better of it, and handed Yut the bowl.

"Easy there, drengr. We've got three stomachs to feed. One more bowl, and *you're* going mushroom picking next time."

A few minutes later, the four vagabonds sat around the remains of their fire, finishing the last of the watered-down stew. Stomach finally filled, Yut stopped shaking enough to take in his surroundings. The trees here had already turned orange and gold, their leaves painting the forest floor. If he had to guess, he would place them in the Northern Trelwoods, where the earth became uneven and hilly. The camp was set inside a natural stone alcove, and Yut noted it shielded them from most of the south and western winds, which had begun their icy assault early this season. They were also well hidden from any observer except where the alcove opened into the forest. Yut concluded it was a great camp spot—almost as great as the one he chose a few days earlier, and with notably less deadly spikes.

He turned his gaze to his saviors as they finished their breakfast. There was Olaf, who seemed like a well-armed thug, but cooked a passable stew and was not nasty like some of the deserters that would occasionally pass through Sanvik. The soldier was glancing at Sigrid, who was eating her stew even faster than Yut. When she finished, she kept a cool stare on Yut. Those gray eyes could keep meat fresh through the summer. Then there was Eira, the blind seeress, who belched so loud after finishing her bowl that Yut felt embarrassed, though no one said anything.

Taking advantage of the silence, Yut cleared his throat. "Um, thank you all. Truly."

Three blank faces turned to him. There was no response, so he shifted slightly and tried again. "For saving me back there. I owe you a debt." He instantly felt that it was the wrong thing to say, as if civilized manners were a strange language to these people. Sigrid looked confused and Eira's expression was unreadable—gods below, what did they expect him to say? Olaf fixed him with a scowl, and to Yut's surprise, was the first to break the silence. "Listen, kid, just how'n the dark did you punch a—"

"You owe us little, child of the rune," Eira quickly interrupted. "I remember you saving our lives as well."

"Well, I'm not quite sure exactly... wait, what did you call me?"

"Now, you all must be wondering why I gathered you here," continued Eira, addressing the group and taking command of the conversation.

Sigrid finally peeled her gaze from Yut. "You didn't gather me."

"Didn't I?"

"No, you didn't."

"Did you...?" asked Olaf.

"No," admitted Eira, "But, in the secret way that the Saga weaves its tales, so this moment has been foretold in the ages of yore, by the very gods that... well... foretold of this moment. Because in this very moment is when our saga truly begins."

Swallowed momentum aside, Eira spoke with refined tone, like the skalds that traveled through Sanvik on the way to bigger towns, telling tales until they were hoarse, all for the promise of a warm meal. In fact, she spoke in a still more refined way, as if she had practiced these words for months.

"We are now a complete party—together with the brutish warrior, a quiet assassin, a promising prodigy, and the wise counselor. The Saga has brought us together, and we have a difficult but rewarding road ahead of us. Together we—"

"Wait a second," interjected Olaf, "Whose saga brought us together?"

"*The* Saga, Olaf. Tale of the gods. Fate. Destiny. I have spoken about this at length with you."

Winds howled, kingdoms rose and fell, and seas dried in Olaf's head, though none of that registered on his face. "Uh, then I'm not the assassin, am I? Unless I'm the prodigy."

Yut looked down at his empty bowl as he tried to make some sense of the situation. What in all of the dark were these people talking about? They were no mere scavengers, but they did not seem sane either. Perhaps that's what the magic chanting did to you. Everyone knew performing any kind of magics was a crime against the gods themselves, and would result in a swift helping of disease and death. Not even Yut's pragmatic father would deny this, and any hint of magic craft in Sanvik was met with a swift investigation. Perhaps that's why the seeress was blind. Though, if that was the case, what did that mean for Yut, who carried a darkened rune on his body? And what did she mean by 'child of the rune'? He gently placed his bowl at his side as he returned to the conversation.

"Now, I didn't say 'oaf' warrior, Sigrid," tried Eira.

"You said brutish, which means 'oaf' in Olaf's case. He's

definitely not the promising prodigy."

"What? Then who's the wise one?" asked Olaf.

Eira cleared her throat loudly. "Look, the titles don't matter. What matters is that we have a diverse group of people in an opportune place and time to do something great. And I am obviously the wise one, ya oaf."

Olaf grumbled something, and Sigrid softly asked, "What are we going to do?"

Eira cleared her throat as she stood up. "We are going to bring about the end of times."

* * *

The wind picked up a few of the leaves outside of their alcove, but no one was looking at those. Yut, Olaf, and Sigrid watched the seeress, who stood proudly with her fists on her hips, looking satisfied. There was a pregnant pause after her announcement, which gave birth to an awkward silence. Eira seemed to be enjoying it.

"Ah," said Olaf eventually.

"What does that mean?" asked Sigrid. She seemed concerned, not at all treating this like a part of an elaborate joke, which Yut was entirely sure that it was. "Why would we bring about the end of times?"

"Not why, but *how,*" beamed Eira.

"Excuse me," ventured Yut, as politely as he could, "but I am also wondering why we need to end the world." He investigated their faces for any sign of humor or jest. A memory of Keld and the jarl's daughters drifted past him. He would not be so gullible again. But there was no laughter, not even a hint of a smirk. In fact, Eira seemed to deflate with his question, and Yut dreaded that he said something wrong again.

"Because some things must be done," she answered, her tone suddenly serious. "Because something is terribly wrong with our world, child, and it falls to us to fix it."

Yut was about to ask about the 'promising prodigy' part, but an obnoxiously loud yawn interrupted him. "Right," remarked Olaf. "Don't know about you all, but I ain't heard of no one bringing about the end of all things waving a stick for a sword, and sporting rags for chain mail. I say we could use a bit more coin, too. And food. And meat." He glanced questioningly at the others as he spoke, as if inviting them to some unspoken plan. He did not need to say it aloud. *Just go along with her ramblings and we'll figure it out later.*

But Sigrid's attention was focused on the seeress. "Alright then, Eira, *how* do we go about fixing the world?"

"We begin," said Eira, "with our ancient enemy, the masters who control the world from their dark corners of malice and dread. We will take down the Cult."

"Cult?" Asked Olaf, his face twisting, "What cult? Of Rothr? Vae? You didn't say anything about cult warfare."

"Not a cult, Olaf. *The* Cult. The only one that matters, and the most hidden and powerful and pernicious. Its existence is an offense to the gods, because they are friends of the Dark and all of its—what are you doing?"

Gods, she's good, thought Yut. He had barely begun to stand, but the blind seeress noticed. Olaf and Sig were looking at him, too. He thought Olaf shook his head.

"Deepest apologies, wise one," began Yut. He assumed "wise one" would be acceptable for a seeress because only one of those had ever visited Sanvik, and that was when Yut was a toddler. And although Tove was the village wisewoman, she was still a far cry from a seeress, who would allegedly deliver messages directly from the gods themselves. Though Yut doubted that anything Eira was saying came from anywhere other than her own imagination. Yut continued, "I just... um, I have the need."

"You did not need to interrupt then, child. Just go behind that tree," said Eira sharply, pointing in a vague direction of where Olaf was sitting. Olaf glowered at him. Yes, he was definitely shaking his head.

I wasn't trying to interrupt, you crazy hag. "Again, I apologize, wise one, but I just cannot go when there are people nearby. It's... an embarrassing condition." He realized if she could hear his every movement, she could probably hear his heartbeat too. Perhaps she would think it was racing due to nerves, not because he was lying through his teeth.

The seeress gave a disappointed sigh. "Very well, I will continue when you return. Do not tarry now, Yut Eriksson."

Thanking her, Yut bowed as he walked briskly outside the alcove, behind it, and up the hill so they would not see him. After a hundred stealthy paces, he looked back, waiting to see movement.

There was none. Great.

He started running.

Chapter Thirteen

The Creek

Yut felt his odds were good. The crazy blind woman would not go chasing after him, and the crazy fat man would not last a mile. The crazy blonde girl might keep up with him, but he stopped every five minutes to watch for any movement behind him. Names? No, who even knew if those were their real names.

He must have run for a league before he stopped at a sizeable creek. Taking a minute to catch his breath, he stooped to wash his face and neck, deciding to cover his scent just in case. He still felt weak, and his meal was trying to escape after the grueling run, but the cold water was refreshing. He forgot to return Eira's cloak before escaping, so he used it to dry himself. It was soft, but grimy, the white cloth bearing stains that looked older than Yut.

He sighed. Gods, what a week. First, he punched an old lady, who turned out to be a Seither, across a ravine. He still couldn't believe that one. Then he stole another seeress' cloak, who was also a witch, as he ran away from the party that fed him. He'd need to beg the gods for mercy once he reached civilization, if he ever makes it that far.

Dark below, considering all the dangers he faced, Yut supposed he should count himself lucky to even be alive. The thought was too much, and he chuckled softly.

"What's so funny?" asked Sigrid.

Yut recoiled, slipped on the wet rocks, and sprawled into the cold water. He scrambled out instantly, but it was too late. He was drenched, and it was to be another cloudy, breezy day. Dark take light breezes.

But then his focus snapped to the impossible fact of Sigrid sitting on the branches of a fallen tree not five strides away, legs crossed, head cocked to the side and studying him. She must have teleported there, because she did not seem out of breath at all. A sliver of sunlight fell on her through the gray clouds, illuminating her flaxen hair and gray eyes in a golden light, making her seem a spirit or an elf, curiously watching a flailing, foolish mortal.

Wow. Yut would call her otherworldly rather than beautiful. Beautiful simply fell short of what she was. Beautiful was for humans, and she was obviously more than that. She noticed him staring, and switched her expression from curious to annoyed, just as that single ray of light was suffocated with clouds. "Well?" She asked sharply.

"I... got lost." Was the best he could come up with. Blinking himself out of the stupor, the shivering caught up to him. Sigrid continued looking at him expectantly.

"I'm sorry," he said, "I should have said something before, but this is all just too much for me. You have all been very kind to me to take me in, but I can't be a part of your group. I'm a... I was a logmar's son, I was to be married to a nice girl, settle in the summer home, catch fish..." Tears betrayed Yut as he tried to blink them away. Where in the dark did tears come from? He was beginning to tremble again, his heart seizing. Gods, not now, please.

Why should he be here? Of all the villages, of all the people, of all the lives that could be touched by tragedy, why did Yut deserve this? He had done nothing, and yet everything he ever had or hoped for was taken away in a night, and for what? Why shouldn't some northern village suffer with their wars, trolls, and witches? It was not supposed to be him. Gods, his parents did not deserve this...

"It was not supposed to be me," he finally whispered, letting the sound of his ragged breathing settle between them.

As he began wiping his tears away, Sigrid jumped from the tree, took a couple of strides to Yut, and slapped him so hard he fell back into the shallow creek.

"Get up," she said sternly. Shock, or grief, left Yut unmoving in the creek, the cold water freezing his spine.

"Dark take you, worthless trelkin, get up," she commanded, making as if to kick him. At that, Yut began to slowly rise. His cheek was already swelling, and he tasted metal. Some distant part of him gauged what she was doing, but that part was not making the decisions now. All other emotions served as kindling for quick, primal anger.

"What in the dark are you—" The second slap was just as sudden, and it bit him in the other cheek with no less force, though he did not lose his ground this time. Blood was filling his mouth, and he thought a tooth came loose.

Before he had time to even look at her, two punches connected with his ribs like lightning strikes, and Yut gave a squeak of pain as he stumbled away from her. "What in the dark is your problem!"

"*You* are my problem," she said, taking a determined step forward. *Not so fast*, thought Yut, and he charged her with a roar. She would have sidestepped in time but did not account for him slipping on the rocks and unnaturally veering into her. Managing to catch her arm, they both fell into the creek.

Sigrid unhooked her hand from Yut's and scrambled to take

him into a wrestling hold. Yut recognized it too late, as she wrapped her legs and arms around him in the Bear's Hold. Yut tried to twist and push his way out as the water enveloped them, but this was no rehearsed fight of the Proving Moon. Sigrid held on, and his vision blurred as his head dipped under the water. Through the creek's foam, he saw blurry torches set in the pillars of the long house, the smoke-covered ceiling, and the shapes of the villagers. Sigrid could not be stronger than Keld, but to struggle against the hold would be just as useless. He couldn't breathe, he couldn't move, and he was freezing.

No. Yut screamed, water filling his mouth, as he pulled against her with all of his strength. Surprised, Sigrid let one hand slip, and Yut instantly grabbed for her hair. At the wrestling matches back home, it was considered cowardly to grab for hair or hit the groin, but this was no wrestling match, and honor be damned. Yut was trying to survive.

He heard some of the wet hair rip from Sigrid's skull just as she shrieked in pain. Unfortunately, it only made her squeeze Yut's throat tighter. Darkness closed around Yut, his strength seeping out and into the water, his senses dulling.

Then she let go, and Yut crawled from the creek, pulling in a lungful of sweet, burning air.

There they were, gasping, Yut on all fours, Sigrid on one knee, looking at each other with dead stares. Eventually, Sigrid approached Yut, and he let her—he was too exhausted to scramble away. Thankfully, instead of kicking him in the face, she simply extended her hand to him. "Better?"

Yut gave a pained gasp as he lifted his hand, his ribs throbbing from her previous punches. She dragged him to his feet.

"Do you beat up every new person you meet?" he asked, flinging away a clump of bloodied blonde hair. He did not think he was feeling better, but he was not crying anymore, either.

"Only the ones that need a beating. But for what it's worth, you scrap alright." When Yut didn't respond, Sigrid sighed. "None of us wanted to be here, logmar, but if it wasn't clear already, the Saga is not kind, even if the gods tell it. The people you met haven't enjoyed a better fate than yours, and if you don't keep it together, this world will pull you apart and take everything from you. Especially if you stand there crying about who deserves what." She spoke with a quiet ferocity, as if she was pulling the words from deep within her.

She turned back toward the camp. "Come on, the others are waiting."

"Wait," said Yut, "Who are you, really?"

"What's it to you?"

"I thought you were scavengers, but you fight like a darkened soldier. And you don't look... er..." Keep on digging that hole, Yut. "Not like a scavenger."

Sigrid let her gaze drag Yut through ice before she answered. "Compliment received. But I am a scavenger, and I happen to have light hair and eyes. No, I'm not a lightfolk. No, I do not sing to starlight, and I don't twirl in the fields."

Yut hesitated for a long moment before taking a step toward her. He noticed that she waited for him. "How... how can I take hold of my fate? I have nothing left."

"Then you have everything. If you can't take anything back, then take revenge."

Yut shook his head. "You don't understand. I'm not a warrior, I can't fight, I have no gold for an army. I can do nothing."

"Well, you're certainly not a warrior," she said, eyeing him. "But you can do... other things." Then an idea seemed to dawn on her. "Go stand in the creek."

"What?"

"Do it, or I will put you in the creek," she said more sternly.

Eira's cloak still dripping, he carefully waded into the shallow creek up to his knees. The rocks were slippery here, so he had to dig in. He thought he saw a couple of fish dart by. Then he realized Sigrid was saying something, but the sound of the creek was drowning her out. Why was she standing so far?

"What?"

"I said you punched a Seither in the mouth," she yelled, carefully stepping closer.

"I... what?"

"Say 'what' again, and I will wallop you. You punched a Seither, a corrupt seeress, a being of the Dark itself, to her wretched doom. And all it took was one punch. If you hadn't done so, she would have drained Eira's, mine, and Olaf's blood for her dark rituals, and she would have fed off your strength for weeks."

Her explanation did nothing for his shivering, which, thanks to a soft breeze, was now growing.

"So, you can do *some* things. Now close your eyes."

Yut was about to ask why, but a sliver of common sense told him to shut up. He closed his eyes.

"How did you feel back then, when you did it?" She asked.

Yut tried to remember the hazy journey from Sanvik—there was pain, fear, panic. The constant *exhaustion.* There was a rune on his forearm, a house shimmering at the edge of a ravine, the kind old woman. No, she was a foul, tall *thing* that spoke in a backward language. The others came to save him, the axe split her head, but she was unharmed. He remembered it then—justice. Strength. The rune spoke to him from the darkness, and he reached out to it. He brimmed with power as everything gained color and focus. His steps gained weight, he began smiling, he felt safe. He somehow saw sense in everything. He even thought he could understand what the Seither was saying, though he did not want to.

Sigrid must have seen his expression change, because she said, "Good, now take that focus and use it. Hear everything around you, hear the tale it tells, and tell the tale back. And I know how that sounds—I felt the same way when I first heard it. Just try."

Yut listened. At first, all he could hear was the sound of the rushing creek, but then a different sound penetrated through the water—a distant, quick knocking. A woodpecker, the sound easily recognizable, drummed on a tree a few feet from the creek. He focused on the sound, which then opened a plethora of bird calls—only some of which Yut recognized. The woods made sounds, like soft branches creaking in the wind and pinecones dropping onto the leaves below. The sound of the creek drifted beneath him, and Yut heard the rustle of leaves, the fish springing out of the water, and the call of a distant raven. He heard his heart pumping warmth into his freezing feet, he heard Sigrid's quiet breath, as if she was standing next to him.

He heard, and then he felt.

He felt the deep dark that found him at that ravine. The rune that called to him, and with it, the entire world.

It came crashing down on him. The sounds, the sensations of it all, everything had its place and story. Everything was telling him where it had been and where it would go. Everything was talking, and Yut was forced to listen. He wanted to scream against the torrent of sensations, to open his eyes at least, but he was bound underneath the weight of it all.

The lark was singing, the creek was sliding against the rocks—it came from the mountains, he could still feel the freshness of the snow that it had been shortly before. How long have these trees been here? How many tales can they tell? Far too many. Their whisperings mercilessly fell on him like storm waves. Yut couldn't breathe, but couldn't move either. How long has he been standing here? Months? Years? But all he could do was listen to the unceasing sound of everything.

Sjaltr.

His voice said it, his ears heard it, but it wasn't him. Yut's eyes burst open as he rushed from the creek, gasping, past Sigrid, and onto the banks. Just then, he realized three things: One, while it felt like he was suspended in a world of sounds for months, it was only a few seconds. Two, Sigrid was watching him with profound astonishment. "How do you know that Telling?" Which brought him to the third, and the darkest realization—he could not hear anything.

He heard his breathing and Sigrid's question, but that was it. No birds, no trees, not even... gods above, the creek.

They stared at the creek as if seeing it for the first time, because at that point Yut and Sigrid saw something neither of them thought was ever possible.

The creek had stopped running.

It was unnatural. The water still moved, but it did not flow. It was like a long puddle, sitting at a slight decline, unheeding of the natural laws that commanded it to descend. A soft blue steam rose from it, and the air shimmered above.

"Dark above, what did you do?" whispered Sigrid, wide eyes still affixed to the creek.

"I... I didn't... It was so loud, too much..." It slowly dawned on Yut. It was all too much. He wanted it to stop, but instead of saying *stop*, the other word came out. And it stopped—everything stopped.

Sigrid shook her head in disbelief. "We have to tell Eira, she can fix it. She can... gods, what are you waiting for?" And she was off, leaping like a gazelle back to the camp.

Yut hesitated for only a moment before running after her.

Chapter Fourteen

On the Precipice of Legend

Sigrid had nearly finished packing her and Eira's things by the time the kid made it back to the camp. She could not say she was surprised, judging by how clumsily he ran when he tried to escape them. He probably thought he was being very clever with that "embarrassing condition" excuse, but even Olaf wasn't fooled. What he needed was a good kick, if not for the disrespect he showed them, then for the audacity to make himself a victim of the situation. She was looking forward to seeing Eira give him a fiery lecture, but when he finally arrived, out of breath and terrified, the seeress was nearly giddy.

"Your first Telling, eh?" she asked proudly.

"I'm so sorry," huffed Yut, "I have no idea what just—a telling?"

"Not telling, you goat, a *Telling*. You must give it the bit of mystery. You changed the Saga of the gods, the very course of nature. You spoke to the water and the trees, and they listened!" Eira was chipper, grabbing Yut by his shoulders like he just caught his first fish. *Interesting*, thought Sig. She was again reminded of that young girl, when Eira taught her to Speak her first Telling.

"*Eldr*," she intoned, and the branch in her hands caught on fire. Eira clapped her hands and laughed, and Sig laughed as well, even though she was frightened. Frightened of the power she was given and frightened at what she wanted to do with it.

Yut looked at her and Olaf, who was still packing, with goat eyes—he seemed to be just as surprised at Eira's response. Altering the Saga bore consequences, if not from the gods then from the people that believed in the gods' punishment. Either way, someone will notice the creek, and they will come looking. Sig told Eira as soon as she was back at camp, but the seeress merely nodded and asked if Yut was with her.

"I... the creek," said Yut through a haze. "The creek had stopped. Please, can you do anything?"

"Peace, child," smiled Eira, "Do not worry about the creek, it will find its natural way soon enough. And so will you. Come, we must be off, young Speaker."

Olaf had already doused the campfire and was now checking that all of his weapons were where they belonged. He periodically glanced at Yut and grumbled under his breath. Sig wondered how much more of this the big man could take before deserting them. It seemed only a matter of time.

Yut awkwardly twisted out of Eira's excited grip. "Aren't the gods going to be... you know, angry?"

"It is not the gods I am worried about," replied Eira. "We should be on our way before the Cult comes. They would have sensed the battle with the Seither, and the creek will only narrow their search. I will also be having my cloak back now, there is a good lad. Olaf, give the boy a—"

"Hold on," said Olaf, who had walked up to them after checking for the dagger in his boot, "again with the Cult. Eira, I know you're wise and all that, but talk straight just once. Is the Cult of Orik real? Are they really out for blood? Our blood?"

The three stood together then, Olaf, Sigrid, and Yut, teetering on the precipice of purpose and legend. Walking up to that precipice, Eira gave them a push. "I've been talking straight to you the entire time, Olaf. The Cult is real. It has been real since the Allwinter and has only grown in power. They have gripped the Saga, and now they twist it whichever way they wish. They would tell you it is for our own good, but their lofty purpose has long been soaked in blood."

Olaf narrowed his eyes. "You sure know a lot about 'em..."

Unswayed, Eira jabbed a finger at Yut, "And now they will be chasing *you,* what with the mayhem you've been causing the Saga. And, by implication, they will be chasing all of us."

"It wasn't my fault!" He stammered, "I didn't mean for it to happen like that, I don't—"

"I said *peace,* young Yut. You have followed the Saga—we all have. There is no shame in that, but we are now bound together, fated for a purpose grander than us. Now we must run, grow, learn. We are hunted now, but we will become the hunters. Are you with me?"

Concerned faces looked at each other. "Well..." started Olaf.

"Always," stepped in Sig, taking Eira's elbow. It was no use denying her path with Eira, not after the years they'd spent together. Not after Eira saved her life. Though the seeress kept some things hidden from her, Sig would rather walk to the heart of the Dark holding Eira's elbow, than be anywhere else without her.

Olaf's face soured. "I don't know about this." He eyed the three companions, and looked ready to say something, but Eira quickly said, "You owe me your axe and your word, big man. That question was not directed at you."

"Oh," frowned Olaf, "Well then... dark take it. Fine."

That left the kid. Hopeless, weak, destitute Yut-the-logmar's-son, who made a creek stop running at his first Telling and survived a fall into a thornbush ravine. Sig saw it in his eyes then, the same fear that she felt when she made a branch burn. A second fear followed, of forests and cities in flames, and the people that made her suffer burned alive. Without Eira to guide her, she might have followed that path, and probably destroyed herself in the process. That is why Sig decided she would not blame Yut for wanting to run from them. This was not a path for many—especially not someone who had just lost everything.

That was when he looked at her, and Sig realized the second fear was absent from his eyes. Instead, two black points pierced her, taking her aback. No, these were not the eyes of fear. Perhaps it was there before, but something else took root now, and Sig understood it too well, she just did not expect it to happen so soon. She slowly nodded at him, and he nodded back. "Alright, I'm in."

"Good," said Eira, "Then give me my cloak back, and let us away to the Red Hill. Olaf, lead the way."

The warrior perked up then, worry replaced by excitement. "Aye, finally. To the market, then." He hefted his pack and was off without further wait.

Yut followed quietly, back to looking like a lost sheep, while Sig and Eira followed behind him. Lost or not, Sig knew what she saw in his eyes, and she was wary. She understood fear and was well-versed in uncertainty. She had lived with it for most of her life and had seen it in the eyes of nearly everyone she encountered. She knew fear was dangerous, though she would rather fight fear than hatred. The person who was afraid would only fight to protect their life. But the person who truly hated you, well, they would have a single purpose in their attack, and their own life would not mean much in the moment. That is why she checked for her knives before following Yut. Eira had better know what she was getting them into, because when Sig peered into Yut's eyes, behind the fear and grief, she found the unmistakable beginnings of hatred.

Chapter Fifteen

The Red Hill

Yut scolded himself for thinking Olaf would lead them to an actual marketplace. In reality, "the market" turned out to be a battlefield.

A fresh battlefield, according to Olaf, and with few survivors. "Prime pickin'," said the big man, "the fighting should all be done, and everyone gone off home for supper." Though he continued humming excitedly, his eyes grew focused and attentive the closer they got. Maybe not *everyone*, then.

As they neared the end of the Northern Trelwoods, the trees became sparse and the land unruly. Several times Olaf stopped at some cliff, bog, or ravine, cursed loudly, and turned to find another path. Yut was glad Sig did not make any remarks about it. From what he could tell, the two scavengers loved nothing more than to snap at one another, like kids that hadn't reached their growing months. By the time they found a semblance of a path, Olaf looked ready to snap a neck, and Sig must have sensed as much.

Eventually they reached the edges of the woods just as a fog drifted in. A lone reindeer caught Yut's eye, feeding on a hill like a ghostly guardian in the fog, allowing them to leave its sacred forest. An inexplicable sadness washed over Yut at seeing the animal. He had only seen them in herds before, the rare times his father took him hunting. He wondered if the wyrm took its family too, or if it lost its way during their migration. Then he thought about how he might never return to the Trelwoods again, if they were to follow Eira's quest. Even if he had never been this far North, the woods were his home, and his family's home, since the Allwinter. After everything that had happened, the woods protected him, and leaving them felt like abandoning a part of himself.

And perhaps that was for the best. Whatever his future held now, he doubted it involved rebuilding a home or governing a village. No, his old self would have to stay behind in the Trelwoods, along with Sanvik. His new self made a creek stop running and destroyed a Seither. His new self would dip his hands in blood and bring about justice—this he promised to the gods, Keld, and his parents.

He looked up at the reindeer again just as it withdrew into the fog. He hoped it would be reunited with its herd soon. Although Yut had lost everything, he gratefully realized that at least he was not alone. He glanced at Olaf, who was staring intently at the animal. "Dark, we just don't have the time..." he whispered. Yut was about to ask him what he meant, when the soldier scowled and looked at Sigrid. "You trackin' him?"

Sig smirked confidently. "I'm tracking him—I'll get it after the market. Hope you know how to cook reindeer."

Olaf chuckled hungrily as Yut sighed. Reindeer did sound delicious.

Eira and Sig followed close behind him through their trip. Olaf's navigational skills were not the only reason for the slow progress through the woods—even though Eira seemed to hear a bird nesting a mile away, she could not maneuver the uneven forest floor by herself. Yut returned her cloak and in exchange, Olaf gave him an oversized, thick tunic. He also gave him a better dagger, an axe, carrying pack, and he even tried to get him interested in a slightly-blooded chain mail, which Yut politely refused.

"New boots you'll nick at the market yourself," said Olaf, tucking the chain mail back in the satchel, "And anything else valuable."

"Won't there be other scavengers?" inquired Yut. He was not worried about seeing the aftermath of a battle. He remembered half-burned lumps of human flesh, frozen expressions of terror covered in the ash of drake fire, the devastating silence. What is a battlefield compared to that?

"Maybe," replied Olaf, "But we won't take long. And you see this fog? The gods are kind to us hungry dogs. We will slip in and out, and if anyone is still there..." Instead of finishing the sentence he checked for his axes. Yut prayed there was nobody there.

Shortly after leaving the last of the Trelwood's trees, they entered a wide hill of yellow and brown grass. There might have been a few lonely trees ahead, but the fog thickened considerably, making the land look like it was drowned in watered milk. The still air gave way to the smell of metal and rot—Yut assumed the mountains of corpses lay just out of view. Strange, though he's suffered through more in the past few days than he had in his entire life, he felt oddly peaceful.

No, it was not peace, but emptiness. Now his life was caught in some wild torrent of runes, gods, magic and monsters, and he was powerless to escape, so he stopped trying.

"Right, we need food, arrows, and silver," Olaf glanced at Yut, "and boots, if you find any."

"Be quick, be quiet," said Eira. "I hear crows, but no footsteps. We are either alone, or someone lies in wait. Olaf will go with Yut, take heed of each other. Sigrid will scout the outskirts and watch for movement. Find me in this spot when you are finished. Now be blessed."

Eira air-traced runes with her index and middle finger, whispering a chant of protection. Standing next to her, Sig bowed her head and repeated the chant. To Yut's surprise, Olaf also bowed his head, and said a few hushed words under his breath. Yut found himself without words. He knew the chant well: "Father Orm, protect and guide your children..." They prayed this chant during hunts, when a bad omen was seen, or when a fever took hold of the town. Now, however, the town was burned to the ground. Now he was without family or friends. Now he was using magic. What good would prayer do now?

He said nothing, but thankfully no one took issue with this. They split up and stepped into the fog.

* * *

The hill was a couple hundred paces across, a grassy rise amid the trees of Trelwoods, but they found the first body within seconds. The fog obscured the entire hill—Yut had never seen it so thick before—so they could not see much more. A blessing, to be sure.

The first corpse was a boy. An arrow protruded out of his skull, splitting the oversized helm. He wore a leather overcoat over a tunic and a sheathed dagger. The helmet itself was a patchwork of wood and leather bound by wire. Yut doubted it could withstand a well-thrown rock, much less a soldier's arrow. He couldn't have been more than thirteen winters.

"Poor bugger must have bolted soon as the fighting started," Olaf echoed Yut's thoughts, kneeling by the youth. "Maybe earlier. Heh, kind of looks like you."

He did not need to say that. Yut took a few steps away, facing towards the woods, feeling the bile rise. So much for feeling empty.

"Well?" asked Olaf.

"What?"

"He's got boots, looks like your size."

"Oh." Yut regarded the kid again. The boots looked much better than Yut's leathers, but it felt wrong. The dead should be buried with their belongings, so they can enter the fields of the dead in comfort. How did this boy come here? He must have family somewhere, praying to Orm for protection over their boy. What would Yut's mother say?

"Could you...?" Yut began, and paused.

It took a moment for Olaf to understand, and then he scoffed loudly. "You want me to feed *and* clothe you? Gods below. Hah!" He adjusted his belt as he walked further up the hill, abandoning Yut by the young corpse. "Cold days are comin', boy. Get the boots or get frostbite."

Yut eventually caught up with Olaf, feeling guilty, but at least his feet were warmer. The big man was examining a fine axe and a sword amid a pile of bodies. Neither the view nor the smell seemed to bother him as much as the weapons in his hands. "Choices, choices..." He muttered as Yut drew near.

"Whose battle was it, anyway?" Yut asked.

"Well, some of 'em are with Jarl Helgi, or King Helgi, if you like. The others gotta be with the twins, from Vessir—maybe you can find one of those fancy Vessir axes, those are worth good coin. And the rest," Olaf paused, prying his eyes from the blades and gazing across the shrouded battlefield, "Others are nobodies, fightin' for their jarl, land, or family. Or, at least they were." The two looked at the dead warriors, still, terrified, and silent.

"I heard Jarl Helgi is trying to take revenge for old Grima's son," said Yut, trying to stave off the eerie silence.

Olaf spat on someone's leg. "And I heard fartin' on a field makes the potatoes grow better. Grima was a proper king. Now all we got is darkened vultures fighting for his corpse."

Yut looked at Olaf in surprise—the big man nearly sounded poetic. "You don't think the twins of Vessir killed Grima's young one?"

"All I know is no one knows nothin'. Everyone's got a good story and everyone thinks they're right. Everyone wants to fight, everyone wants the glory, and everyone wants to win."

Yut gestured to the nameless dead. "Do you know who won here?"

In response, Olaf bent down to an older man in the dirt, his jaw broken and body beginning to swell. Olaf slapped him on the cheek. "Oy, old timer, don't mean to interrupt your nap, but you mind tellin' us who won here? You reckon you did, didn't you? Feeling mighty strong, mighty righteous? I reckon you were a darkened hero of the battle, before gettin' your face smashed in." Olaf grabbed the man's head and began nodding it enthusiastically. Yut did not think it was very funny.

Olaf spat again, stood up, and tossed the sword in favor of the axe. "Remember this, boy, glory's in living. Now, enough lollygagging, we need loot. We should leave soon, too. This place gives me the creeps."

Creeps was an understatement. The sagas never mentioned what happened after the great battles, which made sense now. The stink of blood and feces, the sight of dead warriors immortalized in anguish, the maggots and the crows fighting for eyeballs—all in all, not the most inspirational sight.

The dead watched Yut tread the hill, their faces shifting between terror to awe, as if the corpses were surprised that he was still alive. Yut tried scavenging periodically but soon found that he was not very good at it. Where would someone keep their food or silver on a battlefield? Shouldn't they have left it back home anyway? There were weapons strewn about, but Yut had an axe now, and, unlike Olaf, he really did not see the need in carrying enough weapons for an army.

As he considered going back, a raven screeched not a stride behind him. He leaped in panic, scrambling for his axe, trying to turn around and flee at the same time. The darkened bird must have been hiding in the shadows. Yut did not have time to take out the axe as he tripped on someone's leg and fell face first into the mud. The raven flew away while Yut cleared the mud from his eyes, cursing. That's when he spotted the sword.

The glisten of the jewels on the hilt pierced even through the fog. It stood upright, like an altar of battle, on top of the hill and surrounded by the dead. Yut scrambled closer and saw clear emeralds set in the hilt and pommel, the type that would cost more than the entirety of Sanvik. The wrapping was azure cloth, and the hilt and pommel inlaid with gold and silver. Yut had never seen anything so beautiful—it was like looking at a blade of the gods. He was so mesmerized that he almost missed that it was embedded in someone.

The person killed by the sword was not much older than Yut, though definitely much taller. He had lost his helm, so his golden hair was smeared with mud. The fine chain mail, woven with a gambeson at the joints, was inscribed with runes of bravery and protection, and the blade of the sword mirrored them. This was no mere warrior, it must have been a Heisir, or a jarl's son. Well, they started this mess in the first place, so Yut's conscience was clear as he grabbed the sword.

A bloody hand clamped around his wrist.

Yut yelped and recoiled, nearly diving into the ground again. It was the hand of the fallen Heisir, except he had not fallen yet. Yut could see his eyelids were twitching, and it looked like he was trying to say something.

A few minutes later, Olaf and an out-of-breath Yut stood over the Heisir.

"Not bad, boy. The gems will fetch a good price, if we can pry 'em out. It's no good trying to sell a full sword, trust me. Some swords are famous—especially expensive ones like this. If someone recognizes—"

"Olaf, he's still alive," said Yut, pointing to the Heisir's ragged breathing. Olaf set his pack down—already ringing with loot—and examined the warrior.

"Poor sod. Looks like he got it right under the rib cage. Must have missed all the important bits, so it's the pain, fever, and slow bleeding out for this one." Olaf nudged the man with his foot. "We might as well show some pity, you know, for Vae's sake and all that."

Thank the Nine, Yut expected Olaf to abandon the man after stealing his sword. However, as Yut took out his water flask, Olaf took out his new axe.

"What are you doing?" They said simultaneously.

"I thought we were showing mercy," said Yut.

"And you want to give him water, make him suffer a few more days, eh?"

"I thought we would, you know, patch him up," tried Yut, though the thought sounded naive when he said it aloud.

"Well, if you and your magic friends can heal a man from a sword-through-the-gut-for-three-days, which is probably infected now, and bring him back from the jaws of death herself, you can be my guest. I just thought I would take mercy on the guy, seeing how he's been longing for death for days now."

They stared at one another. Yut did not mention that bringing someone back from the brink of death was exactly what the group did with him, and Olaf must have realized it as well, but there they were. In the silence that stretched, a soft whimper escaped the dying man's lips.

"What was that?" Yut dropped down to the man, straining to hear it again. A man's final words were to be treasured and remembered, so said the wise ones. Olaf shook his head as he picked up his pack.

"...dog," said the Heisir.

Yut leaned closer. "I don't—think he's hallucinating. What is it? What do you see?"

"I see... the dog," He exhaled, his breathing labored.

"He says he sees the dog," called Yut, stopping Olaf short. "Which dog? The hound of Rothr? Is he here now?" It was well known that the god of battle, Rothr, sometimes shifted into a hunting hound. He would run through the battlefield, alighting men with new strength and vigor.

"He *is* hallucinating," said Olaf.

The Heisir strained to get the words out. "The dog..." His eyes wide, with a blood-crusted, trembling finger, he pointed at Olaf. "The dog, the filthy deserter. You came back, you-worse-than-filth, twice-cursed—"

"Actually, I'm feeling very merciful right about now," said Olaf, taking out his axe, "Let the man die in peace."

Yut scrambled to get in the way of Olaf, which was like getting in the way of a rock slide. "He knows you? You're a deserter?" Yut could not tell whether the crack in his voice came from shock or fear. The accusation itself felt like a curse coming from Yut's mouth, though he admitted that it made sense. Why else would a strong warrior like Olaf be hiding out with scavengers? From the way people talked about them, deserters were no better than monsters of the Dark.

"I don't know what he's talking about," growled Olaf, teeth bared. He pushed Yut aside, or rather, walked through where Yut was standing, and put his axe to the dying man's throat. "You *don't* know what you're talking about," he commanded, but the Heisir merely stretched a thin smile over the pallid face.

"Yes... I remember your name now. Battle at the Old Fjord. Olaf... the dog," he finished.

"I'll take your eyes, you bastard!" roared Olaf, raising the axe.

"No!" Shouted Yut, jumping for Olaf's hand.

The axe never landed as something big flew into them both, sending Olaf and Yut sprawling. Lying with them, Sigrid stared with eyes wide and a finger to her lips. Yut froze.

Olaf did not take the hit gracefully but quieted when he saw her face. Slowly, Sig drew her finger away from her lips to point past the Heisir. The three crawled to the dying man, looking past the sword still sticking out of torso, and down the hill.

Milky fog shifted among the bodies of the dead, nothing but shadows looking back at the three scavengers.

"What is it?" whispered Olaf, all traces of the rage seemingly gone.

"I saw someone down there. Tall, wearing armor—could be a soldier," breathed Sig.

Olaf must have gotten nervous because he hushedly explained to Yut, "Soldier is bad. Other looters would have the decency to let us pass without trouble, but soldiers would fight. They think all this belongs to them or the dead, so they wouldn't give us a coin. Greedy bastards."

Olaf peeked over the dying Heisir. "Did you see where he came from?" He asked Sig.

"I did not see him come in, but it must have been from the other side of the hill. There was no one on the battlefield when we came here. He headed towards you when you started bickering."

"We weren't—"

And all three saw him then. Tall indeed, his chain clinking as he walked along the bottom of the hill, just outside of their visible range. It was difficult to make out any detail, but Yut thought he could see a horn on the warrior's helm. Yut stole a glance at his companions as his heart hammered. Olaf and Sig also had their eyes fixed, breathing quickly but quietly. The warrior drifted through the fog like a ghost, finally disappearing behind the sparse trees.

Silence reclaimed the battlefield. The only sound was the fallen Heisir's ragged breathing. He was taking deeper breaths now, as if bracing for something. As if he was about to—

"Kill them!" He shouted.

Olaf clamped his hand over the man's mouth, hard. "Dark take your mother!"

They waited. Soon enough, the soldier appeared again, unhurried but heading straight towards them.

"It's just one man, right?" stammered Yut. "We can take him, right? Are we taking him? Olaf?"

Sig and Olaf lay unmoving, eyes fixated on the approaching figure. Yut focused on him again and realized several things.

He was dragging a longsword along the dirt, his blue face split into a smile that was too wide. His eyes did not hold humor, or hatred, or anything. Instead, they glowed a dull blue color, piercing the fog like two little flames. Lastly, and most importantly, the horn on his helmet was not a horn at all, but an axe. An axe buried in his skull.

It was an axe. And it was buried in his skull.

"It's a... it's—" croaked Yut.

"Draugr!" shouted Sig. "Run!" She slapped Olaf on the back of the head, who sprung up faster than Yut thought possible.

Yut also started running, but for some darkened reason he looked back at the fallen Heisir. His smirk was gone, along with all signs of life. Yut looked at the sword—such value could change everything. He could buy a dozen horses, or a farm. Or a small army.

The draugr was still a ways off when Yut cursed and scampered to the sword, tried to unsheathe it from the Heisir's torso, and couldn't. The blade was stuck to the armor, it was no wonder now why they left it here. He tried to jolt it loose, making the corpse shake. The Heisir, with his final rictus, looked like he was hysterically laughing at Yut.

Yut's heart nearly burst out of his chest as the draugr closed in. "Dark take you!"

With a final yank, the sword came free, and he turned to run after his companions. That was when the dead man spoke to him.

"*You should not be here, little bird.*"

Most voices are heard with ears. Yut heard the deep, smooth voice with his entire being. It reverberated through him, paralyzing him dead in his tracks. The sword fell from his hands as he turned toward the draugr.

The dead man stepped over the Heisir's body, and stood with his head cocked, blue eyes searching Yut.

"*So many dead, so many dead,*" he intoned. Somehow the draugr knew Yut, knew his past. His eyes delved deeper.

"*Yours are the hands of death, little bird. Destruction will spread from you and pass among the living like a disease. Beware the blind seeress. Beware the eight-runed one. Come with me, little bird, I will take you where you belong.*" The draugr reached his hand toward Yut, who had lost all control over his body as complete terror overwhelmed him, crashing down and holding him tight. Yut knew there was no escape, there was only the dead man, and his hand reaching closer, closer to his heart. Yut closed his eyes.

But then there was another sound, like a bear's roar, accompanied by an eagle's shrill cry. Yut opened his eyes, and the draugr's blue hand lay on the ground, cut off by a finely crafted axe. Olaf shoved Yut to the ground as Sig jumped on the enemy's back, repeatedly stabbing him in the neck.

With one arm remaining, the draugr dropped his sword, reached back, and easily threw Sig to the side. She landed hard in a pile of corpses just as Olaf charged again. The draugr dodged the big man's overhand cut this time, and punched him in the throat with unnatural speed. Olaf staggered back, clutching at his neck, making choking sounds. The dead man once again turned to Yut.

Free from draugr's hold, Yut dove for the Heisir's sword, grabbed it, and pointed it at the approaching monster as he scrambled backward.

"*Come with me, little bird,*" repeated the deep voice. The point of Yut's sword was trembling wildly. His voice had been snuffed out by fear, and he could focus on nothing save the draugr's exposed teeth set in blackened gums.

The draugr reached for the blade. "*We will rid the land of your curse—*"

The dead man stopped. He whipped his head to the side, the axe in his skull wrenching out from the momentum. He was looking at Sig, who had recovered from the fall, and was now chanting softly, eyes closed.

The draugr's grin was replaced by fury as he leaped for her, but just then, she opened her eyes and shouted, "Eldr!"

The draugr burst into white flames. It was so bright that Yut had to shield his eyes. A torn, piercing scream emanated from him almost instantly as he desperately tried to extinguish himself, but it was no use. In a matter of seconds, the creature was running downhill and out of sight. It took too long for the echoing scream to finally end.

* * *

The walk back to Eira was silent and quick. Anything living within ten leagues would have heard the screech of the undead. Yut knew it would not fade from his memory. He was sure as the sun that it would come back to his nightmares, over and over. Nothing and no one screamed like the draugr—it was the sound of naked agony and terror.

Neither would Yut forget what the dead man said. Tove said draugr were the only creatures, besides the gods, who could see the future, and they did so without bias or contempt. However, good folk did not seek them out as the creatures were clearly cursed, and where the Dark dwells, the Dark spreads. Yut did not know what the draugr would do to him had he touched him, but he was sure it would not be good.

But how could Yut make many dead? He could not even wield an axe, and his attempt at Speaking was an obvious failure. Perhaps that was it. Yut would fail somehow, and accidentally doom everyone to their death. Maybe he already has. Perhaps the draugr wanted to take him simply to prevent or to punish the death of many.

Gods, Yut, what did you get yourself into? Every decision he had made thus far seemed to have thrown him into further danger and disaster. If this is what it meant to battle the Dark, then Yut would much prefer being a logmar's son in Sanvik. He would even prefer to be a farmer, a fisherman, the village idiot, or anyone else. He would rather worry about the crops and the weather, or even Old Sten's superstitious complaints, than about a draugr cursing his soul. When he imagined fighting evil beings in his mother's garden, injury and death were usually not involved, yet it seemed that is all that awaited him out here. Yut felt tears welling up in his eyes, so he clenched his teeth and tried to steel himself. No, he could not go back to Sanvik because Sanvik no longer existed. It was razed, along with his mother's garden, and the fishermen, and Old Sten. If he wanted a shot at justice, then this was his only path, come injury or death. That is why he accepted Eira's quest. That is why he had to survive.

He looked at his companions. "Thank you. For stepping in back there."

Sigrid said nothing. She tried to look unshaken after the encounter, but Yut could tell she was twitchy. She scanned each passing corpse, her breaths quick, constantly picking at a dagger handle.

"Don't mention it," growled Olaf, who was faring worse than Sig, with his axe and shield out, and his knuckles white with grip. He almost abandoned his loot as they ran downhill. Now he had it tied around his waist, and it was making clinking sounds, which put him further on edge.

"But next time you see somethin' step out of the Dark itself," he paused to wipe the sweat from his forehead and catch his breath. "You run the other way. Even if—" gasp, gasp, "—even if there is loot."

Chapter Sixteen

Paths

Olaf was yelling at Eira as soon as he saw her, though Sigrid did not rush to defend her this time. Instead, she felt the impulse to join him, as much as it pained her. Even so, the icy gaze of the draugr instilled a fearful silence within her.

"The kid is dark bait. That's a Seither *and* a draugr in less than a week!" fumed Olaf. "What happened to 'simple scavengers'? Dark take it, at this rate, we'll be wulver food by the end of the week."

"Peace, Olaf son of—"

"No," said Sigrid. Olaf stopped and looked at Sigrid incredulously. She met his gaze. *Yes, fat man, we are in agreement just this once.* Eira pursed her lips, and even Yut, who looked like he was in the middle of an out-of-body experience, lifted his head.

"It was too close, Eira. If I hadn't used a Telling, if it hadn't worked, we'd be in the ground with the rest of the corpses. Draugr don't just take your life, they take your soul. We were lucky he was fresh, if he had known any Tellings of his own, if he started Speaking—"

"I know what the draugr take, young Sigrid," bit back Eira, "I am a seeress, it is my duty to know these things. Or do you think I wear the white for its looks? Do you believe if I had heard its footsteps prior, then I would have allowed you out there?"

"Then what else could you miss? Olaf is right—we cannot handle these things ourselves. Dark above, Eira, if draugr are attacking during market runs, will they attack while we sleep? How long before the Cult catches us? How will we survive if every cursed thing from the Dark is hunting us?"

Sig couldn't believe what she was saying. She had barely ever raised her tone at Eira, and now she could not stop herself. But the outburst was surprising as well as relieving. These words must have been building up like snowfall in the high peaks, and the avalanche needed to go.

"You think you have seen the heart of the Dark today?" Eira's tone was patient, though Sig could feel a cold fury behind it. She took an involuntary step back. "You were lucky indeed, because the eyes of the world and the gods themselves are upon you now. You have agreed to follow this path, and yet you cower already. We are scavengers no more, but warriors, and we may be the last hope of this wretched world. It is not fair to ask for your courage, since perhaps you are not ready. Yet your courage, and every bit of strength, is what it will take to prevail."

Though she was not using Telling, Eira's words carried power. Sig watched as they settled on Yut's pale face, raising his head and squaring his shoulders as he stood. Olaf's face grew from chronic paranoia to something resembling resignation. Even Sig, who had heard similar words many times before, felt the comfort they breathed into her. If Eira had command of a medium-sized army, she could probably convince them to take over Arthgard itself. Sig deflated. *Guess we keep going, then.*

Olaf dropped the sack of loot in front of him. "Right, well, I reckon we did take care of the blue trelkin right quick. It'll take more than one dead bugger to bring this drengr down. Let's see the goods."

They had a good haul, all things considered. A couple of mint daggers split between Sig and Olaf, a fur for Eira, which was only barely speckled with blood, light provisions, fresh cloth. The kid was still holding on to that ridiculous sword, which should fetch good coin.

As they inspected their prizes, Sig noticed Eira speaking to Yut in the trees. No doubt she wanted to know what the draugr told him. He looked ready to soil himself by the time they came back for him, so she couldn't picture him remembering much. Not that it mattered anyway—the draugr were creatures of the Dark, unnatural things made to destroy this world, no matter how the stories painted them. The most surprising part about the whole ordeal was Olaf; the man ran back for Yut as soon as he realized the kid wasn't with them. In that moment, roaring with rage, he looked like some berserker. It seemed no one was exactly who she thought them to be.

Yut and Eira returned shortly after Sig and Olaf finished sorting through their prize. "We have our next destination," announced Eira. "And don't even start, Olaf. I can hear your moans before they leave your throat."

Olaf frowned in unbridled offense, which was not an unenjoyable sight. Of course, Sig could almost foretell his complaining as well, though that was not saying much. As she walked to Eira's side, Sig gently patted him on the cheek, which earned her an even more enjoyable look of shock. She smiled at him. "Chin up, big man."

He tried to slap her hand away, but she was already gone. "...Darkened hands off me," he grumbled. In return, she winked at him. She had to keep them uncertain, keep them guessing. If it came down to a fight, she would prefer him to be the one that was off balance.

"I suppose it would be too much to ask for our next destination to have good food and soft beds?" asked Yut. To Sig's relief, he seemed to have somewhat recovered from his tragedy. Whatever his motivation was, it would mean the difference between life and death in the wilds. Sigrid had seen her share of war victims giving up on life after losing their families. They became ghosts living in human bodies, wandering through villages and cities, until something or someone eventually claimed their life. Sig was glad she did not suffer that fate, but things were slightly different with her.

Eira accepted Sig's arm at her elbow, though the seeress was the one who began leading her. "Not to worry, young man," she said. "We seek now a place of rest; I should think we deserve as much after the last few days. And there is one place in particular that should serve our needs nicely."

"Is there a village in these parts?" wondered Sig. A wyrm destroyed the closest place she could think of, and the other had to be the village of Orheim. It was a quaint little fishing spot on the river Glammyr, and the locals were nice enough when they last passed through there. Rather, they were more than nice, being so honored by the presence of a seeress that they spared nothing to make Eira and Sig comfortable during their stay.

"Bah, the closest one's gotta be Orheim, that darkened hole," moaned Olaf. Then quieter, he added, "They know me there."

"No village," said Eira, taking a turn West, away from the battlefield and Orheim, and toward the clearing fog. Sometimes, Eira had an uncanny way of navigating herself even without Sig's help. Whenever Sig would ask about it, the wisewoman simply stated that sometimes the Saga guided her. "There is a spot that can fill much more than our bellies."

She stopped for a dramatic pause, which Sig expected by now. She figured Eira loved performing more than any skald in Arthgard, and even though Sig hated skalds, at least Eira had useful things to say in between her flares of drama. Yut jogged up to them, caught wide-eyed in her web. "How else would we be filled? Spiritually?"

"Perhaps," replied the seeress mysteriously. "Tell me, young Yut, what do you know about the lightfolk?"

Chapter Seventeen

Hope of the Saga

Sig watched the landscape shift from dark forests to bright fields, their crimson hues flowing along endless hills, creeks, and valleys. Chill winds swept grass, robes, and hair Northward, as they trekked West, toward the towering and sharp mountains. Toward Eira's secret place of rest. Sig admitted she was frustrated to learn of this hidden lightfolk outpost only now, after years of traveling with Eira. A week ago, she might have dismissed it as a harmless piece of information the seeress forgot to tell her. But after suddenly seeking out Yut, and keeping the Cult of Orik secret, she began to wonder if there was another world that Eira hid from her. And if she kept those secrets, then what else was she hiding? In the past, whenever they traveled through the wilds, Sig would gently hold Eira's elbow to guide her. Now, heading into a seemingly random direction through gods forsaken hills, Sig felt she was the one being guided. Perhaps this was always the case.

She would have confronted Eira herself, but even after two days of their journey, Olaf was never far enough out of earshot, and Yut stuck fast to their side while he pestered Eira with endless questions. Though the winds were unkind to their skin, Sig welcomed their noise, which finally drowned out the young man's inquiries. In fact, she wouldn't be surprised if Eira purposely led them through these hills if only to gain a bit of respite.

At the end of the second day, Sigrid found a decrepit hut for them to camp in. It looked ready to collapse, but a few surrounding trees must have prevented the wind from finishing the job. There was only one room inside, with a few cracked shelves and the remains of a fire pit. Some of the roof had collapsed, too, but it was still better than sleeping outside. After they dropped their packs, and Olaf stretched with all the noise of a cow in labor, and Sig gulped down the remains of her waterskin, Yut began his interrogation again. "So, if our world is the Saga of all of the gods, does that mean you can create a world too?"

Eira slumped down on the ancient floorboards and began massaging her legs. "If only. Even a lightfolk lacks the power to create a Saga that grand. At least, individually." The wisewoman was giving answers in long prose when they left the battlefield. Now Sig noted that the prose had dissolved into simple, tired sentences.

Yut's next question came as soon as Eira finished her answer. "Then it's possible in groups?"

Eira sighed. "It is said that some Speakers could Speak together, in the olden days. This brought them great power, but at an even greater risk. They could level cities, armies, mountains, though this required perfect trust and harmony, and us mortals were not made for such things."

"So what happens to the Speakers if—"

"We need firewood," interrupted Sig, before Eira showed Yut the true meaning of Speaking. She could tell Yut was pushing the exhausted seeress, and Sig still needed her own questions answered. She pinned Yut with a look. "Go now, while we still have light.

Make sure to gather small and large branches. And make sure they're dry."

He blinked, as if jolted from a daydream. Gods, she wasn't like that when she began, was she? Sure, Speaking, Tellings, Runes, and the Saga could become topics so intricate that Sig doubted even Eira understood it all. But that did not mean you had to learn it all in one day. Besides, to her the Saga always came as a feeling, not knowledge. The whisper of grass, the scuttling of a rabbit in the bushes, and the distant croaking of winter frogs focused her mind on the story beneath it all, in the vast darkness. And out of that darkness came her own voice, commanding the world to obey. Sometimes, the world did obey, and those moments made it all worth it. Yut set his own pack in a corner. "Can't we burn some of the hut? Plenty of dry wood here."

"If we rip any more boards out of this thing, it will collapse on us at night. Now, be quick about it. And..." Sigrid looked at Olaf. The big man was sprawled on the floor, using his giant pack as a pillow, and looking like he was a second away from snoring. She gave him a gentle kick. "You go, too. It'll be quicker and safer."

He frowned, one eye cracking open. "Safer? Dark, we're in the middle of nowhere. No, we're in the arm pit of nowhere, there ain't a village within a league, and sure as the dark no bandits. You go yourself if you're so keen."

"There are animals," replied Sig, keeping her voice low and eyes fixed on his. She did not need to rile him up, she just needed him to leave. "And you will be done quicker than me. Which means we'll be eating sooner."

He groaned as popping joints lifted his bulk, but instead of heading for the door, he stepped so close to her that she could count his pores. Foul breath washed over her, and she forced herself to be still and stay her ground. His voice was even lower than hers. "And who put you in charge, eh?"

They stood silent for a second, Olaf staring her down while she clenched her jaw and gently tapped the dagger in her belt. She tried to look relaxed, though her every instinct screamed to either walk away or stab him in the throat. *Breathe in, breathe out.*

Eira's voice drifted from a dark corner of the room. "Go on now, Olaf. I am famished for some of your famed stew." Olaf regarded her a second longer, shook his head, and stepped away.

"Darkened trelkin," whispered Sig when the two left. Eira was still resting in the corner, so she quietly investigated the room. In the days before the war, hunters would leave supplies in these huts for travelers and other hunters, but the lack of supplies flowing between cities put an end to that right quick. She figured whoever hunted in these parts took the last of the provisions, leaving only a few cracked mugs, an assortment of tattered rags, and maybe something that once resembled a fruit. Sig pocketed the rags to use as bandages in the future and moved to examine the grass outside for any recent footprints.

"Don't bother with that, we are safe here," said Eira as Sig opened the door. "I hear no one except for Olaf and Yut. No, there is also a sleeping elk further in the trees, but I don't think we should bother it."

Sigrid closed the rotted wooden door and sat down opposite Eira. The hut creaked and shivered in the autumn wind, as the setting sun peaked through the narrow slits in the walls that acted as windows. It illuminated the room in streaks of yellow, and though it was a cold light, it still felt good on Sig's skin. In the corner, only Eira's extended legs touched the light, making it look like her torso was missing. "You might as well go on and say it," came her voice from the shadow.

"I don't want to sound like I'm complaining," replied Sigrid.

"Bah, there is plenty to complain about, and rightly so. Let it out now or never."

Sig hesitated. Dark, this was harder than she expected. "I guess I would like to know the reason for the secrets. The true reason. I understand you kept me in the dark for a lot of this, I just don't understand why. You should have at least told me about the Cult—if they pose a threat, then I need to know, so I can protect you. So I can protect all of us. Eira, why didn't you tell me before?"

Eira gave an exhausted sigh and leaned forward as she massaged her temples. The light fell on only half of her face, revealing all the worry lines. Sig thought a few new ones were added in the last few days. "You have gotten quite handy with those daggers," said the seeress, catching Sig off guard. She subconsciously moved to feel one of the handles, but stopped herself. Eira would not change the subject on her now. "Eira..."

"It seems the scared little girl from the mire is quite gone, and I should stop pretending she isn't."

Sig tensed for a moment, recalling the stink of that swamp and the fear she felt when she first met Eira. She was not afraid of the seeress but of what she was ready to do to her if Eira attacked. But then Sig imagined her younger self attempting that on the seasoned Speaker, and could not help chuckling at the thought. She relaxed. "That girl's been gone for a while."

"Too right, and now, instead of hiding in bushes, you protect those whom you've been charged with. You use your eyes, your light step, and your daggers. Should you falter, Olaf will step in with his shield and axe."

Sig snorted, but did not interrupt.

"And even young Yut could surprise us, not only with his rune but his good heart. Which leaves me, a blind, useless old woman who has lost track of the world and cannot even go to the privy without a guide."

"Right," scoffed Sig. "Only thing true about that is that you're blind, and old."

Eira grinned. "Perhaps I still have some use to you young folk, but my point is, all of you have means to protect yourselves. What is my weapon, Sigrid? How do I protect you? Make no mistake, Speaking is a useful craft, but not one without dire consequences. No, unfortunately the only protection I have are my secrets. There are many things that I have come to know in my life; few are useful, and most of them are dangerous. Had I revealed the Cult to you, then you would have surely been revealed to them, and I would not have that. At least, not before we have a weapon of our own to challenge them."

Sig blinked. "Weapon? You mean Yut? Eira, I don't know how you imagine him, but he is young, and... not that impressive. He's also been through the dark. You really intend to use him against the Cult?"

Eira stood and walked to where Sig was sitting. Sig reached out to her, and the seeress, having found Sig's hands, sat beside her. The lines of worry on her face were replaced by frustration. "The truth is, Sigrid, the Cult is more dangerous than we can imagine. I hear them, you know. In the Saga, in the story of the world, I hear their twisting and mutilating Tellings. I hear how they push and prod at the very destiny of this world, from determining the outcome of battles to commanding the weather. There is now little they cannot achieve, save felling the gods themselves. Their leader, Aslaug, has poisoned their minds, so they believe they do it for our own good, while the war is worse than ever before. They say they fight the Dark, but Seithers and wyrms abound, even in the peaceful Trelwoods. And no one will challenge them because no one even knows the depths of their evil. But now the tortured Saga has given us a rune-child whom the Cult has not corrupted, who holds one of the most powerful runes of all. We have been given our only chance to destroy them and take back the Saga." She unclasped Sig's hand, which had started to go white from her grip, and walked back to her corner of darkness. "You bet your hide I'm going to use him."

The sun had set, and Sig could hear Olaf and Yut drawing near. At least she had gotten some answers, unsatisfying as they were. She understood Eira's need for secrecy, and even as the seeress spoke, Sigrid felt a pang of guilt at keeping her own secret. She could almost feel the shadows standing outside the hut, watching her through the cracks. Sig told herself she would confess to Eira when the time was right and hoped she would be brave enough to follow through. It took a year of sleepless nights, meditation, and painstaking mental discipline from both Eira and Sig to finally banish them. Having them return now and undo all their effort would be heart-breaking. Some part of her hoped that if she did not address it, they would go away again. Eira would not need to know then, right?

Even with her secret, she would have preferred to know about the Cult, especially given how powerful it was. Of course, what she really did not like was having to stake all of their hopes on Yut. "How can I help?"

Eira did not settle down to rest again. Instead, she donned her leather pouch and felt the components inside. "That remains to be seen. For now, it will be enough for you to be prepared for anything."

The door burst open, and two heaps of wood trudged in. Olaf dumped his logs in the first clean spot he could find. Yut tried to be gentler with his pile, but tripped and spilled it over the entire floor. "Dark!" he exclaimed, sucking his thumb. "I think I got a splinter."

Sig's hopes sank even further, but if this was to be Eira's plan, then she would be a part of it. Their only chance lay in the limited time they had to make him into a proper rune-child. She approached him with one of her smaller daggers, and he recoiled into the wall behind him. Did he think she was going to stab him..?

"I'll get the darkened splinter," she said flatly.

"This drengr can't get away from thorns, can he?" laughed Olaf. "What he needs is a bit of this." He brought his metal flask to Yut's face, who recoiled a second time once the fumes hit his nose.

"Thanks," he wheezed, "I think I'll actually be fine, really. It looks like a small one."

Sig and Olaf nodded simultaneously, then glanced at each other, and immediately turned away. Gods above, they found something they could agree on. *This kid will need to toughen up.*

"If you are quite finished," said Eira, "we have a lightfolk settlement to visit. Now, let us away."

She walked past the three tired scavengers, who blankly stared after her. Olaf sighed and put his hands on his knees. "You're joking."

She did not appear to be joking. Yut looked at Sig with a pleading expression, as if she knew what in the dark Eira was talking about. "It's nearly dark out," she tried.

"That is no matter," replied the seeress, who was now out the door and listening to the wind. "As you know, I don't need light to travel, and I am well acquainted with these parts. We are nearly there, anyway, and we'll be much safer at the outpost than here."

"But the firewood..." started Yut.

"...Will be much needed by the next downtrodden travelers that happen upon this hut. Take some with us and let us go. Our mission requires haste."

Olaf and Yut groaned, faces full of misery, as they picked up their packs and exited the hut. Sig was aching, exhausted, and hungry as well, but she couldn't help smiling as she took Eira's elbow. *Be prepared for anything,* indeed.

Chapter Eighteen

The Lightfolk Grove

"Young Yut, do not think I have forgotten your education," continued Eira when they were back in the trees. The sky had begun to darken, making the land a murky silhouette, as the leaning hut receded into the hills behind them. Sig would have only traveled at this time of night in dire circumstances, but Eira seemed to be completely confident in her stride. "You have asked many questions, now let us see if you remember my answers. Tell us about the lightfolk."

Yut rubbed his eyes, and Sig could only imagine the chaos in his head after two days of hard marching and a constant supply of mystical knowledge. Eira, on the other hand, seemed to walk with a renewed energy, this time taking the lead as she followed an invisible path known only to her. Her energy was almost infectious, even while their stomachs grumbled. The allegedly-old woman weaved through the sparse trees as if she was blind no longer, though after a few minutes, Sig could tell they were headed straight for the wall of a small cliff. She glanced at Yut, who appeared to be deep in thought. *Maybe that'll teach you to keep quiet once in a while.*

"The lightfolk were an ancient race of people whom the gods created to battle the Dark," he said, brows furrowed in concentration. "They were the first Speakers, and were given the power to shape the world as they pleased. However, something happened that caused them to leave our world, abandoning their purpose and the rest of humanity. By the time of the Allwinter, they had become little more than myth."

Sig stared at him. She did not remember Eira teaching him about the lightfolk history more than once, but Yut recited it nearly word for word. The kid was smarter than he looked. "Very good," nodded Eira. "And what do you think about them?"

"Me?" He glanced questioningly at Eira, and then at Sig, who raised her eyebrow. "Ever seen a lightfolk?"

"Well... Old Sten said he saw one at a lake once, but then he said it might have been a trelkin because most of his fish were stolen that night."

"How charming for Old Sten," replied Eira. "I have yet to hear the lightfolk Saga myself, so whether they still exist is up to debate."

"I seen an underfolk once or twice," remarked Olaf from the back. "Dark, even threw dice together. Bugger had a mean streak of luck, 'course I reckon he was cheating, too."

"An interesting tale, Olaf, even if unrelated to the topic at hand," noted Eira. "Though the dvergr are no myth yet, I doubt most of them will be returning to our war-torn lands. At least, not any time soon."

Sig stayed silent while she anxiously watched Eira navigate their path. Occasionally, the seeress would reach out and feel the bark of a passing tree, then nod and slightly adjust their course. Just how many times has she traveled here before meeting Sig? The last light was vanishing quickly, and all her survival instincts begged her to make camp before nightfall. The dead end drew nearer still, and Sig fought the urge to warn Eira. *Be prepared for anything,* said the seeress.

They stopped in front of the cliff wall, trees and hills behind them, and not a living soul within a league. Sig thought the leaning hut they left behind sounded quite cozy right about then.

"A moment," said Eira, letting go of Sigrid and approaching the cliff. As she felt along the rocks, Olaf whispered, "No light, no sound, no beds. We're sleepin' in the darkened forest again. Maybe there's—"

Eira disappeared. Sig did not notice until Olaf stopped talking, but the white smudge of cloak, amid gray and dark rock, was simply gone. They stood transfixed for a moment, and then Sig was darting to the cliff, hand clasped on the dagger handle. "Eira? *Eira!*"

Olaf took out his axe. "More darkened magic. Stay back, boy, but be ready to kill anything you see."

"Calm yourselves," called Eira. Her voice emanated from the wall, but she was still invisible. Sig stared at the rock, wondering if this was some illusory Telling, like the Seither's hut at the ravine. But then Eira's head popped out, a satisfied smirk playing on her face. "Right where I remembered it. *Relax*, Olaf, there is no magic here."

Stupefied, Sig approached Eira's head, and beheld the rest of her body unfolding from the rock. She rubbed her eyes and looked at the stone wall again. In the darkness, she could just make out a jagged line running along its middle. At first and second glance, it looked like a regular cliff, though now that she saw Eira standing in it, she realized a narrow opening was hidden by overlapping stone. It was a perfect trick of the light, where the opening was not seen unless you were looking from a precise angle. But Sig had never seen cliffs like this—or perhaps she has never looked at them right.

"How?" She whispered.

"The lightfolk could shape the world as they pleased," shrugged the seeress. "No need for Tellings, illusory or otherwise, when you can simply mold the stone as you need."

Sigrid regarded the wall again. It did not seem cut or altered, but perhaps that was the trick, you simply direct the stone to grow where you needed it, and it obeyed in its own fashion.

"Wow," said Yut, startling her. She must have been too enamored with the Telling—or lack thereof—to hear him.

"Dark," came from her other side, and she scolded herself for not even hearing Olaf.

"Are they all hidden like this?" asked Sig, following Eira inside the opening and through a tunnel. It stretched for a dozen strides, before bending to the right. Above them the tunnel opened into a slit of azure sky, no doubt hidden from anyone standing on top of the cliff as well. She glanced behind her, and saw what she expected: Yut, wide-eyed and touching the stone as if it was an ancient relic, and Olaf, eyes pinned to the opening above them and shield ready. She felt his alarm—if anyone knew of this passage from above, then the group was the easiest ambush target one could hope for.

"It is very possible," answered Eira, "but I only know of this one, which was discovered by a different seeress through complete chance. Ah. Here we are."

Suddenly, the tunnel turned and opened, and even though Sigrid's daggers were bare, she somehow felt there would be no danger here. The settlement was a round clearing surrounded by tall cliff walls, like a giant pit. On the tops of the cliff walls, even taller trees hid and protected the settlement from above. If their locations were as secluded as this, it was no wonder most people were clueless about the lightfolk.

The settlement itself was not much of one. In fact, Sig had

trouble seeing any signs of civilization at all. A thin creek ran through it, and the center was filled with thick trees unlike any Sig had ever seen. Their meandering trunks and branches wound upward, while their foliage gathered into flat discs at the top like a mushroom's head. The air smelled sweet here, and the chill winds from before felt like a refreshing breeze that stirred the swaying grass. Sig felt like she was in a drastically different land, as if the cliff wall was a portal to a world untouched by humans.

A small bird flew past her shoulder and settled in one of the trees, just as Eira stepped forward. "I've been told this next part is something to behold."

As the seeress walked through the grass, blue lights ignited at her feet and drifted outward. They might have been fireflies, but Sig could not see any substance to them. They spread from Eira, multiplying into dozens and dozens of icy orbs, landing on the trees and rocks. Soon, the entire settlement was illuminated in soft blue light, revealing a garden of flowers adorned in just about every color Sigrid knew. In response, those began to shed green and yellow lights of their own, clothing the dark and naked patch of trees in a brilliant display of flora. Sigrid could not help but gawk. "It's... beautiful."

"Aye," whispered Yut. Even Olaf looked stricken with the lights, though he was silent.

"Indeed," called Eira from within the trees. "This must have been a place of cultivation for the lightfolk, or experimentation. Trees like this are not found anywhere else in these lands, or perhaps anywhere in Arthgard itself. Come, find a good spot to rest. The grass is softer here than most beds."

Sig suddenly pitied the seeress, who could not see the beauty surrounding them. Eira did not like to share the cause of her blindness, save that it was a punishment earned for "peering at something she was not meant to see." Whatever she peered at could not have been worth her sight. It could not have been worth seeing this.

As they walked deeper into the trees, the flowers revealed intricate details in the patterns on their petals. Sig also realized that their glowing lights were actually combinations of differently colored tubes at their center. Before she could say anything, Yut touched one of them, causing a shower of golden sparks to fall from the tubes.

"*Careful,*" she hissed.

He smiled in wonder, the flower's light making his face look otherworldly, like he was some spirit, or a lightfolk himself. He rubbed the glowing residue on his finger. "They're just flowers."

"No, boy," said Olaf, momentary awe replaced by worry. He managed to stay outside the flowers' light, making him look like Yut's oversized shadow. "We don't know anything about this place. They could be poisoned, or worse."

Further in the trees, Eira sat cross-legged next to the stream. It looked like the center of the entire grove, and Sig noticed tell-tale traces of crossing paths. No cobblestone or footprints, instead the trees bent around certain areas, making natural avenues that presumably led to other hidden tunnels in the surrounding cliff walls. They coalesced where Eira sat, where the flowers and lights were at their brightest. It was also where Sig detected a glint of metal peeking out of a rock.

"Nothing here is poisoned, son of Thoran," intoned Eira. "Rest your mind and muscle in this ancient place, and you will feel more rejuvenated than you have been in a long time."

"Magically?" Breathed Yut, whose eyes were almost as bright as the lights around them.

"Places like this are special, and not just for their beauty." Eira's face was downcast, and for the first time in a while, the seeress looked at peace. Throughout their travels, Sig had mostly seen her with something on her mind, something to ponder, some secret to wrestle with. She committed the image of Eira resting to her memory. To her, it was rarer than any lightfolk flower.

"Some places are laden with the Saga, young Yut," she continued. "Ancient places, where Speaking was done at length, where the weave of the gods is at its most powerful. We may use the strength of this place to Speak easier, and produce Tellings that would be much more difficult anywhere else. Here, we can be as the lightfolk were, though we must take care not to exceed our means. An inexperienced mind can drain this entire place, and destroy themselves in the process, with even a simple Telling."

They settled in close to Eira, finding spots where the strange grass was the thickest. Sig had to admit that it was indeed soft, and with their packs serving as pillows it was downright snug. She could not remember the last time she was this comfortable in the wilds, and the fact that they were far from civilization made it even better. She might have fallen asleep right then had her stomach not been roaring.

Using the firewood they picked earlier, Olaf quickly prepared his stew. With the fresh water from the creek, a few potatoes and mushrooms from their packs, a splash of whatever he carried in his flask, and some strips of meat, the warrior mixed the soup with well-practiced motions. Then he looked at them and grinned. "Guess what?"

Sig had to swallow a glob of saliva before answering. "What?"

Olaf dove into his supply bag and produced a small sphere. "It's like I said, the gods smiled on me at the market. Some bugger at Red Hill was carrying a whole onion on him." He cackled and dropped it into the stew before either of them could interject. "We're feastin' like darkened jarls tonight."

Yut stared at the stew, and then at Olaf. "That was on a corpse?"

"Tell me you checked it for blood," said Sig. "I'd rather not catch a disease from your soup."

"Oh, bugger off. You know I'm careful with the pickings. It was clean. Mostly."

Sig could tell he was trying to rile them up, and it seemed to work on Yut. The youth was staring down the stew like he had to make the most important decision of his life. Sig couldn't blame him—the aroma was mouthwatering, which was saying a lot for Olaf's cooking. In fact, it smelled suspiciously good. She looked at the trees above, their flat foliage allowing a few bright stars to peek through. The exotic flowers surrounding them, the soft grass, the little creek... somehow, it all made Sig feel at home. But what was home? When had she truly known safety or peace? It had to be before the forests, before being hunted, before Eira, in her village, where the people accepted her. Memories rose like bile, of playing with the village kids, of harvest feasts, games, and dances. They were bright days, until they were not. Until the villagers awoke her in the night. She remembered how the light from the torches made shadows dance on their faces. She knew they were afraid, which only increased her own fear. "*Sigrid*," they said. "*Sigrid...* "

"Sigrid," repeated Eira. Sig shook her head, realizing Yut and Olaf were watching her intently. She sighed. The stew boiled and the aroma was still there, but her appetite had been gutted. She turned to Eira, who was still in her meditation spot. "Sorry, I thought I heard something." Eira beckoned. "Never mind that, join me here for a spell."

Casting one more glance at the cauldron, Sig walked to where Eira sat, and mirrored her position across from her. They were surrounded by a few boulders, out of which gleaming black pillars emerged upward. Compared to the stone from which they grew, they were impeccably straight, with six sides to each, and their smooth surface reflecting the lights perfectly. So, the lightfolk were fond of cultivating stones as well as plants. Sig had assumed the underfolk, or dwarves, would be into that kind of thing, but it made sense that the original Speakers would not limit themselves to flora alone. She wondered if they did similar things to animals. Or humans. She hoped she would not find out.

"Tell me," asked Eira, "what is the one Telling you wish to learn?" The seeress spoke casually, but Sig could tell that her ever-present worry had returned.

"You know I don't like the riddles, wisewoman," responded Sig bluntly. "You can save those for Yut, I think he'd appreciate them more."

Eira scowled. "No riddles, girl, just answer the darkened question."

"To fly." Sig could not tell if it was an honest answer, since she did not bother dreaming of epic Tellings. It was clear from her training with Eira that she had no great talent for Speaking, and besides, even experienced Speakers would need years of training to command the winds themselves to carry them. Though, she had to admit, flying would be useful. She could fly herself far from these lands, until she found a place that did not stink of war and death.

"Very well," answered Eira, "let us learn to fly. I told you, hard Tellings come easy here, so what better place to bolster your Speaking abilities? You must have felt it by now, that feeling of rest, of peace—that is the work of the Saga as well. I imagine we will have to kick those two awake come morning. Go on, the rune-word for flying is *fluka*. Listen to the Saga. Feel it."

"Didn't you say a novice can destroy themselves here?"

Eira smiled. "You're no novice, Sigrid, no matter how many times you tell yourself the opposite. Besides, I need you to feel the Saga for me. My ears must be exhausted after the last few days, all I can focus on is that damned stew."

Sig examined Eira's face. This must have been a test or a lesson, as she had never heard of the seeress being too tired to hear the Saga. Either way, she would not get any more answers, so she settled in, and stilled her mind. She listened to Olaf and Yut laugh and joke as they inhaled the stew, until their words were stripped to mere syllables. There was the creek, the solitary bird she saw earlier diligently building her nest, and Eira's anxious breathing. There were sounds, there were whispers, and then there was...

"Nothing," sighed Sigrid. "I'm sorry, I don't know what's wrong with me. I'll try again."

She did, and then again, to the same result. By the fourth attempt, she was wiping sweat from her forehead. "It's just... it's just not *there*," she gasped. She must have heard everything in the whole darkened settlement, except the Saga. What in the dark was happening?

She finally opened her eyes, blinking against the lights of the flowers. She could not tell if the seeress was disappointed, but there was nothing to be done. "Eira—"

And then she saw him, standing at a distance behind Eira, at the edges of the soft lights. He was taller than last time, his face was a swirling mass of chaos, and his hands were clasped behind his back. He took a step forward.

"Bah, that's alright, Sig," said Eira, getting up. She blocked the shadow from view, and when she moved aside, he was gone. Sig checked for other shadows around her but could only see strange trees and stones. Sure that none of them wore the shape of her tormentors, she allowed herself to exhale. "I couldn't hear anything either," continued Eira, "must be some elusive lightfolk nonsense. It's not entirely unheard of, I suppose. Perhaps I'll have better luck in a different spot."

"Do you want me t—"

"I will retrieve you once I find it, thank you."

Sig watched her silhouette disappear behind the trees. Eira had a point about the elusive lightfolk magic, though that did not make Sig any more at ease. The feeling of comfort was surely some kind of Telling, which meant the Saga should have been very much alive here. Even without the Telling, Sig expected the strange flora to be whispering their stories. So why in the dark was it so damned quiet? And why did the shadow decide to appear now?

She sat next to Olaf and Yut, still lost in her thoughts, as she scooped herself a bowl of the stew and began to eat. Gods below, the onion *did* transform the entire dish. It took all of two seconds to finish, but she paused before reaching for seconds, as she realized the two were not conversing anymore. Olaf was digging for something in his pack, and Yut was shooting her strange glances as he finished his soup. Sig sighed. "What did the oaf say?"

Yut's head whipped to Olaf, who instantly said, "I didn't say anything!"

Yut looked to her again, eyes wide. "So you really do have lightfolk blood?"

Olaf glared at Yut in betrayal, which told Sig everything. Her dagger was out before Olaf could move an inch. "I promised I'd gut you the next time you called me that, trelkin. And I keep my word." She approached him, dagger pointed toward his throat, as he abandoned his pack and scrambled away from her.

"Let's all just relax, okay? You said not to call you lightfolk, and I didn't say you were lightfolk, did I? Boy, I said *elf.* She has elf blood, which is what *people* say, not me."

"Aren't elves and lightfolk the same thing?" Yut did not appear too concerned for Olaf, which annoyed Sig. He must not have believed she would actually harm him. She determined to prove him wrong one of these days, if not now.

"There's a big difference, you darkened idiot," stammered Olaf, hand outstretched toward Sig and sweat glistening on his forehead. "Elves are just spirits who get up to no good. And sometimes they possess some folk. Again, *people* say that, if you even believe in that kind of thing."

"And then what happens, Olaf?" The point of Sig's dagger slid from Olaf's throat to his groin. "When *some folk* are possessed by elves? What do people say about that?"

The big man gulped. "Well, if you want to talk about stories, then those people can go a bit wild. In the sense of killing people. A lot of people, too, and for no good reason." At this, his eyes met hers, and iron crawled back into his voice. "People say they can slaughter an entire village. Elders. Kids. All in one night, too, with no survivors, leaving the entire place red. Now, I'm not one to judge, but even I'd say that's... not right."

Sig continued watching him, though the dagger eventually fell to her side. There was no point in proving him right with more violence. After all, being possessed by an elvish spirit was one of the milder theories about her past. Maybe the shadows were elves, or maybe she was cursed, but the truth did not matter in the end. This was her burden, and even though it came against her will, she was forced to accept it. There would always be more hunters, either for sport, or justice, or bounty, and she could not hope to kill them all. Eira told her that her battle was against a force no one person could prevail against. Her enemy was not shadows but fear, greed, and ignorance, and sometimes, to fight against it meant to not fight at all.

She spoke quietly as she returned to her seat. "What's 'not right' is hunting down a child because of a rumor. It's 'not right' to have your dogs chase her down while she begs for her life. I don't remember what happened in that village, but I doubt I could have taken out a hundred people when I was barely old enough to lift an axe. If I did get possessed, or cursed, or some other darkened thing, then you can tell me if that is reason enough for my death. And if it's not, then I would kindly appreciate if you kept your trap shut."

The remaining stew simmered above a dying fire, though none of them made a move to finish it. She only realized Yut was standing when he sat down, setting down his bowl like he was retiring a shield. "Sorry," he said, "I didn't realize..."

"Don't mention it." Sig rubbed her eyes as a soft breeze blew embers at her. Other than Eira, she had not talked about her past with anyone that was not trying to kill her. It was only slightly relieving, though mostly she just felt exhausted and exposed. All she wanted to do now was leave this place and these people. Maybe she would give that flying Telling another attempt, after all.

"Well, you know how people are," said Olaf, sauntering back to them. "Always yapping about somethin'. I don't even listen to them most of the time." He sat and began scooping the last of the stew into the bowl he dropped earlier.

Sig tried to shoot daggers at him with her stare. "You don't listen because you're the one who's doing the yapping."

He hesitated. "Maybe, but at least I yap responsibly."

"Didn't you say she can turn into a cat, too?" Asked Yut.

"I swear to all the gods, boy, I'll starve you to death if you don't start keeping your mouth shut." Olaf peered at Sig, ladle frozen in midair, assessing if his life was in danger again. But to Sig's surprise, a small chuckle escaped her as she shook her head. Whether it was the Telling of the outpost, the late hour, or the simple acceptance that these two were not her enemies, she felt a strange lack of control. Gods, what was happening to her?

"I think you're mistaking me for Olaf, who turns into a kitten at the first sign of trouble," she quipped, unable to wipe the smirk off her face.

Yut grinned back. "You're right. I think I've seen him do it, too. He's known as Olaf the Kitten."

Sig burst out laughing. The joke was not even that funny, but she simply could not help it. A wall had collapsed within her, and putting it back was unfeasible. Here they were, a traumatized youth, a coward, a blind seeress, and whatever she was, in a mythical grove, munching stew and trying to save the world. She couldn't have set up a joke in a better way if she had tried. Or wait, weren't they trying to end the world? Just what in the dark were they doing?

"Kitten!" Was all she could holler.

Olaf scowled at both of them, before donning a mischievous look and targeting Yut. "Better a kitten than a darkened mouse." And then he gave an all too realistic mouse squeak. It was so strange to hear that sound coming from Olaf's gruff, bearded face, that Sig collapsed with laughter, kicking her legs like a toddler. Yut was laughing, too, between his own interpretations of a kitten's meowing. Even Olaf joined, his laugh an unholy hybrid of barking and shrieking. She could not tell how long they lay laughing, but tears flowed from Sig's face by the time she tried standing up.

"Hey...hey kitten," she giggled, trying to breathe deeply. Her abdomen was on fire. "Where did you find those mushrooms again?" In response, Olaf started another bout of laughter As she found her balance, the world tilted left, but with plenty of arm-waving, it slowly righted itself. Mushrooms... yes, something about the mushrooms...

She turned to Yut, whose face was suddenly deadpan and pale.

He was focusing on his index finger, which was still covered in that strange flower pollen. “So pretty…” he mumbled. And then a stream of green, stewy puke erupted from the young man, some of it sprinkling her boots. Sig took an instinctive step back, lost her balance, and vacated her stomach of everything it had. Unfortunately, the inebriation from the mushrooms seemed to leave with the remains of the stew.

After a minute of gagging, she managed to look up at Olaf, who was beginning to look sick. “You darkened…” Another gag jolted her, as she shut her eyes and breathed. That was the problem about opening up to people. Sometimes, you opened too much, and your stomach followed suit. She almost wanted to start laughing again at the thought. *Focus*. She would deal with Olaf later. Now, the hour was late, and something was nagging at her. Where was Eira? Shouldn’t she have called for Sig by now?

“Oy,” whispered Olaf, all traces of laughter gone. “Where’d the lights go?”

Sigrid opened her eyes and saw darkness. The flowers, the blue lights, everything had disappeared, leaving only a few stars blinking through the trees. Her heart skipped a beat at the thought of losing her sight to foul mushrooms. She would really kill Olaf if that happened.

Yut gave a muffled groan. It sounded like he was lying face down in the grass. Sig breathed a sigh of relief as her eyes adjusted to the darkness. The strange trees and grass still surrounded them, but not a single one of them shed any light. “Something’s wrong,” she said. “Who has a torch?”

Olaf was already rummaging in his pack, choking out the residual giggles with curses.

“Where are we?” mumbled Yut, as Olaf struck flint and a flame bloomed among them.

"You know this magic stuff," he hissed. "Is it supposed to go out like that?"

Sig found her pack and joined her torch to Olaf's. "We need to find Eira. I don't know what is going on, but it doesn't feel good."

Olaf lifted Yut by the scruff of his shirt and set him on his feet as Sig began walking to where she last saw Eira. In the dark, the trees and flowers looked decidedly more sinister, with their silhouettes casting shadows so black that even their torchlight struggled to penetrate. Sig began calling for Eira, and her stomach dropped when there was no answer. The cautious walk became a jog, and Olaf cursed as he tried to keep up with her. Behind them, she heard Yut's shins impact almost every jutting root, but thankfully he did not fall behind. A dark feeling settled in her—they should have never come here.

She found Eira facing the cliff wall. The seeress was mumbling something, and Sig hesitated to interrupt her in the middle of Speaking. Perhaps the darkness was her doing. Perhaps everything was alright after all.

"Dark, Eira, finally!" yelled Olaf. Sig put out her hand toward him to indicate caution. Olaf picked up on it immediately and put out his own hand so that Yut could run into it. The seeress stopped mumbling but continued facing away from them. The torches did not reveal her face from their position. A shiver ran through Sig.

"Eira?" She asked softly. "Everything alright?"

Eira slowly turned to them, wearing an expression of pure consternation, as if she was in great pain, but was kept from expressing it. And then she was falling into Sigrid's arms, her breathing shallow and limbs trembling. Gods, she was light as a child.

"What's wrong with her?" Barked Olaf. His axe was out and he was looking around frantically.

"I don't...I don't know. She's barely breathing. Gods below, what do we do?" This was not happening. Eira was the guide, Eira knew what was going on, Eira was the healer. What was Sig supposed to do without her? Tears began to form as she suddenly found herself completely helpless. Was this her fault? Would she attempt to Speak again? Perhaps there was something in Eira's satchel that would help. And yet she could not help without knowing what was wrong. She tried to feel Eira's breath again, but this time could not feel anything. "Eira, wake up. Please, wake up!"

Someone picked up the torch she dropped and kneeled next to them. Yut's face was pale but grim, and his eyes had recovered their sharpness. He felt Eira's forehead, the pulse on her neck, and nodded. "She's out cold. We need to... Olaf, hand me your flask."

"Eh?"

"Just do it. Now."

The look Yut gave him left no room for questions. Sig would have been surprised at his sudden change in tone, had she not been worried for Eira's life. Olaf reluctantly offered his flask and Yut snatched it from his hand. Then he gently lifted Eira's head and stuck the head of the flask under her nose. Sig started. "What in the dark are you—"

Eira gasped and slapped the flask away from her. Sig could not believe her eyes. She held the seeress tight as her breathing calmed.

Olaf quickly picked up the flask. "Not bad, boy."

Sig looked at Yut in shock. Not bad, indeed. "How did you know that would work?"

Yut shrugged. "Our wisewoman always kept a Vile Brew in case someone fainted. First time I tried administering it myself, though."

Eira interrupted Sig's next question by suddenly grabbing her cheek and pulling her close. "It's a trap," she whispered.

"What?"

"The Cult...was here. They drained the Saga," explained Eira, her breathing shallow. "Only a veneer left...illusion of comfort. Once I used it, all that was left was the abyss, endless..."

Olaf leaned in with his torch. "What did she say?"

"She said it's a trap..." Of course, if the Saga was drained, it made sense why she did not hear anything before. But if the cult took it all, then perhaps Eira delved too deep, and in those depths heard only the Tellings that the Cult of Orik had left for her. Sig gritted her teeth. It was a trap designed for a Speaker, but not for one traveling with companions. The Cult would not taste victory today.

That was when they heard a deep rumbling from within the grove, and the sound of trees creaking. The three looked into that patch of darkness, and Sig's breath caught. The trees were moving.

Yut stood, pointing the torch toward the trees to get a better view. "Theoretically speaking, if they drained the Saga, what would happen to a place made through it?"

The earth began trembling as rocks tumbled from the cliff wall, and then it dawned on Sig. The trees were moving because they were sliding inside the grove, and under the earth. The entire outpost was being swallowed up.

"Run..." whispered Eira, before going limp again. They needed no further answer or instruction. If a place made through the Saga had none of it left, then that place ceased to exist. The entire outpost was collapsing in on itself, and they were still inside.

"Olaf," started Sig.

"I got her," he said, grabbing Eira by the arm and hoisting her on his shoulder. He managed to pack all his belongings, including the stew pot, before following her. How he was able to carry all of that along with Eira was beyond her.

Yut's eyes were wide as he pointed to the cliffs. "The tunnels are collapsing." Sig followed his gaze, and saw rocks falling from the cliffs and into the dozen tunnels surrounding the outpost. The ground underneath them turned to mush, and if they remained here, Sig was sure they would turn to mush as well. But climbing up the walls with an unconscious Eira was out of the question. Dark take it, if she could not detect the trap before, or save Eira, then by all the gods above and below, she would get them out of this. "There." She spotted the tunnel they used originally. It was wider than the others, and though it was filling with rocks, it was still passable.

The trees bent and broke behind them when they jumped into the entrance. Sig went first to navigate them, Olaf was in the middle so as not to fall behind, and Yut picked up the rear. "Shields!" Roared Sig, as another shower of rocks pelted them from above. Thankfully, none were large enough to crush them, though Sigrid wouldn't rely on that luck for long. The earth jolted as more rocks fell. Maybe it was her imagination, but the tunnel looked narrower than before. It did not matter—they would survive this. They had to. They rounded a bend, and she could see the exit. "Charge!"

The tunnel collapsed as plumes of dust exploded from it, but not before the four scavengers erupted from its innards. They sprawled on regular, real-world grass, coughing up dust and rocks. Behind the cliff walls, the lightfolk grove buried itself in a sound of distant thunder. Sig could spare no thought for the lightfolk history that would forever be lost, as she quickly examined herself and Eira for breaks. She found none, and relief washed through her when she felt for Eira's breath. She was breathing regularly, she was alright. They were alright. "Everyone whole?"

Yut quickly checked each of his limbs and nodded. Olaf spit and growled, "Dark take yer magic."

"Good," said Sig. "Let's put some distance between us and that hole. The Cult might be aware of this." She tensed, waiting for Olaf to oppose her again. But the big man just sighed and moved to pick up Eira.

Sigrid considered their paths. It must have been after midnight by now, but they could not stay here. Eira was the leader, and Sig would do her best in her stead. The hut was too obvious, and should the Cult be looking, it would be the first place they checked. No, they would move North, and hopefully find a suitable hiding spot to camp in. *Yes, Sig, one step at a time. Focus, that's what you need to do.* Focus on the path ahead, focus on survival, focus on getting them through it. There was no sense in thinking about the shadows that led her to that tunnel, and absolutely no reason to pay any mind to the ones that followed her still.

Chapter Nineteen

Goodness of Olaf

Yut was sore in places he did not know existed. In the past week, he had trekked more than he had in his entire life, and to make it worse, last night's adventure in the lightfolk grove had scored him a dozen new bruises. While they were being mercilessly pelted with rocks, he was sure they would be buried, and their quest would be over before it even began. That was when he saw Sigrid and Olaf transform into different people. He was too shocked to see it with the draugr, but when their lives were on the line, the two changed from bickering scavengers to a force for survival. The way Olaf punched through that tunnel and Sig navigated and pushed them on was nothing short of inspiring. As he lay on the mossy forest floor that Sig led them to, watching the sun climb through the trees, he wondered if he could ever become like them.

A shadow emerged from one of the trees, and Sig returned to their camp. They rested in a forgotten patch of trees amid the windy hills—after the last few days, Yut could not tell their exact location even if he drew it out. Sig must have allowed them a few more hours of sleep before pushing them on, seeing how their rest was cut short before. Even though her braids were in disarray, her eyes were red, and her clothes were torn and dirty, she looked calm, which meant the Cult was not chasing them. Wonderful. He probably looked worse than her, but there was nothing to do about it now.

Eira was already awake, leaning against a tree, unmoving and silent. Gods only knew what was going through her head. He was glad to have seen a piece of lightfolk history, though he wondered if they would venture near any interesting place ever again. If the Cult could get them there, then they could get them anywhere. Sig would probably have them crawling through forgotten forests for the rest of their excursion, however long that may take.

The only one unperturbed by their misfortunes was Olaf, who snored fitfully through the night. Yut gave him a gentle tap on the forehead, and then a harder one, making the big man jump awake. Bloodshot eyes surveyed their surroundings, before Sig tossed him a waterskin, and he let go of the axe handle to catch it. She tossed one to Yut as well, who began chugging gratefully. Olaf's mushrooms left a foul taste in his mouth, not to mention swelling his tongue, so the cool water was a mercy.

Sig handed Eira the last waterskin. "How are you feeling, seeress?"

Eira sat in silence for a minute more before coming to some decision. Her face remained grim. "I'm afraid this is where our paths must part for now."

Yut choked on his water. "What?" he coughed. Olaf continued drinking.

"The Saga calls me elsewhere, and I must leave at once. Olaf, hand me that fur if you still have it. There is a good lad."

The warrior unplugged the waterskin from his mouth and caught his breath. "Aren't we supposed to be on some quest of yours? And now you're runnin'?" His face instantly knew saying this was a mistake, but unfortunately, Eira couldn't tell what his face was saying.

"You're the one to talk," she muttered. "Accuse me of running again, and I will put eight and one curses on you. No, I am not fleeing. Call it a detour. I have unknowingly led you into danger twice now, and I fear I am working against the Saga. As such, if we are to have a chance against the Cult, I need to seek advice from an old friend. I am sorry, but we need to separate. Sigrid, you're with me. Olaf, take care of the young man, and we will meet you in Miklor in a fortnight's time. Whip him into shape—I want to see two warriors by the time we meet again."

Yut set down the waterskin. Miklor was leagues North, and they were supposed to walk there with Olaf? By themselves? They barely survived when they were together, so how good were their chances with only him and Olaf? "What about the Cult?" he asked.

"Aye," nodded Sigrid, "They'll pick us off one by one if we are separated. Eira, it's too dangerous."

Eira stood with a groan and stretched her back. "The Cult is attracted to powerful Speaking. So long as we refrain from it, then we will be safe. In fact, we may be in more danger traveling together." Sig made as if to object again, but Eira put up her hand. "My mind is quite made up, Sig. This is not a decision I make lightly. Come, we will travel quicker this way, too."

Olaf cast a disappointed glance at Yut. "Well, that's just great. And what if you don't make it to Miklor? Where exactly are you going, anyway?"

"Peace, warrior. We will meet again—and if we don't, then you can be released from your word, and our bond is broken."

"Should have led with that." Olaf hefted his pack, and glanced at Yut again, who was still coming to terms with this development. He did not want to part with the others, not when he had just begun learning about his power, not when he had just found something resembling friends. Even though he asked Eira some questions about the Saga and Runes, her answers were always roundabout, prompting more questions. They also always led back to the Cult, and how they were the ultimate source of evil in Arthgard. Dark take it, he should have asked more questions. But it seemed the path was decided, and he would need to be strong enough to endure it. He looked at Olaf, whose eye gleamed. "Well? Off to Miklor, we go, kid. And keep up, we got training to do."

* * *

Yut followed Olaf's brisk pace through the trees as Eira and Sig left East. The big soldier was surprisingly light on his feet, even as Yut stumbled through the slippery rocks and the soft earth. They eventually found a hint of a path, at the end of which, presumably, sat the city of Miklor.

Olaf didn't say a word as they traveled, and Yut wasn't sure if he should speak first. Though if he did, he would not know where to start. The dying Heisir recognized Olaf—called him a deserter. That would certainly explain why Olaf was a scavenger now. People who have never stepped foot on a battlefield or even heard of war knew deserters to be evil. Little children were warned not to speak of them, and to call someone a deserter was an insult worthy of a challenge. And yet here was one of the darkened things, walking not two strides from Yut, who did not seem special or evil, and who already saved Yut's life. Twice.

Their path joined a wider road, and they entered a field of flowing gold. He expected barley farmers to be hard at work at this time of day, especially given that barley harvest was at an end. Perhaps the war had gotten to them. Perhaps it was a good conversation starter. "*Do you think the war hit the farmers?*" No, he doubted Olaf knew, or cared. Maybe they could delve into their personal lives to pass the time. *"So, when did you become a deserter?"* Or maybe not that one either. He was thinking of the next question when Olaf suddenly stopped. Yut was surprised to find his own hand already pulling his dagger out as his adrenaline kicked in. Is there an ambush of draugr? Yut glanced around, eyes straining to find movement, or swords, or teeth. The trees could be trolls, the Seither could be hiding in the bushes. Gods, he was unprepared, and weak, and exposed. Dark take his whole life.

But Olaf simply turned around, took out his flask, and motioned to their path. Another path split from it and headed East.

"This is where we part, kid," Olaf said, draining the flask.

"What do you mean?"

"I mean what I just said. You'll go that way, to Orheim, about a league from here, and I'll go to Miklor, like Eira said. Good people in Orheim. I mean, I'm not allowed back there but they'll take a sorry mess like you—put you to work. You can be out of this whole mess, and out of my lovin' care. A few jewels of that sword you nicked should buy you a place, we can split it..."

Olaf continued talking, and Yut understood, and yet he couldn't. Of course, this is the only way it should be. The only way it ever could be. Why would Olaf take on this dark-stained mess? Did he really think he could avenge his family? Learn magic from a blind seeress and fighting from a deserter? Olaf was offering him a mercy, a chance to start over and live as if nothing had ever happened.

"Hey," barked Olaf. Apparently, he was finished speaking.

"I, um, Eira said—"

"I know what she said, but I gave her my word, so I'm stuck. You, on the other hand, are free as a bird."

He was offering him a chance to live as if he still had a future to live for.

"You owe her nothin'. She's got a lot of talk, but in the end, it's all useless to you." As if he had not spoken magic and looked a draugr dead in the eyes.

"You did good so far, stayin' alive and all, but trust me, you better quit while you're ahead. Before you go in the ground."

As if his parents were not murdered.

"Just don't tell them about me, or the magic stuff, and you'll be fine. Now, let me see that sword."

"No." Yut stepped back, hand on the wrapped hilt. Olaf continued forward.

"Listen, I'm not going to take it from you—loot is loot, I respect that. But there is plenty for both of us—"

"I mean, I'm not going to Orheim." Yut tried to make his voice sound resolute, even though his resolution started to melt as soon as Olaf's face hardened. Yut's saga would not end here. He would not end his story as a weakling who needed constant saving. He would not let the death of all those he loved be for nothing, no matter how dangerous it got for him. A power hummed within him, and he would feel it again at the coming of justice, come danger or death.

Olaf's voice was rough. "Listen here, you little runt, not many of us get a second chance like this—"

"I don't want a second chance," insisted Yut, "I don't want to be here, I don't want to be stealing from the dead, and I don't want your pity. You can have the sword, the whole thing, but you will teach me to fight. And I'm going with you to Miklor, like Eira said."

They stood in silence for a while, Yut proffering the sword and breathing fast, but feeling strangely focused. Olaf ground his teeth. It looked like he wanted to start speaking several times but just couldn't get the right words out.

"Here's the thing, kid, I don't want you here, alright? You'll slow us down, which means you will get us killed. You are a—a liability. How in the dark do you think you could be of use to me?"

"I don't know," said Yut honestly, "But that is your problem. I will learn, and you will teach me."

Olaf crossed his arms. "Or what?"

"I—" Damn, that was a good question. "I will use magic on you."

Olaf weighed Yut for a second, and burst out laughing. It was a rich, derisive laugh, enough to make the big man keel over. Or maybe—by the grace of all the gods—was he faking it? After all that Olaf has seen, was there a tinge of nerves around his bellows? Yut had to hope he was faking it. "Yes, a Telling. I will cast a rune on you, and then you won't be laughing. Not without your eyes."

At that Olaf's laugh cut short. He looked at Yut like he was about to pounce. Gods, could Yut do a Telling in the moment? He had no idea, but neither did Olaf. Yut might not be a Speaker, but he at least fancied himself a storyteller.

"Now you're full of it," said Olaf.

"Try me."

"And what if I toss this dagger in your gut? Gonna magic up a stone wall? Will you have time?"

"I guess we can find out, then." The big man was doubting—after all, he saw Yut punch the Seither, and he was far too paranoid to dismiss Yut's threat completely. Still, there was no telling what he was thinking. "But I promise by all the gods above that if I do, by the end, you will be begging to take me with you."

They stood with eyes interlocked, like two titans of the sagas, the fate of both their lives in the balance. Yut understood Olaf, his intentions were for their best—the man was just trying to survive.

There was no sense in taking some kid along with him, dragging the dead weight across leagues of unforgiving wilds. It made complete sense, and that is what infuriated Yut. Again, he thought about how unfair this was to him and everyone else, but in the end, he was also trying to survive. Something awakened in Yut back at that ravine, and whether it was magic, or pure anger, or fate, Yut knew if he went to Orheim, he would kill that part of himself forever.

Olaf still searched Yut, as if trying to find something to exploit in his eyes. His brows furrowed, but that was the only part of his face that changed in those minutes. Could it be disappointment? Resignation? Yut could no longer bear the uncertainty and decided to push him slightly.

"*Fehu, Uruz, Thurisaz...*"

Olaf's face paled. "What are you doing?!"

"*...Raido, Kenaz, Gebo...*" Yut chanted louder, lifting his hands and rolling back his eyes, as he recited the runic alphabet his mother taught him. It's a good thing they don't teach many warriors to read.

"Quit it!" bellowed Olaf, "Hey, I said stop!" The old warrior jumped back, axe and dagger out, eyes to the sky, ready to pounce upon the nine curses that would swarm him in a moment. Yut only chanted louder, and when he ran out of runes to recite, he shouted the formal names of the gods.

"*...Rothr, Vaea, Ormir!*"

Olaf threw his axe to the ground. "You cursed ratkin, fine! I'll bring you to Miklor, you win!"

Yut stopped, refocusing his eyes. He tried to adopt an enlightened expression—in control, unafraid, both sentiments supremely untrue. Keeping his hands outstretched toward Olaf, he whispered with every bit of malice he could muster, "Not. Good. Enough."

Olaf bared his teeth. "I'll teach you to fight, dark take it."

Yut almost gave in then, almost dropped his hands, but a cold voice reminded him that he truly knew only one thing about this man—he cannot be trusted.

"Your word."

Olaf regarded Yut with a look of unbridled hatred, and reluctantly picked his axe back up. Then something seemed to dawn on him, and a realization spread across his face. He spat into his hand and held it out to Yut. "You have my word."

Yut found himself trusting Olaf even less, but the deserter followed Eira because of his word, so it had to hold. Yut did not have any other choice, anyway. The runic alphabet was the one arrow he had, and it had been loosed. This handshake was the only thing that bound him to his fate.

He warily approached Olaf. "You gave your word," he said, spitting into his own hand. Olaf's eyes became empty as they shook, and a cold feeling crawled up Yut's spine. For some reason, he suddenly felt like easy prey.

"Then let us learn to fight, young warrior. Lesson one," he grabbed Yut's hand tighter, erasing any chance of escape, "*never* drop your guard." Just as a meaty fist connected with Yut's jaw, knocking him out cold.

Chapter Twenty

Mercy

Yut awoke to pain and smoke. His head felt like it was clamped in a bear's mouth, shutting out all senses save the thrumming ache. The left side of his face pulsed with it every time he tried to move.

He was lying down, cold rocks and roots piercing his back. He felt that being unconscious this many times in one week could not have been healthy. Nevertheless, he was warm, and a fire crackled next to him. It had to be evening, as the air felt crisp and the last of the autumn crickets were still heard in the distance.

Night. Yut's mind drifted to the nightmares he faced while fighting that fever, the strange visions of the gods. *Be Strong,* said Orm. His mind delved further, to that Seither and the blissful power dancing within him. It had to come from magic, it had to do with the rune on his forearm. Yut always thought magic would involve dark rituals, fellowship with the wild gods, or dealing with the Dark itself. Instead, all he felt was rippling, bursting strength. More so, he saw things clearly, saw the wise tales of the trees, he heard capricious songs from birds miles away, he felt the great tale of the world flow around him—through him—and it felt *right*. As if a veil had been removed from his eyes, and he clearly saw the world for the first time. Gods, if that is magic, then Yut wanted to feel it every second of his life.

He did not let his mind drift further. Further was a bright pain that had just begun receding into darkness. Yut couldn't dwell there—couldn't even look there. All he could do was move. He had to become strong, stronger than any man alive, by magic or otherwise. *Feel the anger,* said a distant voice. *Let it heat and burn and spur you into purpose.*

He tried to peel his eyelids open but got a waft of smoke straight into his face, and his cough alerted Olaf. He was sitting across the fire, sharpening his axe, and as Yut began to twist himself into an upright position, the warrior reached into the campfire and took out a stick with something smoldering on it. The sun had already set, but Yut could just make out the barley fields in the night. Olaf must have carried him up the road, and made camp nearby. There were trees at their back and open landscape in front, bright stars blinking in an open sky. Yut wondered if staying so close to a large road was safe, but he was in no condition to do anything about it.

As Yut rose, bearing the pain of his head and jaw like a heavy headdress, Olaf approached. "You're finally awake," he remarked.

Yut began a half-dazed attempt at scrambling back, snarling at Olaf. "You twice-cursed, darkened piece of—"

"Rat?" Olaf asked politely.

It took a second for Yut to realize Olaf was giving him the sizzling remains of the rodent. The shriveled meat gave off a sickly scent, and Yut shook his head, which he instantly regretted. His jaw and skull led a coordinated attack on his brain and stomach, but anger pushed him through.

"Why did you do that?" fumed Yut, batting away the rat-on-a-stick.

Olaf lumbered back to his seat. "Because you're a punk," he

said matter-of-factly. "And by the way, I knew you were making those words up. You don't know how to do Tellings. Or curses. I should've stabbed you in the throat for that."

"I'm eternally grateful," scowled Yut, massaging his jaw. "I think it's dislocated."

"You'll have to take harder hits if you want to learn battle. Matter of fact, here's lesson two: Winning a fight is about giving hits as well as takin' them. The more hits you can take, the better your chances of winning."

Yut stared into the fire as Olaf devoured his rat and started on the second one.

"You just made that up," said Yut dejectedly.

"What, you're the only one allowed to spout crap? At least what I'm saying makes sense. And I've taken plenty of hits in my time, and I'm still here. The other guys, though, they're back on the Red Hill."

They sat in silence for a time, with Olaf finishing dinner and taking out his new axe to polish it again. Not that it needed it—it was a fine weapon: gleaming serpents framed the butt of the blade, coiling toward the handle where intricate designs in the wood continued the pattern. Yut was so mesmerized he nearly forgot his aching face and pride. "Is that an axe from Vessir?"

"Hah! The Twin Jarls get wet dreams about an axe like this. Oh no, this type of craft..." Olaf paused to hold the axe to the flames. To Yut's disbelief, orange runes appeared on the blade. The flickering shadows made the serpents look like they were moving, as the green gems in their eyes began to glow. "This was not made by any human blacksmith." He looked ready to kiss the weapon.

Yut sat up in earnest now. "Dwarven-make? But how is that possible? I thought the underfolk left after the Allwinter."

"Most of 'em, yeah. Some still muck about with us, though.

They're rare to find, and their weapons even rarer."

Yut took out the Heisir's sword. The jewels gleamed in the firelight like little eyes of some tiny beast. "So, we just *happened* to find a rare dwarven axe and *this* on one battlefield? Seems kind of lucky..."

Olaf found a minuscule blotch somewhere and went back to cleaning the axe, caressing it like a newborn. "Never question luck, boy. You just take it when it comes and run. Besides, if you think we're lucky after the last few days, I might've smacked you too hard."

That made all the sense in the world to Yut, so he set to polishing the Heisir's sword as well, trying to imitate Olaf's technique. There was still blood on it, it was chipped everywhere, and some jewels were missing, but little by little its old glory returned. Yut could even see part of his own reflection in the blade. He wished he hadn't. A dark bruise was blooming where Olaf hit him, and his hair made a bird's nest look lovely.

Eventually, Olaf cleared his throat. "So, anyway, why stay?"

Yut thought for a moment, each possible answer circling around the forbidden topic—where fear and weakness dwelled. "Does it matter?" He asked in turn.

Judging by his expression, Yut might as well have called Olaf a pig. "You will learn fighting," said the appalled warrior, putting the axe down. "Proper fighting, in mud and blood, with and without an axe, in the rain, screaming and pissin' yourself. I gotta know if you have the balls for this. *You* gotta know if you have the balls." He spit out a rat bone. "Or maybe we should go easy. You know, learn the proper forms, share a few sagas, exchange flowers, and the like."

Yut couldn't help smiling at the image and wincing at the pain. "Just pretend that you're training me to kill a very large bear."

"Why in the dark would you—" Olaf's face twitched as several wheels sprung into motion. Then he caught on. "Bless me, you want to kill that dark-spawned thing. Oh yes, I see it in your eyes now, you mad son of a goat. Revenge, that's not bad. Not bad at all—don't get me wrong, sorry about your folks and all, but revenge will take you a long way. I can work with revenge. So long as you know that you can't actually kill a *damned wyrm*."

"Maybe," muttered Yut.

"No, not maybe. Definitely. And finally. Not with your little sword or your little magic—that thing can melt your face off from leagues away. You'd have more chance of killin' me."

Yut regarded Olaf, begrudgingly agreeing with the facts presented. But Olaf wasn't there at the creek, he didn't feel the power at the ravine. That was the power that could take down a drake—a vicious power for a vicious, arrogant drake, who burns down villages with no fear of consequences. Yut will show it fear. He needed to learn Telling soon, but fighting as well, since it would do no good to be impaled by a stray arrow before then. And he needed to control his rune. He needed a lot of things.

"Maybe," Yut said again.

Olaf chuckled and shook his head. "We'll see about that tomorrow. We wake up at first light. If we're to make it to Miklor in two weeks while teaching the sacred art of warfare to a—well, *you*, then it'll be hard marchin' all the way."

"Fine."

"Fine!" barked Olaf.

"Indeed!" chimed a voice behind them.

Olaf was on his feet, axe in his hand, before Yut could even think about covering the Heisir's sword. He threw the wraps on it while taking out his own axe and facing the newcomer, who materialized out of the trees behind them without warning.

He was a short man, maybe a head shorter than Yut, arms spread wide, a bright smile revealing straight white teeth, with a gap in the middle. He wore strange clothes—a white shirt with red embroidery on it, making a design of foreign runes along his collar and sleeves. He approached warily, fully aware of Olaf, who was tense like a hunting hound on a leash. The smiling man did not even have a dagger.

"It is my absolute pleasure to encounter passionate drengr like yourselves on a cold night such as this. My name is Bjarni, I come from the lands of the South, across the great sea, by the way of—"

"Great, piss off," growled Olaf, taking a step forward.

"My friend," said Bjarni, smile slipping as he regarded Olaf's axe, "I am unarmed and wish you nor yours the least of harm. Just a night by a warm fire, nothing else. May I ask, where does the road take you?"

"Miklor," said Yut on instinct, earning a death glare from Olaf.

"What a coincidence! My family and I are journeying to the same city; they say it is a refuge in harsh times like these. If we could merely share your fire to stem the night's cold—"

Olaf took another step toward Bjarni. "Fire's taken, short stuff. It ain't for you or yours. Keep on walkin', or I'll make the cold the last of your worries."

The short man deflated. "Sir, the soldiers took our farm, our house, we have nothing. If I must beg for your hospitality, I shall do so on my knees." There were tears in Bjarni's eyes now. He did look cold in that thin shirt, and gaunt. Empathy crawled up Yut's throat. How long ago did Eira take him in—nothing more than a stray dog? And Yut would gladly give Bjarni any food they might have, but they had nothing—except for the clothes on their back and rat bones by the fire. If only they had taken some of the jewels out of that sword already. Though even if they did, Yut doubted

Olaf would allow it. That deserter was the only wall between Yut and overpowering pity.

"But I know you would not allow this," Bjarni continued, "for I hear a touch of the lark in your own tongue as well, don't I, brother?" He looked up with hopeful eyes at Olaf, who hesitated. Seizing the chance, Bjarni jolted—or at least that's what it looked like. He jumped a yard into the air and landed gracefully into a pose: hands on thighs, one straight foot out, tip of his boot pointed to the sky. Yut thought he would start dancing, but instead he sang.

"*What news from the glorious country, of winding paths and happy homes, of singing larks and dancing trees, of...*"

He sang the wandering melody quietly, but with clear skill of a skald. He kept his eyes locked with Olaf's, clearly hoping the melody would—

"Shut up," said Olaf slowly, placing his axe in front of Bjarni's face, his voice growing cold. "I don't know what kind of one-man act you're playing at, but I've said it twice now. Third time will cost fingers, understand? You can ask the boy—pity is the one thing you won't get from me."

But the song got through somewhere, Yut was sure of it. The way Olaf suddenly became *dangerous*, like a wild beast cornered. Yut imagined emotion was something Olaf had stamped out so thoroughly that he would sooner kill someone than allow feeling to reach his heart. Yut had guessed that Olaf had a slight accent, and this confirmed it. Yut's mother taught him that the land of the lark was the land of Kus, to the Southeast, across the White Sea. If that's where Olaf was born, then what was he doing all the way out here?

"Then I am sorry to have bothered you, good friend," said Bjarni, bowing, "but still I must correct you in one thing. The one-man act has been a five-man act, and the third time will invariably cost fingers. Though, I'm afraid, they will not be mine."

Gods take me for a darkened fool. Yut could see them now, shadows in the trees and bushes. No doubt, getting into position while the actor took their attention. And they both fell for it; Olaf through his anger, Yut through his pity. He thought he heard the creak of an arrow being drawn behind him.

Olaf kept his axe in front of him, but his eyes did not stray from Bjarni, who was smiling again. "It didn't have to be this way, brother, but we will be taking everything. Perhaps if you had offered your fire—"

"Boy-Bjarni." Olaf tilted his head, watching Bjarni's smile slip. "That's what they call you around these parts, eh, shortie? You were a jarl's fool or something, 'til you got kicked out. Always wondered, how dumb do you have to be to screw up bein' an idiot?"

Bjarni's lips were a thin line, contempt clear behind his blue eyes. Yut thought he could have been a shapeshifter, the way he looked like someone else entirely when the smile was gone. Then it returned, but colder this time, barely reaching his eyes. "I was a skald, as a matter of fact, and I see you require further proof, brother." His eyes flicked into the trees behind Yut. "Very well. Dagmar, my dear fellow, would you mind convincing our friend?"

He hadn't finished the sentence before an arrow flew past Olaf's ear, above Bjarni's head and into the shadows behind. Olaf's head whipped around to where Dagmar began reloading his bow, and hurled the dwarven axe into the darkness. Without checking to see if it found its mark, he swung a ferocious backhand at Bjarni, who was too shocked to dodge. The short man began to collapse, but Olaf pulled him close, facing the trees.

All this happened in seconds. Yut's admiration at Olaf's quick thinking was suddenly overshadowed by the realization that he was completely exposed to further arrows. He brought his own axe closer to his chest, and some part of him knew it was useless, but there was nothing else to do. He eyed Olaf's shield, which lay not ten feet away. Stealing one more glance into the forest, he leaped at it, grabbed it, and crouched, so that only his eyes peeked out from above the rim as he watched the forest.

But no more arrows came. Instead, a man strode out from a different place in the trees, holding a dagger in one hand and an axe in the other. So, there were only two. He was taller than Olaf, had a meaner snarl, and had more scars on his face, though the firelight barely touched him at that distance.

Olaf threw the unconscious Bjarni at the bandit, who knocked him aside without a second glance. His axe buried in Dagmar, and armed only with a dagger, Olaf started retreating. The bandit strode up, taking two arcing swipes at Olaf, who just managed to dodge one. The other one glanced off his dagger, though it nicked his hand as droplets of blood began to dot the dirt under him.

Yut stood transfixed by the conflict, his body tense. Both warriors, adept at their craft, fought for their lives, each one's fate balanced on a razor's edge. Yut had seen warriors wrestle and compete in Sanvik, and he thought the whole affair looked intense, especially when coin was waged. This, however, seemed beyond those pale memories. Beyond words and thoughts, this was pure survival.

It was not glorious either. There were no drums, no music. Just two grown men, sweating and heaving with effort, inflicting pain on one another. In fact, it almost seemed inconsequential, except that Yut's life was bound to this conflict.

The bandit knocked Olaf's chipped dagger out of his hand and looked poised to strike death. That moment seemed to stretch, and each second became punctuated by Yut's heartbeat. He looked at his own axe, clutched by the shaking hands of a boy, and looked at the bandit's broad back. Before he could think and aim, the axe was flying across the clearing. Yut caught the fire's reflection in the blade as it coursed for the bandit—it seemed like a strange thing to notice, but Yut's overstretched mind just needed to take a breather and focus on a pretty, shiny thing for a moment.

The axe flew for an eternity, but it was clear it was going to miss its mark. He overshot, the axe was sailing straight over the bandit's head, who had forgotten about Yut.

But Olaf did not forget. His eyes were affixed to the axe as it passed over his opponent, over him, the handle circling over and over, coming just within reach. He snatched it out of the air and brought it straight down on the bandit's head without a moment's hesitation. Blood spattered on Olaf's face as he pulled the axe out with a crunch, and then chopped his head off.

And it was over. The winter frogs croaked in the distance, the fire softly crackled behind Yut, and Olaf breathed heavily as he lumbered past him, shoving Yut's bloodied axe into his hands. He looked resolute, like death itself. Between breaths, he said, "They might become draugr. Get the actor." He did not need to explain, and Yut needed no convincing. He would rather desecrate a corpse than face a living one again.

Olaf walked into the trees where Dagmar lay, leaving Yut to face Bjarni. Swallowing hard, Yut approached the former skald. The short man lay on his back, his face peaceful, blood trickling out of his swollen nose. Which was when Yut realized Bjarni still breathed. *Dark above.*

Yut looked back at Olaf but could only hear the wet chop of decapitation. Back to Bjarni, who was unarmed, and did not even threaten to kill them. Olaf would be coming back any second now, demanding why it was taking so long. He would call Yut coward, a soft kid, a weakling. He would remind Yut of what happened with the Heisir at Red Hill. He might even laugh.

Yut put the axe to Bjarni's throat, then stepped back, desperately trying to control his heartbeat and the rising bile with deep breaths, eyes still on Bjarni. Plenty of youths from the village would jump at the chance to finish off an enemy, claim their first kill, and prove their manhood. It's just that Yut preferred to fish.

He took aim at the skald's throat a few more times. Gods, what if he didn't chop through all the way? What if Bjarni woke up just in time to scream?

"Usually takes a couple swings," said Olaf from behind. Yut nearly dropped his axe. The task before him drowned out all sound and time, as it felt like Yut had been kneeling in front of Bjarni for ages. He looked at Olaf, who was bandaging his hand. He had new boots on, stained with even newer blood.

Yut did not need to ask, his pleading eyes made it clear he could not do it. He braced for Olaf's taunts, but the big man just sighed. "This is the job, kid. You keep your eyes open, put strength in the swing, and forget about everything else. All that matters is you survive—all that matters is you. 'Cause if it's not you, then it's him." He pointed to Bjarni, whose eyelids began to flutter.

"Can't we just tie him up somewhere, make sure he doesn't bother us?" Yut couldn't help sounding like a child.

"Aye, we could at that. But if it's not this ratkin, then it will be the next one, who won't take it lying down. Now, for most, the first one is the hardest. So, get through this and it's smooth sailing—trust me. In fact, consider this part of your training." Hand sufficiently wrapped, Olaf stood and folded his arms. "Now kill."

Yut brought the axe before Bjarni's neck again. The short man was stirring. Gods, this will just be harder later. Yut almost wanted to fight him, earn a sliver of honor, and make this easier. *Nothing will make this easier.*

With a deep breath, Yut lifted the axe, eyes affixed to that throat, the scraggly wisps of hair, the red stitching on the collar, the white shirt, which would be crimson soon—How did he keep it so clean out in the wilds? Yut wondered what those runes said. Were they stitched by a loved one? Where did Bjarni come from, what would he become? Could Yut truly just end it, take his thread from this saga?

This was what he wanted. If he was to exact vengeance, then he would need to kill. He should *want* to kill, and he still burned to avenge Sanvik. Olaf was right. Others will bring him harm, and they would not hesitate, especially not the Cult. That was simply the way the world worked, and it would be better for everyone if Yut just grew up and accepted it. He thought about the wyrm, its golden eyes seeping malice. He hated it with all his heart. Adjusting his grip on the axe handle, he tried to think about all the ones he lost. His mother's face drifted in from the shadows and ash—what would she tell him now? Would she approve of him ending the life of a defenseless stranger? He could sense her outrage at such an idea. His father would disapprove as well. *What are you doing with that axe, Yut?* They wanted him to be a leader, but they were gone, they did not know what he went through, they wouldn't understand.

Bjarni's eyes opened. The axe still hung in the air, but the concussed skald did not register the situation, so his eyes lazily drifted from Yut to the stars above them.

Yut's face contorted with effort, as if the axe weighed infinitely more. In this moment, it did. Several tears fell. Yut strained, heaved, and sobbed and... lowered the axe. He could not do it. He could not disappoint them. He was a coward, a weakling child, not worthy of anything in this world. *Dark take me.*

Head down, he offered the handle to Olaf, who continued

looking at Yut. He knew there was probably disappointment on that face, maybe frustration. Yut deserved it.

But Olaf did not take the handle, and instead walked back to the fire, blowing his nose into his sleeve. "I made myself clear, boy. Kill him or don't. I never promised to protect you, and I sure as dark didn't promise to do your work for you. Boy-Bjarni is your problem now. Feed him, starve him, I don't care. But he won't be leaving us until you do what needs to be done." He threw a few more sticks in the fire.

So Yut sullenly tied the dazed skald to a nearby tree and curled up by the flame. Maybe they should have moved camp, but Yut's mind drifted elsewhere, to the places of shame and dishonor that every man possessed in his heart. In those places, he fell asleep.

* * *

Cold daylight awoke Yut. He felt like his head was on backward, the world was a blurry smudge, his head a bastion of pain, his body sore and cold. Sounds came one by one: sputtering fire, Olaf's snoring, boiling water, soft humming—wait. The buried survival instincts seized Yut's body, and he thought as fast as the morning mind would allow. Soft humming and the smell of something delicious coming from the fire. Perhaps more bandits have arrived and forgot to kill him. Olaf was still alive, though, and no one could miss that mass. Trolls then, getting ready to throw the sleeping idiots into a mass of swirling green goop.

No, the humming was decidedly human, and the daylight would have turned the trolls to stone anyway. The answer was in front of Yut all along, though he would have preferred the trolls. The shreds of the rope that was supposed to hold Bjarni and the shreds of Yut's pride lay tattered by the trees.

But if Bjarni got free, why didn't he run? Why didn't he take their eyes already? Whatever the reason, it was his mistake, and now Yut would not be merciful. Bjarni will defend himself, but Yut would have surprise, size, and anger on his side. He quietly felt for the dagger next to his head, took a couple of quick breaths, and jumped at his captive.

But there was no captive, only Olaf's cooking pot, simmering with a heavenly aroma. Yut's stomach growled, but he forced himself to take in his surroundings.

A movement in the distance, down the hill, heading towards the river. Yut caught a glimpse of white cloth. He glanced at Olaf, sleeping contentedly. *Up at first light—my ass*. Still, this was Yut's problem. He turned back to his quarry—he would not fail this time. He grabbed two axes and followed Bjarni to the river.

Yut could sneak if he wanted to—he had not taken to battle like the other boys of the village, instead he spent time fishing or wandering the woods. There was something serene in treading the mossy forest floor, making little impact, becoming one with the trees and wildlife. This was similar, kind of.

He found the skald squatting by the creek. At first, Yut thought he was relieving himself, but he realized he was just filling a waterskin. That was a funny way of sitting, like a frog. It did not look comfortable at all.

Yut flitted from tree to tree like a bird, coming within a few yards of the humming skald. An axe cluttered behind Bjarni, who slowly stood as he corked his waterskin.

"Defend yourself," said Yut.

Bjarni glanced from the axe at his feet to Yut with a mild surprise, tinged with that ever-present smile. "Do not think I don't appreciate that axe *not* being buried in my spine right now, I truly do. And honor is a fine thing, but perhaps we could conduct our duel after breakfast?"

Yut had forgotten the way the short man spoke in skald-speech, how his regular sentences became prose, streaming like a mountain creek. This way of speaking had Yut and Olaf rooted in the ground while two large, loud attackers surrounded them.

"Breakfast, like honor, is a fine thing as well," said Yut, trying to imitate the skald-speech, "Though what good would it do to a dead man, be it me or you?"

Bjarni clapped his hands, truly looking like a boy in that moment. "He is a warrior and a skald! I should have known. Pleased to make your acquaintance, master…?"

"Yut Eriksson is my name, take it with you to the halls of the dead, Bjarni of Kus." Yut hefted the axe, his heartbeat quickening. He tried to remember how Olaf fought—knees bent, axe eye-level. Time to earn his honor back or die trying. This is how his forefathers lived and died, and today Yut would join those glorious ranks.

"I'll pass," said Bjarni, walking past Yut.

He stood disoriented for a few moments, then grabbed the second axe from the ground. "You can't do that!"

"I shall do as I please," replied the skald. He stopped, then added, "If you have a problem with that, then you may kill me yourself."

Dark take him, either he was a master at bluffing, or he was conscious last night after all. Yut trotted after him. "If you don't fight me then Olaf will kill you."

"I'll take my chances. Besides, I'm a skald, and you seem like a learned man yourself. I suspect a battle of wits and words would be more suitable, wouldn't you say?"

Yut considered how Olaf would take this. A duel of words does not normally constitute a proper challenge, but perhaps that is how they did it in Kus. It would certainly be preferable to spilling blood. As he pondered, they found Olaf already awake and halfway through the pot of stew. He gave a quick nod to Yut—or was it to Bjarni? The warrior emptied his bowl, gave a burp that would have scared off any wildlife within half a mile, and started to stamp out the flames.

"You're still alive," he said to no one in particular, letting the vague words hang like foul air.

"We will settle it later," said Yut when Bjarni remained surprisingly silent, smiling all the while. "Besides, he cooks well, and a little entertainment never hurts."

Olaf spit on the dying embers. "There's no room for entertainment in the wilds, boy. But he does cook." Olaf fixed Bjarni with a mean stare, and the skald beamed back.

"Guess you could have slit our throats in the night," said Olaf.

"Had I wished to, perhaps."

"Could have run off with the weapons."

"Aye."

"Cooked us a stew," tried Yut.

Olaf grunted. "Very well, boy-Bjarni, you wish to join our crew?"

"It would be my honor," bowed Bjarni, "and a personal challenge regarding the entertainment bit. I have stories that would make your blood freeze, and your heart melt."

Olaf just scowled as he continued packing, so Yut and Bjarni gulped down the stew. *Nine, he* can *cook*. One could only hope the mushrooms won't make him see sounds again. Securing their belongings and covering their tracks, the relieved Yut proffered an axe to Bjarni.

In return, he raised his hands. "Oh, I'd rather not." He shrugged at Yut's confusion, "Safer that way."

They ventured through the rest of the golden fields, passing abandoned villages and patches of trees. Olaf was in the front, cutting, pushing, and bullying everything in their way. Bjarni came second, so as not to fall behind, and so Yut could keep an eye on him. The skald tried starting a song an hour into the journey, but Olaf threatened him quiet. He said there were drendir cannibals about, but Yut suspected Olaf hated all things that did not involve killing, stealing, or drinking.

It would be at least two weeks of hard marching to Miklor, which was just fine for Yut. Every step further from his home cleared his mind and hardened his heart. He knew he would return one day and bring death with him. The words of the draugr echoed in his mind again, *destruction will spread from you.* Yut tried not to give the words root. Those that would attack him will pay, no matter how many. And those that stole his family and home will be destroyed.

They rested by a trio of eroded statues—giants of dwarven-make. Bjarni settled at the foot of one, whistling contentedly, just as the sun finally pushed through some of the clouds. Yut was about to settle down too, but Olaf launched his shield at him, missing Yut's head by an inch.

"Catch," he smirked.

Yut whispered a curse under his breath as he grabbed the shield and unhooked his own axe.

Bjarni sat up, sensing excitement in the air. The dwarven axe glimmered in Olaf's hand, staring Yut down. "Just providing valuable training as per our agreement, young drengr. Quick reflexes and all that. Shield up." And he threw himself at Yut.

Yut had once stood close to a giant oak as it was felled by Sanvik lumberjacks. He imagined standing below it, feeling the terror of the inescapable doom rushing in, dragging nearby branches with it as if it was grasping for help. But once he saw Olaf, unrestrained and fully armored, sprinting at him with violent intent, he couldn't imagine the experience being much different.

Yut heaved the shield over his head prematurely as he scrambled backward. "Wait!" But Olaf was a blind and deaf force. He swept Yut's unguarded legs and *fell* on him. Yut thought his ribs would all break at once as the wind left him. But a second later Olaf was walking away, and Yut was getting up and coughing, though he was not sure how.

"Your feet, boy. Everything starts and ends at the base." He faced Yut again. Bjarni was now grinning wholeheartedly, chewing some berries he found gods-know-where. *Who's the entertainment now*, thought Yut.

"Stand firm," continued the deserter, "and do *not* let anyone move you if you don't wanna be moved. But don't be a tree either—*always* be moving. It won't let the other guy get the good hits in."

He paused. "Ready?"

Yut hefted his shield. "Ready."

And Olaf rushed in again.

Chapter Twenty-One

Cannibals

"I am sorry," Sig said eventually.

They walked in deafening silence for hours, as Sig led Eira East, back through the outer Trelwoods. "I don't mean to keep doubting you in front of the others. The draugr, and the Seither—it all just seemed..."

"Overwhelming," finished Eira, holding Sig's arm tighter, "It is alright, child. I have not been forthright with you, and for this I apologize. We have been thrust on this path against our will, or perhaps against our better judgment. What remains is us, and us together. And when the ashes of change and apocalypse are settled, that is all that must remain."

"Didn't realize you were a seeress *and* a skald," smiled Sigrid, feeling the warmth of friendship creeping back between them. "We will remain."

"And the youth, provided he survives." Eira paused. "Olaf will have his part to play as well—he may surprise us all yet."

"You don't think the oaf will lose the kid at first chance?"

"I am afraid neither will survive without the other," said Eira, brows furrowing, "I do not see the end of their saga, but it will be decided in the coming weeks."

"And what about our saga?" All knew divination was only for the divine, and to foresee a life was to bring nine curses on it. A select few knew, however, that foretelling of a particular saga was not so much divination as it was stealing a glance of the general direction of events—hardly cursable stuff.

Eira scowled. "All dark and shadows. I have not been able to see a glimpse for weeks, which is why we must go to her."

Sig stiffened. She did not ask where they were going in hopes of passing the Gray Glades, passing *her*. But Eira patted Sig's arm. "I know you two did not exactly get along last time, but now the Cult will know of us, and they will be closing in. We are in dire need of allies."

"Shouldn't we be staying together then?" asked Sig, trying to change the subject. "What if the Cult attacks those two? They can't fight a full group of Speakers."

"It is as I said: they will be looking for Speakers, people coiled with the Saga. Now, before Yut has gained the use of his abilities, is the safest time for them. I've had... dealings with the Cult of Orik before. They would not attack Olaf and Yut—not right away, at least. They will first watch them, read their sagas, perhaps even befriend them. Only then will they be ruthless." Sig could tell whatever "dealings" Eira had with the Cult were not pleasant ones, but decided not to push it.

After a while, Sig said, "It's the way she stares at me, like I'm a pig with five legs. Like she expects me to do something." Though, it was more than that. The gray seeress' eyes, full of unnatural, childlike giddiness, bored into her as if searching for veins of memory, pain, secrets, fears. Some people could read you—*she* ripped you open, examined each bit, and devoured it.

"Please, she is merely curious," smiled Eira, "We learned

Speaking together, you know, when we were but young and foolish girls. Oh, the mischief we wrought upon poor Seeress Medra, when we Spoke the villagers of Tren... Trile..."

"Trelgen. You made the villagers walk backward for a day."

Eira chuckled. "Right, right, Trelgen. Gods, that was great fun. Though old Gyl does get... enthusiastic about you. If you have anything to hide, anything at all, she might just use it against you."

She knows, thought Sig. Of course, Eira would know about Sig's shadows returning; she wasn't a seeress for nothing. But gray seeress or not, it felt impossible to broach the subject. All the years they have been working to bury them, the sleepless nights spent in agony. She remembered gripping Eira's arms in fear as the whispers overwhelmed her, and the gruesome effort it took to push them out. There was no Telling to remove them—they were a part of her.

It was the gods' twisted joke that the shadowed ones began truly killing her when she started fighting them—when she met Eira. Or maybe Sig merely failed to see how much damage they had already done. The way she lived in the wilds, little more than an animal, ready to kill anyone who would get close, fully under their control. Eira told her who she was, and she fought them. Through anguish, she fought, and she had won, and banished them to the outskirts of her mind.

And now they were back. To acknowledge this would mean to begin the fight again—to admit she was still not free, and might never be free. She looked at Eira, the wisewoman's eye cover askew, red-brown hair damp with mist, mouth slightly open as if she was sipping the air. Admitting defeat was hard, but lying to this woman was impossible.

"There may be something," Sig admitted. "A few weeks ago, when you fell asleep—"

A slight, sudden tilt of Eira's head brought Sig to a complete stop. Only the wisewoman's nostrils moved as she inhaled sharply. Sig reached for her knives. "How many?" she whispered, barely audible, but plenty loud for Eira.

"Twelve, maybe more," she replied. "Armed."

"Not Gyldryn's folk, then. Refugees?"

"Perhaps—I cannot feel their minds." Dark, then no easy Telling to get out of this one. Eira pursed her lips. "We do the *Holy One*."

Sig grimaced. Of all their routines, the Holy One was Sig's least favorite, partly because she had to do most of the talking. Eira was a born talker, the flitting, chirping bird. Sigrid liked to imagine herself as the crouching lynx, though she wouldn't tell that to anyone. Unfortunately, holy seeresses mainly kept their image of the divine by staying silent. Eira continued in low tones. "This one may get ugly—remember, stay calm, read them, and plant your words carefully."

Now Sig started to worry. They had encountered plenty of road folk, and most did not attack a blind seeress in the middle of a forest—the few that did would soon find a dagger buried in their leg. A party of twelve would most likely move on without risking the wrath of the Nine.

After a minute of cautious walking, Sig saw the first shadow of a man emerge from the mist. He was completely bald, his leather tunic plastered with bits of feather, bone, and scale. Dark markings adorned his face; some spelled out runes, others framed his gaunt face. But it was not his clothing or markings that set a dead chill in Sig. It was the mouth. The man's teeth were blackened, with etched horizontal grooves in them. When he spoke, it was like gazing into an opening of some foul abyss.

"That smell..." murmured Eira.

"Drendir," said Sig.

"Cannibals? They cannot be this close to the Gray Glades..." Eira faded as the drendir approached, haunting grin continuing to bloom like a fresh bloodstain.

"Hail, o wise one," he sang, his clear voice resonating through the mists. "I am Crow, of the Seven Tribes." Eira had already adopted the Holy One image: face serene, looking to the heavens, left hand touching Sig's elbow, the other on her staff, her back straight. Gone was the wily wisewoman, this was an ambassador of the gods.

"Hail, Crow of the Seven Tribes," responded Sig. "You stand in the presence of—"

"Interesting thing," interrupted the drendir, "that a mouthpiece of the gods would need a mouthpiece herself." He punctuated each word as if intending to drive them into Sig, though he still watched Eira. Other shadows emerged from the fog behind him, clubs and short bows bared.

"The wise one speaks the will of the gods—you would be wise to let us pass in peace, lest you provoke them." This was the point when Sig needed to show strength. Weakness only encouraged Crow's kind.

The drendir's eyes finally focused on her. "The gods..." His words faded and he seemed lost in thought for a moment. A dozen drendir stood amid trees, all wearing similar face markings and clothing, all bald. One drew a short bow. Then Crow said, "The gods do not care for their children anymore—you and your kind are proof of this."

He turned to the drendir with the bow. "Do not harm the young one, she shall be a gift. The wise one casts spells, shoot her in the mouth."

The cannibal raised her bow.

Sig blinked as a chill passed through her. "You would not

dare—"

The arrow was released. Sig watched in shock, powerless to stop it flying true even through the mist, right at the oblivious Eira. But as it was about to puncture her skull, the blind woman flicked her head to the side, and the arrow merely nicked her cheek before clattering on the rocks behind them.

Her body full of needles, Sig forced herself to think past Eira's near-death. They could not run, talk, or use Telling to control the drendir's minds. Sig could down a few of them, maybe, but that was optimistic. She was also paralyzed in sheer panic, just as more shapes began to appear from the mist around them.

"*Liar*!" snarled Crow. "The witch can see!" The drendir unsheathed their knives, as the archer drew again.

And Eira Spoke.

It was a Telling of unbridled destruction, of storms that rip through tree, sea, and mountain. Dark clouds swelled above them as the wind quickened, kicking up leaves around the circle of drendir. Neither Sig nor the cannibals understood Eira's ancient words, but they felt its power. The words that commanded the tempest to invade this land. The second arrow was taken by the wind and returned fluttering back at the panicking drendir. They quickly dispersed to find cover. Even Sig had the instinct to run, but she knew the danger had not passed yet.

"They have us surrounded," shouted Sig through the howling wind, "Can you take them all?"

Eira, strain plain on her face, shook her head as she continued her Telling. Trees began to bend, then topple, and the quaking ground opened in fissures around them. Lightning struck nearby, decimating a tree, and sparks and smoke filled the air. Blind and deaf, Sig found Eira's arm in the darkness and clutched it for dear life.

When she regained her vision, Eira was hunched on the ground, shivering. The powerful words that woke the storm had faded, leaving the seeress a shell. The clouds were retreating, and the wind had died.

"They had protection staves," whispered Eira, her voice drained.

"The Cult..." breathed Sig. The drendir began emerging from the steaming earth. Sig spotted a few broken bodies under the fallen trees and rocks—the protection staves were strong, but not that strong, and usually did not last for more than a day. It did not matter now, because the gathering mass of drendir around them did not seem to be affected by the storm.

"They are closing in. Dark, there are so many," stammered Sig. There must have been a hundred of them approaching from the shadows. How could there be so many?

"Child," said Eira weakly, "I only hear eight heartbeats."

Sig stared at Eira, her mind racing. She focused on the forms in the mist, their faces a swirling mass of darkness, their movements too smooth, their stillness absolute. Dark above, these were not drendir.

Sig tried to hand her daggers to Eira, dropping them through trembling fingers. Maybe there was still time to run. "Eira, it's happening—"

But her voice was already taken. Her legs and arms had been taken, and the shadowed ones drew closer. Sigrid closed her eyes.

* * *

The sight came back first. Eight bodies lay strewn at her feet. Some were torn open, others still held daggers in their ribcages, most were missing limbs, and all wore a mask of terror. The last drendir,

Crow, was crawling away, her second dagger was in his thigh and there were vicious claw marks on his head. Her own body was drenched in blood and bits of drendir, though it was not her body yet.

Hearing came second. Eira was near, chanting the calming mantra in a pained voice. How many times had she endured it after waking up in a sea of blood? The shadows took her in times of danger, so the blood was rarely hers. Unless, of course, she was the danger. They would not allow anyone, including Sig, to take her life.

Then all the senses returned at once: the sick warmth, smell, and taste of fresh blood, petrifying cold, fatigue. She thought she would collapse, but Eira was holding her—or holding onto her—so she merely went limp in the wisewoman's arms. Finally, shame enveloped her, and as she had done so many times before, Sig quietly whimpered into Eira's chest—she was too tired to weep.

There Eira held her even as the sky darkened, and Sig lost consciousness amid ruined bodies and creeping shadows. Eira held her anyway, until the sound of her quiet chanting hailed the night.

Chapter Twenty-Two

Tova

Yut was the first to smell the smoke. They were taking a rare break from the grueling travel on an even-rarer sunny afternoon. Had he not been sore, fatigued, and blister-ridden, Yut might have enjoyed the warmth. It had been three days of marching through forests, hills, and one big river. They had to swim through the cold waters yesterday, since the raft and the raft man were nowhere to be found. They stopped seldom, and even when they did, a break for the party did not mean a break for Yut. Instead, he barely had time to set down his pack before Olaf took out his axe and shield.

Olaf believed in something called "pain training." Yut was certain the big man made up the term to sound more dignified, because it mainly consisted of Olaf hitting Yut until he fell, started crying, or lost consciousness. Afterward he would ask Yut how he could improve. "Aren't *you* supposed to tell me that?" Yut would shoot back.

"Aye, but that's not what pain training is about," Olaf would reply, or similar nonsense.

So it was during pain training that the acrid smell encroached upon their clearing. Olaf read Yut's face and, bless the gods, lowered his weapons. Bjarni, chewing on bilberries under a sunny patch, perked up a moment later. The skald proved to be a fine companion on an otherwise torturous journey. Full of energy, knowledge of the land, and jokes that made Olaf giggle for hours, Bjarni seemed like the type of person that would feel at home in a jarl's hall, a battlefield, or a middle-of-nowhere forest.

The skald pocketed the rest of his bilberries. "That's no campfire."

"Sure ain't," scowled Olaf, "And no villages around here either." He sniffed the air again, nose always open for opportunity.

"Let's check it out, could be loot," said Yut, eager to avoid training. Olaf grinned. "You're not off the hook yet, boy. You train with the trees tonight."

Dark.

* * *

"Dark," whispered Yut, as he regarded the remains of the encampment. He thought it was an encampment, though he never learned the proper word for it. Really, it was a Tova village. They were different from the Nostvot peoples—his mother said they were ancient, maybe even from the days of the lightfolk. His father, however, said they were just drifters, trying to follow their traditions as much as everyone. They worshipped in different ways, ate different food, and built different things, though Yut remarked that in the end, everything burns the same.

The Tova that camped here had no more than ten tall-tents, with several smoldering totems. Sheep and dogs lay scattered, their throats slit, and a few Tova shared their fate in the mud.

"War-band," Olaf answered the unasked question, hooking his axe. "Took the others as slaves, or ran 'em off. Reckon they stripped everything else clean already."

Yut was about to ask the next hanging question, but the smell of charred flesh caught in his throat. Bjarni asked it instead, "Then why cut the sheep down?" The skald wore a sorrowful expression.

Olaf was already digging through a tall-tent. "They gotta keep moving. Probably didn't even know about the skinnies until they walked right up to them."

"Skinnies" is what the nasty men of the village called the Tova, because most of them were lankier and taller than the Nostvot people, though seemingly no less healthy.

Olaf spat and moved on to the next tent. "But the jarl says to kill, so they kill. And have fun doing it, too."

"The savage survive," intoned Bjarni, as if repeating some proverb. He started to search the wreckage as well. "And Tova are not savage. Barely fighters, even. For these, no more than a skinning knife between ten people."

Yut found his voice as he uprooted himself. "Is it the same?" he asked Bjarni. "In your lands... is there war?"

"There is always war where men dwell. I doubt even the gods can change that."

But Yut wondered as he picked through the collapsed tents. Surely someone with the power of Speaking could make a difference. They could walk into a jarl's hall and tell him to pull back his war dogs or face a lightning bolt to the face. A powerful Speaker wouldn't even need to walk there, they would simply Speak the wars into ceasing. Dark, they could Speak suffering itself into ceasing. No more fighting, no more drakes, though perhaps there are no Speakers that powerful—not ones that care enough, anyway.

And if he learned to use the rune on his arm, and maybe some of that Speaking, would he be able to stop the evil of this world?

Would he want to?

Finding nothing but charred hides and a strange flute, Yut moved on to a collapsed tent outside the encampment. He could instantly tell something was off: the tent was less damaged, and there was a shape lying under the cloth. He took a couple of deep breaths and pulled back the cover. A child's face stared back at him.

Yut stood very still, as if the boy's blank stare put a spell on him. He could not have been more than seven winters, though there were already small rune marks on his gaunt Tova face. Yut would have stood there longer, had he not noticed a tiny flicker in those eyes. "Gods above..."

He scrambled to the kid, gently raising his head, reaching for his water flask. The rest of the boy's body was still under the covers, but judging by the smell, he must have been wounded, and his bone-white face meant he lost blood, and a lot of it. Up close, the boy looked even younger.

Yut touched the water flask to the kid's lips, but the water just dribbled down his chin. "It's alright, kid, I got you now. I got you..." The child's eyes drifted over to Yut, two coal-black dots holding pain too great for words, numbed by trauma.

"Don't take my soul," he whimpered. Yut blinked.

"Hold tight, kid, you'll be safe now." Yut shouted for Bjarni as a thin, cold hand gripped Yut's forearm. The child was looking at Yut intently now. He was shaking.

"The tall one... took his soul." His quick breaths grew ragged, but he only gripped tighter. "Don't take... my... my..."

"No one's taking anything," Yut said, quickly putting the child's head on his lap as he tried to pry the icy hand from his forearm. "You'll be right as rain in no time, kid. You'll see. Bjarni—now that's a guy who knows medicine. Oh, you'll like Bjarni..." And Yut kept talking. Maybe he wanted to distract the boy from the pain, maybe he wanted to distract himself from the dying child in his arms.

He spoke soothingly until emotion choked his voice. Yut was powerless against the memories that came flooding back—the wound that had only begun to heal was ripped open as he watched life leave the young Tova's eyes. How he tried to pull Keld from that wreckage, how he held his parents' charred hands and begged the gods to bring them back. Strangely, no tears came. Instead, Yut stared into the distance as blood rushed in his ears, and something cold enveloped him. He will kill them. By all the gods above and below, he *will* kill them. Through whatever power he was granted, the war band, the wyrm, even the darkened Cult will face a bloody justice. He would not be weak again, he would not hesitate. He would suffer the wrath of the gods and shoulder the Dark itself, but this rot would be cleansed before his vengeance was complete, this much he promised to those who had fallen and those who will perish.

Bjarni found Yut whispering something, to the boy or to himself, even as the skald gently led him away, even as Olaf put the cloth over the body and set it to burn, again filling the forest with the acrid smell. There was no training that night.

Chapter Twenty-Three

The Gray Seeress

Sigrid remained numb. Even though the shadows did not return for the rest of journey, Eira never strayed far from her. She even offered to gather firewood, but Sig just grimaced. Imagine that, a blind woman picking firewood. Hilarious.

She thought about the first time she saw the shadows. It was shortly after tragedy befell her village, and though her memory of those days was hazy, she clearly remembered the tall silhouette leading her through the forests. At times, she considered them friends, the way they kept her company through those dark nights. But then they started to whisper strange things to her, things she could not remember or did not wish to remember. They whispered, and she stopped sleeping and eating, becoming increasingly paranoid. She started to lose consciousness in the middle of the day, only to awaken in a different place. She might have forgiven that much, but then they started to take control of her, leaving behind corpses. That was when the hunters began pursuing her in earnest.

And now there was no denying that the shadows were back. Soon, her mind will be filled with darkness, when the numbness fades. The detachment was nothing new, it usually followed an attack. Eira knew this already, which is why she had not mentioned it since the accident. Gods bless her. The closest she came to the topic was gently asking whether Sig wanted to stay behind for the visit with Gyldryn. But as much as it annoyed her, Sig did not trust herself to be alone for long, not in this state. She needed Eira, and she hoped Eira needed her as well.

That morning they left Trelwoods behind them, and by midday they had crossed the jagged hills, entering the proper territory of the gray seeress. The sun had made a rare appearance, bathing the two women in a spring warmth. For Sig, the warmth provided less comfort as they approached the sparse forests of the glades. She had only been here once before, but she remembered it well.

The two towering, overgrown slabs of stone, covered with runes both great and small, leaned against one another amid a tangle of thorny brush to guard the entrance. The stones really did guard the way, just not physically. Instead, the runes, all or some, altered the Saga so that people passing through this area would never see or hear Gyldryn or one of her followers—the Saga simply would not let them.

The only way to pass was through Speaking, and should one Speak, Gyldryn and her followers would know.

Eira approached the rune stones. "I'll take this one."

"No," said Sig, "I can handle it."

"You sure?"

To answer, Sig walked up to the stones. Opening the way to the Gray Glade was among the first Tellings Eira taught her. Although it would reveal Sigrid's presence to Gyldryn, she felt a frustrating need to prove something to Eira. Or perhaps to prove something to herself.

She placed one hand on each stone and Spoke in the ancient runes, which translated to something along the lines of:

"And the guardians parted, revealing the path inside."

And the guardians parted, revealing the path inside. The thick brush drew away, slithering like snakes. The leaning stones moved through the ground, some of the runes coming to life in a glowing sapphire as they re-arranged themselves. The result was a narrow pathway through an unremarkable wood. Still, even the unremarkable woods held a promise of something more. Few saw this path, and fewer followed it.

She drew a deep breath as Eira took her arm. "Feel better?"

Sig exhaled. "No."

The stones closed behind them as they followed the path. More rune stones were scattered throughout the wild growth, functions for which Sig did not know. She doubted even Gyldryn knew. Cults like hers preferred to occupy ancient places, suffused with the Saga, whether they be evil or good.

Before long they heard the resonance. Both Sig and Eira would hear it at the same time, even though Eira could hear a butterfly's wings beating in the mountains. The resonance was a single clear note, penetrating the air like a needle. It reminded Sig of the tinkling metals worn by shamans, except where theirs was a jumble of rings, this was a delicate melody carried through a person's mind, through their heart. Eira said the resonance indicated welcome and goodwill to the visitors of the Gray Glades, and most found the sound to be calming.

Sig hated it. It reminded her of the ringing in your ears when you hit your head too hard. Maybe that's what the sound was for, getting to her head. *Darkened Speakers.* As she willed her mind shut against any magics of the glades, they emerged into a clearing of flowing grass. There sat about thirty people, all dressed in white, encircling Gyldryn. They swayed with the grass as they hummed, their tones ranging widely without hurting the melody. In fact, they seemed to match the resonance, which was still ringing. Apparently, they did this at least once per day—a song-form of Speaking, believed by some to be the original form of telling the Saga. Even though the clouds smothered the sun again, this place seemed brighter, warmer, happier.

Gyldryn stood in the center, adorned in a cloak similar to Eira's, but with plenty more jewelry, feathers, and colorful things Sig had never seen before. Her face was colored in white resin, and on her head were two large antler horns. Gyl was a tall woman, so with the horns she looked like a giantess, or a goddess. *I guess that was the desired effect,* thought Sig.

"How is she?" asked Eira quietly.

"Same and old," replied Sig, earning a chuckle from Eira. "She's got more jewelry now, though."

Before Eira could respond, Gyldryn began to sing. As much as Sig hated being here, she could not deny the power of that voice. The gray seeress flew upon wings of an eagle, higher than the clouds and the moon, and threatened to take Sig with her. Her melody rose above her followers like a winter dawn, distant and beautiful.

Sig could not blame herself for being mesmerized. After all, this was pure, literal magic. At the sound of her voice, the trees seemed to stretch towards Gyldryn, the grass swayed to the rhythm given by the followers, the clouds themselves would not dare hide the sun from her. As the light bathed the glade, flowers and trees bloomed in the clutch of autumn.

And then it was over. Sig swayed in silence for a moment before flicking a tear from her cheek. The motion was too sudden, and the gray seeress' eyes pierced them both. She nodded gracefully at them.

Sig inspected the camp to avoid eye contact. Tents were erected around the glades, decorated with various skulls, talismans, and totems. In front of these were cooking fires, chopping blocks, tanning racks, animal pens, and anything else that would help these people survive in the wild. Sig also noted the stained altar of sacrifice in the middle of the glade. Vae was a peaceful goddess, but all knew that peace was obtained through blood.

The worshippers began to disperse as they left their trance. Sig often wondered what it would take for someone to leave their entire life to live in the forest with a bunch of strangers. Possibly war, probably cowardice. She watched them, joking and laughing with one another, as others walked silently to their tents. All stole glances at Gyldryn. War or cowardice made them retreat to the glades, but sure as the gods she was the one that made them stay.

Gyldryn's deep voice was full of mirth as she approached them and took Eira's hands. "I had begun to fear the war devoured you, sister." She had removed the headdress, making her look more human, though she was still taller than most people by a head. "It has been far too long."

Eira's face brightened when she heard her Saga-sister's voice. "This is one meal the war would not enjoy. We come in a time of need, Gyl. You remember Sigrid."

"I would not dream of forgetting," smiled Gyl, keeping her eyes fixed on Eira. *Come on, then, look at me,* thought Sig. *Get it over with.*

But seconds stretched, and Gyl's prying eyes remained on Eira, who cleared her throat and said, "Right, can we talk somewhere private?"

Sig stared after Gyl as she led the blind seeress away. What game was she playing at now? The first time they met there was no end to the questions: where had Sig come from? How did she survive? How well did she Speak? And always those eyes, searching, speculating, searing her mind for answers. Maybe Gyl was one of those who thought Sig was a lightfolk, with how infatuated she was with her. Sig decided against it—the gray seeress was strange, but viciously smart. She had to be. Perhaps it was curiosity, after all. Sig watched them enter Gyl's tent, the largest in the camp, and as the tent flap closed, a spell seemed to break. Sig unclenched her jaw and allowed herself to breathe out.

"Who're you?"

Sig turned and looked down. A kid was looking up at her and squinting. Gods below, since when were children allowed into cults? She was barefoot, with a stained white robe and a black eye that she was obviously proud of. At least, Sig thought it was a she—their blonde hair was cut to a finger width above the skull, and nothing indicated a gender. Or maybe Sig was just bad with kids. Or maybe just bad with people in general.

"I'm Eivor," said the child, which did not help at all. "This is my glade. Seeress Gyldryn said so. I asked her if this was her place, and she said, 'it belongs to those much older than us, child, but you can have it if you want.' So, it is mine now, um, and there is a place I like to go to down in the trees..." Sig deafened her ears to the child's story, though she couldn't help smiling at her impression of Gyl. Her—Sig decided she was a her.

She looked toward Gyl's tent again, forcing herself not to wring her hands. Eira seemed to trust her "sister" too much. Surely, she shouldn't be with her alone? Not that Sig wanted to go with them, but friends of old are not necessarily friends of now, and Eira did have a streak for trusting the untrustworthy. Like Olaf. Like Yut.

Like Sig. She came out of her paranoia, realizing that Eivor was pointing toward Gyl's tent. "What?"

"That is Seeress Gyldryn's tent, and sometimes she lets me sleep there when I get the dreams." At this Eivor quieted down, looking off into the distance. *Another sick puppy,* Sig thought. *Of course.* And then her eyes caught Eivor's hand. Her fingers were moving, as if weaving an invisible thread between them. But what stunned Sig was the thistle plant growing in the ground. It wound its way out of the earth, far too quick to be natural, reaching toward Eivor's hand like a viper.

Eivor snapped out of her daydream, glanced to where Sig was looking, and grinned.

"Seeress Gyldryn taught me how to do that." Now motionless, she reached down to pluck the plant and offered it to Sig. "But over in the trees is my *other* hiding spot for when it thunders or when Seeress Gyldryn tells us to hide."

Sig reluctantly took the thistle as she considered this. No more than an hour in the Gray Glades and she already felt the futility of her own Speaking. What was the point of learning to Speak when a kid like Eivor could do it without even saying a word? She had to leave this place soon.

"Tell me, Eivor," said Sig, interrupting whatever the little girl was saying, "Is your secret hiding place behind Gyl's tent?"

Eivor giggled. "You're silly, if I tell you, then it wouldn't be a secret anymore. That's what Seeress Gyl—"

"Fair enough, then let's see how secret it really is. You go and hide, and if I find you, you will teach me this," Sig held out the thistle, to which Eivor furrowed her eyebrows.

"You won't find it, it's *very* secret."

"I'm a tracker, you know. The seeress I'm with, Eira, granted me powers of sharp sight. That is how I know where you're hiding the bread."

The girl's eyes widened—it was a lucky guess, but a good one. Every kid Sig met, mostly orphans and urchins, held something valuable close to them and away from everyone else. And, in the end, what could be more valuable than food?

"You really have eagle eyes?" asked Eivor, wide-eyed.

"Sure," Sig lied. *Run along now.*

"Well alright, but you mustn't peek!"

"I promise." This was no lie; Sig had no intention of seeing where Eivor was going.

As her quick patters faded away, Sig loudly walked toward Gyldryn's tent. She circled around it, making sure they heard her footsteps inside. "Eivor! I'll find you!" She tried to fade her footsteps, walking quietly as if drawing away from the tent. She admitted this was childish and would never fool Eira, but she wasn't trying to fool her.

Sig waited a few moments among the sparse birch, then quietly approached Gyl's tent from behind. There were no other cultists around—no doubt scared of their leader. Sig wasn't afraid. She crept up to a loose tent flap as Gyldryn's deep, muffled voice inside became clearer.

"—but there was no future there. They tried to flee the rune-circle before it broke, but Aslaug already had them in her web."

Eira groaned. "Damn it all to the cursed Dark." At first Sig thought someone else was in the tent, as she had never heard her curse. Eira always said that words, even common ones, held power. The old seeress continued, "I was hoping to speak with Beren next, but I suppose there is no point now."

"I heard his mind was ripped from him along with his rune. He is no more than a slobbering child now."

There was silence, and Sig felt Eira's disappointment through the cloth of the tent. She had no idea who Aslaug was, and whoever Beren was, Sig was glad they weren't there when his mind was ripped away. She started looking for a way to see inside. Perhaps there was tent flap she could peek through, if she moved carefully...

"The Cult is moving," warned Eira, "they know the Saga seeks a change, and they're afraid. Aslaug's grip is slipping."

"You would know more than me, sister."

"This has not touched you yet, sister, but that may very well change soon. Don't you know there are drendir at your doorstep?"

"This is hard to believe," replied Gyl, "considering the monsters cannot stand the resonance. And if they found a way, then I will melt their disgusting mouths shut."

Eira scoffed. "You always did have a way with words. However, they were not after your glade, but after us. I found something special, Gyl. A new rune. The Cult has been seeking him, but I got to him first. There may yet be potential there, and the Saga—"

"It's not Sigrid, is it?" Gyl asked. *No, it's not, you foul-faced snake-pig.*

"Matters not who it is. The point is, there is hope."

"There is no hope, Eira, for your own sake you must accept this. No rune-marked, no shape-changer, no god can change the course of time, or the Cult's desires." Eira grew quiet, and Sig heard Gyldryn move around. She used the sound of the movement to mask her crawling around the tent. "Stay with me, my dear. Let the war sort itself out, as it always has. Can we not spend the winter together, as we have done so often? Aslaug will relent eventually."

"Ha! The Cult will never stop, especially as their time comes to an end—" Eira stopped. Sig dared not breathe as a sudden tension seemed to leak from the tent.

"...who gave that to you?" Eira said, voice full of danger now. Sig started to rise. She still couldn't see much, but maybe there was an angle she could peek through. Her hand slid toward her good throwing dagger.

Gyldryn's laughter cut through the air and stopped Sig short. "Senses sharp as ever, sister. And why must someone give me rune of power? Can I not find one myself?"

Sig finally found a sliver of open tent, though she had to stand on her toes to steal a glimpse inside. Gyl stood confidently, her hand outstretched toward Eira, and a glowing crimson rune shimmered on her palm. It was not on her flesh, but seemed to float just above, like some sort of mirage. It was Hagosz, the rune of destruction, and its red glow bathed Eira's face in an ominous light.

Barely audible, Sig whispered, "Do you need help?" Hoping Gyl's hearing was much worse than Eira's.

"No," said Eira loudly as she stood, "you know very well why you cannot just 'find' one, Gyl. You are not rune-marked, and never have been so far as I remember, so I will ask again: Who did you take the rune from?"

Gyldryn's arm fell, and the red glow subsided. She shook her head as she found a wine flask somewhere and began pouring herself a healthy dose. "Calm yourself, Eira, it was merely a gift. A generous one, to be sure, but freely given. I tricked them, see. They came to the glades, speaking of freedom, a reawakening, and heroes, trying to recruit *me*. Sure, I took their gifts, but I'm the one laughing." Taking the two cups full with wine, she offered one to Eira. "Stay with me, Eira, and more gifts will come. We need only lie in wait..."

"Just say the word," whispered Sig.

"Not yet," said Eira, "the Saga has not ended, and the Cult always gets the last laugh. You are not my enemy, Gyldryn, but if you will not help me, we are done here."

"*Sitja*." It was a strong Telling, made stronger by the suddenness of it. The air grew cold and Eira sat down, hard. "You must always be so stubborn," sighed Gyl, taking a long pull from the cup.

"Hey! You're not even looking for me!" shouted Eivor behind

Sig. Gyl's head snapped to where Sig was standing, eyes locking with her through the narrow opening. Shock and indignation spread on the seeress' face. *Damned kids*.

The dagger left her hand in a blur, straight through the tent flap, straight for the witch's throat. The aim was true, but the cup of wine was already on the ground and Gyldryn's hand was outstretched. Hagosz flashed crimson, the air shimmered in front of her, and the knife melted in midair, leaving behind only sparkling dust.

Then she aimed the rune at Sig, her voice brimming with malice. "Foul darkspawn." The air began to burn around Sig, and at this point she should have been afraid. A few years ago, she would have yelled in rage and let the shadows take over once more. But bless the gods, sometimes the shadows trusted Eira too.

"*Sitja*," commanded Eira, and Gyl crumpled to the ground, Hagosz extinguished. The split second of Gyldryn's rage, and the break in concentration, was all the blind seeress needed. She quickly spoke more binding words on the gray seeress. Sig could almost see them coiling around Gyl as the woman struggled to form words. But binding was rarely broken, even by the most powerful Speakers.

Sig turned to Eivor and froze. The girl was standing still, ashen white, a red rune of Hagosz burning on her forehead. Sig took a step back. "Eira, she is..."

"They are all marked," called Eira. "Get in, quick."

Sig sprinted to the tent entrance, seeing the other followers in a similar state to Eivor. They were rooted in the middle of their daily tasks, looking sickly, Hagosz flashing on their foreheads. A couple of them jerked as if in pain.

"Safety measure," explained Eira when Sig was inside, "They should have felt the Speaking and come running of their own will, but I imagine Gyl used her 'gift' for something more sinister."

"Why aren't they killing us?"

"Oh, they will be, shortly. Their minds must still be fighting her on instinct." A slight smile on Eira's face made her look strangely peaceful. If Sig did not know any better, she might have thought Eira was impressed by Gyl's Telling. Sig was more focused on surviving the next few minutes.

"Then let's finish this snake and be out of here." Sig took out another dagger and moved to Gyldryn, who was curled up and motionless at their feet now.

But Eira grabbed Sig's hand. "I will not be named a kinslayer. And though I cannot see the Saga clearly, I believe in due time Gyl will come to help us, in her own way. She must not die here, but we must run."

"There are close to thirty of them, Eira. I'm not sure..."

"No, silly, we are not criminals. You will Speak us to Miklor."

"Very funny, now the real plan, please."

Eira let go of her hand. "I'm not in a joking mood, girl. Do you not feel the power of this place, the great weight of the Saga? Gyl did not choose the Gray Glades for naught, because this place is as the lightfolk grove should have been. You will *feel* the Saga and use its own power to reshape it. We were never here, because we went straight to Miklor. Understand?"

Sig had no words. In what darkened world did this ever work? She was about to protest again, but Eira's expression suddenly shifted.

"She has them, they are coming. Quickly! You know the runes, now Speak." Eira took Sig's shaking hands. Sig clutched her daggers tighter. "Why can't *you* do it?"

"I cannot focus on two Tellings at once, and one slip is all Gyl needs," said Eira patiently. Shadows, human and inhuman, grew around her. As soon as the first follower entered the tent, Sig would lose her body, she was sure of it. It will be a bloodbath. She might slaughter them all, or she might die. Eira will probably die, too. Eivor...

Closing her eyes, Sig breathed in. She heard the rushing footsteps of the followers, she smelled the panic of their master, felt their hearts hammering. And she felt the Saga. Eira was right—unlike the lightfolk outpost, thousands upon thousands of stories effortlessly unraveled before her, the meaning and purpose of everything laid bare. Sounds became sharper, the smells more pungent, and Sig felt herself floating in the middle of it all.

It felt wonderful.

"Good, child," whispered Eira, "Now, push against it. Make a different saga. We took the North road to Miklor, encountering little, safe and sound."

Sig Spoke. Everything faded, even time. She and Eira floated in darkness, where there was no Saga, no meaning, no past or present. Even Eira did not know what this place was, though some said the darkness was a world behind the world, the source and foundation of Arthgard. Sig figured that to make weighty changes to the Saga, one would need to step outside of it. The shadows skittered at the edges of the darkness, a constant distraction to her Speaking. The grander her Saga-Telling became, the closer they seemed to draw. Still, with Eira's hand on her shoulder, the runes poured out of Sig's mouth until she felt vertigo. Reality stretched, the Saga groaned and struggled, but eventually accepted her tale, and from the abyss came the sound of birds. Then the whisper of trees, then a running creek, and by the time Sig opened her eyes she was standing amid entirely different trees.

She sucked in air as if she just came back from the dead. The world spun, and she retched. Gods, the *power* that ran through her.

Eira told her about this many times, but *dark*.

As the trees righted themselves, her vision cleared to reveal Eira leaning against an oak and smiling. “Well done.”

“Gyl… following?” Sig managed to let out.

“She’d never leave the glades, and I doubt her followers could do what you just did.”

Sig’s blossoming pride was replaced by some more retching and the memory of the little girl Speaking without speaking. Maybe some of them were more powerful than Eira thought.

“We should move anyhow,” continued Eira. Her smile faded, and she deflated. “We got what we needed, even if it was not what we came for. Gyl will find her way, I’m sure of it. And I would not mind sleeping on something softer than an oak root tonight.”

Eira led the shivering Sig out of the forest, and the irony was not lost on either of them.

Chapter Twenty-Four

The Rune of Strength

Yut, Olaf, and Bjarni watched the broken wagon hungrily. They were out of meat and bread, and for all of Olaf's bragging, he couldn't track game to save his life. Berries and water could only do so much, and the wagon had a few barrels and sacks, and no horse or owner in sight. But of course, it could be bait for an ambush, so they merely watched. Hungrily.

"I think Yut should go," whispered Olaf.

"Agreed," Bjarni said, too quickly.

"Go to the dark, I have enough holes in me. If you want meat, then *you* go."

"You're a smaller target than me," said Olaf, "And I'll shoot anyone who shoots at you."

The wagon stood at the bottom of the hill, taunting them. Its axles were cracked as if something heavy had landed on it, in the middle of the path, like an obvious mystery.

"Bjarni's smaller than me," tried Yut.

"Bjarni's as useful as a chicken in combat. You want him to sing to the bandits?"

"Very true," nodded Bjarni.

Yut peeled his eyes away from the wagon and looked at Olaf. Was that an indirect compliment on his fighting skills? "Then I get first pick at whatever's inside."

Olaf considered this at length, then he took out his bow. "Agreed."

This made Yut even more nervous, but he hefted the shield, nonetheless. Then he took Olaf's shield and, like a two-wheeled wagon himself, crept toward the broken wagon. He shadowed the trees, trying to look in all directions at once. With a final burst of speed, he slid towards the wagon and waited, covered with his shields on one side and with the wagon on the other.

But no arrows or axes came. He tried to spot his two friends, but they were well hidden in the forest. He wondered if they were laughing at him with his two shields. Then he wondered if they were still there. Dark.

Glancing around one more time, Yut stole a look inside the wagon. One of the barrels was cracked open and a clear liquid glistened inside. It smelled... sharp. Unpleasant. Whatever was in them, it was certainly not mead.

Wiping sweat from his forehead, Yut slung one of the shields onto his back and ruffled inside with his free hand. There were some potatoes and bread, and he thought he smelled jerky among the sacks. There were also daggers, hand-axes, short bows, arrows, and maybe more. Gods above, this was a supply wagon. Even better, he was sure no real bandit would use weapons and a heap of real food as bait, so he set aside the second shield and jumped into the wagon.

He inspected the goods quickly. Olaf would pick the entire supply clean in less than a minute, finder's pick be damned. Even now, he heard a rustling in the bushes up the hill, followed by Olaf's cursing.

A sudden, sharp pain bit his hand, and he realized that in his enthusiastic shuffling, he brushed against an unsheathed dagger. Sucking on his finger, Yut lifted the blade, only to find a severed hand still clutching the dagger.

Yut flew out of the wagon, unintentionally flinging the blade and hand at Olaf. The veteran instinctively caught it, gave it a cursory inspection, and casually pried the blade away, throwing the hand behind him. Bjarni just managed to dodge it. "What..."

"It's..." stammered Yut.

"Potatoes!" exclaimed Olaf, new dagger already sheathed in his belt, as he rifled through the goods. "And weapons," he continued appraisingly, "this is a darkened war wagon. And, oh yes, fire oil from Rotheim—I heard the stuff even burns underwater." He smelled the potatoes for corruption, and promptly began stuffing his face.

Yut tried to avoid looking at the severed limb lying on the ground, so he turned his full attention to the sack with jerky. He heard Bjarni say, "This was no bandit attack." Gods, the man picked the limb up and was studying it. Unfortunately, he continued, "Ripped from the elbow, but there was also a cut here, and here. Maybe a bear?"

"'Oo 'ares," chewed Olaf, "Mo' fo' us." Yut's growling stomach overrode any argument his brain was trying to come up with, and he grabbed a couple of apples as he chewed on the meat, watchful of other body parts among the supplies.

Bjarni threw away the hand, and then looked under the wagon. "Look here, both axles are cracked in two. Something heavy—very heavy—was on it. But a bear would have gone for the food, and why would the driver not have run at first sight of it? And there are drag marks here..."

The skald snatched the dagger from Olaf's hilt, earning a growl from the warrior as he swallowed the rest of the potato. "Finders keepers," he said dangerously.

Bjarni looked at the dagger intently. "No worries, friend, just borrowing. This is not a hunter's dagger, more like one that the merchants carry. There would be no reason for a merchant to fight a bear for his goods. Unless..."

The way he looked at the wagon suddenly made Yut feel exposed. There was something wrong here, even Olaf felt it. "Grab the food," said the big man, tossing a sack at Yut. But Yut silently finished Bjarni's thought. *Unless the merchant had no chance of running away. Unless the merchant was ambushed and hopelessly outmatched.*

"Why would the bear leave the food and take the body...?" Yut wondered aloud. Olaf cursed and packed faster.

"The bear has no appetite for human food," said Bjarni. Yut could tell the skald did not want to say the next words. "The bear was not a bear at all. Strong as a bear, sure, but too fast."

"And stealthy," said Yut.

"And smart," nodded Bjarni.

Olaf's movements were fluid, his eyes downcast. The sack was half-filled with bread and potatoes, but warrior's sense must have stopped him, because just then the three heard a branch break behind them. It might as well have been the strike of thunder.

Slowly, they turned and saw a shadow in the dark trees fifty feet away. Yut thought he saw the creature's eyes glisten.

It rose.

It was like looking into the face of certain death. Too smart and fast to be a bear, too strong for a wolf, too vicious for a human. And yet it was all three, an undeniable proof that the Dark was approaching the world of mortals, and was perhaps here already.

The wulver's first stride brought them back into reality, but by then it was leaping toward them at an impossible speed. Yut only had time to glimpse the half-human shape, the long claws, and the snarling wolf-like face. It burst through the canopy with hardly any sound, eyes fixed on its prey.

Bjarni threw the merchant's dagger at it, but Yut had no time to see if it struck. There was an axe in his hand and shield in the other, as Olaf dragged him behind the wagon. "Can't run," breathed the warrior as Bjarni slid under the wagon. "Once he's close, we rush him." His voice was gone, so Yut nodded frantically. As if that would ever work—but what other choice did they have?

The wulver stopped on the other side of the wagon. Its steps were padded like a cat's, if it wasn't so heavy it may have been silent. Tortured moments passed. Yut didn't breathe or move, realizing any second could be his last.

The beast sniffed the air, its lungs like a blacksmith's bellows. With a low grunt, it lifted the cart and threw it in the air like it was a child's toy. The barrels and food went flying, showering everyone with potatoes and fire oil.

As soon as Yut saw it up close, he knew there was no chance of a charge. The beast towered over them, and both Yut and Olaf knew they were looking into the face of their end. It stood nearly double their size, with the head and legs of a wolf and the body of a human giant, its muscles taut under thin gray fur. It needed no weapons—each hand had claws the size of Yut's head. There could be no battle, much less a victory, against it, so they stood paralyzed and dripping. Yut thought he heard Olaf drop his axe just as the wagon crashed in the trees.

The wulver raised its claw—it was not looking at danger or even an inconvenience, but at food, so it took its time. There were jagged runes carved in its gray fur, as if with a dull knife, running from its legs to the shoulders. Perhaps that was how they were made.

Perhaps Yut could have used his own fledgling magic abilities to stop the thing, but any further thought was swallowed by that monstrous face and the claw, poised to rip open the two companions in one swoop.

But then it hesitated, and glanced around, not unlike a human. Yut felt like a performance was suddenly halted, and the audience was now aware of other sounds. But the only other sound was of two pebbles colliding. Yut realized Bjarni was behind the beast. He was under the cart before, so he must have scrambled there after the wulver threw it in the air. He was also on his toes, reaching up to the beast's back, and striking something—a flint. Was he trying to start a fire? How in the dark would that ever—

Flames erupted on the wulver's skin. It roared and swept a wild claw at the perpetrator behind him, but Bjarni expected it and rolled out of the way, pocketing his flint and steel. With a certain type of horror, Yut noticed the skald smirking. However smart the wulver was, it knew little of the flammable properties of fire oil, else it wouldn't have drenched itself in it.

Seeing the proximity of the flames to their own soaked bodies, Yut uprooted himself and slapped Olaf—the big man was still in shock, probably. They leaped away from the flames and ran in different directions as the beast tried to extinguish itself first with its hands, and then by rolling on the ground. It was utterly terrifying—a mass of teeth, claws, and burning flesh convulsing and screaming through melting lungs. Yut allowed himself a second glance when he tripped and slid into the underbrush some hundred strides away.

The monster was still aflame, though it had stopped rolling around. Instead, it stood upright, and was seemingly trying to tear its skin off as it roared into the sky. Bjarni and Olaf were nowhere to be seen, thank the gods, and Yut was about to start running again, when the wulver went down on all fours and made a different sound. It sounded like growling at first, but Yut caught its lips moving, even as they burned. Then, brighter than the flames, the runes carved in its flesh began glowing in a shimmering blue light.

Gods below, the wulver was Speaking.

The beast barked another rune, and the blue light became frost that attached itself to its body from the surrounding air, instantly putting out the flames. The wulver's flesh sizzled as smoke shrouded it. It breathed deeply, shuddering in pain, and then it stopped. The sudden silence was interrupted only by Yut's own breathing, which he halted a second later. The wulver's ears twitched—it was waiting, listening. One of its eyes had been burned shut, but the other one darted around, before landing on Yut's path and following it up the hill. But it did not settle on Yut exactly. No, slightly below and to the left.

Yut looked at his arm. His golden rune was burning fiercely, completely giving him away through the dark underbrush.

"Dark." Yut grabbed his shield and ran like his life depended on it—because, right now, it most certainly did.

He ran another hundred paces before he heard the wulver's labored breathing behind him. The darkened fire that would have killed most living things only slowed it down. He hoped it was enough. By then, Yut had spotted the dwarven ruins they passed earlier, and, throwing his shield somewhere vaguely behind him, gave a final mad burst of speed toward the half-buried structure. It was a tunnel entrance, only a couple of feet tall; the rest was swallowed by earth. Still, Yut decided to bet his life that it would be deep enough to protect him from the massive wulver. At least until it died, or gave up. At least until help arrived. None of which seemed too likely.

The shield crunched behind him—gods, the monster was getting closer. Yut focused on the narrow entrance of the ruin, and with a final leap, dove into it just as a claw cut the air where he was a second ago. He scrambled madly into the darkness, squeezing himself through the narrowing tunnel. It led downward into what Yut hoped was a system of dwarven tunnels, far beneath the earth and the wulver.

Hope was not enough, however, as the tunnel narrowed to a dead end, a dozen feet inside the structure. He dug and clawed for all he could, but his bloodied fingers did little. Yut turned around just as the wulver lowered its burned, smoking muzzle into the entrance. It was holding one of its hands to its chest, as it looked burned beyond use. The other hand plunged into the tunnel, clawing at the stonework inches from Yut's foot.

Yut screamed and tried to compress himself further into the dead end. He held his dagger in front of him with both hands, presumably in the same position the merchant held it. Sweat and tears burned his eyes, panic seized him, but he fixed his eyes on that claw.

The wulver retreated, grunted, and threw itself into the structure. Only his head and shoulder fit, but it brought him several inches closer to Yut, so that he could lean over and touch its claw. After a few seconds the monster leaned back and rammed itself into the ruins again. The walls shook and cracked, and still it neared him. The claw thrashed wildly as the beast roared. It knew the hunt was over, though it must have rarely fought this much for a meal.

It leaned back a final time, but before pouncing on the ruin again, it locked its good eye with Yut, and said something. Yut wouldn't have understood it even if it spoke his tongue, since the beast's voice was a gargle of blood and burned vocal cords.

"Please..." begged Yut, tears, and snot running down his face.

The beast was still for a moment, before launching itself at Yut again, this time with the force of an earthquake. The half-buried dwarven ruin crumbled, and the wulver advanced inside. However, its first footstep sunk into the ground and kept sinking.

Yut screamed again as the ground underneath both of them caved in. Before the wulver could bring down its claw, the two fell into the darkness, buried by the earth.

* * *

Rocks pummeled Yut as he descended through the ancient entrance. Damp dirt filled his ears, nose, and eyes, so he could not tell whether the wulver was still with him. It would have filled his mouth, too, had he not kept it shut tight. Though he continued sliding and falling through the collapsed dwarven pathway, and the earth constricted him on all sides, he forced himself not to panic. His heart hammered mercilessly, and the air dwindled from his burning lungs, but he resolved to keep his limbs close and be calm. He would escape this, somehow. He had to.

He knew he had landed when the rocks around him stopped moving. He was upside down, the cold dirt still entombed him, but it did not crush him. He tried moving his arms and found no resistance.

Yut erupted from the rubble and into a dark tunnel. He hacked out half of his lung, throwing up the bit of apple and jerky he tasted earlier. Gods, was that only a few minutes ago? Taking a moment to scoop dirt from his ears and eyes, Yut tried to remember how he got here. Then he jumped back, adrenaline prickling his body. The rubble of fallen earth covered the entrance completely, because he saw no light. Was the wulver still inside? Did it die? He did not want to find out. That he was alive was miracle enough, and that he landed in a standing dwarven tunnel was more fortune than he dared hope for.

Yut coughed out the remaining dust from his lungs as he backed away from the collapsed entrance. He would survive this, he just needed to think. He remembered Eira's voice after he had stopped the creek, when she took him away from Olaf and Sigrid: *The gods themselves watch over you, son of Saga. But the Cult will be watching as well, which is why you must not Speak until I can teach you properly.* Not that he wanted to—he had yet to have a good experience with Speaking. He never told Eira about the rune either, though he assumed she had known, even if she never brought it up. He still had no idea what activated it, only that it burned brightly when he felt the sensation of power. He cursed himself again for not asking more meaningful questions on their way to the lightfolk outpost. Though now he wondered how forthcoming the seeress would be. Perhaps she knew less than he thought.

Then a different memory surfaced. *Yours are the hands of death...*

The draugr was wrong. It had to be. Yut would do the opposite—he would rid the world of that darkened wyrm. And, if it was in his power, he would end the war that needlessly took children's lives. He will protect people and destroy the evil powers that would arise against him, be it the Cult or someone else. Granted, he had no idea how that would happen, but if he could only feel the power of the rune again, if he embraced this new power, nothing would be impossible. And yet a small voice told him the path of peace lay in Orheim. It would not be a path for Yut.

Then, the nightmares swarmed suddenly and without mercy. There were flames, wulvers, his parents screaming, and the golden eyes that watched without pity. The golden eyes that saw through him, that consumed his very soul. He doubled over, trembling hands wiping cold sweat as he struggled to breathe. *Come on, Yut, you got this. You're in an underfolk tunnel, adventuring. Think.*

Yut forced himself to keep walking until the panic subsided. He felt his way along the stone corridor until his eyes adjusted to the faint blue light shed by some of the runes on the walls. It was not his first time in a dwarven tunnel, and it was well known that most were illuminated by the magic those creatures instilled in their home. Some vagabonds even lived in these tunnels, though it was dangerous. Not only were they vast and unexplored, but the dwarves did not appreciate squatters, and filled their halls with traps before they left.

And they were all gone now, of course. When the Allwinter came, just about every dwarf moved deep into the mountains, north and west. They have not returned for fifty years, and their ancient homes remained vacant.

As Yut stumbled through the tunnels, he felt an increasing dread replacing his previous panic. The air felt thick, and his clothing was drenched with sweat. Surely the wulver would have been buried alive, surely it did not have the strength to survive the fall?

Blessedly, the rune on his forearm started glowing again, providing a better light than the runic illumination of the dwarves. Though the strange rune had got him in this mess in the first place, he had grown accustomed to it. Its soft, unblinking light comforted him for some reason, so he decided the rune was good.

A faint writing on the walls caught his eye, so he took a quick rest while studying it. These were supposedly mining tunnels, but he could make out a line of runes at the top of both walls, running down the entirety of the tunnel. The runes were written in some type of dwarven archetype because Yut could not read a single one. He hadn't heard of the dwarves having their own runes—though he hadn't heard about much of the dwarves in general. He was initially interested in studying the runes, but then he was beset by a coughing fit from the dust and decided to move on. Slower, this time, as he remembered about the ancient traps.

He had to approach his predicament logically. First, there was the problem of the wulver. There were runes carved in it, as if with a knife. Perhaps they were once wolves, or men, and were turned into these things by evil magic? Seithers, no doubt. They could also Speak, and this one could see Yut's rune, when no one else could. It also spoke words, as if trying to communicate. As much as the thought horrified him, it also fascinated Yut. Perhaps they could be spoken to—understood, even.

Hopefully not soon, as Yut's thoughts now turned to escape. He had no choice but to follow this mining path for now, but he would need to ascend soon. He wondered if there was even a way to do that, or if dwarves only lived under the earth. *Dark*. Surely, this tunnel led to some kind of meeting place or a center, or maybe even—

And then it stretched out before him. He found himself on an outcropping, a huge chamber that opened above and below him. The blue light was stronger there, illuminating great support beams, buildings along the walls, and tall structures like stalagmites rising from the ground at random intervals. Yut looked closer, and nearly fell off the edge of the outcrop. They were dark-ridden statues.

This was not a mine, but a dwarven city.

He could see paths inlaid in the stonework, winding around the small, squat buildings, which were sculpted out of the ground rather than built with bricks. Some of the buildings were set on the ground, however Yut was surprised to find most of them emerging from the walls of the cavern. There must have been a hundred of them climbing up all the way to the ceiling.

Standing at the precipice, Yut felt like an intruder, knowing how well the dwarves guarded their homes. It was deathly quiet, however, and there was no other way to go, so he cautiously descended the stairs to the city.

Up close, the statues wore no face, only a strange pointy helm and beard. Their bodies resembled stalagmites with humanoid heads, as if the dwarves had a vague idea of what statues were but did not want to put the effort into finishing it. Yut thought they might have seen the wooden statues of the gods among human cities and wanted some for themselves as a novelty. Yut couldn't help smiling at the thought. Several other tunnels connected to the city, and Yut's mood lifted when he saw a lighter shade of blue coming from one of them. It could be hallucination or daylight—a chance he'd gladly take.

And then he stopped short, his smile melting. A glistening pool of dark liquid marked the entrance to the tunnel. Yut's rune glowed brighter as he approached and confirmed his suspicion. It was blood, and it was fresh.

More splotches dotted the tunnel, and Yut had to admit the crushing truth: the wulver was alive and followed the same light Yut had seen. It must have taken a different path of the same tunnel, on the other side of the cave-in, which eventually led back to the dwarven city. Dark take it all.

Yut took deep breaths and tried to think. Perhaps it escaped already, valuing freedom over food. It was losing blood, so it could not afford to wait. Yes, that's it—he must be alone now. He waited bit more to be sure, taking a walk through the city to take his mind away from his imagination.

He studied the dwarven homes, built *into* the wall, extending up hundreds of feet. How did they get up there? Perhaps secret tunnels, or ladders? They reminded Yut of a beehive, the way little windows connected in various patterns, seemingly separate and interwoven at the same time. The more his eyes adjusted to the ambient hue of this place, the more homes he could see. They climbed walls, wrapped around giant stalagmites, some even attached to the ceiling. Everything was carved or built of stone, though Yut noted some structures were inlaid with gleaming black mineral. One dome-like structure was made entirely of it, though it only held narrow slits as its openings.

Yut leaned against it as he stared into the distance. Past the homes and the statues, a sea of blue stone stretched for miles. This was not a cave, but an entire world underneath his own, and they must have lived here for hundreds of years. An uneasy feeling settled in Yut. The elders said the underfolk left shortly after the Allwinter. He hoped it was not in expectation of another calamity. If they stayed here during three years of bitter cold, what would make them all pack up afterward? And if it has been fifty years since then, could they have been wrong?

He continued his walk. "*Empty guesswork makes for empty pockets,*" they would say in Sanvik. Guesswork or not, there was nothing he could pick up—they really did take everything to their new homes in the mountains. He found more illegible runes on their homes, and committed a few to memory, drawing them out in the dust on the ground. Couldn't hurt.

It was then that his finger touched something cold in the dust. It was light, and even through the thick coating of settled ground, Yut could see the shine. A simple necklace with an amulet—a golden disc inscribed with runes that circled the center. So, they didn't take *everything* with them. It felt like a precious trinket, and he might even have a chance to return it to a dwarf if they ever came back from the mountains. And if he survived. Yut reasoned that in this case it was his responsibility to take it. Yes, that's what it was.

As fascinating is it all was, nothing compared to what Yut discovered next—and it was not even about the dwarves, but about his rune. The closer he moved to the wulver's tunnel, the brighter his rune glowed. At first, he thought it was random shifting in the light, but making several trips along the sizeable chamber, it became undeniable. Sweating harder than ever, he tried to approach the wulver's blood from several directions, but that did nothing. No, it was the distance to the tunnel. Or the distance to the wulver.

That had to be it. His rune glowed fiercely when he was within inches of it, and steadily grew brighter as he traversed the tunnels. But what did the wulver have to do with his rune? Perhaps it was like Yut, though the beast's rune was inscribed on its body, whereas Yut's hovered just above his skin. It could also speak like Yut and use its rune to its advantage. Unlike Yut, however, the wulver could actually control its rune and make it form ice when it wished to.

There was much to consider, but Yut stepped into the tunnel anyway. It was not curiosity, he told himself, but survival. There was no other way, and the wulver should have escaped far away into its nest—or wherever those things lived. Except the rune only glowed brighter, and Yut walked slower and quieter. Perhaps if he got close enough, his rune would activate like it did with the Seither, and he would feel that sensation again. He tried not to dwell on it, but that feeling of power and awareness was not something you could forget.

He wanted it again. He wanted to feel it always.

And then he saw it. The tunnel opened into a smaller chamber, filled with stalagmites and statues. Silver daylight washed them all from a narrow hole in the wall. Not so much an entrance as a structural collapse, enough to fit a child through, but not him.

Yut's spirits did not sink from this. His spirits sank when he saw the wulver.

It was lying on a bronze disc some dozen feet wide, which looked like a larger version of his dwarven necklace. The disc was divided into a dozen parts, with dwarven runes inscribed in each section. It sat flush with the ground, surrounded by stalagmites, and gleaming. The beam of light fell directly on the disc, causing the bleeding wulver to steam from the heat. Yut could see its labored breathing as it neared death. Its eyes were closed, and it didn't seem to notice Yut. Still, he crouched behind a nearby stalagmite just in case, and examined the rest of the chamber.

It felt sacred. There were support beams and more of those faceless statues among the stalagmites, and none of the walls were mined. As if the stones were too holy to be touched with tools. And surely that bronze disc held a purpose, sacred or not. Yut wondered if the wulver chose it because of the light, or because of that purpose.

Gods, he was completely ignorant. He checked on the wulver again, judging the distance to that small opening. How long until the beast truly died? Would he dare walk so close to it, even as it lay motionless, hours from now?

Yut knew he needed to think logically. Maybe he could wait it out and explore other tunnels, some of which might even have running water. He could do it—he could survive.

But then he looked at the rune on his arm, its glow soft but encouraging. The closer he got to the wulver, the closer he approached the power. He had not felt it before, but that was because he still had a chance to survive and run. It hummed just beyond his senses, yet it was right before him. At the ravine with the Seither, he felt it in the darkness, and reached out. What if he did so now? What if he was *strong?*

It made no real sense, but this was not a logical situation. He had a rune of power, as Eira called it, and he needed to learn its secrets. The wyrm awaited him. Destiny awaited him. And that destiny lay in front of him, bleeding out on a strange bronze disc.

Yut closed his eyes and let his legs move him. He would not be weak again. The wulver was facing away from him and did not move even as Yut approached.

He took a few deep breaths and stepped into the light. The beast instantly reacted—it was on the edge of death, but its bleeding muscles still convulsed as it jumped back. It bared its fangs, so Yut bared his teeth. The wulver seemed to hesitate, surprised that its prey came willingly. They were on opposite ends of the disc, like wrestling partners before a fight, both mad with adrenaline. A seizing fear gripped Yut as soon as the wulver moved, and he fought with everything he had to stay still.

"Fear me," Yut whispered.

The wulver pounced.

Yut closed his eyes, and felt the claw land hard on his chest. He soared for a moment, and then impacted into a wall with a shockwave of dust. Rocks fell around him, and what sounded like a pillar came crashing down to his right. He opened his eyes and saw a statue in ruin beside him, its debris still settling. Light swelled in the cave. The wulver launched him through the statue and into the wall with the opening, the impact causing it to widen. Yut could even walk through it now, but none of his thoughts entertained escape. He felt his body and neck—there was no pain or breaks, just a sizzle, like heated metal in water. He realized he was steaming.

Yut stood, and the wulver stepped back. It snarled, bit, and roared at the strange human in front of it. Yut would have liked to say he felt no fear, but it was quite the opposite. He felt the mad drum of his heart, the blood racing in his ears. Gods, even being afraid in the middle of a forgotten tunnel felt amazing. Power was coursing through him, and he heard sagas emanating from the stones around him. These were quieter and slower than the ones in the forest, because these stories spoke of things long forgotten and abandoned. No one listened to them now, except for him. Yes, *he* was alive. His mad laughter echoed through the cave.

Yut stepped onto the bronze ring again, dusting himself off, and truly looked at the wulver. He knew the runes carved in its flesh—runes of suffering, hate, cold as ice. He almost remembered what it told him at the ruins entrance, but then the beast pounced again. Its good claw landed hard, but this time Yut was ready. He brought up a hand to intercept the claw, and to his surprise it only managed to push him sideways a few feet, the bronze floor screeching in shock.

The wulver's arm remained interlocked with Yut's, where the golden rune blazed. The wulver lunged to bite his head off, but Yut grabbed one of the fangs with his other arm, holding it in place. It looked impossible to anyone watching, but Yut knew the exact extent of his strength. He knew that a healthy wulver would have been a formidable foe—perhaps too much for him.

But it was not at full strength, so Yut yanked at the fang, pulling the beast off balance. Then he flung the wulver's arm aside, and, grabbing its face with both hands, smashed it against his knee. A bone cracked in the wulver's face, but as Yut wound his fist for a follow-up strike, the monster's arm shot out and scooped his legs. Yut's head banged on the floor just as the wulver's claw descended on him.

He caught it inches from his face, but the wulver was on top of him now, its blood and saliva oozing onto his forehead. It pushed its weight on Yut, the claw closing around his face, and Yut screamed. The golden rune flared once more, and the wulver roared as Yut's teeth dug into its hand. The beast tried to pry it away, but Yut held on, cursed blood filling his mouth. With a jerk, he twisted the wulver's arm, and a snapped bone pierced its forearm from inside.

Yut took advantage of the monster's panic to kick out its leg and quickly rise to eye-level with it. He grabbed its face, and before it could attempt another bite, crashed it into the bronze disc. A loud *bong* resonated throughout the cavern, followed by the wulver's gargled growling. Yut grunted as he brought the head down again and again, until the cavern was filled with the clanging sound of bone on metal.

In the end, Yut was gasping, and the wulver lay motionless in a pool of blood. There was hardly any bronze left to see.

Yut stumbled back. His rune faded soon as the wulver died, and his knees gave out just as he stepped away from the disc.

* * *

Yut watched the wulver carcass for a while, not out of caution but because his limbs were numb. He drifted in and out of consciousness, as if he was in a dream. He jumped when the body moved, however, as sudden squeals of rough metal echoed through the cavern. By that point, the blood had begun to dry, and the wulver's body was long cold. Yut realized with immense relief that it was not the wulver moving, but the disc itself. As it turned, it descended into the earth with a piercing screech. Yut wondered if some ancient trap was activated, but the disc descended harmlessly until silence reigned again.

He remembered emerging into the forest and hearing voices. He yelled—an exhausted, desperate cry—and the voices stopped. He limped and pushed himself through the trees, dismissing visions of wild creatures and gods hiding in the bushes. He remembered falling, and then rough hands shaking him. "Dark below..." Olaf whispered.

Bjarni put his face directly in front of Yut. "Whose blood is that? Where is the wulver?"

Yut felt like his head was miles underwater. "Buried."

Olaf shook his head. "You are one lucky son of a..." Yut faded out of consciousness again, and then awoke by a small campfire, with Bjarni offering him a roasted potato. Yut swallowed that without hardly chewing, though it somehow tasted wrong.

Everything felt...dead. Compared to the exhilaration, the *power* he felt in the cave, everything else was dull. The flames were just flames, and food was tasteless. He was waiting for his normal senses to come back after the power left him, for the relief of being saved by his companions, but all he felt was the emptiness. He was beginning to doubt if he would ever be himself again.

And yet Yut's heart hummed. He went up against a wulver and survived. True, it was an injured and dying one, but a wulver nonetheless. What's more, he was right about his rune. The brighter it glowed, the closer it got him to the state of power. And in that state, he was a god.

What else could it be? The gods gave him this power, so they must have wanted him to be like them. Indestructible. Strong. He just needed to hone it, control it, then he would be unstoppable. Then that darkened wyrm would taste his fury. After all that had happened, he would have his vengeance. After all that had happened, Yut felt a distant pulse of hope.

He needed to learn how to activate his rune whenever he wanted to. He suspected something about the Seither magic made it flare—maybe it was the opposite of the Dark craft, and he was here to destroy it. Perhaps it merely glowed in times of danger. Eira probably knew. She had to. Perhaps his mission was—

"Could've been worse," Bjarni said suddenly, taking a swig from his waterskin.

The other two looked at him, and the short man shrugged. "I'm just saying, no one even lost a limb. I'd call it a success. Downright epic saga, if you ask me. What do you think of this: *The creature stood tall, and seemed even higher. 'Til little brave Bjarni had set him on fire!*" And he raised his waterskin as if it was full of mead, his smile tired but true.

"You ain't the one it was chasing," grumbled Olaf, to Yut's surprise. The warrior looked him straight in the face. "You still look like a pig's ass, by the way. You gonna tell us how you escaped that thing?"

Yut's gaze slipped into the fire again. "I told you already. It was grabbing at me in the dwarven ruin and almost had me. But the ground caved, and we fell into the tunnels. I got out, the wulver didn't." Yut decided to keep his heroics to himself for now. They wouldn't believe him anyway, and it would do no good scaring them like that. He was still unsure of how it worked and did not want them abandoning him out of fear of magic.

"You truly have the luck of the Dark, lad," remarked Bjarni. "Escaping that monster with only a pair of soiled trousers is something any man should be proud of."

There was a moment of tension, expectation, and then Olaf snorted. Bjarni grinned wider, and Yut smirked. "Maybe a little soiled… But not as much as you two oafs, staring at him like it was some darkened fairy tale."

"Hey now, did you not see me set the cursed beast *aflame?* You've never seen anything like that!" Bjarni sprung up and began pantomiming the entire experience. Then Olaf joined in, acting the part of the wulver, and even Yut, his body in pain, made his best impression of soiling his pants. The three laughed as if drunk, the laughter of people who had no business being alive. And in that moment, they found life all the sweeter. Yut's breath caught as he remembered the last time he felt this way. The Proving Moon. He was high on confidence and drunk on mead, dancing and singing until he felt like he was melting. He was also worried about someone learning of his and Keld's scheme to win the People's Brawl. Gods, he would give everything to be worried about that again.

They eventually settled back down, staring into the flames again, which somehow felt warmer and brighter. Yut glanced at his companions and, with a sudden worry, wondered if the Saga would take them away like it had Keld. He clenched his jaw. Not if he could help it. And if he could kill a wulver, he would protect them from harm.

Then, Olaf glanced at Bjarni and said, "I *have* seen it."

The two turned to him, waiting. "Saw what, big man?"

"You said I ain't seen nothing like it. But I saw wulvers, a good dozen of them." Olaf shifted and took a long draft from his flask. How was there still liquid there?

"We were with Heisir Egill's band, chasing down some stragglers from the battle before. It was easy, like the darkened cowards weren't even trying. I was fighting for Vessir back then, before I... well..." *Before I deserted and became a coward myself,* Yut finished mentally.

Olaf examined his flask in detail. "The darkened snakes led us into a trap. Down a ravine, except now they stood smiling like some demons. There was a witch with them, too, front and center, chanting somethin'... *evil.* When the trelkin jumped us, it was too late. We fought like berserkers then, taking out ten, twenty, then fifty of the things with nothin' but our axes and knives. Some of the brothers went down, but we kept fightin'. That is, until we saw the wulvers, which were huge, and came out of holes in the ground, like out of the Dark itself. That's it for the battle, I thought. Poor Egill was the first down—one of the things chopped him up bad." He was gripping the flask and scowling at it, as if he was angry that it was empty. "Anyway, I did see 'em before, and they don't get any prettier."

Bjarni and Yut sat in stunned silence. The coward before them did not run from a war band, or an enemy jarl, but wulvers. Gods below, that didn't count as deserting, did it? Though Yut felt there was more to the story, he was glad when Bjarni finally said, "I'm sorry, brother."

"It's nothing," Olaf said, "Leave the dead in the ground."

"Gods below, is that why..." Yut tried to form his words carefully, not to offend Olaf. "Is that why they call you a... well..."

Olaf continued looking into the flames without emotion. "Nah, I ran plenty of other times."

Yut lay awake for a while after the fire was stamped out. He was exhausted beyond life but could not get the thought of Olaf fighting wulvers out of his head. What was this world he was plunged into, where men fought with beasts and invoked the Dark? He looked at the big man, snoring fitfully, and felt his heart grow heavy.

Coward or not, he felt it was time for a different chapter in Yut's saga. It would be a chapter he wrote. For once, he felt excited for the next day. He may not know much about his power, and he knew dark-all about magic or the Cult or any of that, but he was stronger now. Different. That boy from Sanvik would never survive in the wild. He could never escape a collapsing lightfolk tunnel and explore an underfolk city in the same month. That boy lived a life designed by others, and that boy was gone. Yut would survive. Perhaps he could destroy that wyrm, after all. Perhaps he will find his vengeance, and protect his friends in the process.

Friends, that's right. They were friends now. There would be no more pain training, and Yut dared to hope again. Of course, when Olaf threw a shield at him the next day, Yut learned how painfully wrong he was.

Chapter Twenty-Five

Madness

Heat and steam consumed Sigrid's world. Thin streams of light illuminated little, save empty barrels and rags in the corner of the room. She was submerged up to her eyes in scorching water, feeling the blissful burn on her recent cuts as her muscles relaxed. There was no one with her, of course. Although bath houses used to be common in Miklor, when the war broke out between the cities of Vessir and Rotheim, old Jarl Floki realized brewhouses were far more appreciated by refugees and warriors alike. More profitable, too. Now, most of them were used for brewing beer, except for a few tucked away in forgotten places, reserved for guests of honor, such as a seeress and her companion.

Sig flexed the knots in her back. She would probably need to bathe in lava to loosen those, but the bath did not hurt. No, not at all. She almost felt guilty for enjoying this rare moment of respite, but it was out of her control. Before Eira left her to speak with the jarl, she commanded her to get into the steaming wooden tub, nearly stripping Sig herself. Now, Sig had lost all track of time, as hot water was regularly supplied by one of the jarl's servants, and no one else bothered her. She leaned back in the tub. Surely, Eira would pick her up when she was ready.

Sig thought about the seeress. The shadows were back, there was no denying it, but Eira hardly mentioned them at all during their journey. Sig initially thought Eira was respecting her space, but it had been too long without a word, so she wondered if Eira had forgotten. She wondered if Eira cared.

Stupid, of course she cares. Eira has done everything for her already—the seeress earned the right to worry about her own problems for once. It did not mean she was too concerned with her quest to care for Sig's well-being. It did not mean Eira would not help her with the shadows again. At least, Sig hoped so, because she could never banish them herself. She also hoped they would address it soon, as something told Sig it would only worsen.

She was scrubbing herself with soap and a pumice rock when the knock came. On account of Sig's reputation and Eira's request, the servants were instructed to leave the hot water at the door. Rumors would spread quickly in Miklor, and that is a complication they did not need while they waited for Yut and Olaf to arrive. Sig counted to a minute for the servant to leave, but as she rose from the tub, the door opened.

Sig froze. A pale, small thing trudged in with a full bucket of water, her back hunched and eyes downcast. The hair covering and dress made Sig think this was one of the servants, though obviously one who had missed the jarl's instruction. Sig quickly returned under water, keeping her eyes pinned on the servant girl. *Don't do it,* thought Sig. *Just set the water down and leave.*

And she almost did. She set the bucket near the tub, scanned the pumice rock, the soap, and the herbs to make sure all was in order, and bowed as she made to leave. But when she turned around, her eyes flicked to Sig, once, and again for the quickest double take. And then the door shut, and her footsteps quickly faded down the hallway.

Sig relaxed her grip on the dagger wedged underneath her. Maybe it was curiosity, an innocent look at a secret guest of the jarl, a strange companion of a blind seeress. Of course, who wouldn't be curious? The servant girl looked scared, but that did not necessarily mean she knew about Sig or would tell anyone about her. Perhaps Sig was just paranoid.

"Or perhaps she was sent by someone," seeped a voice in her mind, driving icicles into her spine. He did not sound mischievous this time, but angry, every word coated with disappointment. "*Servants speak. You know this. You know the truth.*"

Sig willed herself to relax, even though the hot water suddenly felt freezing. They will not take her. They are lies. They are not *her.*

She opened her eyes and saw his silhouette through the steam. The dagger flew and thunked against the door, but the shadow remained unharmed. She began to chant through gritted teeth. "Eight gods of old, their saga is told..."

And the shadow disappeared. Surprised, she peered through the room and left the tub, finding them gone. Dark take it, she couldn't tell if them disappearing so quickly was worse than the alternative. She stopped. No, they were not gone. She could sense them, watching her, waiting to catch her unawares at a random moment, just like they did before. Except now she was sure they were getting closer. Sig dreaded what would happen if they closed in—if she would succumb to madness, or go on a killing spree, or end her own life. Probably all of those, though she would not let that happen. Eira would not let that happen.

When the servant returned with another bucket, they found the door ajar and the room empty, save for the thinnest trail of water leading outside.

Chapter Twenty-Six

The Pit

"The pain is good, see," Yut heard. He was lying down but did not know how he got there. It was daytime, but there were stars in his vision.

"Shut up," he growled. His professional respect for Olaf and his darkened training has long since abandoned their journey. It was now replaced by rage and deep, seething regret.

"The young man doubts," intoned Olaf in an enlightened voice. "Heisir Bjarni, would you explain to the young man why the pain is good?"

"Of course, Jarl Olaf." And curse that darkened skald too. Yut sighed as he got up. Rage and regret.

"It means," continued Bjarni, "That you are, for better or worse, and quite inescapably, alive. And that means..."

"You can fight!" roared Olaf, raising his shield.

Dark take him if the two did not become best friends. Something about abusing Yut must have provided an easy connection, though he could not take full credit.

They did not bring up the wulver or the Tova encampment again in their journey. At first, Yut thought they might have forgotten, but then he heard them speak in the night. They spoke of their homeland, battles, and loved ones they abandoned. They spoke of jarls and their ruthless wars, and of those they lost. Those nights, when Yut was too sore to move, he wept.

He wept for Sanvik and for Keld, for the injustice of that Proving Moon. He wept for the Tova boy who was unlucky enough to witness a massacre and die by it. He wept for the hundreds dead at the Red Hill, for the youth whose boots he stole, for the Heisir who died an honorable death. He wept for his parents. He would have wept through the night were he not exhausted, and he would have wept at dawn had they not begun marching at first light. Still, his axe and shield became lighter with every rising, and so did the burden, and the night before they reached Miklor he hardly wept at all.

Soon, their sparring session was over, and Yut took considerably fewer hits this time. At least not humiliating ones.

"We're here," said Olaf when they were on the road again. They were obviously still miles away, but the man must have recognized the path. "We gotta split now."

Yut started. "But Eira said—"

"*Iknowwhatshesaid*. I'm known around these parts, so I got my own way of getting in. We'll meet at the smithy, if Jornar still runs it."

"And if not?" asked Yut.

"Not what?"

"If Jornar does *not* run the smithy."

Olaf thought about this. "He still runs it."

Yut sighed as Bjarni walked up. "You'll like it, Yut. Miklor is a place that appreciates the worth of a skald. And you will get to see the Pit."

Olaf gaped at Yut. "Dark, you've never seen it, have you?"

Yut's father told him about the Pit. A dwarven "relic", though apparently, it was just a deep hole in the ground outside of town. Yut thought he's had enough of dwarven tunnels for a lifetime. Some said Jarl Floki threw prisoners into the hole to rot for the rest of their days, and no one had ever escaped. Though sagas whispered that the dead wandered down there and would moan in the night when they grew hungry.

"I don't see what the big deal is about a hole in the ground," said Yut.

Bjarni just shook his head. "You will."

Eventually, Olaf split East, wading through the high grass and cursing loudly. This left Yut and Bjarni alone for a little while as they approached the city.

"So, you are leaving us?" asked Yut.

"Perhaps. I have some business to attend to in and around Miklor, as I'm sure you do as well."

After a few more minutes, Bjarni looked around and stepped closer. "Does Olaf know about the rune?"

Yut stopped. "How do you...?"

"I know stories," said Bjarni, an easy smile playing on his face. "And I know what to look for. Don't worry, it has not grown visible to others yet, though you are starting to change in other ways, Yut Eriksson. Whatever business you have to attend in Miklor, you should do so quickly, before *others* start noticing as well. When the rune is visible to others, it will be too late."

Yut cursed himself for a fool. Questions tripped on one another before they could escape Yut's mouth, but before he could get the first one out, they crested a hill and saw Miklor.

The clouds had enclosed the world in shadow, but a silver light fell on the city. It stood on a hill, with the jarl's long house overlooking Miklor and its hundreds of buildings. Yut could not believe it at first—he thought that this was where only the gods could dwell, with shields on their walls and the great totems lining the streets. Surely it was too large? Dozens and dozens of smoke trails winded through the sky above it, and there were masses of people inside and outside the thick log walls.

Breathless, Yut tried to gather his thoughts. "Do you... do you know about the Cult?"

"Refugees," said Bjarni, regarding the masses outside the city. "The war drove them to the closest neutral land. More than one orphan and widow hopes for mercy here." Yut was about to repeat the question, but then Bjarni shook his head. "I know plenty of cults, even been in a few for my share. They say it's more enjoyable as a follower, but you can make more silver as a leader. Good place to lie low, too, if you can get in."

"No, the... never mind. What will happen to me? What does the rune mean? Do I just... How do I..."

"I'm just a skald, Yut. I know the stories, and not much more. The new and the old ones, full of magic and rune-children and monsters."

"Rune-children? Why didn't you bring this up earlier?"

"Wasn't sure if you trusted Olaf enough. And yes, rune-children, the agents of the gods imbued with the runes of Orm, given for a specific purpose. I would've thought you heard the sagas—they don't teach you anything these lands, no offense."

"They teach us how to kick a man dodging questions," accused Yut.

"Dodge questions? Me? Well, watch your footing now, or you'll be the one to fall."

"Just answer the—" Yut's next step would not have touched ground, but Bjarni managed to grab his arm before he fell into abyss. Yut stood leaning over and staring into the darkness of the

Pit. It was like looking at some mythical monster, into a darkness that seemed to have substance, which seemed to *move.* Then he was being dragged away, confused.

Bjarni let go of his arm and walked back to the edge of the Pit. "I know of the Cult of Orik, the coward god, and the unseen ones who claim his name for their order. I know one should not utter their name under sun or moon." He affixed Yut with a dark look, "Especially not a rune-son."

"Eira said they are after ones who use magic, and they run the world from the shadows."

Bjarni's brows furrowed at Eira's name, but he continued, "Only gods can command the world, and they will repay the Cult when the time comes. But until then..." He turned and gazed into the abyss, and Yut crawled to join him.

It was not large, perhaps a dozen paces across, flush with the ground, and the most perfectly cut circle Yut had ever seen. Vines climbed down the smooth stone into darkness, and the light did not reach far in. Yut imagined dwarven statues and buildings surrounded the hole in the past, with a continuous stream of the creatures diving and entering their mine shaft, arms, and pockets filled with precious gems.

And then Yut thought that to die of a vicious illness, or even to be sentenced to death, would be better than being thrown into the Pit. Even worse would be to survive the fall. To sit in utter darkness while you gaze at the light above, knowing you would never reach it, would be a torture worse than spending eternity in the Dark.

"Does the jarl really...?"

Bjarni sighed. "Jarl Floki is a gentle old man. His sons, however, are not. I do not know how, but some of the ones they throw down there do survive the fall. At least, for a while."

Yut was about to ask why no signs or fences were built around it, but Bjarni held up his hand. "No more questions, for your own sake. I feel an ill mood approaching. We must separate now. If the gods will, we shall see each other again." He handed Yut a pouch from his pocket. "This will help hide you when they catch your scent. Be vigilant, Yut rune-son, and be strong."

That was the last he would see of Bjarni for some time. Yut stood alone at the Pit for a while longer as the skald walked West. Whatever business he had, it did not lay inside the city itself. Strange. He should have asked Bjarni what his rune meant, or if he had dealings with the Cult, though something told him the short man would have just evaded his questions again. *Does everyone I meet hide a hundred secrets?* But then he remembered Olaf, and thought that there might be some honest people after all. Well, not exactly honest.

Yut opened the pouch, and found it filled with various bark strips, herbs, and nuts. They smelled exactly like nothing.

He left when he thought he heard voices coming from the Pit.

Chapter Twenty-Seven

Miklor

"Oy, red-hair!"

Yut glanced at the refugees surrounding him, realizing he was the closest fit to the description, and looked behind him. There were people everywhere—he was sure he had never seen this many people in one place, and he was not even inside Miklor yet. The giant wooden gate was still a hundred strides away, surrounded by the thick logs of the city's wall. Those were hewed from trees strange to Yut, as he had never seen trunks that thick. He noted the gate itself was shut, but behind it, the city rose like a giant's belly, with its numerous buildings, and the jarl's longhouse at the top. It looked impressive even at a distance.

The refugee area around the city itself was a jumble of tents, camps, cooking pots, the sound of rattling dice, conversations between criminals, warriors, widows, and orphans. Though the latter were not doing much talking. Among the chaos, he saw a man walking toward him—tall, confident, but taking care to avoid the people sleeping. Stepping over a running toddler, he looked Yut over. He had the bearing of a Heisir, still equipped for battle with his black-scaled armor, not to mention the longsword at his side.

Tall and fair-haired, Yut concluded the man was objectively handsome, though a bit on the younger side. The Heisirs that visited Sanvik usually held at least a sliver of gray in their hair, but this one must have been only a handful of years older than Yut. He imagined Yut made him look even better, with his unwashed face and birds-nest hair.

The stranger smiled warmly at him. "Going to the city?"

"No," said Yut coldly, and was surprised. Dark below, he sounded just like Olaf.

But the Heisir just nodded. "Well, if you were going to go, it's locked. No more place for strays, the jarl's boys say, unless someone inside can vouch for you." Then he stepped in close and dropped his voice. "Though if someone *could* vouch for you, I think you'd find no shortage of unfortunate sods who would pay well to tag along."

Yut stepped back, aware of the wrapped sword's weight at his side. Olaf had given it back to him before he left, saying Yut had less chance of being stopped. Yut did not think the man in front of him to be a thief, though he was definitely a soldier, and Olaf said soldiers were worse.

"I don't know anyone in there," said Yut truthfully.

The Heisir continued studying him. "Very well, then we have something in common. Come, join our fire, it's no good being out here alone." He said this in a friendly enough way, but there was little room for refusal in his tone. Without waiting for Yut to answer, the soldier turned and walked back through the forest of people. Yut thought he could bolt for the city gates, but then he imagined twenty stones of chain and axe chasing after him, and decided to follow. The Heisir also held some kind of noble charisma to him, as if there was more to him than what met the eye.

"Name's Ulric, by the way."

Ulric... A shade of a memory echoed from a time before. Yut's mind wandered to the Proving Moon as they entered the camp. There were more soldiers here, men and women, some wrestling, others conversing by the fire. All looked up at Ulric with a light in their eyes.

"He has returned!" Boomed a bear of a man, rising from one of the sleeping cots. He was even bigger than Olaf, except he was also fit and well groomed. Gods above, Ulric *was* a Heisir, and all these soldiers were no doubt under his command.

"You bring us a stray?" Said the woman who had just won the wrestling match. Yut noted she finished off her opponent in an exemplary Bear's Hold. She had glistening metal bits in her braid, which reached the bottom of her back.

"There is more to this man than meets the eye, my friends," announced Ulric. "This here is... well, come to think of it, I never asked your name." But Yut's mind was racing elsewhere as he glanced at the group's standard and the curious warriors around him, then back to Ulric. *It couldn't be...*

"You're Ulric the Tall!" exclaimed Yut, pointing a shaking finger at the Heisir.

"Guilty," grinned Ulric, "And you—"

"Then you're Ysolda, with a braid of lightning!" The woman's expression turned from suspicion to annoyance.

Yut looked at the heavy man. "And you're... well, of course, you're Bjorn the Mountain, bane of armies."

Bjorn smiled and glanced at Ulric. "I like him. Most of this rabble don't know us as they should."

Yut couldn't believe it. Here were the legends themselves—Jorech Sharp-Eye, Axe-head Raina, Sigurd the Small—who did look as short as a child if you didn't look at his face—all real, some of them looking at him. They were all so... human. Yut wouldn't notice them in a crowd, and yet their sagas would no doubt survive for ages. He suddenly felt like a fool, standing in their midst like some gawking farmer.

Ulric watched Yut, allowing him to come to his senses. And then Yut's light faded. *Oh gods, he doesn't know about Sanvik.*

"And your name, if you please."

"Yut Eriksson." There was a pause as the soldiers considered this. Yut felt they expected something more.

"He is being humble!" chimed Ulric, slapping Yut on the shoulder. "This is Yut Strong-Arm! You miserable sheepherders haven't heard of him around these parts, but he's a growing legend."

Ysolda rubbed her chin thoughtfully. "Yut Strong-Arm... You really from around here, then?"

Yut did not know what Ulric was playing at, but now he just felt a bigger fool. He looked at the Heisir. "I'm from Sanvik."

Ulric's eyes flashed and fixed on Yut, just as Ysolda said, "Never heard of it."

"Trust me," said Ulric darkly, "You don't want to. The Pit is nothing compared to that hole." And then he nodded at Yut as if they came to some understanding. "Only the strongest escape."

Now Yut felt truly lost. Did Ulric truly feel that way about his home village, or was he just playing up Yut? Or was this all some joke?

Face still serious, Ulric turned to Bjorn. "Where is the hag?"

"Brother," chuckled the big man, "I've never seen anything the like. The crone bolted not half an hour ago. Didn't think she could even run, but, well, I doubt Ysolda could have outrun her." Some of the legends laughed as well, just like in the stories, and Yut began to feel at ease again. He didn't remember a hag from the sagas, but after his experience with the last one, he was glad she was not around.

Ysolda continued studying Yut. "She was saying some nonsense about a Seither-bane."

"Well, she'll be back whenever she sees fit. Until then, we wait for a miracle to let us into those gates." Ulric winked at Yut and walked to a fire with a pot hanging over it.

Yut's mind raced as he considered the paths before him. Should he tell them about his rune, and the magic, and perhaps get to battle the Dark with Ulric? Was that not what every young warrior dreamed of? Was that not what *he* dreamed of?

"Strong-Arm, come get some grub," called out Bjorn.

They would surely see the stolen sword, and if they recognize it, it will not turn out well for Yut. And what if they despise magic, or worse, if they wouldn't believe him about the rune? He couldn't even get the thing to work when he wanted to.

"Is he praying?"

"Nah, just starstruck by Ysolda."

"Shut up, Jorech."

A cold feeling settled on Yut as something pulled him to look South, toward his home. A raven followed his gaze, gliding over the hunched refugees, weaving between the smoke columns, and settling on the shoulder of a black-robed old man. A cowl obscured his face, but Yut was sure he was watching him. And those eyes never missed a thing.

Yut kept his eyes on the stranger as he spoke. "I can make a way into Miklor, but only for one or two of you."

"Excellent," said Ulric, immediately pouring out his bowl. "Bjorn and I will go when you're ready." Bjorn looked at his bowl, face full of misery, and gave it to another man.

Yut turned from the black-robed elder to look at Miklor. The path of adventure and heroes has been taken from him. A path of vengeance has been offered instead, and it led to a short blind seeress in that city. It was time to move.

* * *

"Who the dark is Jornar?" barked the Miklor sentry. He stood atop the gate, and per Yut's earlier suspicions, it was gigantic up close. There was some kind of tar substance between the logs of the wall, and the gate itself was a thousand stone of plain hardened oak. Yut thought his father would have appreciated its pragmatic effectiveness—it looked simple enough, but you would need an army of giants to force your way inside the city.

He looked to Ulric and Bjorn, cloaked and inconspicuous, standing behind him. Yut admitted he felt a lot more confident of his plan when he was introspecting, but the trusty voice of logic dismantled his confidence the closer they got to the gates. He sighed. It was time to make a fool of himself again.

"The smithy, who else? Tell him Olaf is askin' for him, and he's angry," Yut barked back.

"I look like a messenger boy?"

Yut looked to Ulric again for some kind of help, but the man hid his face behind the hood. *I guess the jarl's "boys" didn't like Ulric in particular.*

Yut inspected the guard again. He was a dog-faced, loud fellow who clearly enjoyed his job. Not the official job, of keeping the city safe, but his natural gods-given job, of being an absolute prick. Yut tried to adopt a look of superior annoyance. After traveling with Olaf and Bjarni, he saw both sides of the negotiation, and in this case, something told him to summon the entirety of his Olaf-ness.

"Listen here, you little runt. My guards and I walked for weeks to get to this darkened city, all because that idiot Jornar sent for me by raven. *A raven,* understand? Now, you can let us in and see our old pal or hear about it from the blacksmith himself. And I reckon you ain't so thick as to get on a blacksmith's bad side, especially Jornar's. So, what'll it be?"

Yut heard Bjorn cover his snicker with a cough, as dog-face dropped his sneer. Yut's own expression was sour, though his heart pummeled.

The guard's eyes narrowed as scenarios and consequences played out in his head. He scoffed. "Fine. But I'll ask Jornar tonight, and if this is some shady business it will be *your* skinny ass, got it?" The double gates creaked open, and Miklor opened her arms for them. Or she raised them.

Yut couldn't help gawking at the world that unraveled before him. It was supposed to be smaller than both Rotheim and Vessir, but he had never seen more wooden buildings in one place. And the *people*. Gods above, they were everywhere. Working, wandering, watching him with suspicion, then interest, then apathy. They were selling wares, begging for coin, entering and leaving, laughing and shouting, singing and sleeping. He wondered where they came from and what their stories were. In Sanvik, everyone knew what everyone was up to, but here, Yut figured it would take years upon years to even learn everyone's name.

Tears of relief crested Yut's eyes. This was not a forgotten forest or an abandoned magical outpost—this was human. Normal. Yes, the city was filled with strangers, and he had never seen anything like it, but gods above, it felt good to be in their midst. Standing on the main road, Yut gazed up at the rising city, where the buildings clamored over each other to reach the jarl's longhouse. It would probably take him a half hour just to make it there. The city was also wider than he thought, as the hill only began to rise further in.

He would have continued staring, but the two warriors took

the lead, navigating behind a nearby outhouse. Having made sure no one was watching, Ulric grinned and punched Yut in the shoulder. "Well done, Strong-Arm."

Bjorn also gave him a healthy slap on the back. "We owe you. Once you're done here, come join us outside the city. We could use a head like yours, not to mention the acting skills. And I'd like to hear the tale of your surname."

Yut nodded as stoically as possible. His back hurt from the slap, but it hurt even more to leave without them. And yet he had made his decision. If he would not be part of the legends, then he hoped he would at least be remembered by some of them. "Gods will that we see each other again," he said.

He watched them disappear into the crowds before becoming aware of the city again. There were plenty of refugees outside the city walls as well as inside. Jarl Floki must have closed the gates when they began to fill Miklor. Some talked and even played music, while others gently swayed as they stared nowhere with empty eyes. Against his better judgment, Yut looked down and thought about the youth whose boots he had stolen. Could the boy's mother be here? Would she recognize her son's belongings?

Yut walked faster through the crowds. He had seen many boys and men dream of the battlefield, but Yut was still searching for that vision of glory. Judging by the Red Hill, and the refugees in Miklor, there was only pain and regret. No, dark take wars and the ones who ignited them.

It did not take long for him to lose regard for time as he explored the city, maybe because he was lost, there were a dozen blacksmiths in Miklor, and no one had any idea who Jornar was. It could have been because merchants accosted him at every corner, peddling fabrics, weapons, and animals for exorbitant prices, all "due to the war", of course. It could have been because varied smells tore his attention into a thousand directions—of roasting mutton and fresh soap, spice and steel, blood and excrement. In truth, Yut wandered because he was young and had never been in a place such as this, so becoming lost in the city was as inevitable as thunder following lightning.

What astounded him more than the grandeur of the city were the details. Though there was a myriad houses, stables, barns, and workshops, each was carved in its own meticulous runes, and nearly all were dressed in colorful fabrics, illustrating clans, animals, and family names. They huddled in groups, while others squatted alone, and still some leaned on trees, rocks, pillars and totems made of stone and timber, presenting themselves in all their glory of brown, light, timber, and unknown wood, standing tall, closed, open, and fearsome. As he wandered among them, it was all Yut could do not to let his jaw drag across the muddy streets.

* * *

Yut had grown dizzy from the blur of faces, buildings, and streets when he learned why no one knew where Jornar was. Most in Miklor referred to him as "the dwarf." Yut had forgotten about the legendary dwarven blacksmith of Miklor, until he tried to wade through a group of orphan kids unashamedly staring at the smith as he worked. Once Yut noticed who they were looking at, he stopped and stared too.

Jornar was half his height, just as Yut predicted, with a short, well-groomed beard that descended from a balding head. His skin was ashen, and tiny rune marks ran up his arms. Those had a blue hue, not unlike the ambient light Yut found in the dwarven city. He was thinner than Yut expected, and clearly enjoyed the rare sunlight as he whittled at some metal bit. Yut had expected some kind of a dwarven hole descending to his workshop, but the shop did not look any different from the other smithies in town. Even Jornar did not look much different from a short man, except for the skin color and the rune marks. Yut wondered if the dwarven image was a trick. After all, who would not want a weapon made by one of the underfolk?

Just then, Jornar snatched a detailing hammer out of his apron and gently tapped his project. There was nothing special to it—no masterful trickery, no dwarven incantations. In fact, he was not even making a weapon, but some kind of shiny decoration. And yet, the ring from that tap did not end.

At first, Yut wondered why Jornar had stopped moving. As the ringing continued, he realized everyone around him stopped moving too—even the orphan that was deftly reaching for Yut's wrapped sword. They were all suspended mid-motion, and Yut was the only one able to move. He instinctively stepped back and saw Jornar's head snap toward him. *Dark.*

And then he was lying on the street, half-submerged in the mud, a dozen curious eyes peering down on him. When he regained his breath, and everything stopped spinning, he attempted to stand. It was a courageous idea, but a far-fetched one. The refugee kids were content to watch him quietly, their eyes trying to peer into Yut's fist clamped around the dwarven amulet at his neck. It hummed softly, and Yut thought he remembered a sudden force exploding from it before his eyes met Jornar's.

Forfeiting the lofty goals of standing upright, Yut managed to kneel, massaging the side where the hilt of the wrapped sword nearly impaled him. Suddenly, a small hand clasped his wrist, and Yut mentally prepared for the possibility of fighting a child-thief today. But for better or worse, the hand was Jornar's, and he did not look pleased. He pointed a thick, metal-dusted finger at Yut.

"You—follow me *now*."

He had a deep, grouchy voice that left no room for questions. Thankfully, the dwarf continued holding Yut's hand as he stumbled through the stupefied children until he shut the workshop door behind them, leaving them in complete darkness.

"Where you get that?" accused Jornar through a thick accent. As Yut's eyes adjusted, he saw two glimmering blue dots where the dwarf's eyes should be. *The fabled darksight of the dwarves.*

Yut instantly took the amulet from around his neck and proffered it to Jornar. "I found it in dwarven ruins south of here. I did not mean to keep it for myself, sir, hoping to return it to whomever lost it. Please, take it. Sir."

Jornar did not move, except that Yut thought he could see the glowing eyes squint. "So, not your? Dvergr not give you?"

"I... well, I took it without anyone knowing, but again, I didn't mean to..." Yut stopped when he heard Jornar mumbling something in dwarvish. It might have been a prayer, incantation, or anything else, but it ended with the dwarf grabbing the necklace from the relieved Yut.

"Thanks," said Jornar. He said a quick dwarven word, and the runes on his arms flashed that same light blue, as a firepit came ablaze at the back of the room, illuminating the rest of the workshop.

Tools of varying size lined the walls, and some were left on tables among opened boxes and barrels. It seemed like the room had only recently fallen into disarray, as if Jornar took up a dozen projects and left them unfinished. There was also a latch in the floor, through which the blacksmith disappeared in short order. Yut tried to peer inside, but saw nothing but blackness. A gust of cold air escaped through it, and Yut nodded. *So he* does *have a dwarven hole.*

"Excuse me, sir Jornar, I was supposed to meet someone here. He looks like—"

Yut barely dodged the vial that flew from the hole. Though even as his body recoiled, his hand instinctively snatched it from the air. Pain training must have accomplished something, in the end. Jornar jumped out with a similar vial.

"Sorry about that," he said, the accent completely gone, "I still forget about the dark thing for you Omri. Anyway, thanks again for the necklace. You're alright, I guess. Drink up."

Yut inspected the green liquid bubbling in the vial. He had given up on people offering him anything good to drink, and this time proved no different. His eyes were watering as soon as he uncorked the vial, and the liquid gave a slight hiss as Yut brought it close. He half-expected there to be something alive inside.

Jornar was already burping from his dose. "Relax—it smells worse than it tastes. Just don't spit it out or I'll kill you."

Dwarven jokes are like dwarven drink, thought Yut. At least, he was mostly sure Jornar was joking. He was a real dwarf, alright, though the fake accent must have made the picture complete for his clients. Rather than take the chance, Yut swallowed the bitter liquid, which pierced his tongue and throat with a thousand sudden pinpricks. It felt like he was swallowing a porcupine, but instead of blood and holes, the drink merely left a fruity aftertaste.

And then he burped half of his lungs out. Eyes wide, Yut clamped his mouth shut too late, but Jornar merely chortled. "Impressive, eh? Brew this stuff myself. Spekta, I call it. It's not for everyone, sure, but that jarl's son whatshisname—the fat one—drinks it like water. Anyway, the ruins to the south, you said? Musta been Raithogradr. Big place, old place. Easy for an old dvergr like me to miss a trinket like that."

Yut coughed out what he hoped was the last of the gas before talking. "Dvergr... You collect the amulets?"

"Aye."

"For your people?"

Jornar snorted. "For coin. It's close to pure gold, ya know. Besides, not like they'll need it."

"Ah." They said in silence for a thoughtful minute until Yut cleared his throat, curiosity getting the best of him. "So... why *did* your people—"

"Nope," interrupted Jornar, hopping off his stool and shutting the latch to the dwarven hole. "I don't talk about that. To anyone. I can get you another Spekta, but that's as far as my gratitude goes. And I'm busy now. Loads of work, loads of work."

Yut stood as well. "My apologies. I was just hoping to wait for my friend here. Olaf said to meet at your smithy once he's able to..." The sentence seemingly died along with Jornar's spirit. The dwarf was facing away, but You could see his shoulders slump as he gave an audible sigh.

"Olaf the hog-chaser?"

"Um... Definitely."

Jornar turned around and started rummaging through the bins and barrels. "Wastin' your time. That darkened trelkin still owes me good silver, which means he won't be showing his face around here until he thinks I forgot. He probably also caught on that our good jarl has doubled the guard everywhere except the Mudwall, and he owes the jarl a lot more than—dark!"

He recoiled from the bins, hissing and shaking his hand. Flecks of black-red blood spattered the floor, and he stuck the hurt finger in his mouth. After a masterful blend of curses in both dwarvish and human, he carefully approached the box again. A strange sound came from it, like a high-pitched growling, and Yut took a step back.

"Damn fanglings too good at their job sometimes," grumbled the dwarf as he edged closer to the box. In one quick motion, he pulled the good hand back as something small and furry leaped out of the box, trailing the dwarf's finger by an inch. Yut caught a flash of sharp teeth. At the same time, Jornar grabbed a pouch from the bin with the other hand, just before the fangling fell back in. It snarled miniaturely.

Jornar shoved the box back under the table and tossed the pouch to Yut. "Remember to feed your fanglings, or they get proper good at their job."

"I don't think we have those," said the stupefied Yut. The pouch was heavy, and by the sound of it, was filled with silver.

"Well, don't just stand there," grunted Jornar, bandaging his finger. "Count it, taste it, whatever it is you people do. I reckon it's close enough to the true value, minus handling fees and all that."

Yut was still confused, and plainly showed it on his face, to which Jornar plainly showed his annoyance. "The *sword.* Hogchaser sent you here for a reason, didn't he? And what better reason than to pawn off somethin' he stole? And I don't do this often, mind you. A sword is a tool, like any other weapon, and stealing a person's tools is punishable by death where I come from. At least, it ought to be. But, seeing how the oaf owes me, and the owner of that sword ain't got no breath left to argue, I figure fair is fair."

Yut reached for the wrapped weapon at his side as things began falling in place. "But you haven't even seen it."

"Three rubies in the pommel, one sapphire at the fore-hilt, inlaid with gold. Beech—no, maple composition. Iron is purified, leather is treated thrice, wrapped in soft cloth, I reckon crimson or azure. Steel is pattern-welded, and it sings even now."

The dwarf grinned at Yut's expression and crossed his arms. "This smith still knows his craft. Now, if ye don't mind, you can leave it right there on the table. And if ye do mind, then good luck sellin' it elsewhere in this darkened town. And you can give my silver back to the fangling."

The Heisir's sword was quickly replaced by the coin pouch, and Yut was gently pushed and kicked out of the smithy. The orphan kids had disbanded at that point, though Yut still made sure no one watched him hide the pouch deep in his tunic. Gods, he met a real dwarf, who was actually a civilized tradesman, all things considered. Somehow, Yut wished to meet him again someday.

But more than anything, Yut wanted to tell this story to Keld, and watch his friend's eyes widen when he told him about that Spekta drink. He might not believe Yut at first, but imagination and curiosity would get the better of him in the end; that's just how Keld was. Yut wanted to tell his mother about the strange amulet and his decision to return it. She would have nodded in approval, and probably tell him some piece of lore about the underfolk that he would forget the next day. How he wished to confirm his father's suspicions that these underfolk were just like them, with a heart, a mind, and a soul that wished to create. If only he had a home to return to, Yut's travels would be complete. Then no amount of discomfort or pain would be too much, and his heart would hold no fear or hatred.

Yut clenched his jaw. *If only.* He scanned the street for watchful eyes again, thankful that his vision was not obscured by tears, and continued his walk. After all, there were plenty more buildings to look at.

* * *

And yet there were eyes on him—mainly, Jornar's. The dwarf watched Yut through a slit in the windows, his face grimmer than usual. Even after Yut disappeared, he stared into the distance, clenching and unclenching his jaw and fists, like he was preparing to jump into an icy river.

Grumbling curses, he eventually uprooted himself and lumbered into his tunnel. It was pitch black, and cold, and though Jornar was fond of the light of the sun, here he truly felt home. Here, he felt safe. Or at least he used to.

His dwarven sight caught the glimmer of the new amulet hanging on the wall, reflecting a bit of light that managed to slip through the latch. It was joined by a dozen others. Had there been more light, they would have gleamed with a radiance of well-polished metal, the result of his hard work. Had there been more light, they would have shimmered, because lately the amulets have taken to moving of their own accord.

Jornar first saw it days ago. The slight vibration and hum of the amulets interrupted his sleep. It soured his suppers, it weighed on his craft, so much that he had stopped working on weapons all together. And now, he stared at them for the hundredth time, eyes twitching. Especially at the amulet in the center, from which the hum reverberated the most. The amulet that he picked up at the temple-chamber Raithogradr.

The amulet that had begun to drip blood.

The timing with the Omri kid was too close to be coincidence, but he dared not question him further. Besides, whatever he did to that altar could not be undone. The amulets hummed, as did a myriad more, out across the mountains of the world, in the cities of his kin. Jornar knew what it meant, but of course, he would not tell anyone. All Jornar did was take a few more shots of Spekta, snatch the stuffed backpack hidden in a corner, and escape into the tunnel, where no human, lightfolk, or dwarf could follow him.

At least, he very much hoped so.

Chapter Twenty-Eight

Reunion

Yut's wandering came to a conclusive end when he was attacked in the street. When he saw a hand reaching out from a group of refugees, Yut dismissed them as another beggar, until they grabbed him by the elbow. Whether it was Olaf's training or the weight of the silver in his tunic, Yut wasted no time gripping the hand and flipping the attacker over his shoulder and into the mud.

The woman gasped, but to his surprise, instantly lashed out with her foot. Yut dodged the well-aimed kick at his face, which allowed him to notice her other leg going for his feet. *Everything starts and ends at the base, boy,* echoed the painful lesson. Yut switched his footing, kicked her foot away, and fell on her.

He managed to pin her and was about to growl obscenities until her hood slipped, and Sigrid's icy eyes stopped him dead.

"Sig? I—"

She used the hesitation to slip her arm free and punch Yut in the throat. He staggered off her, and amid the pain and the coughing, she pulled him into a nearby alley. Adjusting her hood, she looked around furtively. "Didn't mean to scare you there, drengr, but it's good to know you learned something from Olaf.

Eira will be pleased." She seemed healthier to Yut. Or, at least she smelled better than before. Her braids were clean, and her face did not have splotches of dirt anymore. Her eyes still unnerved him, though, especially now that they had a dark, haunted look. Strange, he would have thought she had plenty of sleep in the city.

She patted Yut on the back as he continued coughing. "You look like a rabid rat," she added kindly.

"I would have had you pinned," wheezed Yut.

"Of course, you would have. Where's Olaf?"

"He's not with you?"

"Figures. Follow closely." Before he knew it, she was striding through the throngs of people. Somehow, she managed to step on all the dry spots, while Yut sank ankle-deep into the mud on every other step. Sigrid glanced back at him repeatedly to ensure he was close.

Then she took a sharp turn, vaulted over a fence, and continued through a slim tunnel between two houses. Yut was glad to escape the crowd, though he was surprised at how little he cared about trespassing on other people's property. Gods, he looked like a barbarian and acted like one too. At least, that's what his mother would say.

"Any idea where he's gone off to?" asked Sig over her shoulder, as they hopped another fence to emerge on a street cleared of the refugees. They were closer to the top of the hill now, and the jarl's hall looked more impressive still. Dozens of shields were mounted on its walls, and giant totems stood at its edges. He could only imagine the detailed runes that decorated it.

"He said he'll find another way in, that people know him here."

"Bet they do, though I suppose it doesn't leave many places he could hide." Sig had stopped in front of a large building—not quite a house, but not a long hall either. It reminded Yut of the meeting hall from Sanvik, though this one was made of mostly wood and did not smell of old people. Light and music emanated from within, and a few people drifted in and out.

"She waits inside," said Sig, "Try to keep that thing in your pants, drengr." Yut realized she meant the axe at his side, but not before beginning to blush. And then, by the gods above and below, Sigrid smiled. It was a laughing smile, slightly mocking, and yet it was like watching a lynx pounce at its prey—he wasn't sure whether to feel enchanted or terrified.

"Y—uh, you're not coming?"

Her face became grim as she hid her face in the shadows of her cowl. "I must find the oaf, and I'm afraid I will find him in a fouler place than this. Keep an eye on her, I'll be back soon."

Chapter Twenty-Nine

Truth in the Shadows

Sig waded through the mud-rivers of Miklor, a stolen cloak shrouding the features of her face, all save her eyes. Those flicked between the passing people of Miklor: the broken and lame, poor and hungry, the real ones and... well, the others. Her shadows did not leave after the bath house. On the contrary, they became bold, watching her from the corners and the alleys without even bothering to hide.

After seeing them for days, she realized she wanted to see them clearly. She wanted to speak with them and learn how they could live peacefully, but they always escaped even if she ran after them. They came and went on their own terms, as if she was not worthy of dialogue. The bastards. She would banish them again, she owed it to herself, but that would come later. For now, she had a job to do.

The poor little mouse had become a gnarled rat. That's not a compliment she would give to most, but Yut surprised her. He was gaunt, filthy, and obviously lost when she saw him in the middle of Miklor's streets, and yet there was an unmistakable ice in his eyes. He survived, and he meant to survive. Now, she had to watch her back around him.

Her path led her to the other side of town, to the bottom of the hill, to a place they called the Mudwall. In Miklor, the jarl's mud, sweat, and refuse began at the Great Hall, then slithered down through the streets and alleys and yards of good hard-working folk and their livestock, then through the huts of the poor and the forgotten, and finally rested at a place good, hard-working folk took care to avoid, a place called the Mudwall, where the "mud" now made up half of the city's wall.

The perfect place to find Olaf.

This was the last place she wanted to be and the last person she wanted to see, but Eira wished it, and Sig found that following orders helped her focus. She would need a lot of focus if she were to banish the shadowed ones away again.

She slipped through the descending streets, choked with refugees and excrement, watchful of straying hands. It was quieter here, the sound of hope given up. She noticed the child when she approached the Mudwall. Perhaps it was her recent visit with Eivor, and her abandoning the kid to whatever fate Gyldryn had for her, but he caught her attention. It was the only refugee that looked in her eyes, the only one not afraid. The boy's face was nearly indistinguishable from the street save for two clean lines from the tears.

Focus. She had a job to do. The child kept watching her as she continued past him. There were plenty of other kids here, plenty of hungry mouths, and she was Sigrid, a warrior, a Speaker, and she was... not a monster. The child watched as Sig backtracked and handed him the last of her jerky.

In return, he shoved a dagger at her stomach.

She just managed to grip the blade, a sharp pain blooming in her fingers. It was not a powerful jab, but the dagger was barely smaller than the child, and the tip pierced skin just above her belly button. The kid's hands shook as Sig threw the dagger to the side, and she would have done more had a pair of stronger hands not grabbed her from the back, one hand pulling at her cloak and the other at her elbow.

That left one elbow free, which swiftly smashed the assailant's nose. He fell, clutching his face with one hand, and the other pulling Sig's cloak away. It was another kid, maybe a few moons older. The first one had already bolted as Sig snatched up the cloak and covered herself. The people sitting nearby made as if to move away, but the whole scene took less than two heartbeats, so they were content to pretend nothing happened. At least, as content as they could get.

A kick to the kidneys sent the second youth flying after the first, and Sig slipped away. She saw figures disappearing through doorways and alleys—real figures, she was sure, ones that might be desperate for the blood of a young woman who looked like lightfolk, to sell or drink or worship. The shadow's earlier warning became a reality as excited rumors spread amid the jarl's servants. A lightfolk was among them. The berserker possessed by an elf spirit. A killer who made the jarl's personal guards look like puppies. If she laid eyes on that servant girl again, she might just prove them right.

Focus. She moved deeper toward the Mudwall, feeling eyes creep over her. They had seen her face, and she could feel their imagination painting grand pictures of a captured half-breed, a slave whose blood could heal mortal wounds, extended life, made one rich. To be fair, the last one was true, but only due to greedy, ignorant, foul people who wanted—

Focus! Escaping her thoughts had become increasingly difficult the longer she stayed in Miklor, but thankfully the Mudwall cleared her mind and her sinuses, its stench making her eyes water. It was a man-made hill of mud, refuse, bones, broken wood, and all other unwanted things heaped against the wall. There were rumors that some brave souls dug a tunnel under the city wall and through the Mudwall to find refuge in Miklor. Not worth it for a thousand silver, thought Sig. Still, there were people here, and they were exactly the type of people you'd expect to find here. Sig stayed close to the shadows.

It did not take long to hear Olaf's barking timbre, and it came from a half-submerged shack near the Mudwall itself. Shadows lurked within the gaps in the rotted plank walls, and she heard other voices. Normally she would wait for the oaf outside, but she did not want to stay here a second longer. She slid into the hut, one hand on her dagger.

She found only one room inside, and it was empty.

The door slammed shut behind her, and got a dagger embedded in it for its trouble. Sig already had two more unsheathed as she went low and prepared for an ambush.

But no ambush came. There was less light than there should have been in the silver-lit room, so she closed her eyes and breathed deeply, dreading another attack of the shadowed ones. Were they impersonating Olaf? She wiped her forehead, forcing her heartbeat to slow. Her body remained her own, so she cautiously went for the door. As her fingers touched the old wood, a voice spoke from the back of the room.

"She hasn't told you the truth, has she?" Another dagger flashed across the room, impaling the wall mere inches from the old woman's face. The hag didn't flinch, instead her black eyes bored into Sig, almost accusing her.

"Who the dark are you?" Sig asked quickly, ready to run at the first sign of movement. She would have already been gone, but something about the old woman caught her attention. Her clothing...

"You don't know a seeress when you see one? Do I wear white for nothing?" That explained the dim light and the illusion of Olaf's voice—this was a Speaker. *And I don't know any who are not with the Cult already.*

"You revealed your face, girl, and that is dangerous around here. You should know better, Sigrid Light-blood, daughter of carnage." The seeress' tone was playful, but her dark eyes betrayed no humor. The silver light revealed rune marks on the woman's face, seeping into a thousand wrinkles. They multiplied as the hag smirked. "Or so they claim."

"You are the one who shouldn't have shown your face, hag. Though I should thank you for revealing the Cult's position here. So fitting, right next to the biggest pile of refuse in Arthgard." The Seither began to reply but Sig cut her off. "A single rune-word comes out of your mouth and I will split you. What business have you in Miklor? What do you want with us?"

The Seither sat in silence for a moment, examining Sigrid. "Such talent, squandered amongst the pieces of your shattered potential—and all thanks to the blind one. She is a manipulator, girl, the very best among us. And you fell right into her—"

Sig rushed the hag. In a few strides, Sig had her pinned to the wall, a dagger to her throat. She was lighter than she looked, no heavier than a pile of dry cloth. Sig slapped her twice before talking. "You will answer my question, witch. I'll be doing the entire world a favor if I slit your throat right now."

A gargle came from the Seither and Sig eased the dagger at the crone's throat, blood amassing at her fingers. She came surprisingly close to ending the woman right then. Her vision darkened at the edges, as restraining herself from killing became harder than she expected—why? Every instinct told her to do it, but that would do no good, right?

"The boy... we know what Eira is planning, but she is merely playing into our hands. The Grand Saga will be completed soon. Our champion will stand victorious after the final battle, and your friends will perish. This is the way it must be, this is what Aslaug Spoke, and this is how it will end. But I did not come here for Eira or for the boy, Sigrid, I came here for *you.*"

The Grand Saga? The champion? It sounded like the Cult knew more about Eira's plan than Sig. *She can't get into my head, they're all manipulators.*

Including Eira, said the familiar smooth voice behind her. So, the shadowed ones were here after all.

"You have me now, dark-walker, and if you want to kill us you should have tried—"

"Nobody wants to kill you, Sigrid," chortled the hag, "You must understand this—nobody wants anything to do with you at all! You are nothing to us or our plans. Eira has worked so hard to blind you, to make you feel important, as if your saga matters at all, but I merely wanted to see the look on your face when I told you the truth. And after I tell you, I want you to doubt me, just to see it devour you from inside..."

You are not ready for this truth, said the cold voice, getting closer. Shadowed hands drifted toward the Seither, toward her throat. So this was it, they closed in at last, and it was inside a random hut by the Mudwall. Sig let the witch collapse on the floor.

"Stop," she commanded. To her surprise, the hands halted. They had never obeyed her commands before.

"The voices... are not what you think," gasped the Seither, blood blooming on her white robes. "A pretty story to help you cope with the truth you've known all along, that a—"

Sig's dagger flicked across the hag's throat, controlled by her hand but not by her. The shadows vanished.

Blood flowed freely from the Seither, but she did not crumple to the ground. Instead, as she slumped forward, her skin turned a green-brown color, and piece by piece she came apart into a pile of autumn leaves, sitting quietly in the foul, hot room. Sig's mind did not dwell on the Seither magic, nor whether the hag truly died.

"What did she mean?" She said to the emptiness. There was no sinister laughter, no cryptic answers. "What do you know? *What is the truth*?" Her voice cracked. Her head becoming lighter, she fell to her knees. "Why are you here?" Her heart beat frantically, but this was not an attack from the shadowed ones. On the contrary, she felt more alone than she had in a long time. She did not know what this meant, but it did not seem real.

She remembered the village, but not its name. It was summer, they were preparing for the harvest celebration, and she was running through the mud with the other kids. Then it was night, filled with torches and resigned faces. Strong hands took her, but she was too young to understand what was happening. Her caretaker, an older woman who loved her, was held back by some of the others. There was a flash of white, a dagger, and a hand extended to her. She took it, as she was afraid, and it made her feel safe. She was covered in blood—gods, the villagers were screaming. They were all screaming so loud.

Sig drifted out of the vision with a sharp pain in her head. Mission... she had a mission to do. She was supposed to find someone, but when she finally turned to leave, a dozen shapes covered every way out. Fear gripped her—they were not the shadows. She must not have heard them in the rush of blood in her ears. Their eyes were hungry, and when she saw the chains and clubs, reality rushed in—Sig knew too well what this was.

"Relax, half-breed. The seeress told us not to kill you," said the ugliest one, "but that's fine by us, see. Just wanted to show you a bit of Miklor hospit—" He couldn't finish on account of the dagger in his lung. Sig threw two more, one hitting its mark, before the rest of them caught on. The lack of light was to her advantage, but the space was not.

She got a couple more before they overwhelmed her. She was pinned to the wall in the corner, her face bloodied, when one of the captors whispered, "And for that, we'll be takin' our time with you."

"At least turn me around so I don't smell your breath," hissed Sig. "Your mates know you've been eating from the wall?" She spat blood in his eyes, and he slapped her, hard. *Good*. It was best to get them angry. It may be more painful, but anger meant mistakes, and that meant a chance to escape, though it was hard to imagine a way out of this one. For better or worse, the shadows were not coming, and she was immobilized in a corner of a small room. She might get them angry, but not much else.

"You darkened helseed..." hissed the attacker, wiping his face, "You'll be beggin' for death when I'm done with you."

Before she could respond, he clamped a sweaty hand over her mouth. Sig closed her eyes.

And then a loud *thunk* shook the hut, as if from an impact, followed by muffled, pained curses outside. The captors exchanged confused looks, and then a hand burst through the wall, grabbed smelly-breath by the face, and dragged him *through* the wall into the blinding light of day.

Hands went from Sig back to clubs and chains, but the hole in the wall was more than the hut could handle, and the structure began its loud collapse. The attackers surged for the hole to escape the imminent crash, which effectively blocked it, and soon the hut and the irony came crashing down on everyone inside.

It was not enough to kill, but in the chaos of snapped boards and kicking legs, Sig found escape. She stumbled out of the wreckage, but when she wiped the blood from her eyes, she stopped short. Before her, the foul-breath was in the middle of having his face restructured by a cursing, sweating, mad hog of a man. For the first time in her life, Sig was truly glad to see Olaf.

Upon seeing her, he stood up, and nodded to the ones emerging from the wrecked hut. "We runnin'?"

"No."

"Good." He tossed her a long-knife, and they set to work.

* * *

It was not too long before they sat at the wreckage of the old hut, Sig cleaning her knives, Olaf looking for valuables among the dead. They did not put up much of a fight, probably because they were poor, and starving, and never got any proper training save being beaten in the streets by the jarl's men. This, unfortunately also meant they had precious little to take.

Olaf grumbled with each empty pocket, and Sig watched him from the corner of her eye. It might have been wise to move away from this place as far and as fast as possible, if not for possible trouble from the guards, then from the smell of the Mudwall. But Olaf was a scavenger to his bone, which meant he lived on the principle of leaving no pocket unturned, no matter how empty it was. To her own surprise, an imperceptible smile passed along Sig's face. Sometimes, it was nice to rely on someone.

Olaf eventually sat down not much richer than he was an hour ago, a stride away from her, looking annoyed. He began cleaning his own axe, but suddenly stopped and looked at Sig, a mix of surprise and curiosity on his face, as if he had just noticed her sitting there. Gods above, he might have completely forgotten about her.

Sig realized she was staring back at him, assessing, judging what he might be thinking—no, expecting. Only one person had saved her life before, so this was still new to her. She thought about saying 'thanks' but that didn't sound like her. Then there was an option of a light-hearted "took you long enough" or "guess you could've done worse with that axe" but it seemed like the moment for jokes had passed and they were looking at each other and Olaf still did not say a single cursed word. In the intensity of the moment, Sig pursed her lips and gave a weak but, in her mind, meaningful nod, before promptly deciding that her daggers could use a third cleaning.

Thankfully, Olaf nodded as well and began wiping the blood and bone from his dwarven axe with a piece of unbloodied cloth from one of the corpses. Dark, you really can get used to anything, if you can get used to the smell of Mudwall. After looking at the mountain of excrement once more and deciding that she wouldn't be eating anything for the rest of the day, or possibly the rest of her life, she reached into her satchel. She still had the bit of jerky that she gave to the stupid con-kid. Of course, she took it back from him—she had principles, too. Making the necessary attention-grabbing hand motion, she tossed it at the big man.

The grin that split his face reminded her of a child, so in a way the idea remained the same. She watched him inhale the jerky, lick his blood-crusted fingers, and follow up with an unknown liquid from his forever-flask. He caught her watching and proffered the flask to her. It must have been the shock of the gesture, or simply the strangeness of the moment, as Sig in turn found herself putting the flask to her lips. The fire it contained nearly melted her tongue off. *How could anyone drink this stuff? And why would they want to?* She did not recognize the brew, but it must have been used for cleaning metal.

Olaf stopped laughing a minute after she stopped coughing. Sig thought of fixing him with her stare but thought there were too many tears in her eyes to make it at all threatening. Instead, she found herself chuckling as well.

The laughing stopped abruptly, however, when they heard the dogs. For obvious reasons, no strays lived in the lower city, especially near Mudwall, so dogs now meant only one thing: Jarl Floki's men.

One more look was exchanged, and the two disappeared without a sound.

Chapter Thirty

The Tavern

Yut watched Eira sip her ale. She had a neat way of drinking it, as if she merely wanted to taste the foam. She wouldn't let him order one, insisting he needed to keep a "sharp mind and a sharper eye" in this place, though she was happy to use some of his new silver. Yut, once again, had no idea what she meant, but he surmised that it was better to do as Eira says when it came to these kinds of things.

He decided to distract himself by watching the tavern patrons, keeping a casual hand on his axe, and putting on his best we-don't-want-trouble-and-neither-do-you face. The concept of the tavern was novel to Yut, as the long house was the only place of communal drinking in Sanvik. This, however, seemed more like a meeting place, with a large fire pit in the middle and various tables strewn about. Yut thought it was not very space-efficient, however it was perfect for strangers who wanted to drink in peace. In a town this size, everyone was surely a stranger.

The sun was preparing to set, and the farmhands and miners were coming in for a horn of ale for the day. The city guards seemed to filter most of the refugees out of this tavern, but the mood was not much brighter because of it. At some point, a few of them took out strings, pipes, and a couple of drums. The tables were crowded when the tavern door burst open, and Ulric strode in. He did not see Yut as he made for a table on the other side of the room. Nonetheless, Yut sat a little straighter. Ulric threw himself down at a bench, where some workers cleared the table for him.

Yut considered. He glanced at Eira. "There is someone I want you to meet."

"Is it your quiet, observant twin brother? I'd love to."

She had barely said two words to him when they met, but Yut decided to be a little more patient. At least, until they were outside of the city. There were things he had to tell her, and questions he needed answered. During their journey, he had become keenly aware of how little she revealed to him, though he could not arrive at a sensible reason for the secrecy. He prepared his questions well this time.

"You know," said Yut, "I'm sure if you tried to—and I mean really tried—you might make some friends in a town like this."

"The path we tread allows for no friends, Yut."

"Well, it should allow for this one." Yut narrowed his eyes, "What are you doing, anyway?"

"Listening."

"No, come now."

"Right, I would be listening were it not for the unending fount of noise spewing around these parts." She took a long pull from the mug, abandoning neatness. "I listen to the people, for in the sounds of gossip and rumors lie the seeds of the truths we seek."

Yut stood. "Very good, seeress, but you are still not escaping meeting my new friend, Ulric."

Eira tightened her lips as Yut called out to Ulric. The Heisir glanced from his table, where a few people had already joined him. *If you can't keep company, then you can't be a legend,* noted Yut.

Ulric finally recognized him, hailed him, and strode to their table.

As Yut rose to meet him, Ulric stopped and looked intently at Eira. Yut should have known—he must have seen her condition and was plagued with pity. Or reverence. She still had her lips in a line and communicated about as much friendliness as a stone. *A socially awkward stone?*

"Eira, this is my friend Ulric the Tall, the one from the sagas. Ulric, this is—"

"I know who she is, Strong-Arm," replied Ulric, eyes still affixed to Eira. "What I don't know is why you are sitting with her." His hand inched closer to the axe on his hip. He looked as if he was ready to strike Eira down where she sat.

Yut cleared his throat. "That's interesting. Well, Eira, would you like to—"

In that instant, Ulric decided to strike Eira down where she sat. His axe was out and sailing toward Eira's head before Yut could interfere, yell, or do anything at all.

Incredibly, Eira sprang to the side, avoiding the axe head by inches. It slammed into her chair, and before Ulric could pull it out, Eira turned and spewed ale into his face.

Ulric yelped as he stumbled back, struggling to wipe alcohol from his eyes. People around them scooted chairs back, some shuffling outside, others standing to get a better look. Before anyone could interject, however, Eira tore the axe from the chair and held it up to Ulric's neck.

The drums stopped. No one moved.

Yut had no idea how she was able to move so quickly and keep the axe from cutting the Heisir's head off. Dark take it, he had no idea how this situation even happened. Was it something he said...?

Eira continued holding the axe to Ulric's neck, who had stopped moving as soon as he felt the razor shaving his neck hair.

She had to hold her arm vertically to reach the part underneath his chin, and Yut would have laughed at the disparity between their heights, had this been from one of Bjarni's stories. Unfortunately, this was no story.

"Alright," croaked Ulric, blinking the remains of the ale from his eyes. He looked like he was desperately trying to wink at someone across the room but did not know how. "You made your point, witch."

"Did I?" asked Eira, "I believe we were just getting started."

Ulric's voice was cold. "You know what this means. You are dead. Your friends are dead. You can hide under the deepest root of the highest mountain, but we will find you. We always find the oathbreakers."

"Almost right, little mutt." Eira pressed the blade deeper into Ulric's throat. "*They* will find me. You will only find the inside of your throat strewn across the floor."

Yut noticed small movements throughout the tavern as they stood there: hands grasping for axes, postures shifting, eyes flitting between them and the door. *Some will run,* thought Yut, *some will pounce. Some will fight to protect the seeress, others will aid their friend Ulric.* Gods, they were supposed to keep low.

He had to do something. But what? The tension in the room was impenetrable. Perhaps a good joke? A deft explanation? Yut surveyed the farmhands, miners, and laborers standing around the room. No, these people were not hungry for humor. Half of them were exhausted, overworked, and dejected for most of their day. And the other half were refugees torn from their homes. They were hungry for stew and ale, but they were also hungry for something else. You could see it in their eyes.

Right.

Propelled by the building adrenaline, Yut grabbed Eira's mug of ale and launched it at the tall woman behind him, hitting her square in the face.

"You keep your hands to yourself, you lousy..." He searched for a good insult, as the woman stood back in surprise. He had to have a good insult—something that will get her angry, but not enough to kill him.

"You lousy Rotheim dog. Long live the twins!" He finished lamely. The woman's face shifted from surprise to confused frustration. Then to a sour menace. Yut stepped back and glanced to the side, where Eira and Ulric were still interlocked in their standoff. But people were now shifting their attention between the instigators and their neighbors. Surely, there were some Vessir supporters here? Miklor was a neutral ground, but most of them had to be on the side of Rotheim, and if they were a drawn bow, Yut provided an excellent target. And he called the shooter a lousy dog. In a matter of moments, brows were furrowed, knuckles were cracked, and sides were taken.

And then the room exploded.

Eira and Ulric were forgotten as a chair sailed across the room in Yut's vague direction, but it hit the woman who was already marching toward Yut, who fell and toppled a gang of sudden supporters, who ran into other peaceful citizens of Miklor—who were sick of being treated as peaceful citizens—who, in turn, grabbed the poor drummer, who had somehow begun drumming again at double speed, inspiring the rest of the tavern's patrons into an outraged frenzy of violence.

It worked, thought Yut, as a half-eaten chicken bounced off his face.

Wiping grease off his forehead, he tried to look for Eira's white cloak in the madness. He dug through legs, upturned tables, and slippery floors until he was covered with ale and spit, but there was no sign of her. He began having doubts about putting a blind woman in the middle of a tavern brawl. As a rogue chair leg barely missed his face, Yut's legs were yanked out from under him. Above him stood the woman with ale on her face.

Frantic, Yut looked for something to cover himself with, as she dragged him closer to her. *How is she so strong?!* Around him the madness only grew, but it did not stop his nemesis from growling at him as she raised her fist. There was a clear miscalculation—the one he assumed was a housewife must have been the jarl's personal bodyguard on her day off.

"Look, I'm so—"

A shield slammed the side of her head, knocking her off Yut and into the chaos of people. Eira stood behind her like a lighthouse in a storm, still holding the shield.

"Out!" She yelled, extending her hand.

He was too happy to take it as she navigated them through the coiling bodies of fury. Horns flew, tables splintered, and the drummer played even faster. There was no sign of Ulric, and the part of his mind that was not delirious with adrenaline was impressed with Eira's maneuvering through the battlefield. He still got socked a few times with various blunt objects, but eventually they managed to escape through the tavern's back door.

After a few minutes of sprinting, they sat outside of town, gasping. "Friends, huh?" She breathed. Yut elected not to answer.

Chapter Thirty-One

Answers

They were nearing the woods outside of Miklor when Yut stopped following Eira. The brawl in the tavern continued long after they left, and even spilled into the streets, until the jarl's sons intervened. They said that a wanted Heisir attacked a seeress, and in the commotion of this news, Eira and Yut made their escape.

And now, safe from immediate danger, Yut could not take it any longer. For the past few weeks, his life had been lies shrouded in secrets, and the one person who got him into this mess walked not a stride away.

She heard him stop, of course. "Do not worry, child, Sigrid and Olaf are waiting in the woods. You will need to—"

"I am not a child." Gods, he felt like a child saying that, but Yut had to make a stand now. Eira stopped too, and turned sideways to him, head downcast, which Yut decided meant she was listening intently.

"You have something to say?" she asked slowly.

Yut swallowed. "Yes, er... Enough. I've been trusting you this far, seeress, but, with all respect, there has been nothing to show for it. You told me a great deal about some cult and vanished. You told us to walk to Miklor, and now we are leaving after barely a few hours in the city. You told me that I would learn about the... power, but I know less about it now than before. You told me you'd give me *answers.* But, apparently, you know Ulric, and he called you an oathbreaker, and now we are his enemies? I followed you blindly this far, and now I'm *literally* following you. Dark above, Eira, what was that in the tavern? Are you even blind?" Yut felt a fire building inside him, and he would have erupted had Eira not raised her hand. It should not have had the effect of silencing Yut, but somehow it did.

"You want answers. This is wise—I would want answers as well. But Yut, you *need* to trust me. There are things you must do to destroy the Cult that no one else—"

"And what if I don't *want* to destroy them?" He remembered a time when interrupting an elder, much less a seeress, would have earned Yut a beating out of this world, but indignation replaced those fears now. "You want them gone, but I haven't found any reason to help you. What about me? What about this..." He pointed to his forearm, and though Eira was blind, he was sure she already knew.

Olaf and Sig were standing at the threshold of the forest behind them. They did not interrupt. Yut suspected they wanted answers as well, and Eira must have realized this. She gave a deep, frustrated sigh. "Fine then, let's get this over with." With one quick motion, she untied her blindfold and let it fall to the flowing grasses.

Yut's breath caught as he stepped back. Her eyes were scarred shut, savaged by flame, or metal, or both. She turned to look at the other two, and their reaction mimicked Yut's. He thought Sig would have seen it at least once, but she looked ready to run.

Eira did not replace her blindfold. "My sight was taken long ago, by women who thought they could exchange it for the sight of the gods. They knew little of Speaking. I knew less, and I let them do it. Now I hide the shame of my foolishness under this rag, though I cannot redeem it."

The wind carried the long silence that followed, only the rustle of the long grass offering respite. Yut did not move, how could he? Now he was well and truly lost, at an intersection of a thousand roads. In the end it was Olaf that spoke.

"The witches who did that to you… er, with you, were they…?"

"The beginnings of the Cult of Orik, Seithers, and worse, the lot. Many of us died in the beginning, but through our mistakes and curses we learned, until we could Speak the sun to rise and the stars to dance." Eira looked heartbroken as she spoke, and so very old, as if some spell of hers was broken. "But everything has its price, and the innocents have paid enough for our power."

"And what does that mean?" asked Yut.

"Power only comes through sacrifice, ours or theirs, son of Erik. When I was with the Cult, they were searching for someone like you, the one chosen by the gods, the one for whom an entire village gave their life. Your power is what they need, and that same power will destroy them. I know you want it, Yut. You want the power, and you want it all. But if I give you this weight, will you hold it until the end? Or will it consume you? Understand that I want to teach you everything I know, but I know more than most about gaining too much at once. Besides, only your power can destroy the Cult and get your revenge, and I am the only person who can help you with this. If you trust nothing else, then trust that I need you."

Yut clenched his jaw and looked to the rushing clouds, blinking away the sudden tears. He dared not close his eyes, for he was sure the golden eyes would stare back at him, along with Keld and his parents. What would they tell him now? To seek revenge, to sacrifice his life in pursuit of a power he knew nothing about? Would they truly want him to hold on? An emptiness has been growing inside of him since that day in Sanvik, and although he did not pay attention to it before, he felt it in earnest now. Somehow, it made bearing it all easier. And now he would bear them all.

He found his voice, cracked though it was. "Did they send the wyrm? To find me?"

Eira pursed her lips. "Yes."

Something broke within Yut. Of course, this was the way it must be, the inevitable path of vengeance. He could not tell a better saga if he tried. They were burned alive for him, and now he would die for them. "Then what would you have me do?"

"Make an oath. But first, we put another oath to rest." Eira held out her hand, and Sig caught it, though Yut noticed her steps were hesitant. She wore a new bruise, but if Eira knew what happened to her, she did not show it. "Olaf, I consider your word fulfilled, and release you of my service. Walk with freedom and confidence now, old warrior."

Olaf's brows shot up, and instantly furrowed in suspicion. "Serious?"

"Aye."

"Well..." His eyes darted, and he awkwardly hefted his enormous pack. Yut was sure he would bolt, though now, more than ever, he needed him. He needed an anchor for whatever was coming next, even though it was rusted, old, and smelly. He needed a friend.

But Olaf ran, and they watched his bulk retreat along the forest, until trees and grass hid him for good. Yut did not know why he expected him to stay, or why he felt betrayed. If he learned one thing about Olaf, it was that he was a scavenger and a survivor, and there would be nothing for him on the rest of their path. Yut could not expect him to risk his life for their sake any longer. And yet that did not make it less painful. He watched the place where Olaf disappeared with half-hearted hope, waiting for him to come back. *Don't be a fool.* He also thought he saw a glimmer of betrayal on Sigrid's face, but a stone frown quickly replaced it. "Eira, we need to speak. I saw a Seither in town—"

"Not now, child," said Eira, walking toward the forest. "The Cult is upon us, and we have wasted enough time."

Yut could see Sig tense as if she was ready to break after Olaf, but she only stood for a moment before following them into the forest.

Chapter Thirty-Two

Loyalty of Bjarni

The sky suddenly made up its mind and began pelting the earth with rain that felt colder than snow and sharper than arrows. A hut squatting on the outskirts of Miklor just managed to hold its own against the downpour, and a struggling flame inside kept up an illusion of comfort. Bjarni positioned himself inside to avoid the leaks in the roof, and, managing to find a harpa, he strummed contentedly. But his perpetual smile melted when the beat of the rain became the beat of hooves, surrounding the hut.

The door flung open, and Ulric, more rainwater than man, strode in, nearly flooding the room. Bjarni continued strumming as the Heisir pulled up a chair beside the hearth and hunched over, shivering.

"You walk with a Seither now?" asked Bjarni quietly.

"She has her uses," grunted Ulric, "And she said you have a use too, apparently."

"Perhaps," nodded Bjarni. There was a strained silence; Ulric did not want to leave the fire, and Bjarni clearly enjoyed watching the man shiver.

"You look like the dark," said Bjarni, switching to a capricious, discordant melody on the harpa. He noticed a bloodshot eye and a split lip. "The jarl's boys give you a thrashing?"

"I barely escaped in time." Ulric closed his eyes as a violent shiver passed through him. He clenched his fists, his body jerking as if being whipped by invisible attackers. Then, just as suddenly, he stopped. "You know what I seek. She commanded you to help."

"What, your dog can't sniff it out herself?"

"Not anymore, even though we tracked them this far. She said the rune-child became invisible to her, and that you had something to do with that."

Bjarni allowed a dangerous pause in the melody. "I answer to no Seither."

"Not talking about the Seither. *She* commands you to obey."

Bjarni waited just enough, and picked up the melody again, more jovial now. "Well, if the great Aslaug herself commands it, then obey I shall. She did always appreciate my... subservience."

Ulric leaped at Bjarni without warning, tore the harpa from him, and flung it into the fire. "You will obey her, and you will obey *me.*" The air shimmered around Ulric, as if from intense heat.

"Temper, temper," sang Bjarni, as the flaming harpa strings ripped with a *twang.* "I see the runes are doing their work. Tell me, *champion*, how many days do you have left before they tear you apart? Perhaps you're in more of a hurry than she—"

Ulric's hand clamped onto Bjarni's neck, and he began lifting him with one arm. Only a few people in the world could see the runes on Ulric's body, writhing and shimmering in a spectrum of lights, all fighting for control. Light seeped away from him, leaving only the color of the runes to illuminate his form. A green rune flashed, and the bloodshot eye became white again as his split lip closed.

Though Bjarni's face began to go blue, he did not struggle—he knew it would be useless against such a force. He also realized that when Ulric said he barely escaped the town he was not afraid for his own life, but for the life of every living creature around him. So, Bjarni merely watched the licks of lightning race throughout Ulric's left arm, as tongues of flame began escaping from his right, singing Bjarni's eyebrows. The hut was not prepared for both rain and the power of the gods this night, so it groaned loudly.

Ulric's growl was that of a drake. "Where. Is. My. Rune?"

Bjarni's eyes began to roll back before Ulric dropped him. Sweat droplets fell to the floor and hissed in steam. The floorboards were scalding hot, so Bjarni had to jump up before regaining his breath. He did not see outside but could hear the panic of the horses and the confusion of their riders. He wondered how they would react if they saw their leader now, a vessel of the very magic they fought against. Would they flee or attack?

But Ulric probably did not care, so Bjarni coughed up, "The boy with Eira, Yut Eriksson. He has the rune you seek."

Did Bjarni hear the smallest of gasps from the man above him? Even though Ulric was a silhouette surrounded by otherworldly light, there was a moment of uncertainty from hearing Yut's name. Most would not notice, but most had duller eyes than Bjarni, who could not help but put his head down and chuckle at this game of fate. "I see your master may not have everything in her grasp just yet."

Ulric snapped out of a momentary reverie and turned to leave. "You should hope you're wrong, skald."

The Heisir stepped out of the cabin; dry-heated clothes instantly soaked as if he walked into a lake. Bjarni watched the gallop of their horses disappear into rain and mist, and he continued watching for a while, with only a quiet prayer on his lips.

Chapter Thirty-Three

Divided

They ascended side by side through the Miklor woods, silence broken only by snapping twigs. The forest was old here—much older than Trelwoods. The trees twisted and climbed the rise to the mountains, with their ancient roots crushing the rocky soil underneath them. Yut expected Sig to inquire of Eira again, but no words passed between the two. There was something cold between them, and he had the odd feeling it would not be lifted easily. But Sig continued leading Eira through the underbrush, or Eira led Sig, it was hard to tell. Eira looked so focused it seemed like she was angry. Still, Yut decided to broach the silence.

"So, where are we—"

"I know the secrets weigh heavy, Yut," interrupted Eira, "But you must understand they are necessary for our survival. The day your rune saved you was the day the Cult was sure of your existence, and so it was the day they would dedicate their strongest to track you down. The power..."

Eira drifted off. Yut checked if Sig would complete her sentence, or offer any more insight, but she would not take her eyes off something invisible in the trees. *Gods, this is a mess.* The fear that began to evaporate in his travels with Olaf and Bjarni settled again, as Yut felt increasingly exposed.

"The strongest of the Cultists—would that be Ulric?" asked Yut.

Eira shook her head. "Almost. Ulric is strong in Speaking and Runes, and grows stronger with each new rune he steals. But the strongest of their order is the seeress of the north, Aslaug. The power of her Speaking can split mountains, her knowledge of the Saga alone would be far too much for us. I only hope she has not come here herself..."

Yut stopped listening. He stopped walking, he stopped breathing. Silent, he stood, Eira's words crashing into him like a storm wave.

"...command of the Cult itself." Eira stopped a dozen paces ahead, realizing something was wrong. The stop even made Sig return to reality.

"Eriksson?" prodded Eira.

"Ulric—what did you just say about him?" Yut's heart beat faster as the smell of smoke and burnt flesh filled his mind.

"I said he is formidable, he will be pursuing us, and... Yes, he takes runes, Yut. He has taken many already."

"The tall one took his soul," whispered the trembling Tova child.

"It is as painful and ruthless as you may imagine. The rune is tied to your mind, but if your mind is broken, a powerful Speaker can rip it out. I imagine Ulric has become proficient at that, the darkened trelkin."

Sig peeled her eyes from the trees. "How do they break their minds?"

"All manners of ways. The easier way is to kill their loved ones, destroy their livelihood, make them truly believe the gods have forsaken them. On the other hand, Ulric has become fond of breaking the body first, driving them to madness from the pain."

"Then have you ever..." began Yut.

"No. Even if Aslaug had commanded it, I would never. It takes a particular cruelty, and it is said the runes do not come without cost." Then, in a morose tone, she added, "Pieces of the previous owner's mind are often still attached."

"If he finds us," said Sig, "can you beat him?"

"Perhaps, though he would not seek my life first. Yut's rune is the one he would sacrifice everything for. It is that rune of strength that would save his body from the other ones. I heard them gnawing at him in Miklor, his madness was barely kept at bay."

Yut thought back to when he met the Heisir—he did not seem deranged, though his eyes looked shadowed. Yut now remembered the urgency in his words when they were locked out of Miklor. How could Ulric do something like this? "So, if we just evade the Cult for a few weeks, let the runes do their work, we'll be safe, right? You make it seem like we have no choice."

"I never said he would die, Eriksson. We have not seen what happens if the runes consume someone, but I fear it would be quite dangerous for us. Or perhaps even for all of Arthgard."

"Yut has to kill him," whispered Sig, looking into the trees again. Yut responded with the quickest "no" he ever said in his life.

"And yet you must," said Eira.

"I... can't. I mean—I've never really..."

"Then I will," said Sigrid. "Runes don't make him immune to daggers, do they?"

"Out of the question," stated Eira. "The powers at play are bigger than daggers. He could have all your limbs broken using one of his runes, much less his full might."

"Then I will use Speaking to make—"

"Out. Of. The. Question." Eira said louder, which was

terrifying enough, though Yut could see her shoving her anger down. Gentler, she said, "Your Speaking is special."

"Right. Then I'm sure piss-pants here will get the job done." Yut should not have been hurt by that, but gods it stung. Thankfully there were no more inquiries.

They picked up the pace, moving deeper into the woods, closer to the mountains. It was not until the fall of night, as they sat around a fire and ate the few provisions Sig managed to pick up in the city, that Eira revealed the purpose for their trek.

"We seek an Oathstone. For ages, people from all of Arthgard would dedicate a stone as an ever-standing witness to an oath. Many of these stones are laden with Runes and Tellings, and for a Speaker or a rune-child, they serve to increase their power—so long as that power is used to fulfill the oath. Now, since Ulric and the Cult found us, and we are short on time, allies, and everything else, this is our one chance to stand against them." Eira looked like she was about to go on, but she paused, adding, "Questions?"

Yut was trying to form the words in the proper order when Sig asked, "What are the risks? Side effects?"

"Dangerous and different for everyone, which is why you will not be making the oath, child."

Though Sig seemed distant on the walk here, she suddenly focused on her. Yut groaned inwardly. "What?"

"You are surprised? Come now, Sigrid, I would not risk a proficient Speaker making the oath, much less a young one, and one so unique."

"You would risk Yut doing it." *At least she used my name.*

"Indeed, because this is dire, and he has a rune of power, which should at least provide some protection. We risk one to avoid losing two."

Yut started, "Now, wait—"

Sigrid stood up, the fire reflecting in her eyes. “He cannot do it alone. With Olaf gone, we’ll need all of our power to defeat the Cult. What is the point in sending Yut to die for a fool’s chance? I can make the oath, Eira, and I can *help*. Please. Let me help.”

Whatever comfort the fire brought froze solid as Yut watched Sig. He could see the battle plainly on her face, the tears of urgency gnawing at her eyes. It was more than a simple desire to help. She needed this. Gods knew Yut needed her help in whatever was to come—he needed any help he could take. And had he been stronger or braver he might have stood alongside Sigrid and confronted Eira as well. But he wasn’t. Not anymore.

And Eira sat silent, face unreadable in the flickering shadows.

Sig started again, “I know I failed before—”

“You know nothing, girl,” snapped Eira. “You say you wish to help, but you lie to us and to yourself. You don’t want to help, Sigrid, you only want the power to run from that which you fear. The shadows do not disappear, do they? They are constantly there, even now, at the edge of sight. Tell me, what have you learned from me in all of our years of travel? Was it to run from the shadows, or to face them? I thought I had grown you into a warrior, a fighter, and yet it took one slip to defeat you. Now all I hear is a little girl, scared and ashamed, looking for an easy way back to her mother. But the way is not there, Sigrid, and I grow tired of playing that role. A time of war comes, and those who are afraid have no part to play in it. No, the Oathstone will not help you—in fact, it will probably destroy you, just as Ulric will destroy you if he wishes to. This is my word, and it is final. Now, we have a long march ahead of us...” But Sig was already striding into the trees, the sound of breaking branches growing distant.

Yut found himself standing and looking at the dark spot in the trees where she vanished. Is this it, then? Just him and Eira against everyone else?

“She will be back,” said Eira. And then, again, almost too quiet, “She will be back.”

Chapter Thirty-Four

The Girl and the Lynx

Rage. Sig thought she knew rage before. She would sleep with rage, be jolted awake through it, it would give her energy to keep running. That was a mild annoyance compared to what she felt now.

Rage at Yut, for being a lucky coward and turning Eira against her. Rage at Eira, for daring to speak to her like a child—no, like an animal. A dumb, crippled dog who yapped at the wind. And then, down where the fury erupted from, she felt a seething rage at herself. She was weak, broken, unworthy of Speaking, of being strong, maybe even—

A *snap* of branches to her left, and her dagger was flying. Let it be Yut, or Eira, or anyone in the whole darkened world, let them all die.

But it was not an enemy. Instead, the dagger passed harmlessly through the landvaettir spirit, bouncing off the tree behind it. Sig froze. It looked like a lynx, but its pointed ears were far longer, and it was the color of blue ice. It was also looking directly at her, crouching and ready to pounce.

Sig did not know Miklor woods. They were too close to the

city, which would have made them dangerous for her before she met Eira. She also did not know the vaettir here, though they almost never paid attention to mankind. And yet, they were said to be dangerous for a reason, and so she crouched slowly, hand on her other dagger, staring it in the eyes.

The creature pounced, and she barely managed to roll away, leaves tumbling from her as she pushed herself off the ground. She stayed low, anticipating the next attack, but the lynx was gone.

"*It will return,*" said a deep voice, and she did not need to look to know who it was.

The lynx vaettir disappeared into a large stone, maybe the remains of a ruin, upon which stood a figure. Face of twisting shadows, body only vaguely humanoid.

"Go drown in the dark," cursed Sig, looking intently for the lynx. They traveled through different worlds at a whim, and so it could re-appear anywhere.

"You know why it stalks you." At some point, Sig realized that each shadow differed in size and shape. And although she did not know much about them, the shadow speaking with her now somehow felt like the strongest out of all of them. After all, he spoke to her the most.

"So, we're on speaking terms now?" Sig wiped her palms on the sealskin pants to better grip the dagger. She was not certain how good a dagger would be against a spirit, but surely it couldn't hurt.

"*It surely would hurt,*" said the voice, now directly in front of her, *"Your reliance on the weapon will get you killed against this type of beast."* Sig threw the dagger at him and turned to run, but that's when the lynx materialized again, this time out of a nearby oak. She managed to dodge it out of pure, primal instinct, but not before an ethereal claw snagged her thigh.

The claw passed through her leg without physical harm, and

Sig felt no pain. In fact, she felt nothing at all. The left side of her thigh became numb, and no amount of prodding returned any feeling to it.

"*The vaettir harms your soul and mind, but leaves the body intact,*" intoned the shadow as it circled Sig. The lynx walked alongside it, eyes locked with hers. The numbness in her leg made her limp—she doubted she would be able to dodge the next pounce.

Sig wiped the sweat off her forehead. "It's hunting me because of you."

"*Try again.*" The lynx stopped circling and crouched again. Sig could not help taking slow steps backward as it stalked toward her. This was it, then.

"Is this it, you trelkin? You've already destroyed my life, and now you will take my soul? Is this how it ends?" Sig hit something behind her, and realized she backed into the large stone. The lynx did not slow its approach.

"*She hunts* you, *a berserker, because your rage is powerful and dangerous. This rage would destroy her, and these woods, and it would not stop there. All things must protect their home, Sigrid.*"

"I don't hurt innocents, that is what *you* do," Sig spat.

"*Sigrid,*" said the shadow, and Sig felt her neck seize up. She was forced to draw her gaze past the lynx, past the trailing cloak of darkness emanating from her tormentor, until her eyes were locked onto his face. And in his face, she saw a writhing world of gray and black. It drew her in, deeper, into something inescapably wrong, until the lynx and the woods blurred, faded completely, and she was alone.

Alone, but surrounded by people. Her village, her clan. Sig did not want to be here, to live through these moments again. Every rage, every vision, every waking nightmare brought her closer to that village. Closer to the carnage that made her. Closer to that night. She had heard of what she did, but she could not—would not—approach that memory, much less see it.

"*And yet you must see it,*" said the shadow, his ethereal voice all around her, "*and see it again and again, until you see the truth.*"

Her voice was gone, she could not hope to rebel against this vision. Before, when she was deep in the darkness, she saw glimpses of that night, but it was soon forgotten like a fleeting nightmare.

She knew she would not forget this one. The shadows brought her past the woods, into the village center, and she was helpless to stop them. She saw the villagers' faces clearly, heard the bleating of goats, felt the summer breeze blowing leaves through the muddy roads, among which the village prepared for the celebration. It was not a perfect life, but it was the happiest Sig had felt. After her mother passed, whom Sig had forgotten, pity drove the people to accept and care for her, and so she was happy.

There were rumors, of course, of her mother's past, of her mysterious father, of the way she looked. Icy gray eyes, near-white hair, ears almost pointed. The kids would point, and the adults would whisper, but it was not beyond a child to overlook. After all, she was taken care of. She was happy.

"No." Sig found her voice and *pushed* against the vision. She would not be forced to live it again, not by one spirit or an army of them. Yet even as she pushed, the edges of her sight began to darken with a red hue and her heart stammered. There was not enough air, and Sig felt herself drop to her knees in the real world. As she fought for air, the red edges began to subside, and the vision was brought back into focus.

"*We have done all we can for you, Sigrid. You must see it now or perish.*" The shadow stood with her in the long house of her village, where torches and candles illuminated the stern faces of the village folk. The logmar was speaking to them, but soon he would be finished.

"Why... why now?" Breathed Sig.

"In this we know less than you. Perhaps you changed something, or something changed you. All the truth we have is that this is the right time. The only time."

Sig and the spirit watched the crowd gathered in the long house. This was the night when they would come for her.

"See it, Sigrid, and be free."

"You haven't tormented me enough? You are a spirit of the Dark, you lie with every—" the vision flickered, and Sig saw a glimpse of another figure amid the villagers. It was only a moment, but she was sure of it. She had seen this moment several times, but it had always been the logmar speaking to the rest of the villagers in the long house. He was strangely silent now. "What's happening?"

The shadow echoed her guess. *"A Speaker who does not wish to be seen. But you are a Speaker as well."*

Yes, and it was *her* darkened vision. "Show yourself," she commanded. Another flicker, and the space where the logmar stood twisted. His voice bent with the space, as if different people took turns talking through him. Then that space fractured, and reformed to reveal a figure in a white robe, speaking to the logmar, who sat silent in the high seat with a face as grim as the others.

It was a seeress.

Acting on instinct, Sig walked towards her, trying to get a better look. The seeress was tall, and wore white face coloring, with two black lines streaming down her eyes. Her face continued morphing and shifting, not unlike Sig's shadows. It was clear that she commanded the fear of the entire long house with her height, demeanor, and her deep voice.

"Who in the dark...?" Sig wondered aloud. No one noticed, of course. The vision did not care for what Sig did or said. She looked to the shadow, who was still in the corner of the long house. "Is she real? Or one of your tricks?"

No answer, so she tried to focus on the seeress, who spoke to the logmar of curses and anger of the gods—the crime of harboring a half-breed. And not even a human half-breed, but that of lightfolk and elves, the existence of which was an affront to creation itself. In previous visions, the logmar spoke these words with a furious zeal. The seeress spoke softly, however, and her words dripped with a lifeless malice, as if she was reciting a dark poem. It was a malice that felt ever so familiar.

Hours fleeted past as the logmar pleaded with the seeress, because to refuse her outright would condemn the village to be cursed. But disbelief turned to reluctance, which settled on grim acceptance. Sig grimaced. Though the lead-up was different this time, the result was the same: the villagers would march to her care taker's home. Yes, the memories were returning now, and Sig felt her heart drop as the moment of pain grew nearer.

"*Please,*" she whispered. "I understand, alright? I always did. I was born cursed and so I die cursed, it's the will of the Saga. Isn't that what I'm supposed to understand? It's the truth, isn't it?"

The shadow spirit was next to her again, but it remained unmoving, its twisting face fixed on the villagers. Torchlight illuminated empty faces, the expressions of the self-condemned. At their head was the seeress—who held no emotion as she quietly opened the door to Sig's foster home.

A couple of the women brought her out—she trusted them, so she put up no struggle. Even though her caretaker begged and wept in the distance, young Sig did not realize anything was wrong until they brought her to the village center. Old Sig bared her teeth at her. *Darkened idiot, wake up!* The logmar was gone, too guilt-ridden and afraid to witness the sacrifice he allowed. Some villagers began leaving as well, shaking their heads. Most remained.

The seeress began intoning a Telling as she took out a knife. She grabbed Sig by the hair, who was now crying and struggling, and brought the knife to her neck. The Telling grew louder, and for the second time in her short life, little Sigrid felt the true fear of death. And there, before the silent villagers and under the full moon, she first saw the shadows.

Her village, her family, transformed. Their torches flickered out one by one, and shadows engulfed their bodies. In one breath, a hundred spirits with faces of churning chaos took their place.

Only the seeress kept her form, as she realized the gravity of her mission's success. And while the villagers' forms darkened, hers came into deadly focus.

"Such power," gasped Gyldryn, the knife slipping out of her hand as she stumbled back. She was young here, made younger still by her wide eyes and an awestruck smile. "I had no idea..."

The shadows remained as still as Sig, until the one closest to her, the tall one, offered his hand to her. Her trembling, small hand reached back, and she was led from the village, quietly passing the homes of people she thought she loved, into the depths of the darkness outside.

"That's not what happened." Sig's jaw was clenched, eyes closed against the stream of tears. "They said... they said I killed them all..." Even in the vision, she remembered the smell of blood and the torn screams.

"*You did. But this is truth as well.*"

"You are not real."

"*We are real when we need to be.*"

Sig opened her eyes. "Then you are not the monster."

Gyldryn watched in awe as the young Speaker before her,

threatened by inevitable death, unleashed her wrath for the first time. Sig did not know how she knew the Tellings she spoke that night, but Gyl's white cloak was soon drenched in red, along with everything else in that village. Bodies burst as people tried to flee, though none of them would escape. Some saw a quick death; others had their body twisted and wrung in a wet crunch before drawing their final breath. In the middle of that carnage walked an eight-year-old girl, led by the shadows to a quieter place far away, protected from the sounds of snapping bones and gurgling lungs.

The village was burned to the ground weeks later, after folks gathered enough courage to go inside. And even then, those that had seen the village center did not sleep the same.

In the vision of the ashen village, the older Sig wiped her eyes with trembling hands while the shadow spirit stood close. Her head pounded, but breathing slowly became easier, and eventually she managed to gain control over her sobs. "Why did you hide them from me?"

"*We hid things a child should not have to see, though the seeress was not our doing. When she disappeared from your memory, it may have been her own foul magic, deafening your mind to protect herself.*"

"All those villagers then..."

"*We still walk with you, Sigrid, to protect you from harm—even if the harm would come from your own mind. And we will continue to do so until you need us no longer.*"

She heard their approaching footsteps, the ones she dreaded so many times, ones that heralded bloodshed. The footsteps took control of her and made her into a monster. The ones who protected her against certain death. Though they terrified her before, she never saw them as clearly as she did now—not mere shadows, but smudged outlines of people. They were the spirits of people she knew. People she once loved.

"You are not surprised about Gyldryn?"

Sig wiped her nose. "I suppose I should be. But these are my memories, aren't they? That is why she was so darkened interested in me. I knew it all along, but now it all makes more sense. Now it's all… real."

Sig stood and calmly faced the gathering spirits. "And you are not real." The spirits continued standing there, looking slightly awkward.

"*Are you a lightfolk?*" asked one. It had a different voice from the leader spirit, and this one was shorter, looking up at Sig with that dark, swirling face. Gods, was this a child shadow…?

The answer came easier than she thought. "No. Not possessed by an elvish spirit either. Just a regular old human. Well, mostly regular." She looked around at the village half-buried in ash, starting to turn gold with the rising sun.

"Good," said the leader spirit, "*we can leave then.*"

Sig continued looking at the ashes. "That gods-darkened trelkin crone turned the villagers against me." She looked at the spirits. "She turned all of *you* against me."

"*Yes, she did. But if you focus now then we can leave.*"

"And all you dark-stained trelkin went right along with her lies. How could you?"

"*Yes, they… we did. We must have been afraid. Now, Sigrid—*"

"Oh, *you* were afraid? I have been running all this time—for what? Because of some creepy seeress? She poisoned my mind because I look like a lightfolk? Are they out of their darkened minds? I suppose she started rumors about me, too. Of course, everyone would believe her."

"*If you would just focus—*"

"I'll show them all. I'm a Speaker, gods damn it all to the dark.

And I'm a darkened powerful Speaker, too. You just wait. First, I will tell Eira—"

"*That's enough now.*" There was a stab of pain in her head and the village melted into rivers of darkness. Those waters engulfed Sig, who was still cursing, and brought her back to the forest, where she found herself lying amid the birch trees. The stars shimmered in a bruised-violet sky, and somewhere a bird screamed itself awake. Gods below, how long was she out?

She instinctively made slight movements with her fingers, arms, and legs, making sure nothing was broken. Her left thigh was still numb from where the landvaettir slashed her—hopefully that would heal, though she doubted it.

As she rose, she nearly jumped up the nearest tree. The landvaettir—translucent, light blue lynx—was curled up peacefully beside her.

Sig let go of her dagger as she sat back down. More birds were beginning to yell, and the sky turned orange and gold with the approaching dawn. As much as nature tried lulling her into rest, Sig felt she needed to move. Her head was clearer than it had ever been, but there was still an urgency in the back of her mind. Something important was left unsaid.

"Spirits?" Called out Sig. She had no idea if they were listening, but they were always in her mind, right? They must have been watching and listening this entire time. "Did Eira know I wasn't cursed? Did she know about Gyldryn?"

The lynx raised her head, looked at Sigrid, stretched, and walked off into a different world and out of sight.

There was no other response. "It's okay to admit you don't know something," tried Sig. Proud silence in response. "Fine then, whole lot of good you all are, my imaginary friends. Then I will ask her myself."

Somehow, she knew she would go back. If not for Eira, then at least for Yut. As much as she respected Eira's purpose, the kid was being played like a pipe, and he should at least have a real say in the matter of his life. Yes, Eira was a good woman with valuable knowledge, but it was a lot of pressure to put on someone who had no idea what runes were a month ago. Dark below, probably still didn't have a clue.

No, she would at least warn him, and demand the truth from Eira about Sig's nature—not to mention her power. And then... Well, then she'll have her own choice to make.

Chapter Thirty-Five

The Oathstone

"I don't know Eira, it just looks like a big rock," huffed Yut, standing in front of the alleged stone of legends. They were hiking up the rising forest before dawn, and as the clouds gained light, the trees suddenly gave way to a clearing of white stone ground. Yut was out of breath and drenched in sweat, but Eira pushed him on. The mountains were nearly upon them here, and the elevation shortened their breath.

Sunlight forced its way through some of the clouds, making dappled designs on the largely regular-looking boulder in front of Yut. To be fair, it looked like it was the center of something, especially since a dozen white pillars encircled it. It was also suspiciously smooth. Other pillars were scattered about the clearing like bones of a long-dead giant. Past those, they could see the tops of trees and glimpses of the land between white crags. Yut reckoned he was the highest he'd ever been from home.

"Try to be more specific," sighed Eira, sitting on a toppled pillar, patience already drained, "How tall is it? Are there any markings? What surrounds it?"

Yut inspected the pillar as he walked around it. "It's completely black, as tall as Olaf and maybe another half a head. There are other pillars around it, and... yeah, rune markings, but faint. I thought you've been here b—" And then he stopped himself, but not in time.

"And in your mind that means I remember everything? Or that I even made the trip more than once? Do all seeresses know every little detail about everything? Gods above, save me from the gall of young men..."

Yut continued studying the stone, trying to ignore her as she went on. He made yet another mental mark about muttering within a mile of Eira.

"...should be thankful I even remember the directions here. It is forbidden, you know. Sacred. Gods, are you waiting for it to blink? Here." She approached the stone with her hands out, annoyed but visibly cautious, and placed one palm on the smooth surface of the stone.

Yut did not know what he expected from all this. Perhaps some runes on the stone, or a forest guardian, or a mysterious trickster spirit to confuse them. How would a boulder help him become more powerful?

"Perhaps we should keep searching," suggested Yut. "And I told you, I don't even know how to control the rune."

"This is it," said Eira, her expression suddenly becoming sorrowful, catching Yut off guard. Why was *she* sad if *he* was supposed to take the oath? "Yes, there is a saga pouring forth from here, and I recognize its speech from long ago. Do not worry, Yut, every rune is different, and yours will show you its secrets soon enough. Now, prepare yourself."

"For what? You know you did not actually say what I'm supposed to do here."

"From what I have heard, it is very simple. You put your hand on the Oathstone, like this, swear that you will destroy the Cult of Orik, and that should do it."

"Should?" Yut took a step back. "Can't you tell if there is some kind of... magical protection on there? What if it turns me into something unnatural for my trouble?"

"Could hardly be any worse," responded Eira, returning to her seat. "Maybe it'll make you braver."

Maybe it'll make you braver, mimed Yut, taking care to do it silently. He tried to focus while he stared down the stone. He would be strong, he had to, except that he was about to talk to a magic rock that could very well kill him. He remembered the unconscious Bjarni lying before him, and how Yut's hesitation to kill him stretched to the point of mercy. Somehow, he held a similar hesitation toward the stone. He wanted to sit down and examine everything that happened, but his life had become a blur of quick, life-changing decisions which flung him through the Saga like a leaf through a storm. There was no time to consider anything anymore, something his logical father would never approve of, but what choice did he have? How could he make the right decision when he only had a split second to make it?

"Yut..."

He heard Eira and realized he had not moved for several minutes, though he could not bring himself to snap out of his thoughts. All the paths before him, all the paths he abandoned—what if he had made a horrible mistake? But now Ulric and a dozen other warriors were climbing this very mountain to kill him. Gods below, there had to be another way, if only he had more time...

"Yut, enough."

"Give me a moment, alright? I just need a moment."

He did not know how long he stood there, but by the time she touched his arm he was grinding his teeth to dust, the contact making him jolt. "I just need a moment!"

"Forget the stone." She wore the exhausted expression again, though her voice was gentle. She took his trembling hand while he tried to recover. "Forget the oath, forget everything. Just sit with me."

Taken aback, Yut let her lead him to the collapsed pillar, and sit him down beside her, their back to the Oathstone. She was silent for a while, as a cool mountain wind blew through the clearing, raising puffs of white stone powder that stuck to their tunics and hair. The old trees swayed in the distance, but the rest of the world below stood still.

"You know, this was one of my last views before losing my sight."

Yut looked at her in surprise. She smiled softly, and he could almost see the memories resurfacing behind that blindfold. He forgot she also had a life, and it must not have been an easy one, especially after becoming blind. Gods, all he'd thought about lately was himself. "We were preparing to do something incredible," she continued, "something never attempted by mortals. We were going to see the Saga in its entirety—what was before and what was to come. But for it to work, one of us had to use the Oathstone. So, while she made her oath, I sat here, watching the sun rise. It was wonderful, and I'm thankful the gods gave me that last mercy."

Yut wrung his shaking hands, unsure of what to say. Seeing what was to come did not sound bad at all, especially in that moment. "Did...did you see it?" he asked quietly. "The Saga in its entirety?"

"Yes, I believe I have. But that was the day we learned that seeing does not mean understanding, and I was lucky my mind was not taken along with my sight. Still, I remember glimpses, sounds, colors. They return to me now and then, unbidden, though I remember little from the actual experience. Other than being utterly terrified."

So, that was it, then. Yut gazed at the landscape pierced by rays of light, as the autumn wind gathered its clouds from the East. "It's beautiful," he exhaled. "I don't think I've seen the land from this high. Closest we got were the firs, but I only ever climbed one halfway before snapping a branch."

"I imagine your mother was less than thrilled."

"Oh, you have no idea," chuckled Yut, "When she saw the broken arm, I thought she would kill me herself."

Yut remembered the strange day. One moment he was exhilarated, ascending the sturdy fir branch by branch, the village kids cheering him on from below, as the forest began to bow before him. Then there was a blur, he was blinking on the ground, the kids' faces were pale, and his arm looked funny. Everything became distorted after that, with the sprint back home, his mom's concerned anger, Tove's brew, the pain. It did not feel too different from how he had felt for the past few weeks.

His thoughts drifted back to the Oathstone, and he wrung his hands again. "It's just... How can I be sure if I am doing the right thing? I'm not a soldier or a logmar—dark, I barely make it as a scavenger. I don't know what I'm doing here, but if I fail, then it's all been for nothing. I can't be the right person for this, Eira. You, Sig, and even Olaf are so confident of every decision you make—how do you do it? How do you... go forward?"

Yut dared a glance at the seeress, who surprised him again with a smile. "What?"

"I might as well tell you, though you should know that this knowledge is closely guarded among the seeresses of Arthgard. They will be quite cross with me for divulging a secret so sacred, but I suppose I have nothing to lose. Truth is..." She paused, as is proper for a seeress about to reveal the truth of a thing, and Yut instinctively leaned it.

She grinned. "I have no idea."

Yut gave a deep sigh, but Eira continued. "We do our best with the knowledge we have, Yut Eriksson, and it does not matter whether you are a seeress or a lumberjack. Look at that world down there. You can gaze at it from the highest mountain and observe a thousand roads leading to just about everywhere, but if you cannot see the path in front of your feet, then the extent of your vision does not matter. And that path in front of you is revealed not by sight, but by your heart, and those who live in it. Those that love you best—even if they might kill you for breaking your arm. So, even if this road seems impossible, none of us truly travel it alone, and I think there is some comfort to be found in that."

Yut smiled as he brushed away the sudden tears. The wisewoman was right, of course. The myriad consequences of his decisions blinded him to the reason he was here in the first place. He might have been a leaf fluttering in the wind, but he was still tethered to something true: the memory of those he lost and their wisdom. In a way, they were still with him, and that had to count for something. He looked at Eira, who seemed adrift in her memories again, and nodded.

He approached the Oathstone once more and breathed deep. He would focus on the path ahead and follow his heart; it's what his mother would advise. So long as he did that, he would never be lost. As the last bit of sunlight faded from the surface of the stone, he placed his hand on it and considered the best approach. All the sagas in the world warned of heroes who were too hasty to make an oath with an elf or spirit and paid dearly for it. Yut assumed he would need to phrase it just right, so the Oathstone would not make him useless or a villain.

"You said this would give me more power, right?" asked Yut, his heart picking up speed.

"It will focus it," replied Eira, standing now at a notable distance. He suddenly remembered Sig and a standing creek. "Your rune, the Saga itself, will aid you in destroying the Cult."

Yut turned to address the stone. He cleared his throat. "Alright, then, I—"

And then light took him.

Chapter Thirty-Six

Urgency

Not too far away, Ulric's warriors rested near the remains of a campfire.

"Doubt the kid was the one who split off," said Ofr the Hound, scratching his nose as he read the tracks. "Didn't see him long, but he didn't have much of a stride to him."

"And Eira cannot walk far by herself." Ulric was still mounted, haunted eyes resting on the other pair of tracks. "Their party shrinks. We follow the two footprints."

He did not need to issue the command; his band knew the inflections of his voice like trained hunting dogs. Hushed groans and clinking of metal echoed through the group of warriors as they mounted their horses.

"It is too late," came a rasped voice from the woods. Like one, spears pointed towards the newcomer, and were likewise lowered when they recognized the Seither limping from behind the trees.

"And here I thought our fortunes had turned," called out Bjorn, spitting in her direction. Most would say he was too big to ride a horse for a meaningful amount of time. Most grew silent when they saw his horse. He sat tall on the monstrous beast, derision plain on his bearded face. "I had hoped we left you at Miklor for good, witch."

"There lies your problem, Bjorn No-son," replied the Seither. "That head of yours was not made for thinking."

"Enough," commanded Ulric, with enough menace to wilt the trees around them. "We thought you were dead."

She touched a fresh red scar on her throat. "You could say I was, my Heisir." There were new stains of blood on her soiled cloak, but other than the usual haggard, witchy look, she was as glowing as ever.

Ulric's eye twitched. "Then what news from beyond the grave? Speak quickly, we are closing in on the rune-marked." While the entire band did not sleep long last night, with the rain and the cold, Ulric looked like he had not slept for months.

"You are too late, my Heisir. They have just found the Oathstone. The rune-marked would have likely gained his power by now."

"Then the gods will have their retribution," announced the brave Bjorn, to scattered nods from the others. And then he leaned over to Ulric. "What business do we have in dealing with rune magics? They all belong in the Dark. We should return to Rotheim, regroup, celebrate our victories. Do not tell me we don't deserve it, brother."

"If Ulric says we track them down," said Ysolda, joining them, "Then we do it. Not like you to question orders, Bjorn, especially to battle the Dark."

The big soldier swallowed his retort when he saw Ulric's eyes. They were still affixed to the Seither, who said, "The gods are sending us to destroy the rune-marked, No-Son, is that not reason enough to push on?"

"You don't look like the gods to me, or maybe you fancy

yourself our leader now?" thundered Bjorn, riding up all the way to the Seither, his giant horse snorting snot and saliva in her face. The others began to get restless as well, some even voicing their disagreement. To battle the friends of the Dark was one thing, but to follow the orders of a Seither was close to the dealings of the Dark itself.

"Silence."

It sounded like an echo of Ulric's voice, spreading through the ranks like a disease. Bjorn reluctantly backed away from the sneering witch as Ulric pinched the bridge of his nose, face twisted from the headache. "Gods or not, we still have our mission." He opened his eyes, some clarity returning to his haunted gaze. "We ride for the Oathstone. I will take care of the kid."

"I am with you, my Heisir," agreed the Seither, "But we should be careful. His witch, Eira, is crafty and powerful, and they expect our approach. Perhaps if we send someone else, someone unimportant, to test the waters, there will be no unneeded death among your warriors." The last word came with some malice as she glanced at Bjorn.

Ulric clenched his jaw, conflict plain on his battle-hardened face. "I do not—we do not have that kind of time."

"A little caution will guarantee our success, my lord. And I promise you that the one I have in mind will waste no time in hunting them. He has unfinished business with her, and it is very... pressing."

Ulric looked to the sky, thick with clouds again, and closed his eyes. He was breathing deep, as if trying to calm himself. To others, it might have looked like he was deep in thought or meditating, but the truth was more tragic. Ulric was not thinking.

He was listening.

Or at least he was trying to. In the dark corners of his mind, hidden behind the shadows of the past, echoed the words of instruction and wisdom, teaching him how to listen to the trees and the birds, to understand the Saga. A blind seeress, seemingly lost in the woods, helping a boy fleeing from his father's whip to make sense of it all.

It still did not make sense, of course, except now he could not even hear the trees. Once silence descended, the living runes on his body began to speak. Or rather, yell and scream, and they rarely said anything useful or pleasant. He had worked to quiet them, to hang on until he found the last rune, but something snapped within him when he saw Eira at that tavern. The sight of her brought memories and rage flaring from within, igniting the restless runes into a frenzy.

Ysolda brought him out of his trance. "We are with you even if we need to burn this whole darkened forest to the ground. But we listen to you, Ulric Heisir. Not the witch."

Ulric opened his eyes, though he continued staring into the darkening sky. "Send your people."

One might not have thought it possible, but the Seither looked even more hideous when she was smiling. "I already did, my Heisir."

Chapter Thirty-Seven

The Oath

Yut thought he had felt every type of discomfort in the past few weeks, from freezing, to burning with fever, to great physical and mental pain. Now he could confidently add another to the list: being spun in a hundred different directions at once while being thrown around by a hundred giants. To add to it all, a thousand voices were speaking, whispering, and yelling things at him. He tried yelling back, but could not hear his own thoughts, much less his voice.

Lights assaulted him too, all colors and all brightnesses. A memory surfaced of Tove's mystery drink all those weeks ago. This experience felt similar, but a hundred times worse. Yut thought that if he was in the real world, he would have thrown up a dozen times by now.

Except... he was not in the real world, was he?

Forcing his reeling mind to focus, Yut pieced together the moments leading up to this. He made the oath to the boulder, Eira was standing in the back, he collapsed—no, he did not quite make the oath. Was this the work of the Oathstone? After all, it had to be magical.

The voices grew louder, the spinning intensified, to the point where Yut felt his head ripping apart. He did not know how, but he knew he had precious seconds left before he would be destroyed. Meanwhile, the pain was exquisite.

And what does the pain mean? Olaf's voice drifted in, though it was not one of the myriad around him. *It means,* tried Yut, his mind going dark, *it means you're still alive. It means you can still fight.*

I can fight. And dark take him if he would have killed a wulver to be defeated by some old rock. Yut screamed as he opened his eyes. In the spirals of lights and colors, he saw a new, golden light emanating from his forearm, and he did not need to look to know his rune had alighted. And, as always, not a moment too soon. As the intoxicating strength poured into his bone, muscle and mind, the colors lost their edge. He recalled that the rune showed everything in better focus before—perhaps it revealed the truth of things as well, and the truth was that none of this was as overwhelming as Yut thought.

The spinning began to slow as well, and Yut could have almost made out shapes in the colors and lights, but then a ringing voice above him said, "You'll need something more'n that little trick to leave this place. But I won't kill you yet. Come."

A black hole tore open in front of Yut. Or, as he quickly realized, it was *below* him, so that he fell into darkness, and onto solid ground. Sweet, solid, normal-colored earth was beneath him, and, upon further inspection, that is all that was here. Silver clouds stretched into the flattest horizon Yut had ever seen, making it all look like an unfinished dream.

It was silent here, too, silent enough for Yut to gather his thoughts and memories. The colors and voices might have been some kind of defense against the non-rune-marked oath makers, though Eira said all sorts of folk used the stone. Then, it was a defense *against* the rune-marked, which meant Eira was right about the power of the oath.

In that case, it's now or never, thought Yut.

"I swear to destroy—"

"Not so fast, boy," interrupted the voice from before.

Yut found no one around or above him, and yet the voice was definitely nearby. This time, however, it sounded normal, even with a slight accent.

Yut blinked, and he was suddenly standing at the top of a city unlike he had ever imagined. Even more beautiful than Miklor, it was positioned on a hill, so Yut could see the entirety of the tall and beautiful buildings made of white and blue stone, lined with gold, as they stretched and reached their way throughout a league or more, down into the surrounding forest. Strange trees with leaves of purple and silver decorated squares and streets, where people made their trips, errands, and visits. And what people they were—all tall, ranging in color, beautiful, working, smiling. They wore simple, clean tunics, which somehow looked better than any royal robe.

"Young man," called the voice, this time coming from an older man sitting at a small table behind Yut, leaning against a wall of another building, upon which purple-silver vines made their design. As Yut approached him, the vines seemed to shift colors in the light of the sun.

"'What is this place?'" Said the man impassively, stealing the words from Yut's mouth as he reluctantly sat across. Unlike the people in the city, he was short, round, bald, and covered in rune marks from head to his bare toes. His long black beard flowed freely, covering a rugged coat, which descended to the stone ground. The rune marks on his face were words, most of which Yut did not recognize, though the ones he did made little sense. As he talked, they appeared to move.

"'Where is the stone? Did you bring me here? Who are you?'" He half-smiled, continuing, "And about a dozen more questions that lead to more questions that eventually accomplish nothing and waste both of our time, so why don't I cut straight to it. I'm not the Oathstone, but the sum of your folk's oaths and curses. Yes, you can use the stone to lay curses, but your wise ones have buried that secret. Perhaps for the best. You can call me Etha. What you see around y—"

"That's alright," interjected Yut, memories of Eira's warnings surfacing. "I've had a journey like this before, once. I'd like to make the oath now and go, if that's alright."

Now it was Etha who looked confused. "Journey... oath... This isn't a mushroom trip, boy. You are here by Telling, and you will not leave the same. It's not metaphorical, ya hear?"

"So, my body is not back there, by the stone with Eira?" asked Yut skeptically.

"Your body—of course, it is. But why does it matter? It doesn't mean none of this is real."

"Then how did you fit a city in here?" replied Yut.

Etha's stare was blank. "You must be one of the dullest—"

"This is some spiritual place," interrupted Yut, "and this city is..."

The beautiful people started singing a song in the distance, the melody reminding him of a familiar skald-song. Yut looked at Etha. "This city is of your making, isn't it? You created it based on... what? What others told you about our world?"

Yut could see Etha's jaw clench even through the fat and the beard. "Difficult. You people always have to make this difficult." With a wave of his hand, the city, with its people, buildings, and multi-colored vines, retreated into the horizon. Only the table and the chairs remained amid the gray, lifeless landscape.

Yut shifted slightly, making the chair creak. "I'm sorry. It really was a beautiful place."

"But?" snapped Etha.

"Well... the smiles were a little off. Everyone was too happy. No one is that happy back home."

Etha pondered, sneered, muttered, and then finally deflated. "I give you people perfect joy, and all you can do is criticize it. It's not like there is a point of reference, you know. And all of you have a different story, too—'Oh, they're this tall in my town, they're this color in my village. Why, they speak like so, they smile like this—*but not all the time.* Sometimes it's different!' Chaos is what I call it, ya hear me? You're all just walking bags of chaos."

Yut watched Etha, a doubtlessly ancient being made of magic itself, look off into the distance of the gray horizon with obvious disappointment, and then a thought occurred to him.

"Why did you create that city?" asked Yut carefully.

"That was nothing. I can make hundreds more with a whisper. It was merely for you to feel more at ease, to avoid all this... confusion. And a whole lot of good that did. Or ever does, for that matter."

Yut's thoughts danced, and he decided to risk it. "You also want to feel it, don't you?" He met Etha's eyes. "You want to see the world for yourself, but you are trapped here. Alone."

Lightning spilled through the darkening sky without warning. Yut only caught a glimpse of Etha's furrowing brows before he, too, was covered in darkness. Thunder followed, and the landscape transformed into lush, green trees. The sky was a brilliant blue, with equally brilliant stars blinking in it, even though it was midday. Whether by Etha's wish or some kind of runic magic, Yut was sure this world was much newer than the one he lived in.

He stood atop a hill overlooking a young forest. It must have been the same forest he came from, because next to him also stood the Oathstone. It was larger, however, with more edges and only a few rune marks scribbled on it. Etha's city was beautiful, but he suspected this did not come from his or anyone's imagination. No, these were Etha's memories. The air hummed with an energy that seemed to radiate from the trees and the grass, which soon seeped into Yut. He felt as if something new and great was beginning, and as this world enveloped him, Yut heard something wonderful beyond the animal calls and the rustling breeze.

An all-encompassing melody echoed through the forest, filled with many voices, descending from the sky itself. Many good skalds had stayed a night at Sanvik, but to compare this harmony with anything Yut had heard back home was sacrilege. To Yut, the tones coming from the sky felt like gold and silver, and there was no other way he could describe it.

"I was singing with the High Ones before your kind was even imagined," rung the stone next to Yut, with no small amount of indignation. "Before the grand ending of the melody, when I could still see this world, I saw life abounding. I held the oaths of the lighted, the darkened, and the High Ones themselves. It is *you* who wishes to see my world, son of man. My only desire is to stop hearing yours."

The clouds began to gather before he finished speaking, and suddenly the forest started growing. Time itself flung forward, and the young trees thickened in seconds while the underbrush multiplied. Soon, the forest took a shape closer to that which he remembered from the real world.

But something was wrong. The forest became dark, menacing, angry. Where it was a fresh babe before, it became a crooked old man. It was not the fault of the vision or Etha, Yut realized, rather it was the contrast between what was in the beginning and what it had become.

"You see it, don't you?" said the Etha-stone, its edges becoming rounder and the runes spreading upon its surface. "Your people wandered astray from their mission, for the oaths that you made you did not keep. You have forgotten the song of the ancients, and instead of fighting the Dark you endeavored to master it, not realizing it had already mastered you."

The forest continued growing, and Yut found himself at a loss for words. Or, rather, he had too many words, questions, and none he ever expected would be answered.

The forest had stopped growing, the stars had sunk into the sky and were covered by clouds, and the melody had, depressingly, vanished. Yut doubted he could remember it, much less sing it, though he thought he could feel his body still resonating with it.

"And now you come to me with an oath to kill those you have never met, at the behest of a stranger, unaware of the powers and evil desires that had brought you to this place. You want me to honor such an oath? You want *me* to bow before the same powers that drove your world to the Dark, the powers that all but broke it? By the High Ones, it is enough to make a stone weep!"

"But I want to destroy those powers!" retorted Yut, "I want to return the world to before, to the one you showed me."

"This is impossible," said Etha gravely, "And it would matter little now." Darkness engulfed the trees and the sky, and Yut once again stood among a bare, featureless land with nothing but clouds above him.

"Why not?" demanded Yut.

"Because," said Etha, standing just beside Yut in human form, startling him, "Restoring the ancient melody is not the oath you wish to make, is it? You're just another young rune-child guided by a self-serving seeress on a suicide mission."

Yut blinked. A sick picture started forming in his mind. "There were others?"

The pity was thick in Etha's voice. "My sweet, foolish boy. I tell you that this is how it has always been. But even stones gain wisdom with age, and now I foresee that I will see no others of your kind after you. This must be my end, so I'm afraid I must help you, for the Saga's sake."

"You will grant me my oath?" asked Yut, the impact of what Etha said before still coursing through his mind.

"Yes," answered Etha. And just before he disappeared, he whispered, "But not before I show you the truth."

The landscape took on the shape of houses with thatch roofs. Fire wreathed them, and screams escaped them, as the smell of burning flesh filled the air. Yut was standing in the midst of it, hands already beginning to quiver, forcing himself to believe none of it was real.

Except that he recognized the village all too well.

"Stop," Yut whispered, stumbling back.

"I can create tragedy as well as joy, Son of Erik. And this, unfortunately, is the only way for you to see."

"Don't lie to me, old man!" shouted Yut. White anger consumed him, reflecting the fires that consumed his home. And, for some reason, he could not get his hands to stop shaking. "If this is for your own pleasure, then you're a pathetic creature. You don't know anything about the real world—you don't know anything about *me.* And none of this is real. I'm here to make an oath and nothing more. Either help me or let me leave."

"Nothing more? You wish to gain power, but you are blinded by the blind. Look upon power, son of runes, see how it burns. If you wish for power, then you wish for suffering—and for what, one wisewoman's demands?" Etha's voice thundered above Yut as icy winds whipped around him. Even though the fire grew, Yut shivered as he said, "I seek justice. I will only take life from those who took mine, the Cult of Orik."

"Then we are nearing the truth."

And then he saw it. First, a monstrous shadow behind the smoke, and then the long neck of a black-scaled wyrm, followed by dark wings and a sinuous body, stalking across the burning homes. It crushed them without thought, without mercy, the slit golden eyes piercing Yut and his unspoken words. He now saw that night clearly, the roaring fires of his newly won manhood, the laughter and smell of mead, and the sudden silence of horrified villagers. The roof was swept away, the icy air descended, and the drake peered down at them.

The beast examined each person, as if searching for something, the strange red rune blazing on its forehead. Its eyes passed Yut but did not linger. Someone screamed, everyone attempted to run, to search for cover, but by then the fire was already enveloping them. Yut remembered the wyrm's breath as gentle as a blacksmith's bellows. It overtook the nearest villagers and turned them to ash immediately. But as it raced toward the stupefied Yut, Keld emerged from the fire, himself aflame and screaming. He ran into Yut, carrying and pushing him through tables and chairs until the rest of the crashing roof entombed them both. Yut felt like some dam was burst open in him, and he could not stop the memories or the fear roiling inside him. It was hard to breathe.

"You will make your oath, son of runes and power, and you will tell me the truth," thundered the drake across the village, smoke, and flame escaping his maw. There were giant rune marks covering its black scales. "This is your path, and none but the gods may change it. What is your true oath?"

Yut roared and charged the wyrm, but no matter how hard he ran, he remained in the same spot, forced to watch Sanvik turn to cinders. As the fires died, so did the vision, and an unknowable amount of time passed in silence and darkness. In the end, the memories burned behind Yut, still painful but just slightly lighter. The air around him cooled, and he was back in the infinite gray, in an expectant silence.

"What is your oath?" Etha echoed again.

Yut looked at the flaring rune on his forearm, gold and blue lights tingling, and breathed long and slow. This was his path from the beginning, even if he did not know it. He would always kill for them. He would always die for them. Faces drifted in from the gray, of Tove the wisewoman, and his mother looking at him intently in the dim torchlight. He had a fever running for three nights, and Tove had just finished giving him a bitter brew. He was drifting, weak, and the brew made him shiver. Tove's face was resigned when she left. Another sleepless night was settling, but his mother continued holding his head in her lap. "She said you have a strong heart, my son," she whispered, applying a new rag to his forehead. Yut couldn't tell whether her eyes were red from lack of sleep or from the tears she tried to hide. "Of course you do—you're stronger than all of them, so you will live. And the gods will have to face me before they take you."

And now it all made sense to Yut. He may not be stronger than all of them, but if this was his path, he would leave the rest to the gods. He looked to the sky. "I do this for my mother."

The oath was made, Etha Spoke, and the endless gray became a furious red.

Chapter Thirty-Eight

Purpose

It was easy following their track right up until the thickest fog Sig had ever seen crawled from the earth itself. She would have stopped to wait it out, but somehow, she could not shake the feeling that she had to finish her business with Eira and Yut soon. Fog and darkness were an obstacle for the loud and a tool for the quiet, and she had unfortunately been on both sides of that story before. She kept her ears open, followed the best path that circumstances allowed, and placed her feet gently. She even thought she could tell which part of the forest she was in, until Eira said "Oy," not two strides away from her, which nearly got a dagger embedded in the wisewoman's chest.

Steeling herself, she approached Eira. The seeress was sitting with her back against a white pillar and whispering. *I should've known*, thought Sigrid, feeling and hearing the bending of the Saga in the air. She closed her ears to the fog's complaints, outraged at being formed here and now, instead of the following morning as nature prescribed.

Sig knelt by Eira, trying her best to see, hoping their enemies were not the smart and quiet type. "How many can you hear?"

Eira paused her Telling but did not move. When she got her breath back, she said, "Hard to tell. Ulric's crowd were making good gains but stopped a few hours ago."

"The fog might have gotten to them. It's like wading in milk out there."

"Perhaps. Though I fear they have a Seither, which means things are never as they seem." Sig remembered the Seither at the Mudwall, her words laced with double meaning. She understood now the witch was trying to tell her the truth about Sig's nature, but the shadowed ones knew it was not the right time. She smothered the anger at the injustice of it all, and found it was easier than before.

Focus.

"Where is Yut?"

"I need you to scout," said Eira, not hearing the question. "There are still animals in this forest, and their sounds could be masking skilled hunters. Be wary of Speaking, the Seither could be—"

"Eira," Sig interrupted, laying her hand on Eira's shoulder, to the seeress' visible annoyance. "Where is Yut?"

"The stone, where else? Further in the clearing. We must not rush him; he may just hold our fate now. Now, I can create a clear path through the fog for you. Call out anyone you see, and I will bury them."

It was clear Eira expected Sig to rush off on her new mission, to stalk the prey as she has done countless times before. But Sig continued kneeling by Eira for a silent, tense minute. She wiped the mist from her forehead.

"I see," said the wisewoman. "*Now?* After everything?"

"Eira, this is not about you."

"Stop being a fool. Now that our enemies are closing in, Sigrid.

Now that we are *this* close to our goal, you decide to run away? After all I did for you, all I taught you. When I found you, you were little more than a rabid dog, gripped by madness."

"I'm here for *Yut*, Eira."

"For a silly argument, you would leave me. Gods below, girl, did I not bring you back to the light?"

"But you lied, didn't you?" cried Sig, ripping the words out from her soul, too loud. "I remember everything, Eira. I saw Gyl in my village. The way she talked that night—it was the way *you* talk. You knew the shadowed ones were not real, didn't you? You knew about Gyl and that I wasn't cursed, and you kept it from me. For what, Eira? For control? Poison my mind to have a monster on your leash?"

"You're wrong," whispered the wisewoman, color draining from her face. "Who told you this? I... when Gyl told me about you, I knew she made a mistake. *She* knew it. So I sought to find you, to help you."

Sig threw up her hands, her laugh verging on hysteria. "Well, that's wonderful! Thank you, oh wisewoman, for your infinite grace. You *used* me Eira, and you lied."

"I protected you!" shouted Eira. And then again, quieter, "I protected you, you foolish girl. The lie was a shield for you, the very thing keeping your mind intact. The things you've seen, the things you've *done,* they would have broken you had it not been for this lie."

"The shadows protected me," said Sig. In her heart, she felt as if some great stone began to be lifted from her chest, allowing her to breathe again. Although Eira confirmed her suspicions, her rage did not ignite. On the contrary, that fire seemed to die with every word she said. "They were waiting for the right moment to reveal the truth, but they were always watching. Perhaps you protected me at the start, but only you could have brought me back to the light. And you decided not to. I'm sorry, Eira, I can't go on like nothing happened. I... I need to understand this myself. I had been living a lie this long, I must try to live the truth now."

Eira clasped Sig's hands. "Then let us understand this together, child. I am sorry it happened this way, but we can grow from this. We can heal together. Please, will you not trust me as you once did?"

And she did. More than anything, Sig realized, she wanted to stay by Eira's side, lies and stories be damned. She wanted to be useful, to travel with her, to be safe. So it was with pain that she softly pushed Eira away, and a far-away voice replied to the seeress. "You have broken that trust, Eira, so I must do this myself. I am here to speak with Yut, and then I must leave."

"That's alright, Sig," came a voice from the fog. It sounded like Yut's voice, just emptier and quieter. He emerged from the direction of the Oathstone, still looking awkward, dirty, and hungry. His forearm shimmered as if with intense heat, and bits of red ember flying off and fading. Whatever that stone did, it must have worked.

"I've been told of the ways of the seeresses," he continued, "but it doesn't matter now. I don't have a choice, Sig, and to be honest, I don't think I ever did. But at least now I'm ready for justice."

Sig stepped in front of him. "That is *not* true. Yut, you can have a life outside of all... *this.* Whatever happened at that stone, you are a free man. And that's coming—well, that's coming from me, do you understand?"

"Enough," interjected Eira, her voice like steel, cutting in between them. "He has made the oath. Though Sigrid has elected to abandon us, we still have a job to do, and the Cult is near. Gods willing, the two of us will be enough if we act now. You did make the oath, didn't you?"

"I have."

"Then we make deeper into the—"

Sig thought Eira stopped to listen for something, to the point that her own hands were on her daggers and ready to fly. But there was only an ominous silence. Clearly Eira caught something crucial, something unsettling, in Yut's voice.

Eira hesitated as she tilted her head toward him. "What exact oath did you make?" Whether it was her knowledge of the Saga or just her seeress instinct, Sig suspected Eira did not want to hear the answer.

"I swore to destroy the Cult," said Yut.

"And that is all? That was your entire oath?"

And then Sig noticed Yut's eyes, which before were the hungry eyes of a survivor. Now they were distant, as if his mind was on something far away, unaffected by the world and its cruelty. No anger, no hatred, they were the eyes of a single purpose.

"After I destroy the drake that killed my family."

* * *

An uncomfortable silence stretched through the mountains. The fog, given back its freedom, silently slunk away, eager to escape whatever was about to transpire between the three. For the first time, Yut and Sig beheld a dumbfounded Eira. It was obvious in that moment that a million thoughts fought for dominance behind her blindfold, and her face betrayed the emotions attached to them. There was confusion, anger, and perhaps even fear. It seemed the story Eira had been writing might have finally been torn from her grasp. But there were questions even Sig could not help but wonder.

She turned to Yut. "It let you make two oaths?"

Yut continued looking into the distance. With the fog falling away, you could start to see the mountains above them and the forest of Miklor below, though Sig doubted he was enjoying the view. "I guess he did," he said, "Eth—the stone didn't think it would last much longer, so he let me have two."

Sig looked at the Eira, who was whispering something under her breath. "Can he do that?"

"We can... we can..." muttered Eira, head cast down in thought.

Sig suddenly felt that she missed something important. They had waited too long, Eira had stopped listening for footsteps, and the fog was receding. She looked around at the dozens of pathways that led out of this place, all empty, all quiet.

Too quiet.

She was ready to leave Yut and Eira to their fate when she caught a glimpse of a shadow-spirit standing on one of the pillars surrounding the Oathstone. Though his face was swirling blackness, he seemed to be looking at her. "What..? "She whispered, slowly unsheathing a dagger.

"We can salvage this," Eira nodded, coming to some conclusion in her head. "I can accept this. Boy, is that the set order of the oath, kill the drake and then the Cult, or is interchangeable? You must tell me *exactly* what you said..."

Sig focused on the white pillars again, seeing and hearing no one, and yet sure that they were being watched. But how?

"Eira?" She called cautiously, but the seeress continued interrogating the despondent Yut. Sig looked at the shadow again, who took a startled step back. What the...?

Before rational thought caught up with her, the dagger was already flying at the spirit. She knew now that they were all in her head, conjured up out of a dark experience. Rational thought told her the dagger would pass harmlessly through the imaginary figure, and she would be off to try and find it in the sharp rocks.

Except that it didn't.

The shadowed form dissipated, leaving the dagger embedded in thin air. A slight shimmer, and blood began to bloom around it. Now Yut and Eira were watching, and listening, as green and gold leaves began appearing and falling in that spot. Sig noticed the leaves had glowing runes inscribed in them. In seconds, a mound lay at the foot of a lanky figure, bald, blowpipe poised at her lips, a look of shock on her tattooed face. She looked down at the dagger protruding from her chest, gave one bloody cough, and collapsed.

"Invisible drendir," breathed Sig.

"Seither magic," snarled Eira, "Take me for a darkened fool. Get ready!" She dropped to her knees, both palms on the ground, and exclaimed, "*Syna!*"

The Telling produced a small shockwave originating from Eira. Sig watched the shockwave make little explosions of leaves as it revealed the invisible drendir all around them. There were more positioned at the pillars, but most were encircling them, only a few strides away. In a crystal panic Sig saw dozens of them—some with blowpipes, others with their long knives, their startled faces adapting to the circumstances.

And not a single spirit in sight. *So be it.*

Sig's daggers flew, some even hitting their marks, but the adrenaline was soon replaced with three blowpipe needles embedded in her stomach and neck. She dropped to her knee as her limbs became numb and her vision blurred. The poison spread quickly, and she could only make out the sprawled figures of Eira and Yut before she also began her collapse. "Shadows..?" she managed to whisper.

Other voices drifted in from the gray clouds, but Sig could not even move her neck to look at them. "How in the dark did the half-breed see Fox? The witch mucked up her own magic, didn't she?"

Sig lay on her back, her breath shallow, watching the gray sky before a familiar, bald silhouette covered it. Crow of the Seven Tribes peered at her. "No, the witch led us true. But as you said, this one's a half-breed—gods know what else she can do. Get extra rope for her."

Chapter Thirty-Nine

Old Friends

The limping drendir with grooves in his teeth almost finished tying up Sig, and Yut knew he was next. Whatever paralyzing poison those darts had on them was not effective for long, but gods below did they do their job for the moment. Eira was wrapped completely, with a thick rag in her mouth. Yut felt like he had no bones and was filled with water—even his vision swam. But he did see the drendir around him watching, their blowpipes exchanged for short bows, with another drendir keeping a tight hold on Yut while he waited for the ropes. The fog was thinner now, but he still could not see far into the trees. The drendir did not move or take their eyes away from him, not even for a second. It would not have mattered if they did, because if Yut was able to lift an adult cannibal then this situation would look very different.

Among the other expected emotions, most of all, Yut felt humiliated. His new and supposedly improved rune was silent, his meager ability to Speak was buried under nausea and vertigo, and whatever fighting he learned was useless when you had the physical capability of a seaweed stuck under a rock. Yut stared up the Oathstone, which was currently being vandalized by a drendir with a knife, and thought he heard laughing emanating from it. *Prick.* Yut figured if he survived this, he would destroy that darkened stone himself.

There was a soft crack, followed by curses. Yut dragged his face to the other side to get a better look and saw the drendir leader clutching a bleeding nose. *So, Sig is awake as well.* Stifled laughter scattered among the other drendir grew louder when their leader drove his boot into Sig's ribs.

"That's not even a glimpse of what's coming to you, darkened half-breed," he snarled, saliva and blood speckling Sig, who had her eyes clenched in pain. "You took something from me, you hear me? And you'll pay for each of their lives a thousand times over before the day is done."

"Oy Crow, didn't the witch say not to hurt 'em?" Asked the only drendir still holding a blowpipe. Her eyes were unfocused, and she was picking vigorously at her blackened teeth, a stream of drool running down her chin. Yut wondered what the mental capacities of drendir were, with the whole cannibalism thing. *Probably not great*, he concluded.

There was another crack as Crow straightened his broken nose and blew two streams of blood from it. The pain, which should have been immense, did not register on his face. He looked at the black mouth drendir with eyes of death itself, to no seeming effect. *Definitely not great,* thought Yut. She continued staring into the distance even as Crow limped up to her. The slap was much stronger than Yut expected for a man of his build, and it sent her to the ground.

"I am Crow of the Seven Tribes," he bellowed, pounding his chest at her, "I am the last keeper of the ancient blood, and the gods have anointed me. Should I now be a lapdog for a witch? My father took orders from a king, and I am greater than he."

"But she said she'll hurt us," she moaned.

"*I* will hurt you, Shrew," he responded, visibly holding back another slap, "And for every word that comes out of that disgusting mouth, I will take a finger, understand?"

Shrew seemed to be on the verge of responding on ill-advised instinct, before her eyes focused on something past Crow. "What's that?"

Bald heads turned to peer at the silent fog. Yut could not see in that direction, but he heard the ox on top of him stop breathing for a moment.

"That's just Wolf and Raven, you idiots," called Crow after a pause. "If the witch or her dogs think they can catch us unawares, they will die as well. Hurry up and tie the kid. We feast on red flesh tonight."

Shrew said something else, but it was drowned in the excited calls of various animals from the drendir, which made sense to Yut after he thought about it. Of course, he did not have much time to think about it before the hulking drendir on top of him leaned in, cracking Yut's back, and whispered a humid, "Not much meat on ya, but I reckon I'll make do with some nice and crunchy—"

He drifted off as the animal calls fell silent around them. Everyone, including Yut, stared at Crow while he pondered the arrow buried in his stomach.

It seemed to appear spontaneously, and no one was more surprised at this than Crow himself. Then the ropes he was carrying were on the ground, and so was Crow, silent and still. "See!" Yelled Shrew, joyous grin doubled in its return, "I told y'all there was something—"

Yut pulled his eyes from Crow just in time to see the second arrow go clean through Shrew's throat and splinter on the stones behind her. "They're here!" Someone yelled, and now everyone was moving—some were shooting blind arrows into the fog, while others tried to take cover. Yut knew an opportunity when he saw one, but unfortunately, the mass of hungry cannibal on top of him saw it too. He dragged Yut behind a large pillar, pushing another drendir out. Yut would have tried to struggle, but the poison made his limbs weak.

The drendir that was pushed aside debated claiming his spot back, thought better of it after seeing the size of Yut's captor, and began looking for his next hiding spot. An arrow found him first.

Yut managed to look around him even as he was shoved against the stone. Three more drendir lay pinned with an arrow, leaving five hiding behind cover, and the others having wisely fled.

"Run now and you might live," Yut croaked. He got a healthy slap in the face for his trouble. As he worked life back into his face to spit the blood out, things seemed to quiet down for a moment. The remaining drendir were breathing quickly and trying to look in all directions at once without giving away their position. But then, a movement caught everyone's eye. It did not come from the fog or the trees, but from the fallen drendir in the middle.

In the pool of his own blood, the supposedly dead Crow began to move. Painfully, he shifted to his side, clutching his stomach with a trembling hand. His face was a bloody mess, and blood sprayed from between his grooved teeth as he enunciated each word.

"Idiots. It's. Only. One."

The drendir exchanged glances from their hiding spots. Yes, it all started to make sense—one arrow per target coming from the same general direction. Yes, a few seconds interval between those, no doubt, to notch and aim. Yes, the attacker was close, and could even be out of arrows.

Yut had begun to consider if being eaten alive was worse than having his mind and body broken by Ulric. It was strange—fear did not seem to register at either prospect. Was it the poison...?

While everyone considered Crow's final words, one of the drendir seized her chance and bolted. She got as far as the Oathstone before an axe flew out of a different direction and sprayed the drendir's blood all over Etha.

Having been exposed, the rest of the drendir stood and armed themselves. Yut's captor continued pinning him, though his eyes bulged to notice anything in those trees.

"There!" Shouted one, pointing to the shadow emerging from the fog. The mysterious archer tossed his bow and empty quiver aside, and instead raised a master-crafted dwarven axe.

He was big, and terrifying, armed and armored to the teeth. Olaf the Dog roared and charged at the enemy.

The two drendir with bows immediately fired. One missed, the other would have hit Olaf's helm, but he managed to bring up his shield just in time. The arrow bounced off the rim, and before the drendir could finish nocking the next, Olaf slammed the shield into him, sending him flying. The momentum left Olaf exposed for a split second, when another cannibal dove for a jab with her long knife. It was about to hit home, but Olaf side-stepped, his bulk unnervingly dodging the blade, as he flicked his axe across the drendir's chest. She stumbled, clutching a leaking torso, before collapsing next to Crow.

Three living drendir circled the deserter, knives out, hungry smiles on their faces. They rounded the big man, feinting jabs and lunges, as if toying with their prey. Tense seconds passed, until Olaf barked out, "Seems only a couple ways out of this, boys. You drop yourselves, or I drop you."

Admittedly, it wasn't the best taunt, but it made the drendir in front of him snarl, as the other leaped for Olaf. The big man brought up his shield as it met the cannibal's face. This gave courage to the other two to attack, and they met him with furious slashing of long knives.

Incredibly, Olaf met them with equal force. The man Yut knew to mainly sit by the campfire and complain became someone else. His arms moved with precision ingrained over thousands of hours of training. His feet lithely moved his bulk around as if he grew tiny wings that alleviated most of his weight. His entire being commanded complete confidence and method. Yut could not believe his eyes.

As the two drendir stepped back to recuperate, the third one stood up, wiping blood from his mouth. Behind Olaf, another drendir manifested in the fog, and Olaf's gaze jumped between the growing amount of enemies. *He must be looking for a way to escape*, thought Yut, *his surprise attack didn't work, and now he must retreat. There is no other way. He's a scavenger, he's a survivor, he is...*

And then he met Olaf's eyes.

Dark above.

Olaf stepped back, turning to knock away the jab by the drendir behind him. He counterattacked with a slash of his own, the dwarven axe going half-way through the neck and back out in less than a second.

He turned to meet the three others, who began running to swarm him, but now were forced to stop suddenly, off balance. Olaf took the advantage and threw the axe at the one farthest away. The drendir collapsed with the blade in her face, as Olaf took out another hand axe from his shield hand.

He blocked an attack from the left, countered the one from the right, then used the momentum to move around the enemies, pushing them off balance and forcing them to meet him one on one.

A quick feint to the right, a shield jab on the forehead, and a loud *crack* as the axe struck the drendir's skull. Olaf didn't take the axe out however, but pushed the dead drendir toward the other one, unbalancing the cannibal again. In the blink of an eye Olaf had another knife out, jabbing and pushing at the drendir.

Suddenly, Yut was free. His own captor scrambled away to grab his fallen companion's bow, and Olaf was not looking at him. Yut knew he had precious seconds before the drendir could notch it and shoot his friend's back. He willed his weak legs and arms into motion, but as he tried to pounce on him, the cannibal whipped his fist in a fear-induced haymaker, leaving Yut on his back with the taste of blood in his mouth. The strike split everything into three, and it only came back into focus as the drendir took aim and released.

The arrow streaked toward Olaf just as he cut down his last foe. "Olaf!" Yut yelled, but it was too late.

With a *thunk*, the arrow embedded itself in Olaf's head.

They watched him in shocked silence. His body was about to join the rest of the corpses, there was no doubt. The arrow struck true. Even now, it stuck out of his helmet.

But Olaf the Dog did not fall. Instead, he turned.

His bloodied face twisted from annoyed confusion to something like cold rage as he focused on the shocked drendir with the bow. A new streak of blood flowed from under the helm.

"By the Nine," breathed Yut.

"By the Nine," whispered the drendir.

Olaf took a step forward, and the shooter nearly dropped his bow. He hastily scrambled for another arrow as the Dog began walking toward him. He finally found it, notched it, and fired. This time Olaf intercepted it with his shield without breaking stride. He marched like death itself.

The drendir tried to notch another arrow, dropped it, and began loading again. Olaf was a stride away when he raised the bow for the third time. He tried to aim at Olaf's head again, but the trembling arms missed by a mile. He tried to run, but the Dog was upon him now, hammering his face with a shield, painting the white pillars red.

About a minute later, Olaf stopped, and, breathing heavily, he turned to Yut. His heart skipped a beat as he looked into that stone-cold killer's eyes, the arrow still protruding from the helmet. He gently took it off, examined the arrow tip that penetrated it, and spat. "Thanks for the heads-up."

And with a final smash against the drendir's unrecognizable face, Olaf calmly walked towards Sig and began untying her.

* * *

"We are too late," coughed Eira as soon as Yut took the rag out of her mouth. "They are closing in—half of them will be upon us within minutes. As far as I can tell, the other half is on the forest outskirts. It's over, Yut. They have us surrounded. Gods take me, it's over. Dark..."

The ground was splattered with drendir blood, which pooled beneath each cannibal corpse. Not unlike the Red Hill, Yut realized. Thanks to the gray overcast, Yut could clearly identify their expressions of fear and rage. Of course, some didn't have faces at all, courtesy of Olaf. The big man himself was slumped by the Oathstone, breathing hard as he wiped blood from where the arrow tip scratched his head.

Sig got up with a groan, clutching the place where Crow kicked her. "We're still here, aren't we? We can take out at least a few more before the end."

"Aye," nodded Yut. "Olaf took out all the drendir by himself. We just need a plan." He looked to Olaf for support, but the old soldier was now preoccupied with his flask.

Eira continued facing the earth. "No, we are done. This lot was nothing compared to who is coming. You have one rune, Yut, and the oath wasn't even made right. Ulric alone has eight runes. His warriors are seasoned veterans, and his Seither does not hesitate to utter Darkspeech. I am—"

She stopped as her voice began to tremble. Yut could not see her face, but they could all tell she was trying, and failing, to force the sobs back through clenched teeth. No tears could leave those scarred eyes, but they did not have to. Eira the Blind, enemy of the Cult of Orik, Speaker, liar, manipulator, and the one who saved all of their lives, had finally broken.

"I'm sorry," she gasped between spastic sobs, "I'm sorry. I just wanted to make it right. I thought we'd get help. I thought we could... we could..."

Yut and Sig exchanged uneasy glances. For all her faults, if Eira broke, so did their mission and any hope for survival. Yut could not help but peer into those woods, where Ulric and his soldiers were no doubt preparing themselves for a quick and deadly assault. They could not hope to outrun them, and there was no chance of hiding. Strange, how quickly their fate changed. Just an hour ago, he thought he would gain the power to avenge his family. But now, would they join the drendir on the ground? Would their blood mingle in the rain, and would lucky scavengers loot their remains, not knowing or caring for their stories?

Thunder struck again, and Eira wailed openly now. The smell of blood seemed to sharpen, though this was not new to Yut anymore. Perhaps he could run and deprive Ulric of his rune for a while longer. Then Yut looked at his own axe, and another thought drifted in. *Perhaps I could deprive him forever.*

Yut turned, only to walk into Olaf, who naturally walked through Yut and stood in front of Eira.

"Olaf," she whispered, wiping dribble from her chin. "My child, you came back. You saved us, but for what? I have failed you—"

"*Enough*," he barked, and picked up the silenced seeress by the shoulders, setting her on her feet like a petulant toddler. "We're at war. Your plans went to crap because that's what happens in a war. Now we adapt and continue fighting. You can give up on your life all you want, but you sure as *dark* won't give up on mine. Or theirs." Olaf locked eyes with the stunned Yut and Sig. As if the gods themselves were watching, the last sliver of sunlight broke through and settled on his sweaty, blood-stained, ugly face. "Fight now, die later. Got it?"

"Aye," nodded Sig. "We can still fight, dark take it."

"War it is," echoed Yut, gripping his axe tighter. Three grim faces turned to look at the blind seeress.

They were out of time hours ago, but they were calm as they watched Eira, their expectant silence interrupted only by approaching thunder. After all, every person deserves the time to decide how they will die—even if the gods do not offer this decency to many. Thankfully, it did not take Eira long.

"Aye," she whispered, and suddenly Yut's rune flared, though this time it was bright crimson. It looked like it should have hurt, and he involuntarily flinched. Sig flinched as well, her hands on daggers.

Olaf already had his axe out, eyes bulging at Yut's forearm. "What the dark is that?"

"I don't—the oath made it go red," stammered Yut, "I think that means they're close. Wait, you all can see it?"

"I've seen a crimson rune before," said Sig quietly, "but not one of that shape. How long have you had it?"

Olaf overcame his momentary fright and peered at the rune. "Forget that, will it help us kill 'em?"

"It might—I mean, it depends..."

"*Friends.*" Eira's voice was still scratched, but to Yut's relief she stood slightly straighter now. There was a new emptiness to her as well, though she managed to sound as commanding as a tired mother. "Minds on the matter at hand, please. I cannot promise we will live through today—in fact, the opposite. But, as you said, we can fight, and fight we shall. I dare not assume to still hold your trust, but if we are to have a fool's chance, then we must destroy them one by one, and we must do so together. In this, Yut's rune may help, and it may be our doom. Sigrid, I need you in the trees. Take down as many as you can before they make it here. I will help."

Sig glanced toward an empty space and nodded. "We got it."

We...?

"Yut and Olaf," continued Eira, "you are with me. Yut is Ulric's goal, he will have eyes only for him. You must keep him occupied while I deal with the Seither."

"The old bait and kill," grinned Olaf. "Should have known you had a plan." Yut winced at having to be bait again—a broken wagon and a wulver came to mind. But it seemed to be the least crazy option they had.

"Wait," said Yut, "What about the others? Can Sig hold them off on her own?"

Eira rolled up her once-upon-a-time-white sleeves as she walked toward the center of the clearing, just as the first droplets of rain fell. "I did say I would help her, did I not?"

"More darkened fog," muttered Olaf.

Eira shook her head. "No time for that. And in either case, if this is to be our end, I should like them to earn our deaths. Now, please, remain calm. For the sake of our souls, I will not resort to Darkspeech. But as the gods allow me—"

She slammed her hands on the ground, causing vibrant red runes to spread from her hands, along the white rocks, the pillars, and the pools of blood, twisting over the broken weapons and bodies.

"—It will be close."

Chapter Forty

Breathe

Sig ventured into the trees, in the direction of the enemy. The rain picked up, pattering on the leaves just as she climbed a taller oak tree. Once she makes the first attack, she would need to be mobile, jumping from cover to cover before they realized what was happening. Even now she mapped out the best route to take between dagger throws, between breaths. The forest was ancient and crowded, which was good. The rain was good too, as she heard that The Hound, best tracker in Arthgard, could smell his quarry from a thousand feet away. Hopefully, that was on a dry day. Satisfied with her spot, she tried to focus.

Assuming the enemy knew their drendir plan had failed, they would spread out and approach carefully. Ulric and the Seither would head straight for Yut while the others backed them. Sig-and-friends would be outnumbered, and, by implication, dead within seconds.

She hoped the enemy expected this. She hoped they were sure of their numbers, weapons, and experience. She hoped they felt safe. After all, their dullness would be her only edge. That, and the trees.

It seemed the gods had a twisted sense of humor after all—she was shaped in the woods, alone, hunting and being hunted. She spent long nights waiting in the trees while bounty hunters roamed below. They were hired to kill a killer, but most heard the rumors of half-breed blood and the power it could bring. So they searched, and taunted, and called for her with promises and threats. But she remained in the company of fear and shadow, until Eira found her. Back then, she felt a sliver of hope, but in the end, her journey would end right where it had begun.

"*Different this time, no?*" asked the spirit sitting in the tree across from her.

Sig gave her a nonplussed look. "What are you doing here?"

"*We already said, we are here to protect you.*"

"Whole lot of good you did back there, then." Sig rubbed her rib cage again. *Gods* it hurt. That darkened Crow nearly drove her own rib through her lung.

"*But we did help,*" replied the spirit, gray legs dangling from the branch. She was shorter than the leader—younger, perhaps? She wore a tattered blouse and long-skirt with washed out colors, and no footwear to speak of. Sig could not remember which of the villagers this shadow represented, and she was not sure that she wanted to.

"Then I appreciate you showing me *one* invisible drendir. You know, out of the *hundred* that immediately took us."

The girl-spirit slumped. "*We are you, Siggy. We perceive what you perceive. The difference is, we also see what you choose not to.*"

Great, now they are getting judgy. Sig knew they were right, of course—one drendir was not careful and kicked a pebble down the pillar. And, set against the bland gray sky, there was a hint of an invisible outline moving on the cliff, like creases in the air. She should have noticed it but was focused on Yut and Eira, so the spirits noticed instead.

And then Sig realized something. "With the drendir… Not that I wanted it, but why didn't you all take over as before? If you knew there was danger, and there were too many to handle by myself, why didn't *you* kill them?"

The spirit seemed to think on this for a minute, her face shifting between shades of darkness. "*Something's changed, Siggy. Something has been given and something taken.*"

"All I've gotten is more trauma, it seems."

"*Yes, the pain of memory. The Leader has deemed you ready to receive it, and now you are whole. You need not fear us taking your body and mind ever again. That which is given—peace. Taken—protection.*"

Sig shifted her sitting position to keep her leg from getting cramped. Of course, it's when she wanted their protection that she couldn't have it—just adding punchlines to the joke. She tried to focus on the surroundings to avoid what happened last time, and this gave her the alarming idea that Ulric and his crew may be invisible as well. *Right.* She tried to still her movement, breathing quietly, watching for rain droplets bouncing off spaces they shouldn't.

The spirit remained on the opposite branch, the rain passing through her, which she did not seem to mind. And neither would Sig, as the cold rain started running down her back. Though she wanted more answers before her death, Sig could not risk further speaking.

The spirit turned to her. "*You know we are in your mind, right?*"

Ah. Sig tried to think at her as coherently as possible through the building shivers. *If you want to protect me then help me. They called me a berserker for the things you did through me. Can't you give me something—anything—that can take care of a few dozen soldiers?*

"Hmm... The Leader thinks you have powers that lay dormant, and with time, they will blossom. We will help for as long as you need it, but you need to do some things yourself. I'm sorry, Siggy, that's just how it must be for now. Perhaps later—"

She turned suddenly and peered deep into the forest. This time Sig was looking too. The first of them appeared, a distant silhouette in the pewter light. Rain pattered on a balding head, seeping into his drenched wolfskin and sliding off a beautifully carved yew longbow. He kneeled to examine something on the ground, and Sig realized it was none other than the tracks she made while trying to find Eira. The Hound raised his hand to signal behind him and cautiously walked forward.

At least they're not invisible, thought Sig, as more warriors appeared behind The Hound, shields and spears at the ready. They were spread out, as she assumed, and well-armed, as she feared. No Ulric or Seither, but she counted at least twelve of them covering a sizeable area of the forest.

Breathe in, breathe out. She had faced similar odds once. Maybe. And she was able to run away. And she was smarter now, and quicker, and her aim had improved. Things could be worse.

Which is why she missed a breath when twelve more soldiers appeared behind them.

Hopelessness rose within her. She gripped her daggers tighter, eyes shut as her mind raced through the routes again. She could Speak, which might do some damage but would promptly send a volley of arrows her way. No, stealth was her best option, and in the end, she would unleash whatever dormant power was left in her, for better or worse. She would do her best, which is all she could afford, and hope Eira would be there for her in time. *Breathe in.*

And then she opened her eyes and saw The Hound examining

a broken branch not twelve strides from her, his neck exposed. Sigrid exhaled, and her body trembled no longer.

The second dagger was already flying at the next soldier by the time The Hound's body hit the ground. Sig did not have time to see if it impacted—she leapt to the ground and was on her way to the next spot.

When ambushing, the timing was everything, and she learned early on that the first ten breaths were the most important. In the first ten breaths she was the fastest, most powerful, and, crucially, least seen. She slid into her cover spot, waiting during the second and third breath. Someone gave a confused grunt, and another dagger was in the air.

Three bodies on the ground, and someone shouted—a fourth and fifth breath. Sig leaped at an isolated shield maiden, knocking her off balance and driving a dagger deep into her throat. Her other hand clutched the woman's mouth and nose. She did not dare look at her—the blood spray would blind her, and she was already looking at the next, and the next. Warm blood sprayed at her chest and throat. *Breathe in, breathe out.*

She lunged on all fours, staying close to the ground, seeing but unseen. The soldiers saw their fallen comrades and they shouted, but they were not looking at her yet. A few more daggers flew at exposed necks. *Breathe in, breathe out.*

Three breaths left—no time for thought; only muscle memory. Openings flashed, her eyes caught them, and her body pounced. *Faster.* She lunged off a tree root at another warrior. *Breathe in—*

And she was flat on the ground, her world ringing. His shield connected with her face just in time. Perhaps Sig's last lesson was that she only had eight breaths when fighting seasoned warriors.

The man standing above her was a far cry from the opportunists that would come looking for her. His chain mail glinted even in the shadows, and the spear, a foot from her face, was steady, sharp, and smooth as bone. He must have brought his shield up as soon as he heard the soft creak of her leather boot. Even now he was scanning the trees around him to avoid any more surprises. He yelled for his companions, and Sig would have already launched a dagger at him, had she any daggers left—her last one was knocked out from the impact.

The warrior looked at her again and grunted as the spear drove forward.

"Here."

But she was faster. Sig felt a tug on her shoulder as she rolled toward the spirit's voice. Her braids became undone so that wet hair and mud was all she saw amid flashes of gray sky and earth. Thankfully, she did not need to see, as her hand grasped the familiar handle. She heard the warrior curse and could almost feel the spear point close in on her spine for the second strike.

She leapt to the side again, turned, and *threw* to where she hoped his face might be. Then she heard him drop, the spear clattering next to her. She wiped the mud from her eye and pulled the dagger out of his. *Lucky shot.*

Sig breathed out. Eight breaths, eight warriors down, an infinity to go. They all faced her now, shields and spears raised. A few bows were also up, the arrows sliding back in unbearable tension. She was cold, save for the warm blood flowing down her arm. That spear nicked her good. Some part of her screamed desperate solutions at her: to leap away at the last second, to run, to attempt a protective Telling in the span of seconds. Once, she might have tried that.

Instead, she stood a little straighter, making sure to take in the focused, exhausted faces of her enemies. There was not a Telling she knew that could stop arrows—and if she did, she had no time to say it. So, Sig closed her eyes and listened to the rain.

You're right, she thought, hoping the spirits would hear her. *It is different this time.*

The bow strings snapped as one, and Sig gasped.

Someone grabbed her by the scruff of the shirt and threw her to the ground. Multiple thuds of arrows hit flesh, and Sig looked up at a figure looming over her. An arrow tip stuck out of his chest, but he did not seem to mind. Confusion became terror when she recognized his face.

Most of his barbaric outfit was soaked in blood, but it was not blood that made him move now. A glowing red rune sizzled on his forehead, illuminating the bleak silhouette enough to see the bald head and tips of grooved teeth.

Crow's empty eyes stared past her as a distant voice wheezed out of dead lungs, "I'm here, child."

Whatever horror Sig felt was doubled in the ranks of the soldiers who watched the dead drendir face them with a forced rictus on his face. *Nice touch, wisewoman,* thought Sig. Eira really was toeing the line of Darkspeech.

If any of Ulric's soldiers were unperturbed by then, the appearance of seven more drendir with glowing runes on their foreheads had finished the job. They moved in jerking motions, as if controlled by invisible strings, faces tilted toward their last meal.

Spears were gripped, tattering against shields that suddenly felt heavy. The soldiers still outnumbered the dead, and Sig doubted dead drendir would be much better fighters than living ones. But it was not about fair combat.

It was about how many more breaths they allowed her. She gripped her dagger and slid behind cover as soon as the drendir charged the screaming warriors. *Breathe in...*

* * *

Yut breathed out. He was not sure if the rising bile was from witnessing eight drendir corpses rise from pools of their own blood, or from the nerves of his impending death. He also did not know where the bile even came from—he felt like he had not eaten in days.

Wiping cold sweat from his forehead, he risked a glance at Eira. The wisewoman was facing the forest, arms outstretched, muttering runes in a low voice. Her fingers turned black as she raised the drendir, as if she had touched some corruption with her magic and now it stained her. They still moved in various directions like she was playing an invisible harpa with both hands. Yut hoped it was not enough to damn their souls to the Dark, and just enough to help Sig out there.

His rune was still aflame, making the air around his forearm shimmer, though it was painless. In fact, the red glow provided a strange sort of comfort—and comforts were few lately, almost as few as answers. He still did not know how the rune worked, and he wondered if the rune was now telling him the drake was nearby. He wondered if that drake was Ulric. After all, Eira said some Tellings and Runes allowed shapeshifting. Strange, how there was no rage at that prospect. He wondered if he still wanted revenge, if it meant giving up his own life. His parents would strangle him for even suggesting something like that.

Yut was still keenly aware of the peaceful emptiness, and how it seemed to eat up more of him the further he traveled down this path, whatever it was. Perhaps he could have gone to Orheim after all, just as Olaf offered. If he had gone to Ottervik after the wyrm burned his village—would he have still felt it? Or had he made a terrible mistake?

This was his last thought before Eira opened her eyes with a sudden gasp. "You've done well, Sig. Now run!"

She dropped her arms on her knees. The rain had dampened both of them at this point, though he doubted that was the reason for her shivering. Yut began walking up to her, but she waved him off. "They're here."

And there they stood, a mere fifty strides away at the foot of the forest. Like Yut and Eira, they stood apart, though they walked together. The Seither strode confidently, smiling softly, while Ulric carefully skulked. He looked different now, his bright smile replaced by a haunted, hungry expression. Perhaps this was his true face, now that he was so close to his prize. It was about then that Yut's emptiness was replaced by anxiety. *Gods, maybe this was a bad idea after all.*

"Courage, Yut," said Eira sharply, "We follow the plan. I will not abandon you."

Ulric and Seither stopped, and the Heisir finally raised his face to look at Yut. "Strong-Arm," he called. For a moment, he looked like the Ulric from Miklor, the charismatic leader that Yut snuck into the city. Yut realized that was to his own doom. There was recognition on Ulric's face, as well as concern, as he slowly raised his legendary sword, Staugr. Yut took a step back and gripped his own axe tighter. But Staugr merely clattered to the ground. "I am sorry for the way I acted in Miklor," said Ulric. "It is no secret I have no love for your mentor. I assume she has told you that we are here to torture and kill you for your rune. No doubt she told you many other things, few of them clear or true. I know this because I know Eira. And I know her because I stood where you stand, Strong-Arm, and it led me to ruin."

Yut could hear Eira's teeth grinding. "Lying darkspawn," she muttered.

Ulric paid her no mind. "The truth is that I am dying, Yut. The Cult of Orik has named me their champion, and it was Eira that insisted on the gathering of the runes, all those years ago. But such power was not meant for us mortals, and without your help they will soon destroy me."

"So it is my life for yours, then?" Yut was too loud. *Control your voice, man*. "Not sure I'm taking that deal."

"Your life will be your own, my friend, because the rune can be given freely."

"Liar!" snarled Eira. The Seither laughed—at least that is what Yut assumed based on the rabid squeals coming from her mouth. "So wise for her years," she cackled, "and yet so *stupid*."

"Sometimes it takes a life, or a piece of it, it's true," continued Ulric, "but for one such as you, who had just received his rune, this will not be so. It has not yet been attached to your soul or body, don't you see? At most, I will take some of your recent memories—which I doubt you will miss anyway. Am I wrong?"

Distant thunder and rain filled the silence that followed.

"Is it true?" asked Yut, eyes still locked with Ulric.

"Yut, I have never lied to you," replied Eira. "Though my words were not always clear, I only ever brought you closer to your destiny. Now I tell you truly, the man in front of you does not care for your soul or your life. He admitted it, he's a dead man walking. There are few things he would not say."

"Destiny indeed," whispered Yut. "I thank you, Ulric Heisir, for telling me the truth. But I'm sure you understand that it's difficult to trust you here and now. Besides, how do you expect one more rune to solve your problems?"

"Has she told you nothing? The rune of strength is unlike all others. This is why we have spent years searching for it. It is the one rune that has the power to hold the others in check. And as for trust, I understand too well, though I would question if your trust were wisely placed now. Still, we can do this ourselves, man to man, no seeresses."

"Eira stays."

Ulric clenched his jaw. "To show my heart is true, fine, she can stay."

The smirk melted from the Seither's face. "My Heisir, you *cannot* trust—"

"*Leave us.* No more blood needs to be shed over this." His face suddenly twitched, spasming to his neck and back. He blinked into the distance and stood still for a second, breathing shakily, staring into nothing with that shadowed look. Then he groaned, pinching the bridge of his nose. "I… I don't…"

"It's alright," said Yut, walking forward, his own axe on the ground.

He could almost hear the shock on Eira's face. But this was it, and it had to be done. *He* had to be done.

"Yut, *no.*"

"I'm still not sure I trust you, Ulric, but if I'm being honest, I don't think I care anymore." His voice shook, and his heart beat wildly, but dark could take them both. It was time to end the journey. He thought of his mother, and the last of his strength left him. *Soon.*

He stretched his arm to Ulric. "Take it." The rune on his forearm burst ablaze, angry red sparks shooting into the air, as if aware of the betrayal. Ulric was taken aback, but nodded at Yut, and grasped the arm back.

"*No!*" shouted Eira. The ground jolted under their feet as Eira began Speaking, and a furious blast of wind sent Yut stumbling. But then everything returned to normal—it even stopped raining. Yut saw cracks in the earth spreading from Eira, though they curved around him and Ulric.

"The Seither will protect us for a while," said Ulric, "but not forever. I'm proud of you, brother. Are you ready?"

Yut nodded. Ulric gripped the forearm tighter and began Speaking as well. It was the backwards Speaking of Darkspeech, but Yut felt that did not matter much now. Muffled sounds of thunder and lightning echoed around them as clouds multiplied above. Eira's wrath was finally released, and its power did not disappoint.

He dared a glance at the Seither, yellow teeth on full display in either rage or concentration, or both. Lightning bolts landed around them, though even those blinding flashes were softened under the Seither's protection. She must have been powerful indeed to protect them and herself from Eira.

The seeress herself had her arms in the air, screaming runes at them all. A column of flame shot out from the fissures in the earth, and one caught the Seither off guard. She sidestepped just in time to not be incinerated, though it left a nasty burn mark on the side of her face. In that moment the bubble of protection disappeared, as the Seither changed tactics and focused her full attention on Eira. Wind, rain, and darkness descended upon Yut and Ulric, and the ground trembled even harder. Yut would have lost his footing were it not for Ulric's grip.

"Focus here, Yut," he said softly, "They will be fine. Now, when you feel me pulling, try to let go. It may be painful if you don't."

The seeresses now stood interlocked in an unseen battle, one creating destruction, the other unmaking it. Yut forced himself not to look, and instead planted his feet. *This is it.*

Ulric's grip tightened. He uttered one more Telling, and Yut's body seized. It felt like being tossed in an icy river without warning. His heart rate tripled, and he nearly pulled his hand back. "Dark above," he growled through clenched teeth. It was not so much painful as it was shocking.

And then he felt the power.

Familiar, and yet completely new, it opened his world once again. He was hoping this would happen, that he could taste it once more before the end. He stole a glimpse around him and saw Eira's power in the elements, her complete command of their Saga. The wind and earth obeyed her every Telling as if she was their creator. It was magnificent.

Then there was the Seither, doing everything to take Eira's full wrath and not melt. Her Darkspeech was twisted but beautiful in its own way, cutting into Eira's words and disarming her attacks.

And then his eyes fell on Ulric. He had become a silhouette where only the glimmer of his eyes produced any light. No—there were runes on him, living runes of varying colors, crawling on his arms and neck. In that instant of bliss, Yut saw that Ulric was not the drake that had destroyed his village. He did not know how exactly, perhaps because of the oath, but he did feel that the drake was close. Vengeance was close.

Then his vision went red, and Yut fell to his knees. All of his strength was suddenly drawn out, and he heard the Seither do her squeal-laugh again. Yut remembered the ravine, when he met his first Seither, and the battle that followed. He saw the laughing Seither standing straighter, no longer shaking from Eira's wrath but overcoming it. *The darkened witch stole my power!*

He looked at his arm, which was now white from Ulric's grip. The silhouette continued Speaking, and Yut's vision pulsed. He was thrown into a red memory, Yut looking up at the Oathstone while Eira was telling him something. What did she say? What did he do afterward?

Back in the real world, he heard Eira shout, "Fight, dark take you, *fight!*"

But he couldn't fight, could he? This was his choice, he no longer wished for vengeance, he no longer wanted emptiness. Was that not why he was doing this?

Another memory pulsed, this time they were in the tallgrass, watching Eira as she took off her blindfold for the first time. She wanted their trust but could not earn it. He wanted vengeance. No, that's not—

Another memory, a pit in the ground, empty of everything, even hope. The pain of training. A cave with a wounded wulver. A child lay dying in his arms and he was shouting something.

His mind was becoming numb, but one thought formed clearly—he was not recalling these memories. He was losing them.

Yut forced his eyes open and noticed the rune had shifted from his forearm to his wrist. It drifted towards Ulric, who was watching it intently. Yut instinctively pulled the arm back, but he might have had better luck pulling an oak out of the earth.

He watched the red memories peel away from his mind, powerless to halt them. This was what he wanted, wasn't it? These memories were mostly pain. No one should have to carry them.

There was a fire and an undercooked rat. There was a song in a strange language, and a short man with a gap in his teeth. There was laughter and weeping in the night. A blind seeress. A half-breed warrior. A well-armed coward.

A village, a fire, golden eyes.

A battle for manhood.

No...

A father advising his son on the intricacies of a wholesome toast for a feast.

You can't take these...

A mother tending to her young, bleeding, stupid son. "I was

just being strong, like Keld."

"Keld has fourteen winters already, and has gone through puberty," smiled the strange woman. Her voice seemed familiar.

"So? When I'm fourteen, I will be the one pushing *them* down, you watch. I'll be the strongest in the world."

She chuckled, a beautiful sound. "I'm sure you will, my sweet, fair warrior. If you eat your vegetables and remember that true strength does not lie in strong arms."

"Well, I'll have a horse by then, too."

And then it was gone. Everything was gone. Pure light surrounded him, and a frenzied thought struck him: Was it too late? But too late for what?

He looked deeper into the white abyss and saw it. The very thing he has been dreading, his final companion. Emptiness. This was his soul. This was his vengeance, and he fell deeper until he began to dissolve along with the pain and memories. Alone among nothing, Yut finally became the emptiness. It was... it was...

"It was my mom," he said aloud. But there was no response. There was no rune, because Yut had no body anymore. He suspected there was no "Yut" anymore, either. And yet there was the one undeniable, pure fact that he still held like a festering wound, one that could not heal even if all memory was taken from him.

"She was my mother," he said louder, to no one, to everyone.

"And you killed her."

Yut opened his eyes and saw his rune slipping through his fingers onto Ulric's forearm. *This is it.*

He *pulled* with all of his strength—not against the iron force of Ulric's arm, but everything else. He willed his rune, his memories, his soul back. "Now, now, Yut," intoned Ulric, "I told you what would happen if you held on."

A thousand arrows pierced Yut from all directions. It was a rabid type of pain, one that left scars deep in the mind. He screamed, yes. There were tears and blood and saliva. But he watched the rune, and it did not move any closer to Ulric. And so, even in his agony Yut allowed himself the smallest sliver of satisfaction.

Because, for once in his whole darkened life, something had gone according to plan.

"OLAF!" Yut's howl penetrated even the dark winds of Eira's Speaking.

And it was echoed by a roar.

He had shed his armor and shield. After all, he did not have much time to make it from his hiding spot among the pillars to the enemy. His aim would also have to be exact, so he only kept the dwarven axe and the dagger. And maybe a few others, but he assured Yut and Eira that was it.

And so Olaf charged into battle once more. Sure, he was literally stabbing the enemy in the back through a risky ruse, but nobody said it would be a fair fight.

Ulric's eyes widened as he heard the war cry. He was about to turn to face Olaf, which would spell the end of their foolhardy plan.

"He would never," said Eira in response to Olaf's objection. "The rune is his life, his one chance to escape certain death. And depending on how close it is, he will not let it go for anything. This is why the timing must be perfect."

Instead, the Heisir concentrated on his prize and pulled harder, making Yut nearly blind with pain and effort. *Just a few more seconds, a few more...*

"Witch!" Shouted Ulric, and the Seither, who was still interlocked in the standoff, jumped. She stole a terrified glance at

Olaf, saw him aim the axe at Ulric's head, and her mouth dropped open. Time must have slowed down for her as the adrenaline kicked in, and a thousand decisions were made in that moment. Yut and company had relied on the fact that they would not be smart decisions.

She flung an arm toward Ulric just as Olaf threw. She uttered a desperate Telling, the air shimmered behind Ulric, and a protective half-sphere appeared. Ulric was safe, and their doom was averted at the last second.

That is, not counting the highly mobile dwarven axe sailing directly at her head.

The Seither was happy in her death. After all, she did not realize the bait that Olaf made out of Ulric, and she did not have time to see him adjust his aim at the last second. Focused on protecting her Heisir and battling Eira, there was no time to consider her own health.

She stood still and quiet for a moment as her thoughts caught up with the axe inside her skull. Then, in the way of all Seithers, she began to transform into her true form. Her body twitched and stretched in all the unnatural ways, and she almost became dangerous again.

"In the end, so *stupid,*" sneered Eira through bloodied teeth. The axe might not have killed the Seither, but it did stop her Speaking for a moment. And a moment was all Eira needed.

A rune of pure destruction was uttered, and the Seither exploded into a brilliant light. It was the type of light that made the whole world go dim. Not to be outdone, a shockwave followed, tearing the ground underneath, and sending all of them flying.

Chapter Forty-One

Bait and Kill

Yut was pulled from the rubble by the surprisingly-strong hands of Eira. He blinked furiously, trying to regain vision from the blast of the Seither. Blood trickled from his ears, and he heard a muffled, "I may have overdone it," from Eira. As his senses returned, he saw inscribed runes on the steaming bits of black Oathstone rubble around him.

Yut spat at it. "Good riddance." Steam usually had a way of hissing; this one seemed to be laughing.

The rain had eased somewhat, though distant thunder warned them that it was not over. Violated memories snapped back into place all at once, and relief flooded Yut as the rune flashed crimson on his forearm. It was a close and foolish gamble, baiting Ulric to bait the Seither. But they all knew they stood no chance battling both of them. Now, at least, they could all focus on the Heisir.

Olaf emerged from the rubble with a string of curses that even Yut had not heard before. He expertly checked for injuries, but instead only found his flask in a mangled ruin, which heralded an even brighter set of curses. The Seither explosion left a sizeable crater in the clearing, covering the rest with rubble and a coat of white dust.

"Definitely overdone it," said Eira, and then collapsed to her knees, covering her mouth as she coughed blood into it. Yut moved to help her, and realized she was pale beyond the coating of dust. Dark below, she must have used every ounce of strength in the battle.

Which gave Yut an idea. He put his hand on her shivering shoulder. "Eira..."

"I'm fine," she said through gritted teeth, "We have to finish the job."

"You're a mess. Can't you take some of my strength? The Seither did it somehow."

She shook her head. "I just need a moment."

Yut helped her up and surveyed the destroyed landscape. He glanced at Olaf—even the big man peered at the seeress with concern. It looked strange on his face. The blast did not seem to reach the forest, and Yut wondered if Sig had heard this, and if she was on her way here. What did she tell him before? That he could have a full life without all this? He wiped blood from his ears, flicking it onto the remains of Etha-stone. No, she should be running far away from here. Whatever fulfillment she found, he hoped she could keep it.

A movement underneath a pile of rocks caught their attention. Yut let go of the seeress, and the three of them encircled Ulric. He exploded out of the rubble, looking around frantically. He stopped when he saw the crater and did something they did not expect.

Ulric laughed.

Slow, at first, but building. It was a broken, hysterical laughter, as if some other emotion was trying to escape but couldn't quite find the right way. Yut clutched his dagger, the last weapon he had left, noting Olaf clutched his tighter as well.

"You thought this would hurt me?" bellowed Ulric, joy and pain intermingling in his voice. "No, no... you thought you could take me on, the three of you, without the witch. You sad, darkened cr—"

"Eldr!" Shouted Eira, and Ulric burst aflame. Yut had to shield his eyes from the sudden brilliance. Though more intense, it was the same Telling Sig used on that draugr. It seemed the seeress still had some strength left.

But something was wrong. Ulric stood quiet, wreathed in flames, the sickly smell of burning skin filling the air. Smoke turned into mist and began rising from him as the fire died, leaving behind a badly burned Ulric. A brilliant blue rune glowed on his left arm, and Yut could tell there was plenty of strength left in him as well.

A second rune lit up on his neck, this one a light green, and his burns and cuts began to close up, replaced by clean, unmarked skin.

Behind him, Olaf scowled. "What...?"

Then, all at once, the rest of the runes lit up through his burned clothing. Yut's rune blazed brighter as well, and he was back in the world of power. However, he had no time to enjoy the feeling as Ulric darted toward Eira at an inhuman speed. His fist connected with the protective shield she had managed to Speak just in time, though the impact still sent her skidding across the rocks.

Yut was already behind him, godly strength filling him with bravery. He let the haymaker fly freely, putting his entire weight behind it like Olaf taught him. Ulric barely had time to see it before—

His fist punched air. *Huh?*

Now Ulric was under him, and, as the momentum of the punch twisted Yut's torso, the soldier was in his face again. *Huh?!*

He grabbed Yut by the throat and thrust him to the ground with surprising force, crushing the broken boulders underneath.

More white dust exploded around them, so Ulric brought his face close enough to Yut that he could see his eyes. Pure emptiness gazed back at him.

"The runes make us hard to break, Strong-Arm, but I *will* break you. Body and mind, this time. Just after I break them."

He lifted Yut into the air with one arm. Yut might have struggled, but whether through an exhaustion-fueled hallucination, or his memories still adjusting in his head, Yut did not see Ulric. He saw the people of Sanvik encircling him, excited faces shouting and laughing. "Take his eyes!" One of them yelled. Keld lifted him higher and grunted as he threw Yut into the throng. Yut came back, and in the blur of rocks passing him underneath, he glimpsed Eira preparing another Telling. She flinched just before he impacted, sending them both to the ground.

"Good?" asked Yut when they had finished tumbling over each other. The throw brought them both close to the crater, which Yut now saw was splattered with steaming black liquid. *Still better than a living Seither,* he thought. He should stay away from there, though in the current state he doubted much could hurt him. Save, of course, for an eight-runed death soldier.

"I'm fine," groaned Eira, "The little darkspawn has become formidable. One by one, he will destroy us."

Yut was still shocked at Ulric's power. The man could extinguish flame, heal himself, was strong and fast. And that should have been only a few of his runes in use. Yut looked at his rune, shimmering contentedly. Wasn't he supposed to be the strong one here?

"*Now* will you use my strength?"

Eira started to rise. "I can't. It's... risky. But keep your eyes peeled."

Ulric stepped out of the mist with the care of a wolf on a hunt.

He dug his boots into the rocks to prepare for the sprint, until Olaf appeared from the cloud behind him. The long knife drove straight through the Heisir's neck, the tip coming out the other side. Unfazed, he grabbed Olaf's arm and flicked his hand.

Yut was already running when he heard the bone snap. "Yut, wait!" Shouted Eira, but he could not stand by, not for Olaf.

The big man winced at his arm but did not let it stop him from throwing two quick punches to Ulric's jaw. The third punch was intercepted, so, without losing momentum, Olaf smashed his knee into the Heisir's groin, forcing him to double over.

Yut willed his legs to move faster, even though the wind blasted his face and the rocks flew past. He focused on Olaf. *You're not gonna die now, you fat son of a—*

Suddenly, Ulric released Olaf's broken arm, pulled the long knife out of his own neck, and buried it in Olaf's stomach. The Dog's eyes bulged as he went down to one knee, and Yut nearly stumbled.

Ulric shoved Olaf to the ground and grabbed his head and chin. "NO!" screamed Yut. He was so close. He could make it. He had to.

And then Ulric met his eyes. All of his runes flared, and he leaped, becoming a momentary blur. Then, he was in front of the completely exposed Yut. *The darkened bait and kill.* Ulric placed his hand on Yut's forehead, whose body was still being carried forward by the momentum, and a white rune flashed on his palm. Yut screamed.

And awoke on the ground. The rain had returned, cold droplets pecking at his face. No, there was a roof above him, fires, roasting meats, and the sandy proving pit. This was the night of nights, his big debut as a true man. What was that fighting form his father showed him? Strong indeed. That's right, he would be strong indeed.

"Strong..." he murmured and began to rise from rubble.

Eira landed next to him, her face and hair covered in blood. Gods, she was not supposed to be running through the forest by herself—where was Sig?

"Eira?" he inquired.

Her hand shot out like a viper and slapped him. "Focus!" she shouted. And then it all returned. He still had his rune, but Ulric got to him, and a white rune blinded him, and then... dark above...

"Where is Olaf?"

"Watch out!" Yelled Eira, but it was too late. Ulric was on top of them both, hand to throat and squeezing. Blood covered most of his face, and some teeth were missing, not to mention the burn marks. The white rune immobilized Yut for too long. Eira gave Ulric a thrashing, but even as he held them, the green rune on his neck was ablaze, sealing his wounds. "Watch her, Yut," he growled, "watch me end her like I ended your fat friend. Body and mind, brother. Watch!"

Horrified, Yut realized his own rune was inactive. Ulric's cursed white rune must have somehow dampened it. He felt his forearm burn and could feel the strength returning, but not fast enough.

Suddenly, a shadow loomed over them, dark and terrible. Meaty arms wrapped around Ulric's neck and pulled with all the strength Olaf could muster. Yut did not know how the big man was still standing with that knife in his gut, but he was thankful for it. Ulric screamed but would not let go of his quarry. Yut pushed desperately as well, until he caught Eira reaching for him with a trembling hand.

It was time. They did not know how much strength Olaf had left, and it was clear Eira had none. Risks be damned, they will destroy Ulric together. He reached out to Eira just as his rune flared red again. She hesitated, and Yut attempted a nod of encouragement that she could not see.

"I'm sorry," she mouthed before taking his hand and turning the world dark.

Chapter Forty-Two

An Oath Fulfilled

Sometime later, Yut sat alone in a cloud of hissing steam and ash. Molten rock fell in chunks at various cliffs around him, turning black as it cooled. There were no white stones left, and not a cloud left in the sky.

His rune was active again. He knew because a stream of hot steam blasted him in the face moments before without so much as a blister. He also knew because he heard the Saga around him again, and the outrage with which it cried out. Because the stones were not supposed to be here—and neither was he.

Part of him was still piecing it together, and the other part wanted to run. Eira grabbed his hand and began Speaking even while Ulric choked the life out of her. But she did not take Yut's strength, at least not like the Seither. Instead of simply feeling his strength drain, he felt a connection with Eira. It was like his heart and mind were torn open and intertwined with hers. For a moment, Yut and Eira became one, and everything around them faded into black.

"Some Speakers could Speak together, in the older days," she said back then, "This brought them great power, at an even greater risk.

They could level cities, armies, and mountains. But this required perfect trust and harmony, and us mortals were not made for such things."

They floated alone in the abyss. She still clutched Yut's hand, and he could see red energy flowing from his rune into her veins, spreading through her entire body and making it glow crimson. Eira was trembling—this was far too much power even for her. But she held on fast, no matter how much Yut tried to let go.

Memories flashed before him. Eira's memories, her entire life, just as his memories opened to her. Yut tried to ignore them. He knew Olaf had precious seconds left to live with his wound.

Suddenly, Eira roared. Her voice sounded deeper, harsher, verging on rabid. She was Speaking, one painful rune at a time, and somehow Yut could tell the world was being changed around him even through the darkness. *Gods, are we in the Dark itself?*

He thought he could hear sounds emanating from somewhere above, in a different world. It was like standing behind a great curtain, hearing but not seeing. Something titanic exploded, the ground jumped, and great plumes of flame and steam rose from the ground. Eira was creating something large and terrible, though she herself did not fully know what it was.

Back among the steam clouds, Yut meandered past the pools of lava. He was here somewhere, Yut was sure of it. The initial explosion would have pushed them back, so Yut followed the clearest path into another cloud of ash.

Eira had screamed. Yut could feel her panic, the desperation with which she used the power that would destroy her. His power. He was trying to stop it, to halt the flow of his rune to her. Surely whatever she had released would have been sufficient to destroy Ulric?

But she kept holding on, because under the panic and

overwhelming power Yut felt a more potent emotion. Underneath it all, Eira felt deep, shameful regret. "I'm sorry," she mouthed.

"For what? Eira, end this!"

His rune flared again, and Eira's body was wreathed in crimson. In the real world, something erupted out of the ground with a giant shockwave, and her body was seized once more. Again, Yut focused on the rune, willing it to stop, to end the flow of power before it destroyed her. "No!" he screamed.

"The oath..."

The voice came from the abyss, but it was all too familiar. He realized it was not Eira, but Yut, pouring destruction into her. And he could not stop it.

"The oath is fulfilled," said Etha.

"No..." breathed Yut, "she's not part of the Cult anymore. This was not my oath! You must bring her back! She saved my life..."

And she did. She came back for him, when he was a moment away from being Seither food. She was there during his vision, the fever, the painful night of thorns and darkness. She healed him, brought him back, gave him instruction and purpose. For all her secrets, Eira pulled him from that abyss. Olaf, and Sig, too. They protected him, taught him to survive, and became his friends. By all the gods above and below, he could not lose them. He could not bear that pain. Not again.

All at once, there was silence. The rune had finally fizzled out, and they floated in the cool darkness together.

Yut made his way through the plumes of ash and smoke until he reached a ledge. He was on a sheer precipice, the clouds were gone, and before him stretched the world. Dozens of little rivers wound their way through the many nameless forests of Arthgard, into the little fjords and the White Sea itself, which was now a glistening horizon. He spotted Miklor, the size of his thumb, and could just make out the refugee tents gathered around it. From here, it would not be a stretch to see a thousand roads leading everywhere, just as Eira had said.

He fell to his knees. *Together, they could level mountains.* Steam hissed behind him amid the rumble of falling stones. It seems they could create mountains as well, and this one stood taller even than the Suldrfjall, their peaks far below his feet. A fresh wind blew in from the East, bringing a few melting snowflakes, and Yut shivered. His mind was still in the Dark, where he and Eira floated, nothing left to give or take.

In that eternal quiet, their true forms were revealed. Yut remained the same. After all, he was not quite old enough to hide much. But Eira became younger, filled with life, even as her body began to disintegrate into red flecks.

That was when her blindfold fell, and Yut saw them. In her true form, two golden eyes, slit like a cat's, looked back at him before disintegrating.

"The oath is fulfilled."

The last of her memories reached him as he looked upon the landscape below. They were running out of time. The Cult needed to find the rune of strength before Ulric succumbed to madness. They could not count on finding it anymore, so she decided to create it. It was said that the gods granted runes to mortals to battle the Dark. If a shapeshifter, acting as a servant of the Dark itself, descended upon an innocent village, surely the gods would see fit to grant at least one of them a gift. And if they didn't, she would try again with another village, and then again, until the rune showed itself.

She relied on a fool's chance, but it paid off. That is, until she saw Yut's face, and realized that the world they were trying to build with the Cult would not destroy the Dark but be its culmination.

So, she endeavored to find a different path.

Now it stretched endlessly before him, the great emptiness. Did he really avenge his family and destroy his enemies? No, he had merely played a part in someone's plan. Eira must have known he would destroy her as soon as he revealed his oath to kill the drake. Maybe even sooner. And so, she used him. It was not emptiness that he felt now, but weakness. Too weak to stand up to others, too weak to protect himself or his family. He had been weak since the beginning; it was in his blood, and no rune could change that.

That was when Yut noticed he was not alone at this peak. A bloody path meandered to this ledge and crawled around a boulder. There was a boot, and a hidden dagger peeking out of it. He faced the world, staring into its face as he died. Of course, Yut recognized the boot, as he had to dodge it many times in their training. Sometimes, he even succeeded.

"Your feet, boy. Everything starts and ends at the base." Tears dotted Olaf's bloodied chain mail as Yut wiped ash from the warrior's shoulders. Yut never asked him why he returned to them. He never asked why Olaf remained true to his word with Eira. Perhaps he did not need to. Somehow, Olaf found his mangled flask and the dwarven axe in the new mountain, and he held them to his chest even as he died. In the end, the old soldier passed with a view that none but the gods had seen before.

"We will remember you, Olaf, son of Thoran," whispered Yut, tracing a rune of peace over him. "You saved me. You saved all of us."

Another gust of wind blew against the young mountain, but Yut had already disappeared into the ashes and the mist, and so had the long knife that killed his friend.

Chapter Forty-Three

Blackmount

The mountain, which would later be called Svartalfjall, or Blackmount, stood angry and shivering like a newborn babe. Its appearance was heard and felt all throughout southern Arthgard, and was naturally echoed by thousands upon thousands of terrified prayers. A volcano erupting was a bad omen by itself, but an entire mountain bursting from the ground was something else entirely. Plumes of ash and mist enveloped it as massive boulders fell, were swallowed by abyss and lava, and were replaced by new rising cliffs.

A hand punched out of a sparse mound of rubble. Then another, and then a head that might have once been blonde emerged. Sig was unharmed save for a few burns, plus the cuts from before, but she did not count on her luck for much longer. She held up a dagger as she surveyed her environment. It was not one of her daggers—she nicked it from a soldier before returning to her companions.

After deciding that the only threat in the area was the landscape itself, she pulled the rest of her body out and moved forward at a slight jog. "What in the dark is this?"

"*You saw them just before it happened,*" said the spirit gliding next to her. It was the tall one, the leader, and as usual, he was right. She remembered escaping the forest when she surveyed the battlefield. There were craters and white rubble, and the four of them struggling in the distance. She was afraid she had been too late. And then... Gods below, the power...

"They were Speaking together," she breathed, jumping over a widening pit and nearly losing her footing.

"The power of combined Speaking, Eira has warned you about it. One must consider the result when one of the Speakers is rune-marked."

If this was the result, then the warnings were not dire enough. In that moment she felt a colossal twisting of the Saga without even having to listen, as the ground exploded and columns of mist and ash bellowed out of the earth. She was sure the end of the world had come. It felt ridiculous now, but she had tried to run in and pull them out when it started. She might have become a burned husk had she not been blown back by the shockwave.

After a few minutes, she admitted that she was lost. She was surrounded by a labyrinth of rock in various stages of melting, with plumes of deadly mist and black ash, not to mention the vile smell of sulfur making her eyes water. Before the Leader could give her obvious advice, she started climbing a smaller, more stable cliff, taking care not to burn herself.

She stopped when she noticed a torso stuck in the rubble. It was one of Ulric's soldiers, his whole left side burned to a crisp. When the drendir Telling ended, she was already retreating back to Eira, hoping the remaining soldiers would be slow in coming to their senses. This one might not have been slow, but he was definitely not lucky.

Grabbing his right arm for support, she climbed higher. A vantage point is what she needed, and perhaps a breath of fresh air.

Then she will plan, she will find her companions, they will find a way off this death-rock, and then—

She saw the view beyond the mountain. The shockwave of the emerging mountain must have cleared the storm clouds, as all of Arthgard was laid out for her like a tapestry in brilliant light. Her breath caught, and she had to grab on to the cliff not to lose her balance. Gods above, what kind of power could do something like this?

"*You have powers beyond belief as well, Sigrid,*" intoned the Leader, standing next to her. "*Some day, you will be able to use them.*"

Sig looked at him, one eye closed from the glare of the sun. "Here is an idea: how about you use your powers of enigma and mystery to help me find my friends? No? Then you can get lost. Now. I have had it up to *here* with—"

There was an explosion beneath her, and her peak jolted. She was holding on to dear life when she saw a figure stride out of the explosion into a wide corridor of stable ground.

"STRONG-ARM!" Bellowed Ulric, shimmering runes visible even through the mist.

Sig disappeared behind her cliff. This wasn't right. He should have died already. Was that not why they did all of this in the first place? She peeked again, hoping against hope her cliff would survive a bit longer.

Ulric was pacing and shouting. Anyone who was still alive would have heard his raving, though Sig also heard a muttering in between each call of Yut's name. He would laugh quietly, lash out at something invisible, and call out again. She thought she caught dribble on his chin. *Dark below, he has finally lost it.*

"Would you like my advice?"

"Leave, I said."

The Leader disappeared, and Ulric suddenly turned to face the other end of the corridor. From the mist, Yut's slender shape emerged, a bright red rune on his forearm. He looked terrible, though not too different from the first time she saw him. Of course, now there was that look in his eyes, and he looked deadlier while holding a bloody long knife.

Dark. This was going to get bad. Her preservation instincts were screaming at her to get away from here and find a way down the cursed mountain. Which is why a part of her was surprised when she moved closer, quietly climbing down ledge by ledge towards the two. Eventually she got close enough to hear their voices.

"...as well as I do," Ulric was saying, "They are all gone. This Saga has been finished since the beginning; don't you see? In the end, we were meant to do battle, and the villain was to be defeated by the hero. This is the way we set the world right again."

"Your people are dead too," mumbled Yut, still staring into the distance.

A column of ash burst behind Ulric. "Necessary sacrifices, just like your people, just like you."

"I'm no villain."

"But you are!" Ulric beamed with crazed energy. "Don't you see? This is the brilliance of Aslaug's saga-craft. We are both from the same village, yet I escaped the suffering and torture. *I* chose the path of the hero, *I* chose to save the world from the Dark, and *I* chose to sacrifice my body for these darkened runes. But you are on a rampant path of revenge, and you bring death to everything you touch. You need to be stopped, Yut, for the good of all."

Yut seemed to consider this for a moment. He was standing very still, unheeding of the mountain's rumblings, though Sig noticed he held a long knife in a trembling grip.

"Then let's do this," he said.

Ulric's eyes widened. "Let's."

He became a blur streaking towards the unmoving Yut. Ulric collided with him without any resistance and continued into the billowing ash behind them. Sig heard another explosion as crushed rocks exploded in black-and-gray dust.

She took a moment to think. What could she do? What *was* there to do? Yut had a rune of power but was obviously no match for Ulric. Which meant she was no match for Ulric either. It seemed even Eira could not kill him while having Yut and Olaf at her side. What could Sigrid *do?*

Yut's body came spinning from the ash and skidded on the black rock a few times before impacting another cliff wall. Ulric immediately followed, and, using his runes to blast the rubble away with fire and ice, pulled Yut up by the remains of his tunic. He peered into his eyes and said, "Not yet, eh?"

Yut's head rolled back as he lost consciousness. Then it snapped forward, catching Ulric by surprise. The impact made a sound like two boulders colliding, and Ulric tumbled down the mound of rock. His face was flattened, and as he began to heal, Yut jumped down and grabbed him from behind. Sig recognized the wrestling pin, and tiny hope flared. Ulric's years of combat did not matter in the Bear's Hold, Yut just had to hold on.

Ulric struggled as his face turned blue. Sig was looking for an opportunity, but Ulric was sending waves of fire and ice all round them in desperation. Yut just held on with his teeth bared and the crimson rune flaring. That is, until the Heisir brought up his right arm to Yut's face. A white rune flashed on Ulric's palm, Yut's eyes widened, and he threw Ulric to the side.

They recovered for a moment, Yut furiously rubbing his eyes and Ulric forcing air back into his lungs.

"I'm going out there," said Sig quietly, already expecting the subsequent *"This is dangerous,"* and *"Your mind is not ready."*

"That was Yut's one chance," she told the Leader. "Now Ulric will beat the life out of him and take the rune. You want that to happen?"

Yut's hand inched toward a nearby boulder, and he launched it at the warrior without so much as a grunt of effort. Ulric lunged sideways on all fours and leapt towards Yut, driving him into a cliff, *through it,* and out the other side somewhere, leaving flows of lava in their wake.

"But you are not r—"

"I know you're afraid. You think we will die, but this is war, and we can't just run anymore. I could not live with myself if we did. Now, you get me whatever power you think I have. Otherwise, I'll have to do this without you."

The Leader's voice came close to something resembling despair. *"We don't just want you to survive, Sigrid. We want you to be whole. We want you to be at peace."*

Sig began climbing towards the sounds of fighting, smiling gently. *As do I.*

* * *

Ulric's knee drove into Yut's face again, making powder out of the rocks behind his head. Yut did not feel the pain as much as he felt the weakness of his body. The strength of the rune was still there, but what could it do against a man he could barely see?

He dodged another knee slam and shoved at Ulric, sending him flying into the mist. He will be back, of course. He was always back. Yut imagined that if he pushed the Heisir straight off the mountain, he would scale it in a matter of minutes, hellbent on stealing his rune.

Still, Yut tried to run. He jumped across ravines, through plumes of ash and mist as lava speckled him. And his sharpened eyes did not let him miss the bodies.

Ulric's soldiers lay buried in this mountain, and others. How many villages had this mountain incinerated? Was it self-defense, or did he really want to kill them? After all, he had made two oaths, and both involved killing. *Yours are the hands of death.* Perhaps he *was* the villain of this Saga. Perhaps the world would be made right by his death. What good did vengeance ever do?

"I will have a horse then, too," said Yut.

His mother laughed. "I'm sure you will. But true strength comes from the heart. And when you have a strong heart, my son, then your weakness becomes your strength."

Yut stopped at a ledge and saw the world before him again. He closed his eyes.

"I can't do this. I don't have a strong heart. I shouldn't have survived. I can't..." He felt the hot tears on his face, and they were more painful than any blow Ulric could deliver. Something broke inside him—he could not imagine fighting Ulric anymore. His destiny was not a destiny at all, but an unfinished plan, a bad story. The entire Saga aligned against him, so the only thing left to do was to accept his defeat. "I'm sorry, mom."

The wind picked up, and would have been freezing had it not been for the furnace of the mountain. He breathed in the Saga all around him. The breeze brought news from the Southeast, where great ships departed the ports of Rotheim, carrying timber and ore to strange lands. The mountain cried out and shivered in the light. It was brought into this world kicking and screaming, but now it merely grumbled as it tried to adjust to the light and the wind.

Yut stared into the sky while he awaited Ulric. He felt a growing awareness that he would die on this mountain. And yet his rune would not let that happen. It had always come alive in times of danger. It had always protected his life...

Except it didn't, did it? He faced plenty of dangerous moments in the past weeks, and yet it only awoke at a precious few of them. When a Seither tried to kill him the first time, or when he fought the wulver.

Yut blinked. It awoke when he fell among those spikes, the day after leaving Sanvik. And what could have tied those moments together? What was the one feeling Yut had felt then, and now? "*When you have a strong heart, my son...*"

"He is ready," said Ulric behind him. "Let us take the pain, Yut."

Yut stared at his rune. His breath caught. *My weakness... You were with me the entire time.*

Ulric stood at a distance, wary of surprises. The rune of light flared on his palm. He would not have Yut be awake during the transfer again. "Approach me slowly, Strong-Arm, and we will save the world together."

Yut turned, and Ulric nodded. The Heisir had seen a similar face at least seven times before. It took patience, taming a rune-marked, and this one took the most patience of all. But it was worth it. It had to be.

"I can't do this, Ulric," called Yut.

"It's alright now, brother."

"I'm not strong. I'm not smart or fast either. You, and the Cult, and everyone else showed me this much; I'm not strong enough."

Ulric's face twitched, he muttered something, and came back to. "Yut, we need to do this now."

Yut raised his hands as the wind, having finally found its way around the unexpected mountain, picked up its pace. He smiled as his tears dried. "But my mother said that first you should have a strong heart. And then it doesn't matter how many horses you have."

Ulric rushed in. In half a second, he was in front of Yut, grabbing his forearm, and whispering the runes of Darkspeech. And then, by pure accident, he glanced into Yut's eyes, which were staring back at him.

"I may be weak," said Yut, "but someone has to stand up to you people."

This time Yut expected the white rune and grabbed Ulric by the wrist before it landed on his forehead. Ulric's eyes widened. "It's too late, Yut. I've broken you."

Yut's eyes were manic. "Yes, you have."

He flicked and Ulric grunted as his forearm folded in half. The Heisir planted his feet and punched Yut's torso, blue rune flashing and leaving icy residue at each strike. He might as well have punched the mountain.

Still holding Ulric's broken arm, Yut grabbed his face with the other hand and shoved it into the ground. Cracks spread underneath them, so Yut moved away from the ledge, dragging Ulric through the brittle rock the entire way. A flash of ice and lightning, and Yut was blasted into a nearby cliff. Ulric got up and snapped his arm into place as the healing rune activated.

Yut walked out of the dust cloud calmly. He did not feel much more powerful—it was only a feeling of being somewhat whole. He accepted his weakness, and the rune of strength responded according to its purpose: to lend its power when Yut was at his weakest moment. It was a strength that came from weakness. A strength that his mother taught him. He still felt the great emptiness, but at least now it was in the proper place.

"I cannot kill you, Ulric. But you must pay for the runes and the lives you've taken."

The Heisir cackled, though his face twisted in agony. A fissure in the mountain opened between them, and a curtain of steam and ash poured forth. Before Yut could walk around it, Ulric flew through, hand with the white rune outstretched.

Yut caught it and twisted the freshly healed arm, followed by a punch to the gut. "For the Tova child." Ulric's blood spattered on Yut's chest. "For Sigrid." Jab on the face, and Ulric's nose shattered again. "For Olaf." The sound of ripping flesh and Ulric's scream echoed through the cliffs as Yut tore the arm away from him and tossed it over the ledge.

They watched together as the limb twisted in the air, the rune of flame on the forearm fading, and the rune of blinding light on the palm... was not there.

Yut's head snapped to Ulric, right into his other palm, to where the rune of light had crawled. Light exploded, and Yut fell to the ground.

He could see little red veins in the light, and he tried to fight the brilliance, but it was useless. He felt numb, not even able to breathe. And then the pain started, ripping his skull apart and paralyzing him completely. Were it not for that, he would have laughed. How else could it have gone? But he tried his best and hoped his parents would be proud of him. Maybe Keld would be as well. Maybe he will see them soon.

But the pain stopped as suddenly as it began. The light diffused, and Yut's heart dropped at it being over, at having to live out the rest of his life without memory.

Except that Ulric was still above him, his left arm in the air. It looked like he had seized up again, eyes wide and staring into the sky. *Gods below, his runes*. They were like little fires before, but now they were dull. Even the green rune on his neck, which had begun healing the stump at his shoulder, had gone dim.

The air around them shimmered as golden runes blinked in and out of existence. The entire space seemed to bend, as if they were looking at everything through the surface of a clear lake. Above Ulric, far in the sky, something dark began to undulate and grow. But all of this was overshadowed by the sudden song of a grand choir. Their voices were many, yet each was perfect, and they were not singing mere words.

They were Speaking.

He looked behind Ulric and saw her. It could not have been Sigrid, because she looked like a goddess. Her ash-ridden hair was undulating, and the floating runes revolved around her, outlining her in gold. Her, and what looked like others, invisible, standing all around them. But then Yut looked back at her, and realized her lips were moving to the Speaking of the choir. All of creation sang with her, she did not have to command it to do anything. The song reminded him of the singing that Etha showed him in the visions, with voices of gold and silver. It was magnificent.

Her song grew, and she locked eyes with him. He nodded. The dull runes on Ulric's body had coalesced at his chest—they did not need much convincing. Ulric himself appeared paralyzed, though his eyes jumped wildly at the display before him. Yut felt something ancient and permanent was happening, something with consequences. But for better or worse, this had to be done.

He grabbed at Ulric's chest. What should have been impossible became possible, as Yut's fingers curled around the runes, and he *pulled*. Ulric's eyes bulged in pain and panic, but Yut did not care much for either. He pulled with all of his strength, roaring with effort, as the runes stretched, tore, and finally ripped free. Ulric made a hollow gasp and fell limp on the warm rocks. Meanwhile, the runes burst from Yut's palm and flew to join the ones blinking in the air. A few seconds later they disappeared, and the shower of runes began to dwindle.

One by one, the invisible shapes faded. The singing had ended as well, to Yut's disappointment. Sig's radiant glow had vanished, leaving behind ash, dried blood, and sweat. She sat down hard, taking in trembling breaths as if she had nearly drowned. She stared at him, and he stared back, neither finding the words that could possibly make sense of all that had happened.

* * *

"How...?" Yut started, but Sig just shook her head. She wore the expression of someone thoroughly bewildered at what they had just done—a sentiment Yut knew well.

"Eira? Olaf?" she breathed, and Yut shook his head. He could tell she had already guessed the answer before she asked, but still a small gasp escaped her. She momentarily looked at Yut, expecting him to say anything else, but when no answer came, she clenched her jaw, limped quietly to a ledge and faced the wind. The clear autumn sun did not do much for the cold at this height, and the heat of the mountain was waning. Yet she continued facing the world, her undone hair fluttering like flame on a torch.

Yut began to rise as well, breathing deeply to stave off the deadly exhaustion that followed each time the rune was activated. It was asleep now, of course, as the moment of weakness had passed, and he was relatively safe again. Though now he was aware of the power within, a steady fire ready to ignite his limbs when there was nowhere to run.

He stepped carefully toward the ledge, aware of the dancing dark spots in his vision. He suspected it was the work of the white rune, and he doubted a good night's rest would be enough to heal his eyes.

He stood only close enough for Sig to hear him. "What do we do now?"

At first, he thought she was lost in her own world again. But then she turned, settling red-rimmed eyes first at Yut, and then at Ulric. "Why don't you kill him?"

Yut looked at the Heisir, whose breath was shallow but regular. His body was contorted, as if each of his muscles and tendons seized all at once. His left arm was a bloody stump, though the wound managed to close just before Sig stopped him. The moment Yut pried those runes away was the moment he felt Ulric's soul rip apart. The pain alone should have been enough to kill him, yet somehow, he lived. Somehow, he hung on.

"The mountain will kill him," said Yut. He still had not willingly killed someone, and he did not have enough rage or energy left to make another attempt. Between Eira's betrayal and Olaf's death, he did not have much of anything left.

Sigrid stepped away from the ledge, keeping her eyes on the Heisir. "Then maybe it shouldn't."

She noticed Yut's confused expression and continued. "Ulric was the Cult's champion, but the runes were their biggest weapon. Whatever they planned to do with him, it involved nine runes, and eight of those are gone now."

"So, he's useless to them."

"As a champion, yes. But they don't know that yet." She looked at Yut then, blue eyes filled with warning. "If you kill him now, there will be a blood feud. Ulric was their most powerful rune-child, but he was not the only one, and now they would send them all. That is, unless Aslaug herself comes for you and your rune. Eira barely spoke about her, but from what I understood, she is far worse than Ulric."

Yut glanced at his forearm, where a dark imprint, like a rune mark, began to take shape where the rune usually appeared. "I think they'll come for me either way, Sig."

She nodded gravely. "Aye, but at least this will buy you some time."

"Time for what? If there was more help to be found, Eira would have told us. And even if she didn't, I would know."

Sig furrowed her brow but did not question the last comment. "Not time to fight, Yut. Time to sail away. Far from these lands, and then farther still. You go until you are lost, far enough so the Cult cannot reach you. Even with the rune of strength, they're far too strong for you."

"Too strong..." murmured Yut as he regarded Ulric. There was a moment of contemplation, half-second of battling wills and winding paths, a conflict that comes in every man's life when he must decide between doing what is right instead of what is good. In the end, he pursed his lips, stood a little straighter, and placed a hand on Sig's shoulder. "Thank you, Sig. For everything, truly."

"I would help if I could, but I—" she stopped, and Yut understood.

"I owe you my life, Sig. I will never forget this, and I won't be in debt forever. I hope you recover well."

"That's the problem," she said, some of her steel returning as she knocked his hand from her shoulder. "I think I already did. What will you do with him?"

Instead of answering, Yut kneeled down to the broken body and put a small pouch under Ulric's charred chainmail, making sure it would not tumble out. Then he closed his eyes, muttered something under his breath, and a red rune sparked to life on his forearm. He effortlessly lifted Ulric's body onto his shoulder, nodded to Sig, and was about to turn, before Arthgard caught his eye again.

Wordless, they stood amid boiling rock and singing winds until snowflakes began to land without melting. Looking out at the world together, they both wondered how it seemed to have grown smaller.

Epilogue

The Madman

The Madman stretches his feet by the tiny flame, taking a long draw from the bottle. A few coughs and burps later, he contentedly smiles at the Visitor. "And that about does it, ya persistent bugger. Got your story, neatly wrapped and powdered. Make sure the door is closed tight on yer way out, it's got a loose hinge."

The Visitor waits silently. The temperature seems to drop, and the fire at the Madman's feet fights for its life.

"The dark more ya want? I gave you everything." But the Madman knows what the Visitor wants. It's just, as a skald, he wants to make sure people really *want* it before he gives it to them.

"Fine! Fine, this one wants a bit more. Something extra, eh? Every good story has something extra, and the skald only tells good stories." He throws another plank in the fire. Before, sunlight would have streamed through the shuttered windows of this hut. Now it stands frozen in the shadow of the Blackmount.

"They say," begins the Madman, "That sometime after the Blackmount appeared, snow began falling and it did not end in autumn, nor winter, nor spring. Of course, everyone knew the mountain was an ill omen. The folly of the Speakers and witches and rune-children had finally reached its peak, and the retribution of the gods would be swift. And cold. Yet that day, while everyone stared up at the mountain, no one thought to look down at the shape of a man and a woman emerging from its shadow. They parted ways then, looking back only for a moment. The woman went south, to find peace in nameless forests and mountains. The man, a bright red rune on his arm, was carrying someone on his shoulder. He ran for a day, never tiring, never sleeping, until he came to a pit in the ground. It was a pit from which no light escaped, and some heard the moans of the dead emanating from within. It was there that he dropped the body of his one-armed quarry, leaving his fate to the gods alone. And, of course, to whatever dwells in that hole."

The Visitor stands suddenly and approaches the Madman. The chair squeals, and the Madman grabs his bottle a bit tighter. The Visitor leans down and looks into the yellowed eyes, a single word and question penetrating the ale-addled mind.

"*Where?*"

"No one knows where Yut Eriksson is," stammers the Madman. "Some say he traveled across the seas, far from his shame. Others claim he threw himself into the same volcano he created—"

The Visitor makes it clear this was not the question. Realization dawns on the Madman and, slowly, his twisted grin returns. "You will find the Pit just south of the city of Miklor. Can't miss it."

The door shuts, and the Madman does not move until the footsteps, creaking on snow, fade completely. Only then does he begin laughing.

Acknowledgments

Acknowledgements

Erin Bledsoe, you may have provided the developmental edit, but really, you taught me to write good. Thank you for your dedication in transforming the manuscript.

Misha Sagun, you read it in two nights while under a tent in the middle-of-nowhere woods. *And* you gave instant, good feedback. I salute you, sir.

Raven Anderson, your edits, constant support, and unwavering positivity will always be an inspiration. The best coworker (friend) a guy could hope for.

David Munkres, a spontaneous shadow from the past, to be sure, but one with a heart of gold. Thank you for your feedback, and sorry again for only sending you half of the book on accident.

Sandra Gamble-Navarro, thank you for connecting me with Evan Murphree Gamble, who gave invaluable feedback.

Mary Crocker, for combing through the *finalized* version and finding typos, all in record timing.

Lilya Verlan, my partner in crime since childhood. I might have started writing because of a mental breakdown, but your encouragement saw this book through the end. Thank you for being there since day one, Lilshe. Maybe one day I'll be able to express how much it really means to me.

And to the dozens of folks who kept asking, encouraging, and motivating me, I am eternally grateful for your goodness.

Photo Credit: Joseph Fedorov, Young and Wise Media

Michael Verlan is an accountant, preacher, violinist, and writer. Immigrating from Eastern Ukraine in 2005, he had no desire to read—mainly because he didn't know English. But once he picked it up, he devoured every book he saw. He now lives in Lynnwood, Washington, where he enjoys drinking coffee, discovering stories, and playing Dungeons and Dragons.

Instagram: @michael_verlan
Twitter/X: @M_Verlan

Gotquestions.org

Milton Keynes UK
Ingram Content Group UK Ltd.
UKHW021928190224
438095UK00007BA/301